MW00774456

MERCY'S REQUIEM

A. C. MARTIN

ISBN — hardcover —979-8-9903828-0-0
ISBN — paperback —979-8-9903828-2-4
ISBN — ebook — 979-8-9903828-1-7

For every LGBTQIA2S+ person who grew up having to scour the internet to find fantasy stories with queer main characters: this is for you.

CONTENT GUIDANCE: This novel contains aspects of blood, torture, child and adult abuse, mentions of sexual assult, death, grief and loss, and weapons. Please read with care, and prioritize your mental and emotional health.

This list is not all inclusive and should be used as a guide for the content ahead.

N
W
E
S
Solaris
ASHWOOD
Romalta
ORION
CYRENE
SILAS

CHAPTER ONE

THE CREVICE

The moment Arden stepped into the hazy, caliginous building, she knew many men would die that night. The scent of sweaty musk, piss, and cheap booze assaulted her delicate nose, nearly as offensive as the garish, color-alternating lights. Before her eyes could adjust to the central room's boisterous ambiance, her heightened senses picked up a subtle breeze to the left.

Reacting on preternatural instinct, she ducked and spun forward, the belligerent man's fist kissing nothing but the empty space her head had just inhabited. Unable to control his momentum, the human stumbled forward and crashed into a black lacquer table adjacent to the dance floor, splintering the wood as cards, coins, and beer flew.

Incensed voices roared, and men jumped away from their spilled drinks, drawing their weapons as their buddies collected the money spinning on the floor. A gleeful laugh rose above the musical vibrations from someone
Arden assumed was the idiot's original target, seemingly delighted at the violent outcome for his attacker. The blubbering apologies from the inebriate fell on merciless ears as they descended upon him like a pack of winged pterolycus wolves,

determined to have their pound of flesh for the minor transgression.

Disgust curled her lip beneath the fabric face-covering as she watched the level of bestiality from the same mortals who claimed they were not nearly as ruthless as their immortal neighbors.

"Take your garbage outside before you stain the gods-damned floors!" a burly bouncer shouted, shouldering past the cluster of cheering spectators. A huge vein bulged from the side of his reddening neck as spittle flew from his mouth.

Arden spared one last glance toward the full-on brawl that was now tussling out the heavy double doors and into the night air.

Slinking toward the large slab of gray stone along the back wall serving as the main bar's countertop, her lithe body easily weaved through the dancing locals and claimed a spot in the far corner. With one elbow resting casually on the rough surface, Arden did a brief mental inventory of the weapons hidden within her clothes. With two pistols and four blades accounted for, she raised one index finger to flag the bartender down for a drink.

Within moments, he slammed a pint down, the urine-colored liquid sloshing over the brim. She tossed him a few more pieces of copper than the cost, her stomach roiling at the unappetizing brew. Lifting the smudged glass, she toasted a second bouncer as if promising not to repeat the trouble she had walked into.

Luckily for him, she was not planning to participate in any brawls; unfortunately for this establishment, her plan was to raise a different kind of hell tonight.

Amusement curled the edges of her hidden lips as she cradled the mug in her left hand and surveyed this entertainment hall's main level. How *The Crevice* had not been shut down permanently was a mystery to every thug, thief, and sleazy drug lord whom the Silas Private Investigatory Unit had interrogated.

Sure, in the three years Arden had been in this territory, it had been stormed by Silas's enforcement patrol regularly enough. They had even torched the place a time or two, but the city's criminals continued to raise it from the ashes, a new owner ushered in with each revival. Interestingly enough, each man who succeeded in taking ownership of this original plot kept the original name.

Or murdered for it is more accurate.

It was doubtful that keeping the name was a display of sentimentality. It was far better for business endeavors to keep the reputation—and debauchery—it provided.

The Crevice was a well-recognized beacon for all things questionable and immoral and happened to be the perfect place to find the man she was hunting down tonight. Rumors had spread that this cesspool's newest owner had an affinity for weapons, poisons, and intel about Silas's most elite citizens. While she was *technically* here to complete a high-paying contract outside her legal job, he was also rumored to have exclusive knowledge about the castle grounds and its residents.

Unfortunately, his intrigue was not won simply by waving around money or status. He was a collector of a vastly different kind. Whispers in the slums inferred that he enjoyed stealing young children and selling them for entertainment or debts, with no care for their fate once he received his coins. Despite the abhorrence of claiming ownership over any cognizant living being, Arden had learned the only way to find oneself under his attention was to have similar interests. This was just another role she had to play by order of the Council of Elders to save her failing kingdom of Orion.

The color-changing lights nearly blinded her as she verified that all the previously gathered intel was correct. Per the usual denizens of this putrid place, it was newly renovated to be three stories. The current level was set up like a typical club, complete with a mist machine and people dry-humping each other on the dance floor. The basement level was where the fights occurred; nothing was off limits, and at least two people per month lost their lives. Tonight's unlucky target mostly reigned from the upper level, where the most illegal deals occurred.

After reviewing the exits and patrons one last time, Arden purposefully sauntered toward the stairs leading up to the exclusive access areas. As she drew closer to the stairwell, a towering man stepped in front of her path, his grip casual on a sawed-off shotgun. Her hand drifted closer to the only visible dagger held to her waist via a leather belt. She slowed her steps to a stop merely five feet before him. When he stayed silent, her head cocked to the side, gloved hand slowly drifting to the weapon. With him being human, she would certainly impale him before he could even aim his shotgun.

"What do you desire?" His gravelly voice was completely devoid of emotion, and his dull eyes never blinked. Based on his vacant gaze, he was high on something. The academic side of her brain shuffled through a dichotomous key of possibilities, rapidly narrowing down the list.

Perspiration was present, the scent of which was cloyingly sweet. Blown pupils. Unfocused gaze. Slight tremors in his hands. Noticeable agitation from his jerky head movements. There was no trace of powder rimming his nostrils. His long-sleeved shirt hid any confirmation of needle tracks, but if she were a betting person, Arden would have placed next month's rent on it being Clarity Candy. The new lab-created stimulant had been all the craze since it was spilled into the black market a year ago. The utter lack of intelligent thought in him was unsettling. She took a calming breath and hoped the information she'd tortured out of the pedophile earlier was correct.

"Redemption." The lowered pitch of her voice sounded far closer to male than female, a tactic that had never failed for her before. The man she was looking for loved to lean hard into the metaphorical bullshit, so she was begrudgingly participating in it.

For a long moment, nothing happened. Just as she concluded she would have to find a separate way through, the guard merely stepped back toward his original post, allowing a clear path up the stairs. Underneath her midnight black hood, Arden warily watched him as she ascended the steps, only pausing once she was well out of range. The drug increased his processing time, making him far more of a threat. Any high person was unpredictable, but Clarity Candy had a reputation for causing sudden changes in character.

Nausea overcame her, and a slight regurgitation of an earlier meal threatened to crawl up her throat as she walked by stall after stall of scantily clad children; none of the girls were past their first bleed. By the time she finally stopped in front of the man who labeled himself Deliverance, she had counted twenty stalls. Some contained children with hollow eyes, while others remained empty. A few scraps of torn fabric were utilized as useless door coverings, a mockery of modesty. Her molars were grinding together so harshly that she had a fleeting moment of concern they would crack.

Deliverance remained reclined against his velvet chaise as he sipped from his cup with abandon. Arden's nostrils picked up the scent of whiskey, most likely far classier than anything they served downstairs. Three girls wearing collars and leashes—and little else—were sitting around him on the floor. His dark facial hair was meticulously trimmed to outline his jaw and grew fully over his chin. A belly laugh escaped him at whatever his colleague had said, and he handed him one of the leashes.

"Let me know how she likes it, Gerald," he nearly shouted, his hairy chest visibly shaking with mirth as the girl was forced to crawl toward one of the VIP rooms in the back. "Just don't break her. She is a crowd favorite."

Rage licked up her spine, the fire so hot that Arden briefly looked down as it settled in her chest, half-expecting smoke to rise from the burn. Justice demanded she snap his neck. Creatures like him were worse than the damn nightwalkers infesting the continent.

Not yet. She forced her clenched fists to release before he noticed them.

Arden gathered that inferno of undiluted fury into the back of her throat and transformed it into freezing ice as she exhaled out of her parted lips.

It was foolish to risk revealing this ability.

She knew humans could not feel or wield quintessence, what they colloquially referred to as magick. Since they could not feel it, they did not understand its complexities or just how difficult harnessing the transcendental elusive element was. King Julius of Cyrene had all beings entering his domain who were even suspected of possessing that ability murdered. The suspicion itself was a death sentence, so she rarely manipulated it in this backward kingdom.

As careless as it was, Arden only felt a twisted satisfaction watching Deliverance's smile drop as rapidly as the temperature in the room did. The cold did not bother her, but she knew he would be uncomfortably chilled for a moment, forcing him off-kilter.

Finally, he deigned to give her his attention. She released the quintessence swirling under her skin, allowing the temperature to return to normal as the aether settled into the background of her consciousness.

He shook his head and warily looked around, snapping his fingers. Another guard broke away from the shadows and leaned his ear toward Deliverance. She mentally added a mark to the number of people who would not be leaving this establishment tonight.

"Ensure all the windows and doors remain closed. I felt a draft, and the clients will not want a case of blue balls. My ability to make money revolves around their ability to get it up."

The privately whispered conversation was clear to her slightly pointed ears, the top halves of which had been meticulously covered this morning with a black piece of fabric tied across her forehead and knotted tight in the back. For all intents and purposes, Arden was human, just like the rest of them.

She kept a neutral look in her eyes and waited patiently for the whole conversation to finish. Just as smoothly as he had appeared, the guard melted back into the shadows clinging to every corner of the room, presumably to fix the temperature.

Deliverance's beady eyes kept darting over toward Arden, as if he subconsciously knew she was the top predator here. It was too bad for him that his arrogance overrode his common sense.

"Hello, good sir. I have not seen you around here before." His smarmy remark would not get a clear answer. She did not reward people who attempted to gain information in convoluted ways, especially not regarding the pimp of children. Still, he was expecting a response, and she needed to play nice a little while longer, much to her vexation.

"You would not have."

Saying nothing else, Arden let him squirm slightly in his seat as he decided the best course of action. Little did he know that his fate had been sealed weeks earlier when she had learned of his proclivities, the payoff from his headhunting contract merely a bonus. Nothing he offered or said would change his demise, but she could be lenient if he cooperated.

Maybe.

"What is your interest? Metal, earth, or flesh?" His teeth flashed in the candlelight as he offered an arrogant smile. Her jaw ached with the urge to bare her own teeth despite her face being hidden. She wondered briefly if he would remain so egotistical while watching her canines elongate. Arden choked down the rising fury and loosened her shoulders to look less threatening. His defenses immediately dropped, and he stood up to clasp her hand. Humans were so easy to manipulate. It was almost no fun. Almost.

When she ignored his offered hand, he chuckled and slid it casually into his pocket.

"I am interested in all." Tucking her hand into one of her pant pockets, she flashed several gold marks. His eyes lit up greedily as she continued. "I desire only your best wares."

"Of course, sir. Allow me to show you my collection of toys first. You can take your pick."

A shallow dip of her chin was all Arden allowed, and he held up the remaining two leashes. Taking stock of the young girls, she shook her head. A brief frown morphed Deliverance's lips before he recovered with a wide grin.

"I can assure you that Jasmine and Ayla are quite popular."

"No."

His eyes turned into a stony glare at her immediate refusal, but his smile did not waver this time. The expression was almost comical.

"Alright." His voice was clipped, and he dropped the leashes. "Do not move."

The girls shrank away from his thinly veiled anger, further confirming how poorly he treated his so-called possessions. Arden forced herself to look away from their petrified faces and stiffly walked beside him as he presented stall after stall of children. She just needed to wait until she cornered him alone. Then, he would pay. Of that, she was sure.

With each shake of her head, he became increasingly irritated. He was clearly not used to being denied or refused anything. That arrogant sense of status would aid his downfall.

At the second-to-last stall, Deliverance prefaced his presentation. "If you like your pets to be less docile, this one would be a good option. It was recently acquired and hasn't quite lost its bite."

Her attention shifted from him to the young girl crouched in the far corner, her eyes burning holes into Deliverance's skull. If looks alone could kill, he would have expired the moment he'd stopped at her stall. A sharp thrill swept through her at the violence in the child's gaze. When Arden began to approach her, the pimp stepped forward as well. She quickly held her arm out across his chest, stopping him.

"I'd like to see my investment alone." When he opened his mouth to protest, she continued. "I want to see how it reacts without its master present."

Guilt turned her tongue leaden as she spoke the acrid words, but it was essential to her success. Understanding dawned on him, and Deliverance eased his shoulders back and laughed, roughly clapping her shoulder.

"I see. I'll give you a few minutes alone to evaluate. Remember—" His voice turned threatening. "You break it, you buy it."

With his final warning issued, Deliverance turned on his heels and sauntered to his velvet throne, apparently convinced thoroughly of his future sale. She rolled her eyes at his back and walked carefully toward the child. When Arden was within five feet of the balled-up figure, she crouched low until her left knee met the wooden floor.

"Hello, little one."

The words had barely left Arden's mouth before the girl's entire frail body launched forward. Despite being blessed with Fae speed, sharp nails clawed into her forearm through the black tunic, undoubtedly drawing blood. As she removed the vice-like grip from her arm, the clear *snick* of unsheathing steel resounded. Arden's head jerked backward, eyebrows climbing toward her hairline as her sharp blade passed mere centimeters away from her bicolored eyes.

It was much harder to disarm and subdue an opponent *without* causing irreversible harm than she had originally thought. Despite the girl's element of surprise and balls of steel, Arden quickly regained the upper hand by twisting the girl's wrist until she yelped and released the dagger. Arden snatched it out of the air as it dropped, flipping the handle deftly so the back of the blade rested along the outside of her forearm while the tip pressed into the child's throat. Although Arden's primal side demanded retribution, she bit down on the snarl threatening to emerge.

Despite the turn of events, the girl glared up at her with defiance. Unlike the others, this one's spirit was not broken. Even once the others were freed, they would likely never recover. They had been so abused that she could not figure out how they could ever get past the trauma to take hold of their own lives again. They had gone through far too much for being so young. The tiny thing being held at knifepoint was a warrior in a child's body, and the predator in Arden recognized an equal in spirit.

"If I release you, will you allow me the opportunity to explain how we get you out of this shitshow?"

Unease furrowed the girl's eyebrows, but the bravery did not leave her sharp gaze. Tentatively, she nodded, careful not to allow the knife to press further into her skin. Immediately, Arden released the girl's wrists and stepped back, remaining crouched and close enough for her to hear the quiet voice.

"I am not here to buy you. I am here to get retribution for the crimes against humanity that the bastard back there has committed."

The girl gaped in surprise.

"You have a choice to make. You can stay here and remain in this cesspool, attempting to escape amidst the havoc I am about to wreak." Arden's head lowered to meet her stare head-on, allowing the girl to see her honesty.

"Or?" The child's voice was quiet but not weak.

The half-blooded woman's lips quirked beneath her face covering. "Or—" she emphasized. "You can come with me, play along with the ruse, and earn your guaranteed freedom this very night."

Her decision flickered across her face far before she voiced it. Those warrior eyes hardened with resolve, and she slowly nodded, processing everything. "I get to see you end him."

It was not a request.

It was simply an expectation. That small kernel of respect grew even larger within Arden, appreciating the directness.

Arden's studious attention traveled over the small form in front of her again. The girl's tightly coiled black ringlets were matted with blood in places, and grime dulled what Arden was sure would be a lustrous natural shine. Big brown eyes, which reminded Arden of hot chocolate in winter, watched her wearily. Most noticeable, though, were the myriad of bruises and welts across her skin. The choice was by far the easiest of the night.

"As you wish." She deserved far more than that, but it

was what Arden could offer. "Don't get in my way."

The resulting smile was sinister, and it was returned despite the mask obscuring most of her features. Within a minute, a plan had been formulated, and the girl knew her role.

Arden slipped the rope leash through the hoops of the tight collar as loosely as possible and looked at her regretfully. "I am sorry about the leash. We need to keep up pretenses until we get him alone."

"I know."

"The knot is self-releasing if you tug backward sharply. Do you understand?"

"Yes."

As the girl stood fully, the proud curve of her shoulders became apparent. She shook her head as if physically throwing off any nerves she had. Just as the child began to step forward, Arden held out a hand, immediately stopping her in her tracks.

"Remember, you belong to no man, woman, or creature."

"I know." There was no haughtiness in her tone. It was simply a statement of fact.

"Don't forget to look feral."

"Trust me, not a problem." That blood-boiling rage rose to the surface and flushed her face again.

Arden chuckled in delight at the pup before schooling her face back into neutrality. The eyes could give away hidden intentions far quicker than anything else. Gloved fingers tightened on the rope just enough to keep a convincing grasp on it, and she led them back toward Deliverance.

As they stepped forward, the girl dashed to the side as if to escape, and Arden quickly caught her upper arm and shoved her to the ground with a glare. Although little real force was used, she was quite convincing with her acting, allowing her body to collapse roughly on the ground.

Deliverance chuckled darkly at the abusive behavior, further cementing Arden's resolve that he would receive no leniency for his atrocities.

"I can tell the kind of man you are, sir, by your choice.

Why don't you leave your bitch here while we go in the back to talk shop?"

"I will not."

Deliverance spared her a glance before ignoring the comment. "My men will watch it." He continued walking, and Arden merely followed him with the girl by her side.

"All the same, I don't like people touching what's mine. I'm possessive." The older woman exhaled a suggestive laugh and winked at him as bile coated her throat. "Besides, I'm not convinced she won't gnaw through the rope if left to her own devices."

The disgusting innuendo and speaking of her new charge as little more than a rabid animal provoked a full belly laugh as he seemed completely at ease again.

Dumbass. So *fucking* gullible.

Seeming to allow it, he continued down the back halls, with overhead lights few and far between. The ceiling was festooned with abundant cobwebs, and upon rounding the corner, the ambiance was far less welcoming. Arden's almond-shaped eyes narrowed in displeasure. She had been raised with the ideology that people should keep their places of residence—both work and living included—orderly and clean.

Deliverance could have kept his office space less of a clusterfuck, at the bare minimum. The lack of pride or professionalism irked her more than she cared to admit, and she nearly scoffed at herself. Leave it to her to judge a literal pedophile for his lack of decorum.

While he fiddled with his ring of keys to open the locked office, Arden silently withdrew the dagger strapped to her left arm beneath the sleeve of her tunic.

Just as the key slid into the lock and twisted, releasing the mechanism, the blade was discreetly slid handle-first into the girl's hand.

Without hesitation, the child grasped the sharp object and crossed her arms haughtily, obscuring it from sight.

Deliverance's office was as cluttered and dirty as the man

himself. Vials upon vials of unnaturally colored substances lined one wooden case, while another housed documents and ostentatious wares.

Arden purposely looked slowly around the space, pretending to be interested in the various artifacts while actually looking for threats and escape routes. The human's teeth gleamed in the low light as he smiled smugly. At his direction, her body dropped carefully into a hard wooden chair, its joints emanating a loud groan with her weight upon them.

She gently tugged the girl's leash and pointed to the ground. Attentively, the child obeyed and pressed against the desk with her back, staring up demurely to wait for the agreed-upon signal to begin her retribution. Arden studiously ignored her and watched Deliverance as he steepled his fingers in front of his face.

"So," he drawled, perfectly at ease in the greedy realm of his own creation. "You've selected the flesh. What kind of metal are you searching for?"

"Xaliar." The metal's name was listed softly, her voice still pitched deep enough to be mistaken for a male.

His head reared back, and the whites of his eyes visibly showed his shock.

"Xaliar?" Deliverance's voice rose an octave incredulously. "Don't be daft! That metal is merely a myth. A legend for the delusional."

Arden's eyes narrowed at his scoff. One more disrespectful word from him, and to hell with the plan. Few of the Fae race would stand for the dismissal in his tone, and many Lycans would have allowed their wolven side to take over already. She came from both lineages, and her temper had always been a fickle thing, but she retained a modicum more control than a juvenile. Her patience was wearing thin, and she would not be disrespected again without consequence.

"Do not be deliberately obtuse. I have it on good authority that not only do you know it exists, but that you have a piece of mine in your selection. I am prepared to offer you a deal you can't refuse."

For the first time since their initial encounter, wariness gave way to fear potent enough to drench the room with it. Her nose wrinkled, annoyed that neither human had to suffer the stench.

"Who are you?" His wavering voice betrayed him. Deliverance sat up straight in his chair, his hand attempting to creep closer to the gun tucked in the waistband of his pants.

"Tsk, tsk, Deliverance." Condescension dripped from her words like venom. "You were *almost* doing well."

As he rushed to pull out his handgun and switch off the safety, Arden was upon him. The girl had silently undone the rope and collar upon seeing Arden's foot tap twice—the agreed-upon signal from their earlier haphazard plan. Utilizing the rope he had forced her to be leashed with, the girl grasped his wrists and wrenched them in the wrong direction behind his back. His shoulder popped out of its socket at a grotesque angle, and the kid smirked.

Deliverance inhaled to scream, maybe from pain or for his men, but Arden quickly chopped his throat with her hand, causing him to choke down the noise. Within mere moments, he was bound completely with his face shoved against the desk. She tore his nice linen shirt off his back and shoved a large wad of it in his mouth. Only when she was sure he could not be heard did she rest her hip on the edge of the desk with him.

"You mentioned earlier that we had not met, and that is true." She drew a wicked-looking serrated dagger from the inside of the well-worn black boot propped up against his chair. His pupils dilated at her gloved finger lightly tracing the jagged edge. "However, I know all about you."

The girl, free now from her confines, walked around the room, seemingly taking inventory of Deliverance's possessions. The casual way she swung the blade in her hand had Deliverance unsure which of them was the biggest threat. Arden bit back a pleased grin.

"You know, I don't really blame you for taking up a moniker. Not with a name like Gilbert." His eyes narrowed, and he tried to protest through his gag. Faster than the human eye could detect, the dagger point Arden had been playing with was deep into the wood, mere millimeters from his nose. His head yanked back as far as it could from his prostrated position.

"The problem I have, Gil—can I call you Gil?—is that you need to live up to your chosen name." Arden continued, ignoring his panic. "Unlike what you parade around town, you are not the embodiment of deliverance, nor do you provide redemption. I, for example, decided to use a name very fitting to my purpose. Would you like to know what they call me?"

He hesitated before slowly shaking his head. His hands were turning purple behind his back.

Good.

"Well, Gil, I'll tell you anyway. I've been called many things. Bastard. Psychotic. Vigilante." Each common insult was ticked off on her fingers as they were listed. "But my most commonly recognized name here in the glorious city of Silas is the Reaper."

She gesticulated broadly, enjoying the unnecessary flair for the dramatic. All color drained from his face, and the stench of his fear grew even more potent. The girl froze her perusal in surprise, eyeing Arden up and down curiously.

Deliverance began to shake.

"You have a choice to make, Gilbert." Forcefully, she gripped his hair and shoved him backward into his chair, forcing him to look up at her. "You either tell me what I want to know, or you don't. You return the Xaliar sword, which rightfully belongs to my kingdom, or not. The consequence of any option is ultimately the same. You are not getting out of here alive."

The bitter smell of urine pervaded her nostrils, and a wet area now darkened his trousers.

"You get to choose how quick it is and if your family goes down with you. If you cooperate, I'll go easy on you. Waste my time and—well, I'm going to really enjoy our very long night together."

He could not see Arden's face to gauge her seriousness, but the promise of violence in her eyes was warning enough.

"Will you answer me truthfully?"

He nodded.

She pressed, "Will I need to pay a visit to dear little Jory?"

Arden had never harmed an innocent, harmless child, no matter who sired them. Still, she was not above dangling the threat over him, waiting for him to fall for the bluff.

The frantic shaking of Deliverance's sweaty head indicated this night might not be a waste after all.

CHAPTER TWO

THE REAPER

"Fuck!" Teyla swore, narrowly avoiding becoming roadkill as a car weaved treacherously in and out of the gridlocked downtown traffic.

As it was, the driver's tires splattered what she desperately hoped was water mixed with beer and not human bodily fluids all over her warm joggers. Recovering quickly, she shook off the spiking adrenaline from the near-injury and stepped fully onto the crowded pavement.

Yet another fight had broken out in the most nefarious entertainment spot in her beloved city. *The Crevice* was just as disgusting as the last time its doors were open. Unfortunately, when she had discreetly convinced the city law enforcement to shut it down the last time, she had not been specific enough.

Apparently, she had needed to specify for them to burn it until nothing remained but the ashes of those who had made a living off it coating the cobbled street. Seeing as the enforcement officers had blanched at that concept and failed to do anything correctly yet again, she was sneaking out once more and wasting her night surrounded by filth.

Teyla did not normally condone the killing of her

civilians, but this particular den of promiscuity and questionable life choices was now bartering the lives of children. In her opinion, no being should be shown mercy for that level of atrocity. During her studies, one of her maids had snuck in a few requested prohibited texts that referenced how immortals were punished for severe crimes. Each volume instructed to make an impact. If it was good enough for the ever-elusive Fae and Lycans, it was good enough for humans.

The only way to deal with monsters was by being monstrous. Learning that particular lesson had broken some integral part of her many years ago.

For many years, Teyla had remained suffocated by the intense protective services her father and his council had deemed necessary for safety. There were too many years where she was little more than a shell of uncertainty and fear. Continuing to hide away from her people and allowing them to suffer against the Orionian fiends alone was unthinkable. She could not tolerate it anymore, and one night, her resolve to obey simply snapped.

It took numerous attempts, a lot of injuries, and many sleepless nights to figure out how to sneak out and not get caught by her guards or the general populace. Out of the four years of helping her people from the shadows, she still had not been successful in shutting this place permanently down. Hopefully, tonight would rectify those failures.

Not for the first time, her heart ached for the children kept here. They were sold against their will and suffered terribly because of it. She wanted this blight against Silas removed. Sometimes, a woman simply had to do the work herself. Earlier in the day, she had decided that she would no longer leave it up to the city officers or the rebel group who called themselves the Ghosts. Neither cared enough to make this project a priority.

Teyla entered *The Crevice* with ease, noting that the bouncer did not even request the flash of an ID. They truly let anyone into this place.

Just as she started to weave through the sweaty crowd, a

man yelled out, "Fire!"

Chaos erupted.

Immediately, it was every person for themselves as gamblers, drunkards, and ladies of the night alike bottlenecked the main entrance. She winced as a sharp shoulder slammed into her smaller frame, knocking her off balance. Sure as the gods, a hungry conflagration was eating through the building predominantly made of wood. This was no accidental fire caused by an overturned candle.

No, this was surely intentional.

A pang of disappointment shot through her as she realized somebody else had reached this place first.

As the flames continued to lick their way down from the upper level, devouring all in their path, a flash of black caught her attention. For a split second, a tall silhouette of a man was visible, racing down the steps leading from the upper level. One blink, and he was gone, along with a girl in his possession.

Absolutely not.

Not a single detestable man was escaping the chaos here tonight. Teyla dashed between the frantic, sweaty bodies attempting to flee, a fish swimming furiously against the stream. After much shoving and elbowing, she fell out the other side. The wall of human bodies was reminder enough to find an exit quickly. She sprinted across the old plank flooring to the back until she reached the worker's door, discreet enough not to be noticed by the masses.

Body slamming against it with an "oomph," the momentum cracked the latch and swung her out into the blessedly less smoky outdoors. She greedily gulped deep breaths of clean air and rested her hands on her knees, searching for any sign of the man from earlier.

Straining ears picked up the slight scuffle of a shoe against cobblestone about two blocks adjacent. Without further hesitation, Teyla's search renewed with vigor. She forced her footfalls to be as silent as possible as she attempted to track the girl and her kidnapper.

Ducking and weaving between the people gathering on the sidewalks to watch the fire consume *The Crevice*, Teyla kept sprinting in the general direction she had last seen them. The masses were stepping upon a long piece of bloodied rope, most likely left behind during the struggle. Pushing herself even harder, she felt the air slice through her lungs like a knife.

Seeing a momentary break in the congested crowd, she leaped around the corner, her momentum too fast to correct silently. She winced at the loud drag of her leather boots on the loose gravel, and she flew past the protection of the wall and straight into the open.

The toe of her shoe caught on a raised stone, and she swung her arms rapidly so as not to fall flat on her face. Before Teyla could regain her balance, her body was hauled backward and thrown into a small alcove between the doors of two establishments.

She scrambled for her blade, but her assailant was too fast. Before Teyla could palm her blade, he pinned both her arms harshly above her, leaving her completely helpless.

Fuck, she thought bitterly.

The flash of steel in the neon store signs caught her undivided attention. The stranger spun the dagger on the palm of his gloved right hand before slowly raising his head to look at her.

Despite the predicament, her breath caught in awe—his eyes captivated her. His right eye glowed a stunning light amber, caught somewhere between burnt orange and copper. It was as though every passionate emotion flared to life within that swirling molten lava.

His left eye was even more striking—blue so light it was almost white. A wicked-looking scar bifurcated his left eyebrow and crossed the bridge of his nose, his vision seemingly unimpacted by the old wound. Teyla wondered how far down his face that scar went. His left iris had a deep blue ring outlining the startling blue. All warmth died in its frigid depths.

The stranger speaking startled her out of a trance, heat rushing to her cheeks upon realizing she had just been staring at him. "Why are you following me?"

His voice caused her head to cock to the side curiously. The slight lilt and cadence indicated he was not from Cyrene, but something nagged at her. Before she could figure out what it was, the stranger raised the pointed end of the dagger until it was level with her face.

Fear increased her breathing's cadence, but she knew she could not back down. That captured child deserved a chance at freedom, and Teyla would make that happen even if it was the last thing she did. Just as she turned away, the knife tip snagged her hood and threw it backward, garish neon purple lights from the storefront illuminating her face.

Blonde hair ripped free of its binding and whipped her face from the force of the movement, obscuring her vision momentarily. The intimidating man dropped her hands like he had been burned and stepped back out of hand-to-hand combat range. His captivating eyes scanned her figure up and down curiously, tingles traveling along her body at the intense perusal. Without another word, he returned the tactical-looking dagger into a sheath along his left arm and stalked away.

Surprise left her dumbfounded. He had originally looked ready to gut her. The only thing that had changed was the revealing of hair. Surely, he had not recognized her simply by that. Many women in Cyrene had blonde hair.

Teyla had been sure to cover her face, similar to that of her assailant. Nobody outside the special protection service agents, maids, and ladies in waiting had been close enough to recognize her in a decade. She snapped out of her residual shock upon seeing him reach the girl and turn her around, leading her away to some horrible, unknown fate. Teyla pushed off of the hard alcove wall, her resolve returning. "Stop!"

The stranger continued to walk away, pulling the girl along by her upper arm. Teyla was more than a little annoyed; she was angry that he had not heeded the command. Very few dared to defy her family, and the insult did not go unnoticed. Before she had time to think the action through fully, she cocked back her arm and hurled a lean dagger straight toward the back of his stupid hooded head.

As the knife rotated through the air, the man reacted far faster than any human had the right to. Stepping quickly to the side, he snatched the still-rotating blade straight out of the air as it flew where his head had just been. Ever so slowly, his body turned to look at her incredulously.

"I spare your life, Princess, and you try to send a blade through the back of my skull?"

His voice was as soft as the wind, whispering through the twenty feet between them, caressing her and attempting to lull her into false security. Teyla would not be fooled. Dread filled her stomach at the use of her title. He recognized her, then. She needed to figure out how he had managed to discover her identity so quickly. Her nighttime outings relied heavily on her anonymity.

"So, you are aware of who you just disobeyed a direct command from?" Voice sounding haughty to even her own ears, she winced internally. His chuckled response was borderline sinful, with shivers of pleasure tingling down her spine at the sound.

"You truly are a ruthless little thing, aren't you? I suppose you take after your father more than I thought."

She bristled at the insult.

"I am nothing like him," Teyla spat, hands curling into balls.

"Tsk, tsk. Surely, you know it is considered treason to speak ill about the Cyrenian Crown."

Her jaw dropped at his audacity. As Teyla struggled to devise a retort, the man pulled back his hood. It hardly revealed anything, much to her disappointment. The lower part of his face was still covered by cloth, and a thick strip of black fabric was tied around his forehead and ears. The only discernible features were those damning eyes, which were currently dancing with amusement. Glaring at him, she pushed her fascination with his complete heterochromia to the back of her mind.

He was mocking her.

The simple fact that he even dared to speak so flippantly toward her put her on edge; this man was surely more dangerous than she could tell if he did not fear their king's retribution.

"Very funny, asshole." Her glower would have made lesser men flinch. He was right that the wrath of the Cyrene royalty was well known to the public. He did not seem to care. "Release the girl, and I'll forget the offense and allow you to live another day."

A soft laugh escaped him, and his head tipped backward in his mirth. A flash of his neck escaped the cloth, the skin a light golden brown and sweaty. Teyla forced herself not to linger on that brief, tantalizing bit of flesh. This man was an abomination, kidnapping and selling children for his own gain. No matter what he might look like underneath the black obscuring his identity, she refused to be attracted to him, even superficially.

What has come over me?

"The girl is not mine," the mysterious man spoke.

Surprised, Teyla's attention flew back to him as he continued. "She is a free human. I was simply escorting her through the slums of the city."

Bullshit.

"Allow her to speak freely, then, and represent herself," Teyla challenged, raising an eyebrow at him. A nonchalant shrug was his only answer. The girl stepped forward.

Teyla's heart fractured even further as she fully focused on the girl's appearance. The disheveled rag she wore barely covered her, leaving little to the imagination. Jaw ticking angrily at how mottled and broken open her skin was, Teyla clenched her fists. The girl's eyes were far less meek than her body appeared. Defiance flashed in them as she beheld Teyla's scrutiny.

"This man saved me. He pretended to be an interested

buyer to get close to my previous *master*." She spat the word like a curse. "He feigned interest in my purchase and did not let me out of his sight. He gave me the choice to escape with him or find my own way. As I am not dense, I chose the path of least resistance."

Disbelief lit the princess, her brows raising. Surely, this was just another ruse. "Did you burn the others with no mercy? My eyes in *The Crevice* reported at least ten, upwards of fifteen children in there."

"I would never harm children." The stranger's voice was clipped with barely restrained anger.

Teyla held her hands up placatingly. "All right. What was done to them?"

"They were cut from their restraints and set loose prior to the unfortunate *accidental* blaze currently burning that cess-pool to a crisp. Also, your spies are terrible. There were twen-ty-three total."

Either this man was exceptionally good at lying or, less likely, he was telling the truth. No matter how hard she searched those hypnotizing eyes, there was not one flicker of doubt or a lie. Teyla cared deeply for her people, but the pos-sibility of a Cyrenian man hunting down pedophiles without demanding payment was next to zero.

"Who are you?" The question was out before she could stop it.

"An ally, Princess." He sketched a grandiose mockery of a bow. "Now, as fun as this is, we must be going. Those thugs will begin searching for us soon enough."

When he turned to walk away, she took a step forward. "Wait!"

Teyla could see his ire from his posture, but he did listen. Taking advantage of the moment, she shrugged off her expensive cloak and held it out to the girl.

She looked at Teyla haughtily, raising her chin. "I am not ashamed of my body or what they've done to it." Her words were caustic, so the princess chose her rebuke carefully.

"You shouldn't be. Let them see they hold no power over you."

The girl's anger eased as she beheld the complete lack of judgment.

"But it is not a weakness to accept kindness from a stranger. Just as it is not a failure not to allow others to take the same advantage of you," Teyla continued gently.

She did not lower her outstretched arm, nor did she break the odd staring contest they were having. Teyla simply waited. The man watched the interaction with his head cocked almost curiously, allowing the girl to make her own choice. His story had just become a fraction more believable. Finally, the girl reached out, her small hands accepting the dark gray cloak.

Teyla smiled victoriously. "Good luck, child. May the gods bless you abundantly."

Having said her piece, she turned around to return to the castle. Now that she had lost some of her protection, she would have to take a less direct route. Apparently, she was not as discreet and anonymous as she had believed.

She had made it only two blocks before the hairs on the back of her neck stood up. The gods had not let her down with her intuition yet. Swiftly turning, Teyla scanned the alley. Not a soul was in sight. A frown tugged her lips further down as she could neither see nor hear anything.

When she turned on her heel, she immediately froze, noticing the black folded fabric placed on a wooden crate directly in front of her. It had not been there moments prior.

She nervously gripped her curved blade in a fist and stepped forward, noticing a scrap of paper lying on the top. Her left hand shook in trepidation as she unfolded the wrinkled paper. It looked like a list of supplies. It was not until she flipped it over that the note was revealed.

Until next time, Princess.
—Reaper

Teyla had just been face-to-face with the most notorious, well-known criminal in Silas, and he'd allowed her to live. There was no doubt about that. She would not have stood a chance against a killer like him. The blood drained from her face at the revelation.

The public held mixed feelings toward the Reaper. The man was like a wraith in the night, slipping in and out of his targets' homes without a trace. As far as anybody could tell, he was a vigilante, and his work of killing horrible people in Silas was well known. The Council thought he would eventually attempt to attack the Crown, but that was obviously false since he had known her identity and called himself an ally.

The scrawl on the note was somewhere between elegant and hurried, not what she would expect from the man based on what little character she'd had time to derive about him. Unsettled by how thoroughly he had snuck up on her and disappeared, she reached for the fabric. It was soft on the inside but thin leather on the outside. Durable and water-resistant, but light enough not to weigh the wearer down.

Teyla should leave this gift here. If she accepted it, the man might believe she owed him something in return later. Still, the words she'd said to the child rang through her head.

The sentiment was one she thoroughly believed. It was not a weakness to accept kindness, so why was she hesitating? She was just as much of a threat to the girl as the man was to her. A total stranger with an unknown agenda.

A crisp wind stirred litter up from the pavement, causing bumps to cover her skin. It was oddly chilly for a night at the end of spring. The dip in temperature made up her mind, and she quickly pulled the cloak onto her shivering figure.

Instantaneously, warmth seeped back into her limbs. It was well-worn but had been taken care of diligently. This stranger was full of contradictions, making her mind crazy trying to figure out the puzzle. Fascination was the last thing Teyla needed on her plate. Pulling the dark hood up, she was internally pleased with the total coverage it had over her golden hair and feminine features. She crumpled the note, shoved it into one of the many pockets, and began her way through the city's underbelly.

As she raced back to the castle, she could not help but appreciate the fit of the cloak. It was slightly too large for her more petite frame but did not engulf her or impede any movements. That was advantageous to her nighttime excursions. By the time she reached the sewage tunnel, the faintest of red rays were cresting from the eastern hill. Dawn was fast approaching, and the window of time she had to finish sneaking into her private rooms at the castle was rapidly diminishing.

Her lungs burned as she held her breath and dashed along the tiny concrete ledge through the worst-smelling section of waste. Sliding to a stop by the thick metal grate blocking the way through the wall, she finally breathed again. The leftmost corner was covered with moss.

Carefully, Teyla pulled a thick layer of foliage away from the grate to reveal the small hole she had discovered four years earlier. It was far too narrow for most adults to fit through, let alone a full-grown man.

She slid her left leg in first, squeezing her thighs through. Snug but manageable. She sucked in her stomach as she bent sideways to slide her torso through. Her chest and back scraped the edges of the rough crack as she forced her upper body fully to the other side. Once that ordeal was done, she allowed herself a sigh of relief. She'd never gotten stuck, but she still worried she could not get back through and be caught outside.

Soon enough, her other leg was through, and the walls stopped caving in; claustrophobia was the worst. Teyla reached her arms back through and trussed up the greenery to cover the hole again until it looked like it had never been disturbed. Another few minutes brought her outside the tunnel, seven stories below her bedroom chamber window.

The sky was turning a beautiful golden pink. Her time was up. She scrambled along the ground and dug up the hidden rope and anchor. With practiced ease, she made a lasso and launched it upward with a whoosh. Teyla winced as the metal scraped loudly on the stone before snagging firmly on the concrete pillar of a balcony on the third floor. She tugged it sharply to test it. Satisfied she wouldn't fall to her death, she began the ascent.

Crouching on the balcony ledge, she quickly wrapped the rope across her torso. Once it was secured, she flexed her fingers and grabbed onto the stone's slightly protruding edges. This was the worst part. Scaling the wall was no easy feat, especially up four more stories. Luckily, balconies were on every floor except for six and seven.

Her breath was punching out raggedly as she heaved her shaking body through the bedchamber's window. Wasting no time, she stripped out of the dirty clothes and hid them along with her boots in the loose floorboard by the foot of the bed, dragging the chest back over it with a grunt. She had just pulled on her nightgown and thrown the covers over her when Gierda knocked and walked in with a dress in hand. Teyla slowed her breathing to appear in a deep sleep and feigned waking up when the maid lightly shook her.

"Good morning, Princess. The King has requested your presence."

Fighting a groan, she simply nodded. Gierda herded her into the bathing chamber and helped Teyla through the motions of bathing and dressing. Despite raising her eyebrows at the dirt that came off the princess' skin, Gierda did not comment.

A sigh left Teyla as she took in her reflection. The King had ordered her maid to dress her to look, as he lovingly put it, "presentable, for once." She looked hideous. Gierda had specific instructions to choose the royal colors. The purple and silver would not have seemed so bad if they were not intertwined in this dress.

Teyla loathed these stuffy dresses. They made her feel constrained, uncomfortable, and sweaty in the summertime.

Well, that was not entirely true. She hated the dresses she was forced to wear to court events.

Outside of those pompous occasions, her usual attire consisted of pants and a well-made blouse or a loose summer dress. Instead of heeled shoes, she preferred to wear boots or canvas shoes. The maids almost always pulled her blonde hair out of her face in the court's traditional fashion, which she also hated.

Her sunshine golden hair was the one attribute Teyla had inherited from her mother, and she had many fond memories of her mother's hair being down. Secretly, she suspected the resemblance was why her father made them pull it up.

Being the King's greatest disappointment was nothing new. She had been letting him down ever since she was a young child. He'd always wanted her to be a proper lady and was rewarded with a daughter who enjoyed roughhousing more than tea parties. More than that, he expected her to bring a solid ally to the kingdom through an arranged marriage.

It was an agenda the lords of the court had been pressing for years—how revolting. She was not opposed to the idea of serving her people. Teyla adored what little she had glimpsed of them while sneaking out but hated that she might end up stuck with a man of the King's choosing.

"This dress is hideous. Where did you even find this terrible pattern?" Disgust coated the words, and her maid flinched at the bitter tone. Instant guilt flooded through her, and Teyla exhaled a deep sigh.

"Ignore that, Gierda. It was uncalled for." Everybody knew that once the King gave an order, it was expected to be obeyed without question or resistance. The horrors that occurred when people did not heed a request from their malicious ruler haunted her nightmares.

The frigid memories of the innocent blood coating the tiles in the throne room resulted in a full-body shiver. She could almost hear the sickening thud of their heads hitting the floor seconds before their bodies did the same.

Most of the kingdom knew the kind of monster their King had become, but nobody was powerful enough to challenge his reign or usurp the throne. Not after he'd slaughtered every magick wielder who'd lived in Cyrene or crossed the borders.

Shaking her head to clear the mutinous thoughts, Teyla glanced at her reflection again. Gierda did her best to meet the requirements while allowing her some breathing room. The dress had a form-fitting bust, but at least she was not forced into a corset that had, unbelievably, come back into fashion last year. It was a small mercy.

The bodice had purple lace sleeves. The lace extended in a triangular shape over the top of her hands, securing itself via a small loop over each middle finger. The lower half of the dress flowed around her legs, the ends grazing her ankles in a soft caress.

A sharp prick to her scalp cut her perusal short. The angry blue eyes of her reflection shot up to make eye contact with Gierda through the mirror, who was already frowning and mumbling her apologies before Teyla even thought of reprimanding her.

The young girl finished fastening Teyla's hair and plumped the dress one last time before standing to the side, waiting. Teyla fought the urge to roll her eyes. This particular maid always wished to be dismissed quickly. Instead of fighting about it or allowing another sharp word to cross her tongue, she nodded once.

"You're free to leave. Please be available if I have more need of you."

Gierda did not wait to be told twice. She curtsied and left out the servant's door in the living area of the chambers. It was the only exit besides the main door, one she knew was only to be used in case of an emergency.

Teyla had been sequestered away in the upper-class section of the castle for most of her life. Only the nobility, guards, and specific maids had been close enough to know her features.

The common people had seen pictures of her at public events, surrounded by agents, but never with her face fully displayed.

Security increased heavily after the war with Orion began. Near the end of the war, the Queen had been brutally murdered, her throat slashed open by Orionian spies. Teyla could barely even recall her own mother's voice, being a small child when it all happened. As she aged, the security tightened until it nearly choked her.

While her father had turned into a monster, he did care about the Crown. To preserve an heir, he had her freedom revoked. This allowed her to stay safe, according to the royal council. However, the rules designed to protect her felt like a load of shit. They just wanted to keep her compliant and pure until she could be bartered off.

Still, allowing the maid to leave early provided the opportunity to grab her dagger. Teyla unsheathed the sentimental blade and looked at it once more, admiring it. It was gorgeous. Three polished emeralds studded its hilt's length.

The weight was in perfect balance; Teyla knew the exact specifications, as if the dagger was an extension of her arm. The blade was thin but strong, about seven inches long. When she moved it around, the inscription on the blade became noticeable in the sunlight. The letters were small and barely visible. The phrase she had long ago memorized rang through her.

Shine bright, little moon

Tears sprung as she read the phrase once. Twice. Then, a third time. Her mother's last words floated through her head. One of her previous maids, Penny, had a cousin who custom-made it for her as a gift. Teyla had simply asked for a smuggled dagger and had not expected the inscription.

S he had been young and terrified of being unable to defend herself. Penny had put her life on the line to procure this blade, which was now the princess's most prized possession. Penny had passed away a few months ago from an illness of the lungs after caring for her since her birth. No handmaiden who had replaced her had come close to being good enough to fill her shoes. Instead, Teyla treasured the gift and hid it from the maids who came after.

Shaking out of her reverie, Teyla ran a hand along the leather thigh harness. It was well-worn and would need to be discreetly replaced soon. That was an issue for a later date, and she blindly secured the strap around her right thigh, years of practice making it easy.

The dagger's weight was almost negligible, but it took her another moment to adjust her gait and ensure the dress rustled just the right way for the blade to remain unnoticed. Just as she stepped toward the door, one of the guards knocked.

"Coming!" she called, crossing the greeting room.

Teyla bit her cheek to suppress a disgusted grunt as she saw who was waiting. Nicolai was the worst of the Royal Guard. Despite her being the princess of Cyrene, he treated her like dirt under his boots. Worse, though, was his affinity for looking at her like a piece of meat. Like he was hungry.

The King allowed it simply because he reveled in anything that punished Teyla for her uncanny resemblance to her mother. Nicolai's entire countenance bothered her, so it was unsurprising when he called out her dismay.

"Why so annoyed, little lamb?" He spoke with what was meant to be a seductive lilt but simply led to an angry inferno in her veins. His grin was cocky, and his eyes were mischievous; he knew exactly how much he was baiting her. He was traditionally "good-looking," but only objectively. To know him was to loathe him, and to her, he was heinous.

"Your job is simply to escort me to the greeting room. There is no need to open your mouth to speak as well." Her voice was firm, and she was proud that her bravery did not waver. His response popped her newfound courage.

"Don't give me any reason to report any transgressions to the King. You know he loves to let me play with you when you misbehave."

With her stomach in her throat, she nodded demurely. Teyla was not eager for another one of Nicolai's playtimes. The last one had resulted in her sleeping off the effects of his venom for days, which was only a week earlier.

"There you go, sweet lamb. Do as I tell you." Nicolai seemed to inhale his victory and swelled even larger with triumph. She tried to ignore him and the terrible innuendos he made throughout the walk. Instead, she focused on her prim shoes and the castle's scenery.

The hallways that connected her small room to the rest of the castle were covered in gray stone, built to withstand a siege. She lived in the oldest section of the building; it was dusty, and the light fixtures were old. Some dripped cobwebs whose shadows played on the walls. She essentially lived in a glorified dungeon, and everybody inside the castle knew it.

As they neared the castle's newly renovated wing, light began seeping through the windows lining the walls. At the change in the sound of their footfalls, she looked down in anticipation. This was possibly the most beautiful part of the castle. Nobody except the King and the contractor—unless the King had already killed the contractor—knew how the floor was made so shiny that it carried reflections in its tile, like walking on a silver lake or mirror.

Simply put, it was a masterpiece. Nicolai must have been in a hurry to arrive if he was taking them through the Great Hall. Usually, he avoided it so she could not enjoy its spectacular, one-of-a-kind beauty.

Lost in thought about what could be so important, Teyla did not notice that they were in the throne room until Nicolai shoved her shoulders down with surprising force, and she landed on her knees. Her skin barked with pain as it hit the stone, but she refused to give him the satisfaction of making a noise. Instead, the princess simply lowered her head and eyes in supplication as the King required.

A deep chuckle reached her ears, undoubtedly at her pain and forced posturing. The King was a true sadist, and she had watched the horrors he enjoyed before sitting down for a meal. Countless souls had been sent to the After due to nothing other than his vanity and lust for dark entertainment.

Teyla remained stoic as she waited for the command to rise. It never came.

"I have come up with the most wonderful game." His lazy lilt crawled like spiders down her spine. "I am going to host a competition with a reward that nobody can refuse."

The hair on the nape of her neck stood straight up. The King's games were never good, and no one could ever win. They were designed for maximum pain to the contestants, and completing the final task was nearly impossibl. He must be bored again, which would only lead to more *playtime* between Nicolai, the King, and herself.

Against her best efforts, her body trembled with trepidation, a fact neither man in the room missed. With a malicious smile, the King continued. "The reward will be you, my dear."

He paused again as if for dramatic effect. "Whoever wins will become your spouse. It is an esteemed honor, no doubt, to become my heir. No thanks to you." He did not even try to hide his distaste for her. Despite all the years of cruelty she'd lived through, the dismissal still pierced her heart. "These tests will show which men are the pinnacle of grace, strength, determination, and skill. It will be announced today, hence your attire."

His cold, stone-like eyes showed disappointment as he looked Teyla over from head to toe. "Your maid did a decent job of dressing you, I suppose. Truly, you are still not much to look at. What a pity for my heir."

He turned his back toward her and Nicolai; the conversation was over. As they turned to return to her pretty cell, Teyla heard him chuckle again—a low, terrifying noise.

May the Mother help us all.

CHAPTER THREE

REVELATIONS

Arden had not slept for more than a few hours in days. She needed to return to her small pack in the suburbs of Silas, but both of them needed a break. It was a minor miracle that the girl had not collapsed yet. Arden was half-convinced she was sleepwalking at this point. The girl had not spoken a word since accepting the cloak from the princess—the *fucking* living, breathing princess of Cyrene.

Thoughts spun rampantly as she remembered the last several hours. After leaving The Crevice and the run-in with Princess Teyla, they'd had to slink around the city with dozens of miscreants on their tails. Those they had not been able to avoid, she'd slaughtered.

Unease churned her stomach at the sheer number of lives she'd ended in one night. The six pedophiles at *The Crevice*, including Deliverance, deserved far worse than the ending they'd received. Not a speck of remorse or regret was wasted on their demise.

The other casualties simply felt unnecessary. Had Arden been alone as originally planned, the murders would have been avoidable. Stealth was her friend, and she would have disappeared like a phantom on the back of the motorbike she had stored nearby. The human girl was not as agile or quick as a Fae or Lycan, and her bike had been surrounded by thugs by the time they'd arrived.

While Arden could have murdered them, she could not bear the thought of more citizens being pointlessly slaughtered that night. So, they'd detoured, and she'd needed to be faster and wiser than them. Surprisingly, the girl had done everything she'd been instructed to do without question or hesitation.

Arden was already thinking fondly of the girl; with enough training, she could make a fine addition to the pack. There was one minor problem: the girl was human.

While all Cyrenian humans knew about Lycans theoretically, very few had ever met one in the past twenty years. After the royal family of Orion was massacred, Cyrene's army searched their entire territory to wipe out any trace of her people. Many humans believed they had succeeded and thought they were now extinct.

Most of those were *happy* with the thought that the Lycans were gone for good. Some children believed Lycans were nothing more than a haunting bedside story. A growl at the insult began to rise in her throat before she clamped down on the urge. Arden did not want to startle the girl.

Now, Cyrene's royals, nobles, and high priests taught their inhabitants that only humans, Fae, and nightwalkers existed at this point. They told people they were hunting nightwalkers to extinction as well.

However, with the sudden change of the ruler of Cyrene four decades ago, they seem to have slowed the hunting of those succubi down. Those in positions of power had to be aware some Lycans still existed. Any Lycan unlucky enough to be discovered was instantly sent to gods-know-where to be examined and cut up, their pieces left to decay in the woods.

The information Arden had discovered at one of the Cyrenian lord's houses a week earlier might finally shed some light on how the castle had been tracking her people down and what information they were searching for.

The child's labored breathing brought her back to the present. The forest terrain was rocky and climbing in elevation, and the kid was exhausted. Arden was well aware of the enormous risk this girl was taking by remaining around her.

Not for the first time that night, she mentally berated herself. She should have made the right decision and dumped the girl off somewhere on the way to her pack once she was sure it was safe. The dominant, protective wolf instincts inside her left no room for debate. The girl would only be left somewhere safe.

The soft trickling of yet another stream came into earshot, as good a time as any to rest after the breakneck pace Arden had set. Her feet switched directions, heading to the water's edge, her legs quaking beneath her, aching after so many hours without pause. Grimacing from the deep pain in her legs, she stiffly bent over to dunk her canteen into the running water. After she had raided a nobleman's villa earlier in the week, she'd ridden with very few breaks across the territory to get to Silas. Immediately upon her return, Maximus had assigned her to Deliverance, leading her to this moment.

"Where are we?" The girl spoke so quietly that even Arden's advanced hearing could barely hear over the running water.

"It's hard to say in these parts of the woods."

The girl looked at her incredulously, knowing she hadn't been led unfalteringly throughout the city only to get lost in the woods. Smart girl.

Quickly deciding there was little threat in telling her, Arden sighed. "Based on the time we traveled, I would guess we are roughly half a day's journey away from the next town, east." The girl nodded. Sitting down, Arden pulled out half a loaf of bread and two apples from the black travel sack and held out the food as a peace offering to the girl, who tentatively grabbed it and sat on the forest floor. "I will take you to the closest town and drop you off there before continuing my journey."

Arden's words were muffled, spoken through a mouthful of bread. The only way around her new, poorly timed protective instincts would be to leave the child with a dominant, protective figure. Hopefully, they could find one there.

The girl shook her head vigorously. "No! I want to stay with you." Her face had paled, and the acrid taste of fear crept into her voice.

Interesting. Gathering her thoughts, she looked at the girl and offered her an ultimatum. "Tell me about yourself—how you ended up in that hellhole and why you want to travel with me. After your story, I will decide if you can stay." Internally, the possessive wolf grumbled with happiness. Arden secretly wanted to keep her.

The girl looked taken aback. Again, Arden found herself surprised to be enjoying the company. It had been a while since her travel companions were so expressive and spirited.

"My name is Xara." Her human body remained stiff, but her eyes glazed over as if lost in distant memories. "I was born into a greedy family. My father is a merchant specializing in ceramic wares. He was expecting a boy so he could have a valuable heir. When I was born, I was nothing but a hindrance. He beat me for most of my life, sending me to work in the fields to make money for his trade. My mother was barren after me. One day, she became extremely ill and made my father give his word that he would provide for me until marriage. He sealed that oath with his blood."

One blink was the only sign of surprise Arden allowed. Blood oaths were the oldest form of magick that bound all creatures in this world. The person was held in an unbreakable contract by uttering such an oath. Attempting to betray it brought immediate death.

Most Fae and Lycan folk only took two blood oaths their entire lives: to their partner and possibly an oath of fealty. Humans made them even more infrequently. The more oaths taken, the higher the likelihood of that person accidentally breaking one. That Xara's mother managed to bind the girl's father with one while on her deathbed was quite the feat. Arden would fight Deliverance and all his thugs again before she allowed Xara to return to that detestable man.

Her mental deliberation was hidden well enough that Xara carried on without pause.

"After she died, he was even more vicious." Xara took a shaky breath as if the memories were being relived. Arden's heart ached to console her, but she denied that urge and forced her body to remain still.

"He remarried within the year to a new woman, only five years my senior. Father used all the money I made in the fields to cover the bride price. Then, he sent me to work for a new farmer. This field worker was cruel and took an interest in me. Once I had my first bleed, he asked my father for my hand."

Xara's mouth curled in disdain. "My father did not care much if I was married off or not. He just wanted the money. It also allowed him to get rid of me while keeping his promise to my mother. So, he gave me away to this cruel farmer. Even while I was being thrown out of the house, he sneered at me that he was lucky to make anything off such an ugly girl like me."

Xara took another calming breath. Tears began to fall as she continued to recount the tale.

"The farmer took me away on horseback to Silas so that he could 'christen the marriage,' where none of the neighbors would hear me scream. I was with him for less than two weeks before his gambling addiction had damning consequences. To escape death and pay his debts, he sold me to Deliverance. I had been in *The Crevice* for only a couple of days before tonight. The town east of us is where my father lives. If I return there, he will kill me. I cannot go back."

Arden felt like she was choking on the ice coating her throat. Xara was just a child. If anybody could understand what it was like to have been dealt a hard life, it was her. She, too, had lost her mother. When she looked up from examining the dust on her boots, the absolute grief and devastation on the girl's face made her decision.

"Sweet child, Mother Ambrosia has given you a hard path." Her voice was soft, and she did not bother to sound like a man. She removed the face mask and cloak, and the girl gasped.

"You are a woman?" Disbelief showed on her face. Arden allowed a roguish grin to stretch her lips, fangs surely glinting in the faint rays of dawn. "Surprise."

Shocked, the girl shook her head and laughed. Maybe hunger and lack of sleep were having a bigger impact than she had given credence to, but Arden laughed with her. It felt refreshing and carefree to laugh, as if all the horrors they'd experienced had never existed, if only for just a moment. Too soon, the laugher died down, and a somber air settled in.

"I am beyond thankful you came to save me. I just turned thirteen."

That white-hot anger settled in again. Maybe the deplorable men's fates were far too merciful. How Xara's father and her husband could have even sold her was a mystery. The King of Cyrene had passed laws that required brides to be at least sixteen, although even that was abhorrent. Her stomach churned like butter as nausea engulfed her, thinking about the egregious things that had been done to Xara.

"What is your name?" Xara's soft voice floated toward her, knocking the thoughts away.

Allowing a mischievous glint to alight her face, she grinned. "Well, little one, I need to ask you a question before I can answer that."

The girl nodded.

"Would your opinion change if you knew you were traveling with someone not even part human?"

Her reaction was instantaneous. Fear sliced through the air, and the girl leaped to her feet. Arden's muscles remained locked not to scare the child more, watching Xara's face as she processed her emotions. Most humans would have already bolted. Arden was already impressed with the girl's resilience. Slowly, Xara's shoulders rolled back with a newfound determination.

"With all due respect, I have already faced monsters. You cannot hold a candle to the darkness of men. If you would have me, I would still like to travel by your side."

The wisdom in her voice made her seem so much older than thirteen. Arden studied Xara's expression, scanning for any signs of deceit. Xara's chin was held high, her brow set in a line of renewed resolve. Her deep brown eyes bore holes into Arden, waiting for her decision. This girl was unlike any human she had been around on this continent. She had gall.

"Welcome to the pack, Xara." Just like that, any doubt or worry dissipated. A huge smile swept over Xara's features. Her shoulders caved in with relief.

Arden leaned back, relaxing as she contemplated what to share. Her history was complex and deadly. Secrecy had always been the most important aspect of her life.

She sighed and began. "Officially, I am best known as the Reaper."

Xara's lips parted but quickly sealed again as if she thought better of the question they wished to pose.

Arden winked. "But my friends call me Arden."

Xara nodded and smiled. "Ar-den." She drew out each syllable of the name, trying it out on her tongue. With an impish grin, Xara stated, matter-of-factly, "I'm going to call you 'A.'"

Nose wrinkling in disgust, Arden quickly shook her head. "That is…" She paused, trying to think of the words to convey how much she disliked it. "That is not an option. You will absolutely not, under any circumstances, call me that. My full name will do just fine."

Xara just nodded, that fiendish grin still gracing her mouth. "I have heard of the vigilante using that moniker. I was under the impression the Reaper was male." Xara looked her over from top to bottom. "And much older."

It was no surprise that the little one had heard of the Reaper. Her temporary pack had ensured that tales of her work had reached all ends of Cyrene. The title came from the underground jobs she completed. Wherever the Reaper went, whatever she stole, there was sure to be a trail of bodies in her wake. Of course, she made sure not to kill everybody. Survivors spread ghost stories.

When she'd begun the gritty work three years prior, her technique was simply to knock people out and tie them up while she took whatever the contract instructed her to steal. The rebel pack needed the funding desperately. In time, the Reaper's reputation grew. With the growth in popularity came the requests to expand the targets.

While some people still requested stolen items, more prominent people tasked the Reaper with killing crime lords and people threatening their positions. Since the general population was begrudgingly appreciative of the thorough extermination of the vermin harassing their towns, she quickly became known as the poor people's vigilante. The free publicity was fine as long as nobody knew who the Reaper truly was.

"It is essential that people continue to believe I'm male," Arden told Xara firmly. "The Reaper is feared precisely because he has remained unidentifiable. He could be your neighbor, part of the Royal Guard, or your average criminal. I let the rumors turn the Reaper into feared lore. The mystery keeps the general public invested but still wary. A good myth is like a wildfire—hard to extinguish. It would not bode well if they discovered it was just an almost-thirty-year-old female."

The threat was clear: while she was trusting Xara with this information, one step out of line and she would handle her. Viciously. The girl's throat bobbed up and down, but she voiced her understanding.

Arden grimaced at her own tone. "Listen, I don't mean to be a hardass. I have worked extraordinarily hard to make a name for myself and to protect the people I love while doing it. I meant it when I said I would view you as my pack and family.

I will claim you as my blood, and it will become official."

She paused momentarily. "You will have to swear the oath of fealty to me and, by extension, the pack."

Xara stood up as the gravity of the situation started to take hold. "Pack? What species are you?" Although obviously concerned, she did not make a run for it.

"What sentient species do you know of that form packs, little one? I believe there is really only one that categorizes their inner circles as such."

"Surely you can't be, though. Aren't Lycans extinct?" Doubt crept into her voice. Her brows furrowed as she tried to reconcile what she was being told with the narrative she had grown up believing. "Why would the Crown lie about the extermination of an entire species?"

"You'd be surprised by all the lies the King is responsible for." Arden snorted in false amusement. "If the public believes the current royal family has done such a thorough job at protecting them, they are far less likely to revolt or demand a new ruler."

Xara still looked doubtful. It made sense that changing her mind would take more than a stranger's rebellious politics. Arden methodically removed the bandana covering her slightly curved ears, a dead giveaway of half her heritage. Xara's mouth fell open, and her pupils dilated in surprise. Instinctively, the girl's trembling hand reached out to touch the outer shell of her ear.

Arden jerked her head backward out of reach, Xara's hand falling limply into her lap.

"Never touch a Fae's ears, sweetie. They are… sensitive. It is an intimate gesture only to be shared with a lover."

Xara's face grew red as she processed the information. Arden refused to be embarrassed. Both sides of her heritage were incredibly open with physical affection, and that was nothing she would be embarrassed about. Lycans were closer to their primal side than humans, which meant those instincts were closer to the surface.

"I can tell you are struggling to believe that I am a Lycan." When Xara's mouth opened to protest, Arden merely held up her bare hand. "Watch."

When Xara's doe eyes were focused on the outstretched hand, Arden allowed the shift to begin. The nails of her left hand elongated into sharp points, and her thumb shortened into a dewclaw. She forced the shift to pause there, all of her focus and energy holding the change still for a few moments.

Arden released the quintessence trapped in her chest and allowed the shift to reverse. Once her fingers returned to normal, she extended, flexed, and curled them to release the slight ache in the joints.

"How?" Xara breathed, looking amazed.

Pride flooded Arden's body. "I'm just that amazing," she quipped.

Xara laughed, the shock still leaving her slightly breathless. Her eyes were wild.

"All Fae and Lycans have some ability to control the quintessence. This is because of the aether in their blood granted to them by Mother Ambrosia. As the legends tell it, their gift is representative of their truest selves. Whatever that means." She offered Xara a lopsided grin.

"So, your gift is shifting into a wolf?"

"Sort of. I am a bona fide halfling. My father was a full-blooded Lycan, while my mother was a full-blooded Fae. The races rarely mate and dilute such pure bloodlines. Over the centuries, the powers have grown weaker with each generation mixing, so the most powerful bloodlines only procreate with their same species."

"But your parents did not." It was not a question.

"Nobody was sure what gift I would get from my parents when I was conceived. Some thought the Lycan side would dominate my genetics, while the others—mostly Fae, as I'm sure surprises you—thought the elemental powers of my mother were sure to be passed down. Nobody expected what actually happened."

Xara was on the edge of her tree stump, leaning forward in anticipation.

"Instead of the aether competing, it intertwined. As far as abilities go, I am fully Lycan and fully Fae. I am not graced with merely the ability to manipulate quintessence in one way but two. Two complimentary sides of the same coin. Wolf and water. I believe the love between my parents caused their magick to work in harmony."

"But that would make you one of the most powerful beings to exist."

"Maybe." She admitted with a shrug. "Or one of the most out of control. The aether can drive any being crazy. The ability to feel the quintessence is twice as hard to ignore for me as most. It is a living thing, and the aether in my veins dances with it, pushing the power against my skin. It constantly demands to escape the confines of my Fae form."

It felt like admitting something shameful. Instead of adding to that feeling, Xara simply took the hand that had been deadly claws mere minutes before between her small ones. Arden rolled her shoulders backward, stretching out the weight of carrying her inner wolf.

"Anyway, the Orion Council of Elders decided that only a being of my power might complete the task I was sent here to do. With Princess Calliope of Orion nestled safely deep in her territory, I came here and formed a pack alongside my mentor. It is that same group of Lycans you will soon meet."

"How do you know that they'll even accept me? I am just a human. I have nothing to offer."

It was a very valid question. A human had not been initiated into a Lycan pack in hundreds of years. There are no laws banning it, except in the context of enslaved humans or using humans to breed. Immersing one into a pack was more taboo than illegal.

Arden released a deep, stressed breath. "They will. I am not sure how yet, but they trust me and value my opinion."

Xara looked at her skeptically.

"We will be traveling for another half hour. I'll figure it out. For both of our sakes."

Arden rose from her spot against the large tree, sufficiently relaying the ending of the conversation. While she busied herself with reorganizing the items in the satchel, Xara drank from the canteen and prepared for the rest of the journey.

CHAPTER FOUR

DEN OF WOLVES

The thirty-minute trek took close to an hour because of Xara's slow pace. She had the princess's cloak to keep her warm—made from some of the finest material Arden had seen while in Cyrene—but it had taken her far too long to realize why the girl was limping. It was not until she stumbled forward, and the tangy iron smell of fresh blood clouded the air, that she glanced down at Xara's dirt-covered feet. No shoes to be found.

"Sit down, girl." Arden's voice was rough with frustration.

Xara shrank into herself at the abrasive tone and immediately sat on the ground. Mentally chastising herself for making Xara feel worse, Arden took a deep breath as she knelt by her. Gently taking the girl's bare feet in her hands, she inspected them closely.

"I am not angry with you; I am upset at myself. I should have noticed hours ago that you did not have shoes."

As Arden spoke in her most soothing voice, she opened the canteen of river water and tugged on the invisible thread of aether in her blood, allowing her to manipulate the quintessence. Just as eager as a moth to a flickering flame, the power—invisible to the eyes—rose to the surface. A tingling sensation spread from her chest, traveling down her arms and dancing along her fingertips, begging to be used.

She bid the water to float out of the canister, fingers waving in a beckoning motion from pinky to thumb. Ever eager and obedient, the water particles flowed toward her through the open air, clustering together to form a visible floating stream.

Tension immediately released as she controlled the aether, offering it a tangible outlet. She directed the water to cleanse the grime coating Xara's feet and ankles, hearing her hiss quietly at the burn. When her skin was as cleansed as it could be without soap, Arden turned her attention to washing Xara's hands. Once satisfied that the risk for infection was as low as it could be in the middle of the woods, she released the tether to the quintessence in the water and watched it fall among the grass.

"That was…" Xara's awed voice trailed off.

"Magickal?" Arden offered with a skewed grin as she inspected the gashes on Xara's soles. Only one of the wounds was deep enough to be concerning.

Xara swatted Arden's shoulder. "Shut up. I'm serious!" Her throat bobbed with emotion. "Most humans under thirty have never seen magick used in real life. The King outlawed magick in Cyrene decades ago and killed those who disobeyed. It feels as much a myth as Lycans and Fae."

"I can assure you that magick, Lycans, and Fae are very much real and just as deadly as in your scary tales."

Arden did not bother to sugarcoat her response. This particular child had seen enough of the savagery of life without her pretending the world was not a dangerous and fucked-up place. She could not go back in time to protect Xara from the trauma she had already endured, but she could offer her unwavering truth and respect.

"Your magick does not seem that threatening." Xara's eyes widened comically. "No disrespect intended."

"I understand, pup." The chuckle eased some of the tightness from her chest as she finished wrapping Xara's feet with bandages. "I hope you never have to see how ruthless it can be. The risks of using magick here are numerous, especially at the castle. I don't even know if the King has witches employed with their abilities to detect it. Even without it, you have already seen me kill twelve men within the last day."

"Fourteen."

Arden's left eyebrow raised as she did another mental headcount. "Fourteen," she amended as she picked Xara up at the waist and slung her onto her back like a travel pack. The girl's squeal of delight warmed Arden's stone-cold heart, and her cheeks were aching from how much she had smiled and laughed within the last day. Arden could not remember the last time she had felt so light.

No longer slowed by the human girl, the rest of the journey to the pack hideout passed quickly. They entered the densest part of this forest, swallowed by the foliage.

Arden felt Xara press harder into her back, hands nervously tightening on her shirt. It had always confused her that humans did not feel peaceful in the woods immediately.

Wanting to assuage her anxiety as her heart doubled in pace, Arden reached up to squeeze one of the hands still clinging to her with a vice-like grip.

"We're almost there, Xee." Her lips twitched as she awaited her reaction.

"Hey! Don't call me that, A!"

Along with her indignant voice increasing several pitches, Xara poked the shaved side of the woman's head repeatedly, despite the half-hearted efforts to dodge the onslaught.

"All right, all right, you little hellion! I'll offer you a bargain." The poking assault paused.

"I'm listening." Xara's voice sounded playfully threatening.

"If I can call you Xee, I will let you call me A."

As Xara pondered the offer, Arden leaned sideways and

helped the girl gently slide off her back. Except for one slight wince as she adjusted her stance, Xara seemed to be tolerating standing on her wounded feet.

Arden eyed Xara's pointer finger tapping her own with mock suspicion and extended her right hand. With an exaggerated eye roll, Xara placed her much smaller hand within Arden's and shook it firmly. "I agree to your terms."

Now that their mini spat was resolved, Arden slowly surveyed the area, checking for threats. Outside of a seemingly overtly aggressive squirrel, nothing stood out.

She relaxed the tight control keeping her in her Fae form and allowed her senses to stretch out even further than usual. Partially shifted like this, distant noises of the river running nearby and the surrounding forest's rustling became much more distinct and obvious.

Sorting through the various scents and flavors, Arden ensured nothing was amiss within damp leaves, drying mud from the recent rain showers, and the gritty scent of the rocks and stones; the warbling of awakening birds and scrabbling squirrel's pinpoint nails darting around the trunks of the proud oak trees. Even straining her senses to the point of a headache revealed no bipedal creatures except themselves.

Relaxing, she gently pushed the wolven form into the background of her mind, allowing the more muted senses of her Fae form to take over. She shook her head to get rid of the last traces of discomfort from the partial shift and turned her attention back to her companion.

"Nothing in these woods but us, little one."

Xara looked at her like she had grown a second head. Bewildered, Arden checked over her shoulder in case the girl was looking at something else. She was not. Arden faced her incredulously.

"What? Is something on my face?" Self-consciously, she rubbed at her cheeks. Maybe she was covered with debris.

"Did you know your eyes glow?" The question was blurted like it was forcibly pulled from her.

Oh.

"I do. I sort of forgot humans don't do that." Arden smiled sheepishly, rubbing the back of her neck. "It's not special to me. All magick wielders' eyes glow brighter when utilizing the aether to control quintessence." Shoulders shrugged.

Xara crossed her arms over her chest with a huff. It was the closest she had come to looking like a petulant child.

Arden bit back a laugh, not wanting to provoke her further.

"Being a human sucks. There are literally no perks. We are weaker, slower, die sooner, and have nothing as cool as your magick."

A startled laugh burst from Arden's chest before she could stop it. At Xara's stony glare, she firmly pressed her lips together as her shoulders shook from silent laughter. Only once she was sure she could speak without laughing did she respond. "I think you're pretty amazing, little one." Xara rolled her eyes, but Arden grabbed her upper arm. "I'm serious. Humans are incredibly important to any kingdom. They make up more than ninety percent of the population and are responsible for the success of any ruler. Not only that, but they are the most resilient species out there. Don't sell yourself short."

When Xara finally conceded and nodded, Arden rose back to her full height.

"Welcome home, pup."

Pulling aside foliage on the ground and against the rock wall revealed an opening. The vines naturally hid the entrance but branches and leaves also fell to the forest floor, adding additional coverage for the crack in the stone. Sensing Xara's apprehension, Arden went into the small crevice first. The fissure was narrow enough to make her feel claustrophobic for several paces until it suddenly widened into a large alcove.

Xara followed her through, then turned in a slow circle, taking the area in. She jumped when a loud growl interrupted the peaceful ambiance. Several more growls joined in, and four large, pissed-off Lycans in their human forms began to circle the area. Arden waited for their bad attitudes to subside, unfazed by their territorial bullshit.

She sniffed, annoyed. *Males.*

"All right, all right, don't get your fucking panties in a knot, Theo," she snapped at the loudest one with dark hair.

His growling only became louder. Xara stepped back a half-step in fear before Theo's tall, muscular figure lunged closer. At Xara's cry of alarm, Arden whipped around and grabbed the girl's arm, shielding her protectively. A snarl echoed around the chamber before Arden recognized it as her own.

Upon realizing she was ready to shift into her wolf form to protect the girl, the room bled into a puzzled silence.

"What is the meaning of you bringing this girl here? This *human* girl, who is now in our den," Theo spoke, aggression still pouring from him in waves. "We do not take in strays."

"Theo, enough." A firm voice cut him off with a commanding tone. "If you give our packmate time to explain the situation, I'm sure we will all become enlightened."

"Thank you, Maximus," Arden cut him a grateful glance. His familiar brown eyes and shaggy black hair calmed her, as his presence always had since she was a child. Maximus, the eldest of the group and the leader by proxy, sat on a bench made of large slabs of stone and offered an encouraging smile.

Arden spun in a circle to peer at the rest of the pack. Theo backed into the corner nearest to the entrance with his arms crossed over his broad chest, his face promising death. The other two Lycans, the wombmates, simply looked at each other for a heartbeat before sitting down on the ground. Satisfied that the threat of an imminent attack was gone, Arden began her explanation for breaking an unspoken rule in pack life.

As she offered up a brief synopsis of the events from *The Crevice*—sans mention of the princess—sadistic grins grew as they intently listened to the brutal deaths of the despicable men. Maximus' jaw clenched with fury upon hearing how many children had been in that cesspool. When Arden explained her decision to save Xara, the twins shared another impassive look. A flicker of jealousy and longing ate at Arden's insides at the subtle display of Lycan mind-linking. It was the most intimate sort of aether, only existing between wombmates or a true alpha with their mate and pack.

Theo's gruff—and unwelcome—voice cut through the silence. "You took in a stray because your mothering instincts got in the fucking way?"

His tone was scathing. Had Arden been in her Lycan form, hackles would have risen higher than the four-hundred-year-old oak tree within the Orionian castle's courtyard.

"Jace, Aeri—any thoughts or opinions you'd like to get off your chest?" Arden eyed the twins as she attempted to keep her tone light and inquisitive.

Aeri piped up dispassionately, "Arden is the least mothering figure I've ever met."

"Thank you, I think." Arden was bemused, unsure if she should be offended by the nonbinary twin's comment.

Aeri flashed an amused smirk with that cool androgynous vibe only they could pull off. "Regardless, I want to know more about the child. She seems…" Aeri's voice trailed off, their eyes looking distant.

"Older than she appears." Jace finished for them. She raised an inquisitive eyebrow at the girl. It was Xara's story to share, if she chose to.

Arden listened as Xara bravely shared her history. This human girl held more tenacity than many Orionian adults Arden had encountered. Despite Xara's obvious trepidation—pronounced by her shaky hands and sweaty skin—and the fact that the very monsters she grew up fearing surrounded her, Xara was keeping her head high, spine straight, and chin tilted up. Even when large tears fell, and Xara's voice broke as she recanted her past, the girl remained staunch in her stance and determination not to shrink down in shame. When Xara finished, Arden took that as her cue to continue the plan they had discussed.

"And so, we come to the pack to request an exception to tradition. I know humans are not typically initiated into packs, but many extenuating circumstances led to this request. Additionally, Xara is prepared to make the blood oath of fealty to me and, by extension, our pack."

All the Lycans stared in disbelief. In unison, the twins tilted their heads in surprise, the movement almost entirely lupine. Had she not been entrenched in such a serious moment, Arden would have laughed at their synchronicity. Raised eyebrows were the only change in expression Maximus allowed himself. Theo, unsurprisingly, kept his scowl.

"And what exactly does this thing bring to the pack? It sounds like we'll just have another mouth I need to feed," Theo began to complain. Arden moved to smack the disrespect out of him, but a small hand grabbing her shirt caused her to pause.

Xara snapped her cloak tight intrepidly. "*She* is more than capable of contributing to the pack. I slaved in the fields before I could speak and have suffered more in this life at the hands of a family than most will ever experience. I am often seen as small and inconsequential—"

Arden saw the withering look Xara shot Theo as another example of the balls of steel the girl possessed.

"I will spy for the pack. I can pick up a legitimate job at the castle. Nobody checks what they say in front of the maids. I will be as invisible as a ghost and can report any information you may need while earning my keep with a small salary."

Arden struggled to press her lips together and withhold a smile. Only Maximus appeared unfazed. "Just what kind of operation do you think we are running that we would have use for castle insider intel?"

Xara gave a knowing smile before answering with a small chuckle. "Arden is the Reaper. I am not naive enough to think the rest of you don't follow in those footsteps when your home is a secret den in the forest. Plus, she disemboweled several child predators right after robbing a mansion for information. That's not sketchy at all, right?"

When Maximus looked her way, Arden merely shrugged. If he did not approve of how she performed the job, he could do it instead. She respected him more than anybody else, but she would be damned if she would be shamed for the monster she had to become to save their kingdom.

The price for their people's salvation was partially the blood on her hands and the splintered fractals of whatever remained of her soul. If he wanted to take over the mantle, Arden would happily let him. Until then, it was her burden to bear and her decision alone how to carry it.

The twins stood up, identical in their mannerisms but very different in appearance and personalities, perfectly balancing each other. Jace possessed long, wild, flaming red hair and green eyes as emerald as the Orionian forests. Always the joker, the ever-present grin was on his face as he made his way closer to them.

Aeri's mussed blond hair stuck out in every direction as if they had just woken up before Arden and Xara's arrival. Based on their tired green eyes, that seemed highly likely. They always enjoyed sleeping in when able. Aeri paced along one step behind their twin.

Jace looked impressed as he scanned Xara from head to toe. "Not much gets past our observant friend. I say we keep her. She's cute, fierce, and smart."

"And cutthroat," Aeri added quietly.

"Yes," Jace continued. "And cutthroat. Just my type of packmate. Even for a pup."

Arden's heart warmed. If half the pack accepted her small companion, it was only a matter of time before the others did too. Max walked up as her thoughts bounced to him, and he kept a comfortable distance from the girl. With almost three decades of knowing him, Arden knew it was not to scare the child.

Max said, "Arden, I have known you for your entire life. I have never known you to bring an untrustworthy person into our family. Something about Xara called to you and your wolf. I trust those instincts."

Relief washed over her, and her shoulders fully relaxed for the first time since entering the den. She wondered if Xara's trembling came from happiness, trepidation, or both. It seemed to ease only through pure willpower as Theo prowled closer to Xara.

"Make the oath. Then, we'll see your mettle and if you are worthy," Theo said rather harshly.

Xara held out her hand. "Dagger. Now."

Within a single breath, Arden unsheathed one of her blades and placed it in her waiting palm. They had discussed the ritual extensively on the way, anticipating some of the pack's distrust.

They'd practiced the recitation tirelessly until it was perfect, and both understood the implications. Swearing an oath of fealty was not as common as in the old days. In Orion, only those sworn into the royal court were required to do it, but it happened rarely between others.

Both of them had stumbled through various wordings to honor each other. Arden's wolf had never demanded to protect a person before this. For her, it was not a choice but a necessity.

Xara locked eyes with Arden before pressing the blade against her own palm. Swiftly, she pulled down and sliced it. She winced, but barely, and pride bloomed inside Arden.

"I, Xara, swear this blood oath of my free will, knowingly entering into a binding contract and all it entails. I swear loyalty to you, Arden, and to always do the best for you. I swear to honor you and protect you to the best of my abilities. I promise to integrate into your pack and your family and to remain loyal to you and all you stand for until my last breath."

Without hesitation, Arden slashed the blade into her own palm, briefly watching crimson blood swell out. "I, Arden, swear this blood oath of my own free will, knowingly entering into a binding contract and all it entails. I accept your oath and, in return, swear to honor and care for you as if you were of my own blood. I promise to always treat you as family until the Mother and the gods call us home, and I will remain with you in the After."

Without another moment, bleeding palms were pressed together, human blood and halfling blood mixing. A sudden flash of light pierced the den as the magick took over, the brightness ensconcing them. After a moment, the den was cast in darkness once more. The oath settled on Arden's shoulders like a warm embrace, not suffocating but reassuring.

"Welcome to the pack, pup. You can share Arden's space since you are so close now. Stay out of my way." Theo shoved through them, disconnecting their clasped hands.

Arden rolled her eyes at his immature antics, and Xara covered her mouth to hide her grin. Examining her palm in the dim light, Arden saw the blood had already coagulated and begun to dry. Xara did not have the same quick healing. Arden gestured for her to sit down so she could tend to the wound.

Although it would have been easier to use quintessence, she wanted this to be more hands-on after the intimacy of binding their souls together. Pouring some lukewarm water out of the canteen over the fresh wound, she washed the blood away from the cut.

Arden's tattered heart thumped an extra beat as she beheld the mark on Xara's palm. A perfectly healed scar lay in the place of the previously jagged open flesh. Instead of the various red hues of a new scar, the line was shimmering silver. Arden hastily wiped off her hand on her pants and beheld a matching line. She had assumed the stinging had stopped due to the adrenaline rush, not because it had healed already.

Maximus nodded, seemingly amused at the shock mirrored on their faces. "I suppose neither of you have sworn the oath of fealty before?"

Xara shook her head. Arden did not bother to answer, as Max already knew her history.

His eyes turned glassy as he spoke wistfully. "The most

honorable thing I ever did was swear the blood oath to your father, Arden."

Her surprised gaze flew to each person in the room, rapidly assessing their reaction to his confession. Maximus's background had been painstakingly crafted by the Princess of Orion to minimize any chance of him being recognized, even by his own people. The twins did not so much as look up from the parchment they were reviewing. Theo was nowhere to be seen, perhaps in the back area of the cavernous room. Her shoulders visibly relaxed, and she subtly dipped her chin for Maximus to continue.

"Being blood-sworn to him has been the single most important thing I have accomplished in my many years. The blood oath is a gift from Mother Ambrosia to honor those faithful to it."

"And punish those who are not," Arden muttered darkly.

A wry smile lifted the corners of Max's lips. "Touché, Arden. Quintessence is a living entity, as cognizant as any of us. Instead of being contained in one physical form, it resides everywhere among us, even among the beings who can't sense it. The oaths work primarily based on the intent of those using them. For oath marks, the magick takes into account the commitment each party is making to the other and is, therefore, slightly personalized to each. The one thing they have in common is the color of the permanent mark."

He examined the matching scars. "The permanent oath mark reflects your commitment to never stop caring for and protecting each other, even in the After."

"Can we see yours, sir?"

Grief tugged at the edges of Maximus's eyes, dimming the light in them as he looked at Xara. "Of course, little one."

He unbuttoned the top of his gray tunic, baring the left side of his bronze chest to her. Arden's eyes shuttered, and she purposefully did not look at the mark. The ache from the memory of her father was still as sharp as ever, even after all those years. She knew what she would see. His oath mark was a thin line crossing his pectoral muscle diagonally.

Despite guessing what Xara's follow-up question would be, Arden's heart squeezed in renewed grief as the girl spoke. "Why is yours not reflective like ours?"

Ever patient and kind, Maximus did not even flinch at the reminder. "All blood oaths shine because of the magick imbued in them. Your father's mark was white, yes?"

"No." Xara frowned in confusion. "His was always just a scar, like yours."

"Ah." He paused, thinking about the implications of that. "Did you lay eyes on it prior to your mother's passing?"

"No, sir. Only afterward."

"You can call me Max, sweetie." He clasped her fingers, dwarfing them with his huge hand. "Oaths are distinct colors depending on the type. Oaths of fealty are silver. Gold marks are oaths between mates, general blood oaths that are not the previous two types are white, and oaths of vengeance are black. When one of the people within the oath passes on to the After, the mark will return to regular scar tissue, as the surviving member is no longer bound by the magick."

Xara asked, "Your father is dead, A?"

Her soft voice threatened to break Arden's carefully built mask of indifference. She could practically scent the pity. "Yes, Xara. My mother too. Max basically adopted me, which is just one of the many examples of the poor life choices he has made in his old age."

Maximus roared a full belly laugh at her verbal jab, causing Xara to giggle along with his mirth. Arden could not bear to dwell on the traumatizing past any longer.

Refocusing on business, Arden changed the topic. "Maximus, I also have intel from Lord Caine's manor. A bunch of paperwork and a vial with green liquid in it. Could we have Aeri examine the vial and have Theo break down their underground network?"

"I did not think you had finally tracked it down. How

do you know it is accurate?" Theo appeared out of seemingly thin air, and Aeri crept closer, listening intently at the sound of their name. Jace noticed everybody's attention on them and followed after his sibling.

Undeterred, Arden answered firmly. "Unless hiding information within an alcove lined with quintessence-imbued spikes is common practice for most, I am fairly certain it was not anything they wished to be found."

Her voice was flat, daring any of the men to second guess her surety again. When silence persevered, Arden gestured toward the bandages on her right arm and hand. "As you can see, the spikes were an actual threat instead of a mere visual deterrent. The rest of the documents in my satchel had adorned the large desk within Lord Caine's chambers, along with the King's invitation."

"What invitation?" Theo demanded.

"I am unsure, but the talk in *The Crevice* was that the King has an official announcement planned for later today. Xara and I are planning to attend."

If Xara was shocked by the turn of events, she did not let it show. The neutral look she wore did not waver a modicum as she nodded her agreement.

The rest of the pack looked disturbed. The King of Cyrene had not convened the lords back into the capital of Silas since before the queen died. Security was doubled, and nobody saw his daughter either. Prior to being chased down by the princess the night before, Arden had remained sure that the king kept her sequestered safely within the castle walls for her protection. Apparently, the King did not have as tight of a grip on her leash as he believed.

Faithfulness to the pack demanded she inform them of her sighting, but a soft voice whispered in the back of her mind.

Wait. Not yet.

History and experience led her to trust that voice of reason despite going against her instincts. Some secrets were necessary in war. They would not understand why she did not take the princess then. She did not understand why she not only allowed but helped her escape. However, Arden had no doubt she would understand soon. Luckily, Xara kept her mouth closed about the encounter too.

"Despite the announcement, our mission remains unchanged. Theo—see if you can gather how the Cyrenian Crown is tracking down our kin utilizing the illegal market. We know they have a system. Maybe this swiped paperwork and thumb drive can help."

Theo was nodding his head as he considered. "I will need to go back to the SPIU to use their tech."

At the mere mention of the Silas Private Investigatory Unit, Arden wrinkled her nose. The brief leave she'd requested to complete her trip to the Caine manor ended the next day, and she would have to spend half of her time pretending to work for the enemy again. The brief reprieve from agency life had been nice. A good night's sleep would seemingly continue to evade her.

Max's voice was firm and commanding as he continued to hand out assignments. "Aeri, let's put your genius mind to the test and break down whatever chemicals and ingredients are housed in the green vial. Hopefully, you can reverse engineer it to discover its purpose."

"Maybe it will be a useful new substance to add to our arsenal." Aeri's excitement was palpable.

Jace smiled at his sibling, ruffling their sandy hair. Arden noticed the sweet look of affection Aeri shot Jace. She swallowed thickly as homesickness hit her like a punch to the solar plexus, and she looked away.

"Arden, go back to the SPIU and work that angle while I find new contracts for the Reaper. Jace, you will—"

"Be in charge of being the handsome one. I know," Jace cut Maximus off, and Xara giggled at his shenanigans.

An exaggerated long sigh blew out of Max's mouth as the corner of his lips twitched upward at Jace's antics too.

Seeming to ignore the commentary for the moment, Max settled his brown eyes on Arden. "Keep an ear out for this announcement and continue forward as planned until changes are necessary."

Differing levels of enthusiasm followed, but all pack members agreed with Maximus. Xara started packing their travel belongings. "Come on, A! We have to get to town to hear about the announcement!" When Arden opened her mouth to argue that they needed to come up with more details for the operation, the girl cut her off.

"It will take us a while to get there, and we don't want to miss it." Arden could not disagree with that point. She said goodbye to the pack and started back toward the capital of Cyrene with her newest packmate

CHAPTER FIVE

PROCLAMATIONS

The city of Silas was vibrating with energy and anticipation, unlike anything she had seen before. A dull roar rose from outside the announcement balcony as the residents below continued to speak excitedly, heard even above the nobles' conversations. Teyla tried to ignore the sheer volume of the crowd as her focus narrowed in on the King.

He was pacing back and forth across the reception room, his black robe billowing in his wake; even the disgustingly expensive silk dared not get in his way. Several of the dukes and duchesses were murmuring amongst themselves, but overall, they kept a better handle on their excitement and curiosity. A fairly familiar face, Lord Johan Caine, sipped his wine as he watched the King like a hawk.

Johan had not arrived until this morning, cutting it quite close to the deadline for this announcement. He was relatively new to the noble role after his father, Lord Betor Caine, had been slaughtered while on a hunting trip less than a year earlier.

Rumors swirled around the elite within the castle walls that Johan himself had orchestrated it. After watching him socialize for the last twenty minutes, Teyla would not be surprised if it was true. His deep brown eyes were so dark they almost appeared black, and his tongue was sharp whenever he spoke. It would not be the first time that ambition had caused changes within the ranks. She vowed to stay as far away from him as possible during his stay.

Teyla wished in vain that the announcement was already over so she could take her blasted dress off. Dread curdled in her stomach, and an acrid taste climbed the back of her throat as they all awaited the announcement. A silly competition was all it apparently took to win the hand of the elusive Cyrenian princess. What was the King thinking?

He had remained firm for years about utilizing marriage for long-lasting treaties with other kingdoms. After Orion's king and queen had fallen and their orphaned daughter had retreated to the deep recesses of her mountainous kingdom to rebuild, he seemed less persistent about needing allies but still determined an arranged marriage would benefit the kingdom. Not love. Never for anything so inconsequential.

As far as she knew, the King did not even believe in love after her mother had died. At complete odds with her father, she desired to marry someone she loved instead of for propriety. Still, the King and his court of nobility focused on what exactly they could leverage from using her.

A delicate clearing of a throat made her glance up from her fidgeting hands to see all eyes were trained on her. A flush of embarrassment rose to her neck and cheeks as she met the King's eyes.

"Your Majesty, please forgive me. I was so enraptured by excited thoughts of my upcoming engagement that I was unable to hear what you said."

Audible gasps left the noble women, and men's voices rose in outrage. The dark promise of excruciating pain and suffering crossed the King's face through the clamoring. Teyla's jaw clenched as her stomach somersaulted at the realization that she had been very, very wrong in her calculations.

Her statement ruined his announcement. Despite trying

so hard to be the good, demure daughter, she'd taken the "glory" and excitement of his dramatic announcement away from him. What an idiotic mistake.

A glance toward Nicolai at the door revealed a hungry smile. *Playtime* would occur again much sooner than she'd hoped. Anxiety and suppressed rage battled inside of her, righteous anger threatening to reveal her traitorous thoughts. Nicolai noticed she was slightly shaking with disquietude, and his eyes flashed a warning.

Message received.

He delighted in her fear and pain, but if she made more of a fool out of the King, there would be hell to pay.

Right.

Bitterness swirled like smoke in her mouth. Not even the nobility should know she felt anything but love and loyalty toward the King and Crown of Cyrene. Her chest expanded painfully as she focused on breathing deeply, tunneling so far inside that only her name remained. All that existed was her at her most basic, primal level. There, she was safe. No matter what happened to her mind or body, nobody could take away that sweet, dark pit within. Slowly, a faint light began to emit from the darkness of her soul.

The slight trembling stopped. Carefully, like her first attempt to calm a wily mare in the fields, Teyla reached out to the magick. This ability to control it was kept shoved so deep inside her that not even a Lycan's superior senses would be able to sniff out this truth. Here lay the secret that so many had died to keep from everyone, even her father. Joyously, the quintessence swirled around her, begging her to allow it out to dance. She felt exhilarated.

Such a deadly thing this magick was. Teyla would be put to death if it was discovered, but she *felt* invincible. So, so dangerous was it to feel this brazen attitude toward the monster within the King.

As the power thrummed inside her, a small, wicked smile broke free at the pandemonium. Let the King recover this mess of his own creation. It was his problem that he wanted to be so overdramatic about the reveal of his stupid game. There would be pain in her future; that much was sure.

However, triumphant horns rang in her ears, negating even anxiety over the future. A thought struck her. This was what it was like to feel powerful. People killed for less. It was addictive. No wonder the King had attempted to eradicate this threat to him.

This little setback was the least the King deserved. That treasonous thought alone brought her out of her righteous reverie. Ruefully, Teyla mentally caressed the magick with love and willed it to hide. She wiped the satisfaction from her face, but it was too late.

The King's cunning eyes were locked on her victorious smile; it was as if he had immediate access to her very thoughts. The scorching wrath pouring out of him was world-ending. He was cataloging this moment to punish her later; of that, she had little doubt.

Instead of his usual bored, unimpressed face whenever he happened to pivot his attention toward her, pure malice lit his face. At that moment, she could practically feel the dynamic shift. Instead of being used as a plaything for Nicolai, the King would up the ante and the suffering.

A tiny, fucked-up part of her sighed in relief. Nicolai's treatment of her had turned very possessive and entitled. Nausea rose at the memory of how brashly his hands had caressed her the last time. If the King allowed it, she had no doubt that he would have raped her that night. Drunk on her blood, alcohol, and control, and high on her terror and pleas for him to stop, his coy teasing of her had evolved into something far more sinister.

The King demanded quiet, and despite the wild feelings running rampant in the room, all obeyed. Taking a deep breath, Teyla felt the tension released from his neck, and he held out his hands as if calming a feral beast.

"Silence, please, my friends. Have you forgotten who

your King is?" he hissed. Those words alone squashed the rest of the whispers in the room. The King was not just upset. He was furious. The last time he'd been this angry, heads had rolled.

"I demand and deserve your respect and your trust. Have I not earned that?"

Immediately, the nobility responded with affirmations and declarations of their trust. Nobody was foolish enough to remain silent, especially her. Teyla murmured the engrained attestation of loyalty and fidelity to the Crown and surreptitiously glanced around, noticing the men were more emphatic than the women with their responses.

"While my lovely Teyla was too excited and ruined the surprise, she is correct." The thinly veiled verbal reprimand lashed against her face like a visceral blow. "I have designed a competition for our entertainment and pleasure. At the end of the competition, the victor will become engaged to the Princess of Cyrene."

A pin drop would have felt like an earthquake at this point.

"The competition will consist of extremely mentally, physically, and emotionally grueling challenges designed by myself so that only the strongest competitors can survive." He paused, looking around the room. Not a single brave soul met his gaze.

"There are no rules for entering the contest except for one. The contract is binding. You either pass each round hoping to win and become victorious or become eliminated. A new wave of my ingenious competition will occur every other week at the end of the work week. This will be brutal. People will die. Many will give up once inside, become eliminated, and crawl back to whatever hovel they came from. But some will succeed. Bets will be made. Money will change hands. We will be entertained and well fed."

She remained ramrod straight in her chair, trying not to disappoint him any further as her mind raced with the possibilities. How many people realistically wanted to compete for her hand, the princess they had not truly seen in over a decade? Surely not that many.

Lord Caine, in heightened elegance, rose formally from his seat and bowed, addressing the King. "Your Majesty, may I ask a question?"

His eyes remained fixed on the floor while the King assessed him. Whatever the King saw in him, he appeared to be pleased. He inclined his head, the only permission the lord needed.

"Thank you for your generosity. My King, will there be a limit on the number of contestants? I'm sure many people will see the value of this competition and will want in."

The King considered. "You bring up a fair point. Only one competitor per family name."

Lord Caine nodded and sat back down, appeased. One noble was not so gracious. Lord Marcus Mace exploded out of his seat, red-faced with anger.

"What of us, Julius? We have served you well for decades. How will you repay us for *our* loyalty when you offer your daughter's hand in marriage to commoners like a common street whore!"

Teyla winced as the nobility gasped, but he barreled onward. "We have not pushed the matter of her marriage for years because you said she was reserved for furthering your conquests and making relationships with other kingdoms. This is unacceptable, and I demand only the nobility have a right to her hand!"

For fear of further disturbing the peace, Teyla did not dare to breathe too deeply. The tension in the room around her grew taut with the King's rage. He turned toward the lord and slowly walked over to him.

His voice was a soft lilt as he addressed the man.

Lord Mace stiffened almost imperceptibly. The King laid a hand on each of his shoulders and drew him in for a hug.

"Marcus," the King continued, still speaking softly. "Of

course, the nobles have a right to her hand. You all may enter the competition to prove your worth to me. I will even offer you all the extra knowledge you need beforehand to give you an advantage over the rest. No mere commoner should be able to defeat these tasks, anyway. It is merely for my amusement."

Lord Mace relaxed within his embrace, a smile of relief on his face. He did not see the King's eyes harden or his face contort with his rage, but the rest of the party did. It took everything in her to keep silent and simply bear witness to what was about to happen. The noblewomen did not have the same restraint or common sense.

At the sound of the gasps, the Lord tried to pull away but met the relentless resistance of the King's embrace. "All of you are to receive a chance. Everyone, that is, except you."

With a strength he should not possess at his age, the King wrapped his hands around the lord's neck and twisted, effectively snapping his neck. A scream ripped free from one of the ladies, cut short by a different lord desperate to cover her mouth. Alas, it was too late.

With a wave of the King's right hand, Nicolai prowled forward, grabbing the lady from her seat and forcing her to her knees in front of the King. He bowed low, offering his large handgun, grip first, to the monarch. No hesitation was found as the King grabbed the gun and spoke.

"Lady Elizabeth Mace, you have been found guilty of treason by the King through the association of your husband, Lord Marcus Mace. Both of you have been sentenced to death."

The metal glinted as he pressed it directly against the lady's forehead and pulled the trigger. Blood and chunks of brain flew, and everybody but Nicolai and the King jumped out of the way.

Taking out a pure white handkerchief, the King wiped the blood from his hands and face. Nicolai grabbed the dropped gun, tucked it back in its holster at his hip, and returned to his post, covered in blood and not looking the least bit bothered.

Instead, he looked rather feral and delighted.

Teyla vaguely heeded the rest of the room as they all went silent and obedient. Her mind replayed the sequence on a loop, only refocusing when the King's announcement to the general public occurred. Even with his stipulation of only one person per family being eligible to enter, the crowd roared with approval and excitement.

Her mind raced just as it always did after witnessing the King, her father, murder people without just cause. His trials were nonexistent, and each time he was displeased with someone, he became the executioner himself. He relished the kill. What kind of monster did that?

She was exceedingly grateful when she was allowed to return to her chambers, trapped within the prison of her own mind. It seemed the gods blessed her even more, as the blood that soaked the folds at the bottom of the skirt made her horrid dress unsalvageable.

Bummer, she thought dryly.

Eventually, during her hot bath, thoughts shifted away from the execution to who might win her hand in marriage. Would he be kind to her or be just another power-hungry man like Nicolai or Lord Caine? Another shudder rippled through her despite the heat of the water at the thought of Lord Caine becoming king once her father died. Either way, her future betrothed was almost guaranteed to be awful.

"Soon," she whispered to her heart. *Soon, we will escape and never look back.*

CHAPTER SIX

STRATAGEM

Sweat ran in rivulets down Arden's shoulder blades under the infernal heat as the entire pack leaned over the rudimentary map that Aeri had quickly sketched. The King had announced the first event of the competition only three days prior, and obtaining Theo and Jace's aliases had been a hassle. Acquiring last-minute IDs required "borrowing" them from unregistered dead people with no next of kin. Due to her reputation as the Reaper, Arden had a few contacts who owed her favors for *not* killing them.

Many tears and pleas for mercy later, one of the young men who supplied kids with fake IDs within Silas had provided her with two sets of identification. They included IDs, heritage patents, and medical records. She scrutinized them meticulously, comparing them to other citizens' proof of identification.

When they'd electronically registered the two fake names for the competition, they'd waited a nerve-wracking few minutes to see if Arden had been conned. Luckily for them and the damn hacker, the IDs passed the test. After a lot of huffing and puffing, the pack deemed them sufficient.

As the brains of their operation, Aeri had snuck out

alone to the arena every night for the last three days and early this morning for the last time to get a layout and a general idea of what they would be facing. Just as Theo began to argue with them over the best battle strategies, a horn blew overhead, signaling an announcement from the King.

The large screens zoomed in as he rose from his makeshift throne and climbed the stairs, raising his hands wide, commanding silence. With the cameras projecting his face clearly, there was unlikely to be a single soul that could not see his gleaming smile. When the crowd fully hushed their excitement at seeing him so up close, he began, a microphone amplifying his words.

"Citizens of Silas and the surrounding towns within our great kingdom of Cyrene, the wait is finally over! Today marks the first of five challenges that mark this competition. The prize? Glory. Not to mention the hand of my beloved daughter, Princess Teyla."

Theo snorted incredulously. Arden attempted not to smile at the glare Max sent his way. She actually agreed with Theo this time but would never pass up an opportunity to see him put in his place. If the Princess of Cyrene was so cherished, why did the King sequester her for so long? Surely, the solitude would wreck anybody's mental well-being.

A tingle ran up her spine at the memory of the irate princess throwing a dagger straight at her head. She was more ferocious than expected, and Arden's body thrummed in excitement at the princess's accuracy. Arden secretly hoped she might present a fun challenge after years of laborious work. Maybe the King did not know the backbone she possessed.

"While I know all of you brave men are anxious to see your princess clearly for the first time in fifteen years, the council and I have decided that she will be fully unveiled to the champions of round four of the competition."

Angry protests erupted, but the King silenced them with brutal efficiency. "My friends, please understand. I cannot lose my only daughter like I did my wife."

He paused for a moment as if overcome by emotion. Clearing his throat, he continued. "I know there are parties in the city right now plotting my demise and the fall of the Cyrenian Crown."

More outraged cries followed that statement. The number of phones that were up recording as if this was a concert was ridiculous.

"Who knew we were so popular as to make the announcement?" Jace joked under his breath.

Before Max could react, Aeri boxed their twin over the ear and cast him a reproachful look. The King carried on, encouraged by the crowd's reaction. Arden's attention was pulled toward the siblings.

"Just because you think we are surrounded by only humans does not mean that we are. Try to be less careless, dumbass." The Lycans in the area easily heard Aeri's hiss, but Xara looked confused. Arden shook her head with a slight eye roll and watched the King create his spectacle.

The King continued from his raised podium. "Yes, I know. Some people plan to slaughter my daughter and me daily. There are raids almost weekly by the Orionian scum along our borders, killing our most defenseless brothers and sisters and laying waste to our land! While I am willing to be in harm's way as your King, I must be much more careful with your princess."

The crowd's tone shifted to understanding and sympathy. The King easily manipulated the crowd, lying as they blindly believed every word from his lips.

It was easy for them. The Queen of Cyrene had been adored by her people prior to her murder. The memory of her kindness and grace remained, especially within the stone walls of Silas. They never publicly caught the perpetrator, but the King would not rest until she was avenged.

The King brushed his hand over his purple robe. "The first phase of the competition is a strategy game. My champion must be smart and strategic, able to speak up in council meetings and back up what he says in physical combat if necessary.

Therefore, I have split the competitors up into teams of roughly fifty men. Each team is color-coded with dye. They will have the objective of stealing the other team's Cyrenian flag, also dyed."

The crowd was mesmerized, trying to grasp the information like a lifeline. There had never been a game like this in Cyrenian history, which was fitting since a princess historically had never been betrothed to a commoner.

Arden's eyes skimmed the crowd on the raised platform, holding the King, royal guards, and nobility. Although she suspected the princess would not be present, she felt a dash of disappointment when she could not pick out the princess's striking golden locks.

"There were so many people who stepped forward to join this challenge that today's events will occur in four waves. Just under four hundred Cyrenian men will prove their mettle and their mental worth." The crowd roared in encouragement for their families' competitors.

After a long pause, the King added, "Half of them will be eliminated after today."

Arden watched as the crowd was stunned to silence.

The King continued. "Let's not delay any longer. Round one teams, make your way into the playing field. This is a reminder that there should be no stepping out of the confines of the area marked by wood. Trying to leave the arena will be grounds for immediate expulsion from the games."

Once the first wave of men entered the arena, blue dyed shirts versus a red clay dye, the King held up his hand again.

"Let the games begin!" he bellowed to the crowd. The roar was deafening to Arden's sensitive ears. The wincing of her pack mates assured her that they were suffering just as much.

"Aeri, show us what you've got," Maximus commanded. Jace and Theo were assigned to the final two waves, so they needed to finalize a plan quickly.

The arena was a short horse ride outside of the walls

of the city, where the terrain turned far rougher. Instead of the rolling hills with bright greenery, the ground was riddled with rocks of all shapes and sizes, making it very uneven to cross, especially on horseback. Trees grew in abundance, their gnarled roots intertwining to create even more danger.

Some space was cleared enough for spectating, but for the most part, it was kept wild. There were areas of large rock formations, a natural stream running through, along with lots of trees and shrubbery. In a few areas, the trees had been thinned out so the spectating could be more enjoyable. A pang of sadness shot through Arden at the senseless loss of arboreal life.

Some of the chopped-down trees had been laid in a rough oval shape to mark the competition arena. Per the announcement earlier in the week, people were allowed to spectate anywhere outside of the oval. People congregated toward the middle section of the arena, unwilling to miss the action.

The royals and nobility—not including the princess—enjoyed their own covered, private section to spectate. The platform was raised for the best view, and the castle servants had even brought padded chairs for its occupants.

It was very different from the glory of their usual cozy areas within the castle, but it did seem to do the trick of keeping them out of the dirt and allowing them to have the best seats. The King undoubtedly demanded these arrangements for maximum comfort for the nobility. He left all of the "lesser" people in the literal dirt. Orion's deceased king and queen had never treated their people like that; in every way they could, they treated everybody with equal respect and dignity.

Aeri's sketch showed the oval boundary, as well as the largest components within the arena. When Arden squinted closer, it was obvious that they had even shaded it to accurately represent elevation changes that could benefit them. The topography was incredible, and Arden amusedly thought that Aeri had missed their true calling as a cartographer. She was grateful their path had brought them to this gathering so the Lycans could carry out their insurgency once and for all and be rid of the King.

Aeri said, "I know this might piss you off, Theo, but I don't think you should be the one competing in the games."

Arden's head swiveled to Aeri in surprise. What the hell were they thinking?

Maximus seemed to be on the same wavelength. "We decided three nights ago that Jace and Theo were our best options. What has changed your mind?"

Ever the diplomat, Maximus allowed Aeri the chance to explain. Despite not being a blood-born alpha, he ruled with respect and logic, which Arden admired.

"You cannot be actually considering this right now?" Theo's voice dropped to a low register.

Arden discreetly tucked Xara behind her left arm in case she needed to move her quickly. Theo was extraordinarily hot-headed, and she did not trust him; he could easily cause a scene or hurt her, accidentally or otherwise. Getting the message, Xara crept behind her fully, gripping the back of her button-down top. Despite her wariness, Xara peeked around Arden's torso to keep watching.

Max sighed. "I am giving them the same respect of hearing their logic that I would permit you."

Theo snarled and crossed his rippling forearms as he clenched and unclenched his fists.

At Maximus's nod, Aeri continued with their chin held high. "Theo is great for brute strength, but we don't know what the other challenges will be. We should optimize the members of our pack who are the most well-rounded in their skills. In hand-to-hand combat, Theo might win. But anything requiring other weapons or agility does not play into his strengths."

"You think you're a better fit?" Theo's tone was mocking, causing Jace to stand to full height to defend his wombmate.

"Not me. I know I am better utilized behind the scenes like this." Aeri gestured to the well-drawn map, then tapped their temple knowingly. "The obvious choice is Arden."

Arden's spine stiffened, and she braced for the argument about to break out. Theo had hated her guts from the moment she'd turned his advances down when they'd first met. Partner that with his sick misogyny, and she was the bane of his existence.

Just as Theo opened his mouth, another horn sounded.

An announcer spoke into a microphone. "Moving on to the next round of the competition is…" Arden's eyes nearly hit the back of her skull at the exaggerated dramatization. "The red team!"

The announcer cheered along with the rest of the crowd, making it impossible for Arden to think, let alone hold a conversation. Once the noise settled down, she rushed to answer before Theo did.

"I disagree. I am needed more as the Reaper, and I'm technically clocked in as an SPIU agent right now. I don't have time for this as well." Aeri opened their mouth to argue, so Arden lamely continued. "I would need to wear my all-black ensemble. I will stand out like a torch in a cavern, as I would have to stay masked."

It was mostly a good argument. Theo looked suspicious, as if he could not imagine a situation where she would take his side. It seemed to be a theme today.

Maximus tapped his lips with his pointer finger as he thought through all of the pros and cons, weighing the opinions of each pack member. Wisely, Xara and Jace stayed silent, although both were intently watching the situation unfold.

"Theo, you're out."

Before Maximus could continue, Theo growled with anger. He turned around and punched a tree as he left, causing the bark to splinter. Everybody looked around to see if any humans had noticed the use of unnatural strength, but when nobody yelled or approached the damaged tree, they relaxed.

Maximus rubbed his eyes as if staving off a headache. "Arden, go change. You know the drill. Take Xara with you. I will discuss the battle strategy further with the twins so we have a plan when you get back. Your group is last, so don't rush, but don't mess around either."

"Yes, sir." Arden's voice was clipped with annoyance at the change in events, but she respected Max enough to obey even as her instincts roared at her to challenge his orders.

It took most of her focus to suppress the wolven need to dominate and the rage threatening to rear its ugly head. Xara glanced at her from the corner of her eye. Whatever she saw in Arden's face led her to grasp Arden's hand firmly as they wove through the camping grounds the spectators had set up for the event.

Arden unashamedly clung to Xara's comforting grip like a lifeline, pushing the irritation down until her lungs could expand again uninhibited. The girl remained a silent presence, a steadfast anchor to the outside world, allowing Arden to wrangle the base instincts within.

It was not until she released a deep, settling breath that Xara squeezed her hand and offered a sympathetic smile.

"If you want to talk about it, I am here to listen. There is nothing you could say that I would judge you for." The girl halted her footsteps, jerking Arden to a stop as well. Her big doe eyes looked up with total sincerity. "Except if you tell me you want to date Theo."

A startled laugh escaped Arden, and Xara's chocolate brown eyes twinkled with amusement. Somehow, this girl had pulled her out of one of her destructive spirals quicker than she had ever been able to do alone. Filled with a fondness she had not felt in decades, Arden ruffled Xara's curly hair, whose indignant protest only served to increase Arden's amusement.

Despite the offer, Xara did not push for any answers over the next five minutes of walking back to their tent, hidden inconspicuously at the encampment's edge. Hesitant thoughts and explanations swirled around in Arden's mind as she attempted to determine what was safe to tell her blood-bonded friend. Slipping inside the tent was a brief reprieve from the sweltering heat, putting Arden slightly more at ease.

Her hands were shaky as she dug through her travel pack. If Xara noticed, she did not comment on it. Instead, Xara helped pull out the supplies Arden usually wore on excursions as the Reaper.

"If I tell you this, you cannot breathe a word about it to any of our packmates."

Xara kneeled and helped Arden unlace her well-worn boots to pull them off. Once they were removed, Arden quickly shucked off her beige button-down shirt, brown pants, and underthings. If Xara was uncomfortable at Arden's sudden nakedness, she did not even bat an eye. She simply motioned for Arden to lift her arms. Arden recalled the condition Xara had been in the night they'd first met a few weeks earlier, and it suddenly made much more sense. Arden did as she was instructed, and Xara began to walk around her body with a long scrap of white cloth, wrapping her chest firmly to bind her breasts.

As she worked, Xara calmly spoke. "Even *if* I were not blood-sworn and bonded to you, I would never betray your trust."

Arden ignored the discomfort gradually increasing at having her chest bound. It was the worst part of hiding and pretending to be male, but a necessary one. She had always been pleased with the size of her bust, but it would be a dead giveaway that she was not male if not secured properly.

Arden frowned before replying. "How do I know that to be absolute truth? Others have said similarly."

Hating how insecure she sounded with that admission, Arden looked at the dirt. Xara mimed stretching side to side and swinging her arms, so she followed suit, pleasantly surprised at how comfortable the bindings were. She had never been successful at binding tight enough while allowing for an almost full range of motion. Color her impressed.

"Well, I owe you my life, to start." Arden continued to dress in black clothes while Xara spoke. "But even if that wasn't the case and betraying you could not potentially kill me—" She smiled wryly. "You are single-handedly the most honorable woman I have ever met. I want you to survive and succeed because I know you are going to change the world for the better. To harm you would be to hurt not only myself but the entire continent and every kingdom within its borders. I may be young, but I am not foolish."

Emotion tightened Arden's throat, so she choked out the easiest thing. "Female."

"What?"

As Arden sat down, she attempted to tame the wildness that was her mane of hair. "I am not a woman. That is a word solely befitting to humans. You are a woman—barely, if we consider your bleed to be that determining factor—but I will never be a woman. Fae and Lycans are inherently male or female, or nonbinary in Aeri's case."

Arden yanked at the knots in her hair with frustration. Doing her hair was her most hated chore.

Even after shaving the left corner of her head, she had far too much hair to manage easily. Xara stopped Arden's furious tugging and smacked her hands away. Giving up, Arden huffed and let the girl try.

"Why does the wording matter so much?" Xara's voice held no judgment, only unfettered curiosity.

"It is insulting to ignore the aethereal half of us. I am not simply a human woman. I am incomplete without my Lycan and Fae half. I have one foot in the wild, and that will never change. The verbiage is important and can show a large lack of respect when ignored or used improperly."

Bi-colored eyes closed in relaxation as Xara's fingers brushed her hair and scalp. Nobody had really touched or arranged her hair since her mother, except for Max one time early on after she had been orphaned. He had quickly given up on the unruly hair.

"So, what you're saying is when I really want to piss off Theo, I should call him an incorrigible man?"

The snort that came out of Arden was very unladylike.

Good thing she was not a lady.

"Yeah, pup, that would do it."

A playful tug on her hair was the only response as Xara continued to plait it. Her soul knew she was a safe person, and Arden always trusted those instincts.

"Sometimes I lose some of my control when commanded by others to do something I don't want to."

Xara hummed under her breath.

"What?" Arden was incredulous at the girl's lack of surprise.

"That seems to be a common trend among Lycans, A."

"Well, you're not entirely wrong. We are a stubborn race. But it is different for me. It goes against my very nature to obey a command from a beta Lycan, even one I respect like Max."

"A beta?"

Ah.

This would be more difficult to explain to a human who did not know about Lycan hierarchies. However, if there was one person she was willing to put in the effort for, it was Xara.

"Right, okay. Let's do a quick crash course into Orion races and rankings, shall we?"

"Absolutely." Interest laced Xara's voice.

"Before Cyrene formed its own kingdom, there were four main species of intelligent life. They consisted of humans, Fae, Lycans, and nightwalkers. Underneath the umbrella of humans were witches, which were humans who were blessed with the ability to control magick but did not have an animal form like the Fae.

"When Cyrene rebelled and formed their own kingdom, they slaughtered Fae, Lycans, witches, and nightwalkers, claiming that humans never stood a chance of equality without magick. Most magick wielders fled to Orion, leaving humans and any nightwalkers who escaped the poaching to remain in Cyrene."

"I know all of this, A."

Xara twisted the now-plaited hair around itself into a bun at the base of Arden's neck and secured it with a hair tie. Quickly kissing Xara's cheek in thanks, Arden tugged on her headpiece to cover all of her features except the horizontal sliver for her eyes. As she continued, she strapped a few hidden daggers to her body. One could never be too careful.

"Orion's royal title passes down by birthright or decree. If the ruling king or queen thought their offspring was unfit to rule, they would put their suggestion for an heir to vote by the Council. The Council consists of two representatives from each race, except for nightwalkers, obviously."

Xara grunted her understanding.

"Besides the king or queen, each race has equal power within the governing council to allow for the most equality. So much power, in fact, that the Council could vote out the throne if there were enough cause and support. Anyway, I digress."

Arden pushed through the tent and picked Xara up so she could continue to whisper as they returned to the pack. Xara giggled as she was carried, and Arden was immensely glad to give her childlike experiences again after she had been shoved into adulthood so forcibly.

"Within the Lycan community, there is a natural rank that differentiates us. This follows the way wild wolf packs operate too. The rankings are alpha, beta, and omega. Omegas in the wild are considered the weakest and are often bullied by other wolves. Laws were passed centuries ago abolishing the omega ranking, using magick to mesh it into the beta ranking due to the inequality of that practice. Therefore, packs now consist of one alpha and betas. Whichever Lycan mates with the alpha gains the honorary title of Luna and the respect it deserves.

"We can talk politics later, but a pack of wolves without an alpha in charge is not truly a bonded pack. Maximus is a beta, as are Theo, Aeri, and Jace, so we are not a bonded pack. That means we cannot use magick to mind link and communicate mentally. This is considered a weakness, as a pack cannot be fully bonded without the link. The lack of it can lead to danger and deadly power struggles."

"You said Max, Jace, Aeri, and Theo are betas."

The sentence sounded like a question, but one was not asked. Arden merely nodded, waiting to see if she would connect the dots. Xara slowly leaned backward away from the shoulder she was leaning on, looking surprised. Arden continued walking to the rendezvous point, allowing Xara to digest the information.

"You are not a beta?"

Arden shook her head and raised her eyebrows at Xara meaningfully. It was practically possible to see the gears turning in her head.

"You are too strong to be an omega…" Her voice trailed off, silently prodding Arden to answer her unspoken question. Arden merely grinned and nudged the girl with her right shoulder, prompting her to continue.

"If you are an alpha," Xara spoke slowly, as if piecing together her thoughts. "Why is Maximus in charge?"

Finally, a question that could be easily answered. "Max is older and demands respect without needing to be bonded. My presence here is not to form a pack. My purpose is much bigger than that, as is Max's. The Orionian Council commanded us to complete a top-secret mission that the others only know the bare bones of."

Using her left arm to gently pull Xara's head closer, Arden's mouth close to her ear, Arden spoke so softly not even a Lycan could hear.

"We are to capture the Princess of Cyrene and bring her back to the stronghold of Orion."

Xara reeled back as if struck. Allowing her time to absorb the shock of the statement, Arden continued a bit louder.

"Anyway, that's why I have a hard time obeying others sometimes."

Her voice was cheerful, as if she had not just dropped a bomb in her blood-bonded partner's lap. They were close to where they'd left Max and the twins, so she gently set Xara down on her own two feet. Before she could continue walking, Xara pulled on her sleeve. Arden leaned down attentively.

"Why did you let the princess escape the night we ran into her?"

Arden's gut coiled at the memory. "Honestly, I don't know."

CHAPTER SEVEN

PHASE I

As the princess hid from yet another group of men tramping through the underbrush, she could not help but wonder what the hell possessed her to register in this wretched competition. Letting loose the breath she had been holding, Teyla slowly stood back up from the crouched position and warily looked around for more enemies. The truth was she knew exactly why she'd signed up for this blasted competition, even though it was incredibly stupid and reckless.

For the past two weeks, she had stayed up far too late reading up on the bylaws of Cyrene and the competition's reward. Based on everything she had read, the King's agreement was binding. Whichever man won the competition was guaranteed her hand in marriage by law. That meant if Lord Caine or any other corrupted man won, she had no choice in the matter.

It seemed clear the night she realized just how screwed she was that the only answer was to compete. If she won, no man had the right to her hand. The King might kill her for that impetuous decision, but he would have to do it himself. Teyla was not convinced he would show leniency. She had seen him slaughter for far less severe slights. Still, she would rather die free than live chained to a man just as bad as her father.

By the time she heard the twig snap behind her, it was too late to do anything but dodge. The swords had not been dulled. As the King had put it, "What would be the fun in that?"

The weapons were just as lethal as always, and she barely managed to avoid getting slashed in the face. Her arm was not as lucky.

Crying out in pain, she felt the blade cut through her skin like butter. The burning sensation started mere heartbeats later, and she cradled the arm to her abdomen. Teyla wryly considered that she was lucky no guns had been supplied in this round.

"Look here, boys! We caught an imposter!"

The man sporting an orange strip of fabric around his waist laughed cruelly as she stumbled backward, farther out of his reach. She kept her sword pointed upward, ready to fend off his attack. Dread turned her blood to ice as her frantic gaze swept across the area. A quick headcount revealed five men in orange paraphernalia stalking toward her.

"What is a woman doing out here dressed as a man? Are you some kind of fucked up dyke?" He swept his sword in a wide arc, vaguely gesturing to the whole arena.

The disgust from his words rendered her tongue silent. There was a very slim chance of making it out of here alive. One-on-one, Teyla stood a chance, but she was vastly outnumbered. At least they were on the outskirts of the orange side of the ring and were too far inside to be heard by any spectators—the only positive thing at this moment.

"You don't have to answer, bitch," the man continued undeterred as the other men laughed. "Women are only good for one thing, and that is spreading their legs."

Fury caused her spine to snap straight. The second-hand helmet hid her face enough for them not to know just whom they spoke to. If this was how they talked to a random woman, she could only imagine how they would treat their future wives, princesses or not. He turned to rile up his friends, and she struck like a viper.

Pure, unadulterated anger gifted Teyla the strength and speed she did not naturally possess. The blade struck true, slicing into his ribs before she twirled further away. An unexpected surge of satisfaction rose within her at the sight of his crimson blood dripping off the sword's edge.

"You bitch!" he cursed as he grasped his side. "Get her!"

The roared command was all the warning she had before the men charged. Quickly spiraling downward into her magick, she searched desperately for the dormant quintessence within her. Only to avoid death would she risk exposing this lethal secret. However, magick would do her no good in the After. Just as she grasped the particles and willed them to the surface of her skin, a figure landed mere feet in front of her.

She scrambled backward in shock, her hold on the quintessence vanishing, but he was not facing her. He must have leaped off of the large rock her back was pressed against. How he landed in such a controlled crouch was beyond her. A sigh of relief left her as she noted the bright green cloth tied around his left bicep. Relief turned into confusion as she noticed he held no weapon. His surprising presence alone caused the men to pause.

"Now, now, gentlemen. Surely, I misheard that you were planning to rape and kill a woman?"

That soft voice promised death. Although he had not spoken to her in the same lethal way he'd just spoken to these men, Teyla would recognize that voice anywhere—the voice of the man who had piqued her interest those weeks ago.

"Reaper?" The name was merely a whispered breath of disbelief. Almost as if he heard, his head turned slightly back toward her, but his attention never left the five men, who were looking toward their leader in confusion.

"What the fuck are you waiting for? He's not armed! Kill them both!" Spittle flew from the leader's mouth as he yelled his command. Still, nobody moved as if their instincts warned them of the predator in front of them.

"If I were you, boys, I would walk away while you can still go home to your families. I will not be so lenient next time."

The stranger dressed in black cut a swaggering figure. Normally, she found that characteristic disgusting, but right now, all that swept through her was gratefulness for his arrogance. This man had spared her life the last time they met. While Teyla had yet to see him in action, based on how quickly he had moved out of the trajectory of her dagger, she knew he was not bluffing.

A few of the men looked toward each other, uncertain. Just as she thought they were going to disengage, the man who had originally attacked kicked one of them forward.

"Don't be such pussies! Attack!"

Nothing made men more violent than offending their manhood. Their egos wounded, the leader's lackeys shifted their feet with uncertainty one last time before they charged.

Fear melted into pure awe as Teyla watched the Reaper in action. He did not shift even a fraction until the first man was upon him. He ducked the sword attack and spun, tripping the next man who fell into his comrade's blade. Shouts of surprise and pain rang around them, but her ally did not falter. He spun around like the god of death, moving so fast her eyes could barely track the movement.

In under a minute, all four of the lackeys were dead on the ground, or soon to be, based on the gurgling noise from one of the crumbled bodies. The orange leader's face slackened and turned white as a sheet. He took a half step back, which the Reaper matched, his striking eyes focused, as if he were an asp gearing up to strike. Her jaw dropped in disbelief as the front of the attacker's pants darkened from fear.

"Come on, buddy. Don't be a pussy," the Reaper taunted him, using his own words against him.

Just as the man turned to flee, the vigilante pulled a

dagger seemingly out of thin air and hurled it at him. It struck the base of the man's skull, and his body tumbled unceremoniously to the ground.

Teyla remained standing in stunned silence at how quickly this man had just dispatched five armed men.

He had been armed the entire time.

Instead of using his own weapons, he'd just taken down the first four men with their own. Was it just to prove a point? If so, what was it?

He yanked his dagger out of the man's neck, the crunch of bones sickening. Without a care, he wiped the blade on the dead man's shirt before sheathing it somewhere on his forearm. His eyes flashed with anger as he stalked back toward her.

"What are you doing here, Princess?"

He did recognize her for the second time then. This time, her hair and face were completely hidden under a helmet. How the hell did he know it was her?

He stopped less than a foot away, glaring down with those startling eyes. The anger radiating off him in waves made her throat dry. Teyla tried to swallow, to say anything, but nothing came out.

His head whipped to the left suddenly before he let out such a crude curse that her ears turned red. He yanked the sword from her loose hold and ran straight into her, sweeping her off her feet. Smacking his shoulder in anger, Teyla attempted to twist out of his hold desperately. He did not say anything else as he sprinted away with her in his arms.

She briefly wondered how he was carrying her while covering such a distance so quickly. Maybe adrenaline was giving him extra strength. When she opened her mouth to demand he let her down, he let out a harsh, "Shh!"

He did not just shush the princess of Cyrene. Her hand whipped forward, slapping him hard across the face. A low grunt was the only noise he made, despite the major throbbing in her hand, affirming it was a solid smack.

"Take off your helmet. Now, Princess!"

The harsh demand startled her, but she obeyed. He grabbed it and chucked it backward to the right, creating a large clatter. He leaped off of a raised area into a small valley. His knees gave out as they landed, and Teyla braced for the impact that was undoubtedly about to hit. The breath left her as they landed, but she did not have any pain. Somehow, he had twisted, taking the brunt of the damage.

Despite the pain he must be feeling, he pulled her toward him and dove into a small overhanging area underneath the large boulder he had just launched over. It was a very tight area, only large enough for both of their bodies to lay flush against each other. He gently clamped a hand over her mouth as he breathed hard, his eyes scanning the valley as if waiting for something.

Seconds after he settled them into the crevice, the sound of many people crashing through the foliage reached her ears. Understanding flooded through her. He had known they were coming and had hidden them. Her right hand was trapped between her body and his chest, so she gently nudged his chest to get his attention.

When his attention landed on her, Teyla shifted her head into a small nod, hoping he understood the silent plea. The Reaper must have found whatever he was searching for in her gaze because he removed his gloved hand from covering her mouth and shifted enough to grab another dagger. She could not figure out where he was storing all of them.

The crashing grew louder before coming to a halt. Several pairs of boots were visible just over his shoulder. Her eyes grew wide with fear.

Moving slow enough not to rustle the various leaves under them, the man shifted to wedge his leg between hers. He insistently pushed until his thigh fully settled against her core, startling her. His torso shifted slightly to block her view, and his right arm carefully tucked her head to his chest, being mindful not to stick her with the blade in his hand.

As all the light was blocked out, she understood his

positioning. He was wearing solely black and had completely covered her from view, especially her bright golden hair that was no longer hidden by a helmet.

"Quiet your breathing, Princess."

His breath whispered into her ear, causing a shiver to wrack her body from the gentle caress. Despite knowing he was being quiet for tactical reasons, a forbidden, wicked delight at the sensation caused her toes to curl in her boots.

As her vision adjusted to the darkness, she could just barely make out the glint in his eyes as he studied her. Teyla could vaguely hear the muffled voices of the men talking to each other, but her entire being was focused on the man lying completely on top of her. His face was covered enough that she could not tell what he was thinking.

After several agonizing moments waiting to be discovered, her heartbeat slowed to a steady cadence again, and her breaths came out soundlessly. When she had matched her breathing to his, the mind-numbing fear faded enough for irritation to creep in. She was still terrified but was once again fully in control of her faculties.

"Good."

That single raspy word had her closing her eyes to ignore the reaction the praise brought her. She mindlessly shifted, causing his thigh to press against her harder. Only then did her mind fully register the position they were in.

Their bodies were pressed as closely as they could be, leaving little to the imagination. In the Reaper's effort to fully hide her body and easily seen clothes, his hips were draped over her. One very strong thigh was shoved against her center, meaning any small movement caused a delicious heat to travel through her.

The realization made Teyla stiffen in mortification. The man's brows furrowed in confusion. After a moment of them simply breathing, his entire demeanor changed, and she could see the moment understanding dawned on him.

He lifted his hips slightly away from her, allowing a

brief reprieve from the sensations. Relief and disappointment warred inside. It was short-lived, as he very slowly shifted forward again, pressing firmly against her as he watched closely. She inhaled sharply at the pleasant sensation and glared accusingly at him.

"Reaper." Her tone was full of warning as she beheld the laughter dancing in his eyes. At the sound of his name, his gaze seemed to get even more molten. His focus dipped to her mouth, and she realized she was biting her bottom lip.

"Where the fuck did they go?" one of the men less than three feet away spoke, exasperated.

The loud voice jolted her, and fear replaced the pleasant sensation in her abdomen. It was as if a spell had broken. The Reaper's previously passionate gaze shuttered back to a very guarded look as he eased his body weight off her as best he could in such tight quarters.

Giving herself two heartbeats of horror at her lack of self-control, Teyla shoved the self-loathing away to be dealt with later.

"How did they run away so quickly? We were right on their heels!"

"Maybe it's for the best. Did you see those bodies they left scattered around out there? Whatever man did that is a monster."

The Reaper's eyes remained impassive. She wondered if their opinions even mattered to him before reminding herself once more that she did not need to care about his feelings. They were strangers.

"At least they were heading in the opposite direction of our flag," the first man spoke again, dragging the tip of his sword through the leaves on the ground carelessly.

"Enough. Let's run the perimeter again."

A smattering of muttered agreements rose before their footsteps faded. Teyla strained her ears to hear which way they went but was unsuccessful. After another moment of complete silence, the Reaper rolled out of the crevice into a crouched position. His gloved hand tapped on the rock, signaling all clear.

She crawled out into the sunshine, a wave of heat hitting her face. The man looked at her before turning to head in the direction they'd just run from.

"Wait!" Her desperate call made him pause. Capitalizing on his hesitation, Teyla hurried forward. "I *need* somebody to train me, if I hope to survive."

He turned back toward her fully, his head cocked slightly in confusion.

Teyla barreled onward, hoping she was not making a huge mistake. "I would have died today without your help. I have no hope of surviving this competition without your help. You are the only one who has protected me multiple times. Help me."

"Why should I?"

Could she detect a hint of bitterness in his tone? Why would he be upset?

"You told me you were an ally. I'm asking you to prove it. I need a chance to survive this thing. Please."

The Reaper was silent for a long time while her heart beat a mile a minute. However, she remained silent. Her fidgeting hands must have given away her nerves, but she waited.

"We will need to meet at night. It will be easier to meet you and train that way. Meet me at the quarry in three nights' time to discuss details."

"Where are you going?"

This time, the Reaper did not even turn back around.

"I'm going to go capture their flag so we can move on in this stupid competition."

Despite their predicament, Teyla grinned. Something about him that she could not explain drew her in. That was dangerous. Above her, she watched as a sliver of sun floated out like a revelation from behind a cloud. Perhaps she was making the biggest mistake of her life.

CHAPTER EIGHT

THE INTERVIEW

"If I were you, I would just tell the truth. We already have the information we need to put you deep inside the Trench for the rest of your life. If you give us the few missing pieces we need, I'll cut a deal with you."

Arden leaned her shoulders back against the frame of the two-way mirror in the interrogation room as Aeri worked their suspect for answers. In her opinion, Aeri was the best out of all of them at getting a perp to talk. Something about their steady countenance and absolute surety in everything they said put humans off-kilter.

The buzz of the watch wrapped around Arden's left wrist clued her in to pull her phone out of the back pocket of her black jeans. The text message had her eyebrows raising as her curiosity piqued. Maximus did not usually message her on her work phone, knowing nothing was really secured at the Silas Private Investigatory Unit.

As she pushed off the wall, Aeri's attention landed on her. After waving the phone and receiving a brief nod from them, she knocked on the door to be let out. A buff-looking enforcement officer ushered her through into the white hall.

Ignoring the curious looks of the other workers, she pushed her way outside, where there was a tiny bit more privacy.

Maximus answered on the first ring of the call. "Arden, I have intel for your next case."

She kept her face carefully neutral despite the confusion racing through her. Max knew they did not have another client right now and rarely helped with this aspect of their jobs anyway. Still, he would not have called if it was unimportant, and she could not risk anybody spying on her knowing anything was amiss.

"Go ahead, sir."

"There is a personal protection job opening up for a member of the nobility."

Arden's breath rushed out of her. This opportunity could be the perfect way to infiltrate the castle and get further information on the princess. Max knew that.

"Have I been offered the position, or am I meant to be applying? We both know it's not the usual case type for the SPIU."

"After speaking with the recruiter, you are one of three applicants entering the final round of consideration. You came highly recommended as the most successful agent in the SPIU within the last three years."

His praise warmed her, especially because they both knew it was true. Despite the various directions she was pulled in daily and averaging only two to three hours of sleep per night, her performance never diminished. Arden completed the agency work efficiently and accurately, partially due to her ability to pick up trace scents of the unknown subjects.

Even when she did not have all the evidence to help the city officers convict them, she could track it down or coerce a confession from their lips with Aeri's assistance. Between the two of them, the agency's success rate had shot up, putting the SPIU on the map of the most sought-after private investigatory units.

"Give me the details."

As Maximus provided the interview location and time, Arden swore colorfully. She had less than an hour to change into something better and arrive at the castle. A tinge of guilt hit her as she abandoned Aeri and sent them good vibes that they would get the confession.

Loping over to her motorcycle, she tugged the helmet on and kicked it into gear, tearing out of the parking lot far faster than the speed limit allowed. She just hoped she would not get pulled over as she hightailed it to the apartment the pack kept in the city just for instances like these.

Arden reached the apartment building within ten minutes, which was a new record. Before the front door was even closed, she whipped her casual V-neck shirt off her body and walked over to her bags. Jace looked up from his laptop and shot her a bemused look but did not question her sanity as she dug through her options.

A frustrated growl escaped her as she realized she had nothing fancy enough for this interview, and she refused to wear a dress to an interview for a protection job. Surely, there was *something* that would make her look more presentable.

"Here, try this on." Jace threw her one of Aeri's white long-sleeved button-down shirts. When she pulled on navy dress slacks with it, it was halfway there.

"It needs something else, Jace."

"I agree." He looked her up and down thoughtfully, his head cocking to the side. "Wait!"

His outburst startled her, and she pulled the hair she was trying to tame too hard. Hissing at the sharp pain in her scalp, she watched him rush out of the room only to return seconds later. She yanked the tossed jacket out of the air just before it hit her.

"Just put it on and try it."

Realizing she had less than thirty minutes to be at the castle, she did not argue further. The blazer was light gray and remarkably close to her size. It must have also been Aeri's since they were the only one close enough to her in build.

Shrugging on shoulder holsters and verifying that the safeties were clicked on her pistols, Arden felt more steady. Once the blazer was on and buttoned, she looked at her reflection. It was surprising how well the borrowed clothes suited and fit her. The colors looked particularly good against her glamored appearance.

Upon entering the kingdom of Cyrene, Max had felt her heterochromia was far too recognizable. Since then, she used some of the quintessence to glamor her appearance when acting as Arden, the agent.

It was just enough change to hide her in plain sight. She changed her eyes to be the same amber color she was born with before the incident that had affected her left eye. She removed the scar across her face and the side of her head and rounded out her normally pointed ears. The tattoos and piercings decorating her skin were also hidden, making her look far more respectable.

As the glamor required a constant flow of quintessence, she did not use it when she was not at her agency job. She was a strong wielder, but she did not want to grow tired by tapping into the aether all the time. The small amount of energy it did take helped relieve the pressure constantly pushing against her skin, begging to be used.

It did not matter if her appearance was glamored when operating as the Reaper, as she covered ninety-nine percent of her body anyway. The duality of her eyes would ensure that nobody traced back her illicit activities to her agency job. It was a win-win.

"Undo two more buttons."

Arden's attention shifted to Jace in the mirror, a frown tugging down her mouth. As if he could hear her inner dialogue, he explained further.

"It isn't slutty but will pull most men's gazes to your chest just enough to be a distraction. It is another tool in your arsenal and highlights the advantage of your femininity. It is useless to try to hide that part of you. Instead, prove to the interviewers just how distracting and useful it can be."

"You make a fair point. Wish me luck."

"You don't need it." Jace's boyish grin stretched across his face, and she could not help smiling back at his confidence in her.

Arden strapped on the last few weapons as she raced back down to her bike. Deciding to ignore the mess the helmet might make of her hair, she sped off to the castle. Since it was early afternoon, traffic was not bad. Arden thanked whatever gods were listening for that fact as she pulled up with five minutes left to spare.

She tossed the keys to the valet along with her helmet begrudgingly, but she did not have time to park it elsewhere herself. Her steps slowed to a stop at the entrance, and she pulled her hair up into a tight bun and hoped the flyaway strands were presentable.

"Invitation."

The palace guard seemed unnecessarily grouchy for having such an easy job, but Arden wisely kept her mouth shut. She pulled up the interview information Max had sent her along with the invitation on her phone and presented it to the guard.

"We've been expecting you, Agent. Remove any weapons on you."

Arden pursed her lips but complied with the order. As she shucked off her guns and blades, she questioned, "When will I get them back?"

"It depends. If you are hired, immediately. If you aren't, upon leaving the premises."

"You keep them separate from others? This collection was not cheap, and the pistols belong to my agency." Arden could not help but push, ensuring none of her weapons would go "missing."

"Yes. Here is your ticket."

Sure enough, the guard handed her a ticket number as a different guard placed all her weapons in one bag with a matching tab. When directed, she lifted her arms and allowed them to scan her body to check for other weapons.

Her breath stuttered slightly as the metal detector passed over the Xaliar dagger tucked into a sheath on her ankle. As expected, no noise went off, and her anxiety bled out of her and was replaced with acute relief.

Once the guard was satisfied that she was not smuggling in anything dangerous, he handed her the phone back and directed her down several halls. Arden reached the correct door and glanced down one last time at her slightly visible cleavage. A soft snort exited her nose as she hoped that Jace was right.

As she raised her fist to knock on the wooden door, it swung open inward. An upset-looking Theo stalked out, ramming his shoulder into hers in his haste to leave. Maximus had not told her that Theo was also being interviewed. Arden could not help but wonder if he'd intentionally left that little detail out.

Theo had a job in the city's enforcement office as his cover, and it seemed that his interview did not go as well as he would have liked.

"Come in."

Shaking off any thoughts unrelated to this interview, she obeyed before freezing mid-step. Arden had expected to be interviewing with the head of the Royal Guard, which it appeared she was partially right about. What she had not anticipated was the King's presence.

Going against her very nature, she bent her waist immediately in a deep bow to the King. The anger she tried to keep leashed tightly inside rioted, demanding retribution for the crimes this human had committed against her people. Every synapse of her body felt lit at the knowledge that she had never been so close to the King.

"Rise."

Body functioning on autopilot, Arden stood up straight and shook hands with the Captain of the Royal Guard, who was standing closest to her. His grip was firm but not enough to cause harm, and she copied that same force. As their hands dropped, the man gestured to the free chair on the other side of the table. "Please, sit."

As she settled into the chair, Arden looked around the room for threats and escape routes and counted the number of guards in the room out of habit. Crossing her ankles, the familiar weight of the Xaliar dagger soothed her, and she could claw her way out of the initial shock of being so close to her kingdom's biggest enemy.

"So, Agent, I am sure you are hoping to know more information about this contract." The Captain began, and she forced a smile, nodding. "Excellent. Well, first, my name is Farrow, and I am the Captain of the Royal Guard."

"Well met, Farrow." Her response came out smooth, much to her relief. "It is an honor to be in the presence of such a renowned guard."

The statement was not just to blow smoke up his ass. The pack had heard of Farrow and his role in tightening the security within the castle. While his efforts made their job of extricating the princess much more difficult, Arden appreciated a man who took pride in his work and took his role seriously. It was a shame he worked for the viper currently reclined in his chair, barely paying attention.

"I read the resume you sent over and have to admit that I was impressed. You seem quite young to have such a successful career."

"Thank you, sir. I can only attribute my success to my mentor and my team."

The King huffed a laugh at that. The captain seemed equally confused at the laughter as his eyebrows furrowed momentarily before recovering his poker face.

"Tell me, Agent. Why did you decide to pursue a career in private investigation instead of joining the prestigious palace guards or even detective work with the city enforcement?"

"I've never been huge into politics," she answered casually. It might have been the wrong thing to say, but she trudged on. "Where I grew up on the outskirts of Cyrene, it was simply about surviving nightwalker attacks and defending my family. As I grew older, I realized the passion I had for solving mysteries and prided myself on a job well done. Private investigation seemed like a place where I could experience both."

The practiced lies slid off her tongue easily. Maximus had run through a series of possible aliases before they left Orion, and she had picked this one. The information was close enough to the truth that she did not need to worry about being caught in a lie. Arden did live in the outskirts of Cyrene, if Orion fell into that category. Nightwalker attacks used to be much more common in Orion, and she often protected her cousin when they occurred.

"Why apply for a protection detail contract then?"

Arden answered conciliatorily. "Honestly? I want to find a new challenge. I have yet to find a case I couldn't solve."

"Is that arrogance I detect?" Farrow challenged.

"Confidence, sir." Arden leaned forward, equal parts pleased and disgusted, when the captain's attention dropped to her chest. *Good call, Jace.* When she cleared her throat softly, Farrow looked away from her cleavage, a light pink hue tinting his cheeks at getting caught ogling her décolletage.

"How are you with weapons?"

"I have yet to meet a weapon I haven't excelled in. My record is exceptional. I'm sure it is in that file you have of mine."

Before the captain could respond, a deep voice interrupted.

"You are a woman. Tell me why we should consider hiring somebody of the lesser sex," The King drawled, malice glinting in his blue eyes.

It was a trap. It had to be.

He must be testing her, either her tolerance for misogyny or her willingness to be spoken down to. Regardless, she needed to tread carefully. Arden had a feeling that this answer would determine if she got the job, which the pack desperately needed.

"While I do not know the exact reason for the protection detail, I can imagine that discretion is necessary. Most people will not be expecting a woman to be a trained guard with lethal precision. It is easy for me to blend into any crowd or be a demanding presence when needed. That versatility is paramount and not an ability any man you hire can have."

Following her explanation, silence reigned. The King appeared to be pondering her point while the captain continued to look disarmed by her tits. If it was not such an important moment, Arden may have laughed.

"You are hired. Farrow, show this agent to her new room and give her the details of the assignment. Dismissed."

Arden could hardly keep up with the whiplash of emotions but followed Farrow and the other guards out of the room as directed by their King. As soon as the door closed behind them, the shift was palpable. Each man relaxed, some of them even joking around with each other.

Captain Farrow walked her to a small room containing a bed and dresser as well as a weapons rack. It was plain but more than enough for her. Arden was elated that she had a reason to be in the castle now. As he finished explaining the kitchen hours, training times, and where to get outfitted in the Royal Guard attire, Arden could not wait any longer.

"Who am I going to be helping protect?"

Farrow laughed at her enthusiasm before clasping her shoulder. "Your first shift starts tomorrow. I would recommend spending the rest of today bringing any belongings you need here. You will follow around Nicolai for your first shift to learn the ins and outs of the detail."

She thanked him for the information before staring at him expectantly. Farrow shook his head in amusement before finally answering.

"Tomorrow, you will begin protecting Princess Teyla of Cyrene."

CHAPTER NINE

HUMILITY & HISTORY

She was going to die, and it would be entirely Madam Heyesworth's fault. Even worse, it was to be a slow, torturous death from boredom. This particular tutor was infamous for her brand of monotonous intonation. Surely nobody could blame Teyla for drifting off under those harrowing circumstances.

Half convinced she was sleeping with her eyes open, a prickling awareness settling on the back of her neck jolted her back to the land of consciousness. Teyla's spine stiffened at the feeling of being watched. As discreetly as she could manage under Madam Heyesworth's astute observation, she snuck a surreptitious glance over her shoulder.

Nicolai sauntered in impetuously as usual; however, the typical dread that occurred upon seeing him was not what attracted her attention. Accompanying him was a lean woman dressed in the standard colors of the Royal Guard—complete with a mask—but looking highly out of place in it. Bright sunlight filtering through the tall windows illuminated the intense golden irises that flickered toward her.

Each guard inside the castle was required to wear face

masks per their uniform, covering the top half of their faces. Only their eyes, jaws, and mouths were visible. The objective was anonymity, discouraging personal relationships from forming. Teyla's relationship with Nicolai was entirely against her wishes, but everybody else she interacted with outside of her ladies-in-waiting was intentionally distanced from her.

Nobody within the castle staff—with the exception of Nicolai's leering—ever looked the princess directly in the eyes without explicit permission.

Teyla remembered vividly the last time she had dared to get too friendly with an unfortunate worker. The messenger boy had only been a year her senior, and her teenage crush on him had preoccupied all her mental faculties. Eventually, he'd started making special stops just for her, and one thing led to another, as it often did. Axel had been her first crush, kiss, love—her first everything.

Her father had made it abundantly clear what he thought about their bond by having the guards beat him, drag him to the back of the stable, and put a chrome barrel to his skull.

The sound of the bullet echoed in her ears as Teyla relived the memory. Axel's punishment had been death. Her punishment for daring to fall in love, especially with a commoner, was being forced to bear witness to his execution. Since then, nobody except her ladies-in-waiting dared look at her for longer than a glance.

The laser focus this woman had on Teyla's face was becoming alarming. Maybe she did not know the rules.

As the princess thought to warn her, the new guard broke their impromptu staring contest and nodded along with whatever Nicolai was telling her. Teyla waited for several sickening heartbeats before relaxing to see that Nicolai had not noticed the prolonged glance. If he had, he would undoubtedly be on the way to inform the King.

It seemed to be the woman's first day on the job, and she did not want it to end in another execution. As the pair of guards drew closer, she could barely overhear their hushed conversation.

"The princess is in the middle of her history lesson. The ladies-in-waiting join her in all of her lectures to better learn how to assist with her needs once she is crowned," Nicolai explained, boredom lacing every word.

Curiosity more than piqued, Teyla continued her arduous task. Despite there being digital copies of all of their more ancient texts, Teyla was forced to copy down the entire history of Cyrene at least once a year by hand.

The Council had determined that the heir needed to know it thoroughly. If she did not, they did not think she would serve the kingdom well when she ascended into her role as queen. Teyla wrote:

There are many gods, none more known or more infamous than Ambrosia, who is often referred to as "the Mother." Goddess Ambrosia went against the gods' wishes and created humans who could manipulate magick, whom she called witches. These witches only reproduced through the maternal lines, passing down their control of the various elements from mother to daughter.

Cramping pain filled her hand, but Madam Heyesworth kept her beady eyes on Teyla, offering no reprieve. Any disobedience would be quickly and succinctly reported to the King, who would not hesitate to dole out swift punishment. Teyla allowed a small huff of annoyance and continued, keenly aware of Nicolai and the new guard quietly talking in the corner by the door, which she found far more interesting. Her ladies-in-waiting were scattered throughout the room, either reading or sewing. They were not subjected to the same torment that she was, which left her quite bitter. Her writing continued:

Eventually, the Mother's witches went against the Divines' wishes, and they created two unnatural beings, Lycans and nightwalkers. Both moon-cursed creatures of the night became mindless when their bloodlust took over. During the full moon, Lycans lost their sense of who they were and attacked humans, increasing their numbers to…

The clock tower chimed two hours past noon. Teyla

shot to her feet, disturbing Madam Heyesworth with the rapid movements, smiling apologetically at the uptight woman. "Forgive me, Madam, but I have another appointment I mustn't be late for. Here are my copies of our esteemed history, just as you requested. I can't wait for the next installment."

The lie slid off her tongue far easier than she would have liked. It seemed that the princess had gotten much better at lying ever since her powers had surfaced when she'd turned eighteen. Still, lying, for her, was unavoidable.

Forcing herself to bow her head as a sign of respect to her tutor, Teyla grabbed the paper and pens scattered across the table and hurriedly threw everything into a bag. Ruby, one of the ladies, rolled her eyes almost imperceptibly as she picked it up for Teyla, always reluctant to help in any substantial way. Walking past the guards, clothes rustling indicated the ladies were following behind.

Teyla almost tripped over her own two feet when the female guard asked Nicolai, "Are all the ladies-in-waiting to complete the lessons along with the princess?" Her tenor was husky, slightly lower in pitch than most women. It sang with an unfamiliar lilt. Perhaps she was from the western edges of the kingdom, although it was rare for somebody outside of the cities to become enmeshed with the Royal Guard. Granted, it was also quite rare for a woman to climb the ranks to reach a highly coveted position within the castle walls.

Most women who deigned to pursue a protection-centered career either wound up in the investigation agencies or beyond the city's boundaries to be used as mere fodder against nightwalker attacks. The King defended his actions by stating men were more important to the continuation of Cyrene, and whatever the King wanted, he received.

This woman immediately interested Teyla, though she did not want Nicolai to know, or he would use that knowledge against her.

"The ladies are expected to follow Teyla to her various appointments throughout the day. Her schedule varies depending on the day of the week. The ladies are expected to learn womanly tasks alongside her, although the curriculum is not the same. They will assist Teyla as needed while they contribute to the court with their wombs, as that is their main value to the court."

Nausea threatened to spoil Teyla's lunch at the familiarity with which he referred to her despite her royal standing. She clenched a fist within the folds of her dress to avoid punching something, preferably his stupid face. His grimy voice sounded as pleasant as sand scraping against glass. Ignoring how harsh and unpleasant he sounded compared to his trainee was difficult.

"I had assumed men within the Royal Guard would lack the comprehension abilities to understand the complexities of a woman and her inherent contributions to society, but I must admit that I am disappointed my suspicions were proven correct."

The new guard's pleasant delivery was at complete odds with the grating words uttered, just as casual as if she were commenting on the weather. Teyla coughed harshly to cover the stupefied laugh that had begun to escape. Nobody in her lifetime had dared to speak to a Royal Guard that way.

Harlowe's loud guffaw had not been as successfully muffled, and Nicolai's scowl made it even harder for Teyla to contain her snickers. This was quickly turning into the best day of her week.

So entrenched in her thoughts and amusement, she did not notice the lump in the carpet until the top of her foot caught on it, flinging her body forward. Her muscles braced for the harsh bite of the ground, but it never came. As fast as her body had fallen forward, something reversed its momentum. Strong arms hauled Teyla backward into a firm yet supple body. Exclamations of surprise rose from the ladies following further behind.

A gasp escaped Teyla's throat as gloved hands wrapped around her forearms, holding her back against her rescuer's front.

"Are you all right, Princess?"

The warm breath blowing strands of hair against her ear made her entire body lock up. A burning sensation tore through her lungs as she felt she could not breathe so close to this woman. She forcibly coughed in a futile attempt to stop the stuttering breaths wracking her chest. Luckily, yet too soon, she released Teyla's body and walked around in front, bending slightly at the waist to make eye contact.

"Princess?"

The concern in the woman's voice melted Teyla's heart as she became entranced with the human looking into her soul.

From what Teyla could see of her face, the woman was stunning. The intensity in her eyes reminded the princess of the Reaper, startling her. Teyla immediately calmed once she verified that this guard's eyes were the same color. It could not be the same person, even though the color was similar to one of the Reaper's eyes.

It was striking against the deep purple mask she wore as part of her guard uniform. The slope of her nose was pleasant, and her pink lips were turned down in a slight frown. Her strong jawline complemented her prominent cheekbones, and Teyla could see her jaw clenching as she waited for a response.

A pointed throat clearing broke Teyla out of the odd trance the woman held her in.

Nicolai's obnoxious voice was directed at the woman. "She is fine, guard. You should step back now."

"It's Agent," the woman corrected him calmly, still assessing the princess with a concerned look.

Teyla's cheeks flushed bright red with embarrassment. Of course, the one time she was about as agile as a newborn fawn and almost fell while in a dress was in front of this gorgeous human. Was it too much to hope for a hole to open in the ground and swallow her just to escape this mortification? Despite his apparent annoyance, Teyla had little doubt Nicolai was soaking up her embarrassment as always. *Asshole.*

Stepping a healthy distance away, the agent bowed her

head in penitence. "Forgive me, Princess, for touching you without explicit permission and maintaining eye contact. I saw an imminent danger to your person and acted on instinct. I meant no offense to you or the Crown." She kept her eyes on the ground, waiting for Teyla to speak.

This woman did know the rules and had intentionally broken them twice now.

Interesting.

Clearing her throat and still flushed around the neck and ears, the princess responded. "It's all right, Agent…" Her voice trailed off, realizing she did not know her name.

"I am merely a lowly contracted agent, Princess. My name is of no importance," the agent filled in the silence graciously, one corner of her lips curving up in the smallest movement. Teyla briefly wondered what it would look like to see a smile stretch entirely across her face. The thought startled her, and she decided to catalog that reaction to analyze later. The gods knew she did not need to act any more strangely in front of the mystery woman.

"All is forgiven, my humble agent." Amusement coated Teyla's tongue as she tried to keep a stoic face. "I appreciate your assistance with my imminent threat. Please, resume your… conversation. You need not stop on my account."

Teyla tripped over the verbiage with almost as little grace as she'd had when physically catapulting forward. It came off as more of a question than a statement as she tried to avoid harming Nicolai's already wounded ego.

White teeth flashed as the agent bit down briefly on her lower lip, as if physically trying to restrain a grin. It was a valiant effort from the agent despite failing to keep a straight face, and Teyla was supremely grateful that Nicholai was too far behind her to see her answering smirk.

Breathing came easier once the agent returned to her spot beside Nicolai. Despite the conversation resuming between the guards and the ladies, Teyla swore she still felt the agent's penetrating stare on the back of her head. It was not unpleasant like Nicolai's negative energy, though it made her slightly on edge. Nobody had dared to look at her this much. It was too soon to determine if the agent was bold or simply had a death wish. Time would tell.

The group was walking toward her next appointment when a royal messenger stopped in front of them. Apprehension flooded Teyla's body as she waited for the boy to catch his breath. He held out a parchment scroll. As soon as she accepted it the messenger bowed low before racing off again. Teyla's stomach felt leaden as she unraveled it.

The King requests your presence in the private office.
Immediately.

There was no signature, but there was no need for one. His handwriting was seared into her mind from all of the summons she had received over the years. Teyla attempted to steel herself, rolling the scroll back up.

Without a word, she handed the scroll to Nicolai and began the walk to his office. The verbal lashing she would receive later for accepting the scroll before her guard had read it was nothing compared to what awaited her in the beast's den. The glee in Nicolai's voice as he dismissed the ladies sounded muffled, as if her head was underwater.

"What are you doing?" Nicolai sneered, glancing back at the new agent who was following them.

Teyla's panic rose with his piercing voice. Despite the nearly overwhelming nausea she was experiencing, she was impressed at the agent's gall—she must have come from a far less strict district of the kingdom.

The agent glanced at Nicolai. "I was instructed by the Captain of the Guard to accompany you today. I am not interested in disobeying his directions."

Nicolai's annoyance at the statement permeated the air, but even Teyla knew there was nothing he could do. Despite his role as one of her personal guards, he also answered to the captain. He grunted his acceptance and began leading them through the halls.

The five-minute walk to the office felt like seconds. The princess was so intent on tamping down her anxiety she was surprised she'd managed not to trip again. The new woman's observant stare became more frequent as they approached the King's private office.

Teyla thought to snap at her for staring but found herself outside the office, with both of them waiting for her. *Great.* She was making a fantastic impression today.

Refusing to look at either guard, Teyla shoved against the heavy oak doors. With a groan, they swung inward, revealing a softly lit interior.

Nicolai instructed the guard to remain outside the doors to keep watch. "It is personal business that has nothing to do with you."

His pedantic tone was obnoxious, but the agent simply responded with a nod and posted herself at the door.

The sound of the door closing left Teyla feeling more alone than usual. It took a moment to realize with a jolt that she felt safer with the agent. That should have worried her, but the reality was that she knew anywhere was safer than being with Nicholai and her father.

Teyla continued walking through the dimly lit, small personal library of the office and pushed through the internal set of doors. The King sat regally at his desk, looking down his nose at her upon their entrance. The wicked gleam of amusement in his eyes was a telltale sign that this was not just a social visit. Teyla went to the center of the room and bowed, waiting for the King's command to relieve her from the uncomfortable position. It never came.

"Before we get to business, I wanted to inform you that you have an extra protection detail," he began dismissively, as if it were below his station to talk to her. "I am assuming that as the competition continues, we will need to up security in the castle."

"Thank you, Father." Her murmured response was met with silence for an excruciating amount of time.

"You ruined my announcement, Teyla," he continued, his volume low. The calm demeanor did not fool her. He was a cobra, poised to strike. He had not permitted her to speak, so Teyla's lips remained pressed together, the tension in the room building to a breaking point.

"You were not only wholly ignorant of the situation but then somehow found amusement in the pandemonium your idiocy caused!" His voice rose with every word until he was yelling. The princess flinched, then wished she had not given either man the satisfaction of noting her fear.

"She also accepted your summons before me. Again."

Teyla shot a glare at Nicolai. His saccharine smile was the picture of innocence.

"Kneel." The King's injunction left no room for protest.

The bark of pain in her knees barely registered as Nicolai shoved her harshly onto the stone. Teyla's mind was far more preoccupied with the trepidation of what was to come.

"Nicolai, loosen her top."

She shuddered with disgust as his fingers undid the lacing of the dress. The debasement of these punishments they called "playtime" was nearly unbearable. They fed on her humiliation almost as much as they did on her pain. After years of their dehumanizing behavior, Teyla was ashamed that it still bothered her. For the millionth time, she hopelessly wished she could control the flush creeping up her neck as the tops of her breasts became exposed.

The King stood up from his regal chair, not even glancing at her kneeling form. Nicolai, on the other hand, was gazing hungrily at her exposed flesh.

"Nicolai, the ferrule."

Teyla kept staring at the stone as she heard the swish of the fabric moving around. Her jaws were clenched so hard she was surprised her teeth did not crack.

"Remember, girl, I would not have to punish you if you behaved. You alone are to blame for your pain."

The King reigned five lashes down on her bare back in quick succession, barely allowing time to breathe in between. Each smack left a welt low on her back. A whimper escaped with the last two, causing the King and Nicolai to share a terrifying smile. When the King finished the lashing, he turned toward Nicolai fully.

"Enjoy your treat, Nicolai. Don't make a mess like last time."

Nicolai merely smiled at him and chuckled, not at all berated. He stalked closer and murmured against her ear. "You smell divine as always, pet. I hope you taste just as delicious."

As the King returned to his paperwork, Nicolai tugged the top of the dress down further, shoving the fabric beneath her breasts to present them fully before him. Teyla closed her eyes, trying not to react.

He used both hands to roughly twist her nipples, smiling mockingly when they became firm from the unwanted touch. Without warning, he lunged forward, his fangs sinking into the flesh on the top of her left breast, pain flashing through her with the impalement and each gulp of blood he consumed. Her entire chest felt like it was on fire as he drained as much as he wanted.

Like always, the fear that he might choose to inject his venom and turn her into a nightwalker was paralyzing. It was her fear of turning into the monsters that tortured her and kept her complacent. The threat of the turn kept her docile and made her the perfect snack. A single tear dripped down her cheek. Teyla's last thought was, *what would my people think if they knew?* Then, everything faded to black.

CHAPTER TEN

GLAMOR

Arden knew that glamors, like all enchantment magick, worked when precisely woven. Still, she'd had reservations when Maximus had instructed her to weave one while operating as Agent Arden, protection specialist extraordinaire. He'd reminded her that her eyes were far too recognizable ever since the old injury to her face, a fact with which she begrudgingly agreed. Therefore, she'd spent all day with part of her focus on steadily threading quintessence into her glamor disguise.

After a few hours, it had become second nature to hold the magickal threads in place, hiding her scars, changing her eyes and ears, and hiding her tattoos and piercings. Arden had barely been able to look at her reflection early that morning as she'd beheld her long-lost childhood features before violence had left its permanent mark.

Between the glamor and the fact that the princess had assumed the Reaper was male, Teyla had not recognized her. It would be difficult to switch identities so frequently, but it was necessary to slip into the castle. Since applying a glamor was a tiny, constant flow of quintessence, it was far less likely to be detected than her other powers.

Arden stood anxiously outside the external doors of the King's private study, trying not to fidget. Her attention went to the courtyard clock; once again, she was impatient. It must have been an important meeting, but Nicolai's dismissing her outside like a dog infuriated her, and the irony did not escape her.

Arden was already itching to kill that creep, and she had only been stuck with him for a few hours. Getting close to the princess like this to gain her trust would be harder than Arden had anticipated. She paused that train of thought as soft footfalls came toward the door.

She stiffly remained at attention and pretended she could hear nothing, like a human. The scent of fear that flooded the area around the princess just before the door opened made her throat constrict.

Something was very wrong. Arden shook her head to clear her mind, an old habit reminiscent of a canine. She could have slapped herself for these small mistakes that would identify her as more than human to anyone who knew better.

The door swung open, and Princess Teyla reappeared alone for the moment.

All thoughts of capturing the princess emptied out of Arden's mind when, at last, she saw her. Arden rapidly looked over the princess from head to toe, her trained eyes missing nothing. Her pallor was startling; her skin was several shades whiter, waxy, and diaphoretic.

Princess Teyla's normally lustrous blonde hair was plastered to her forehead with sweat, and the tight smile in place of a greeting did not assuage any concern.

"I don't mean to overstep—" Arden began.

The princess sharply cut her off, "Then do not."

Taken aback by the bite in her response, Arden raised her eyebrows behind the mask. A flush spread across her face at the chastisement, and she desperately hoped the mask came down low enough to conceal it. Not a soul had so bluntly chastised Arden since she was a pup. She allowed one more glance over the princess before releasing a deep breath and nodding.

"Understood, Princess."

Instead of risking angering the princess more, she looked out one of the windows. The sun was still out, the blue skies absent of clouds, when an idea began forming in her head.

"Do you wish to return to your quarters, or would you prefer to meander into the courtyard with me and catch some of the sun?"

"You do not need to accompany me anywhere."

Princess Teyla's voice was tired but firm and seemed a little defensive. Arden bit back the snarky response begging to come out and responded. "What if I just want to?"

The princess looked over, surprise lighting up the blue eyes that were becoming familiar. Princess Teyla's mouth opened and closed without making a sound.

Arden's brows furrowed at her reaction. In Orion, royalty always spent time with those within the castle. The royal family was expected to learn about their companions and to solidify relationships with them. Not only was it courteous, but it was also important to gain loyalty through devotion instead of demand.

The interactions Arden had cataloged throughout the day flashed back to her, one after another. There had not been a moment when the princess had spoken casually to those around her. There was even a rule about eye contact without express direction from the royalty.

Arden's eyelids squeezed shut as she processed her foolishness. Cyrenian culture was vastly different from where she was raised. Orionians were social, far less formal, and definitely less direct.

"You are a guard unlike any other I've ever met," Princess Teyla mused aloud, tapping her finger against her lip while she thought. Arden tracked the movement, appreciating the shape of her rosy lips.

The princess was stunning, a fact that had nearly struck her stupid beneath that damned rock during the competition.

She was the most visually appealing woman Arden had ever seen, which troubled her greatly. Arden stopped looking at the princess's mouth and tentatively attempted to skirt the cultural blunder that had just occurred.

"I apologize if I have done something untraditional that upset you, Princess Teyla. I merely thought it looked pleasant outside and thought you might enjoy the temperate weather compared to the unforgiving heat of the last few weeks. Please forgive me if I have foolishly inserted myself into the equation."

Saying her name had felt almost decadent rolling off her tongue, something she decided immediately never to speak of. It truly was unfair that the most beautiful creature in existence had such an incredibly delicious name.

Arden's thoughts slammed to a halt. *Princess* Teyla was nothing more than her greatest enemy's daughter.

The Crown of Cyrene had brutally and mercilessly destroyed everything she loved: her family and the glorious kingdom of Orion and had even tried to destroy her entire race. She would never forget or forgive those crimes.

While the princess had been merely a child, like Arden, at the beginning of her father's conquest, she was the enemy by extension of the King. Ultimately, it did not matter that the princess's physical appearance took her breath away. She was the enemy. Arden needed to get her head back on right.

"You did nothing wrong except perhaps talk to me like I am a person instead of your princess, although some may report that as a punishable offense."

Arden's attention whipped back to her at the casual threat. It was a great relief when the princess smiled, her eyes twinkling. Was she teasing her or warning her? Deciding to take yet another risk, Arden asked her, "Are you included in the list of those who would divulge that information?"

Teyla's eyes resembled a thunderous storm as they darkened. "No."

Her firm voice left no room to doubt her. After a brief

moment of silence, Arden cleared her throat and gestured for the princess to lead the way. She walked slightly closer behind the princess than etiquette demanded, still concerned about her pallor. If the princess keeled over, Arden wanted to be there to catch her.

Arden's instincts were rarely wrong, and they did not lead her astray this time. Princess Teyla took all of five steps, and her knees buckled beneath her. Arden surged forward, catching her by the waist once again and easing her back into her arms. The princess's head lolled to the side as she completely lost consciousness.

Clamping down on the initial panic, Arden swore colorfully under her breath and bent down, scooping the princess into her arms. The agent carried her bridal style the last few steps to the courtyard. They passed a worker scuttling by, and Arden's voice was demanding as she barked orders out. "Fetch water, strips of fabric, and the castle healers. Now!"

Arden waited only for the verbal affirmative before continuing onward. Her eyes adjusted to the bright light, and she scouted a flat area on some grass in the shade of a large flowering tree. Changing the trajectory of her steps, Arden gently lowered the unconscious princess to the ground, her face ensconced in the shade.

It took only a harsh "Find somewhere else to be now!" to the rest of those gathered in the courtyard for them to scatter.

The wolf inside was clawing at her mental barriers, demanding to *provide for and protect* the woman lying in front of her. The demand was so deafening in her head that she closed her eyes tightly to suppress the possibility of shifting into her wolven form in the middle of the enemy's courtyard.

Arden's gums throbbed as her canines threatened to extend fully, and her nails pricked her palms through the leather gloves. Her protective instincts overrode her self-preservation as her eyes opened to startling clarity before falling closed again. Tapping into the aether and invoking the quintessence was undoubtedly causing them to glow due to the proximity of a shift, and she was exceptionally grateful everyone had fled.

Teyla was still lying there, hair splayed across the grass. Arden scanned her body to look for external injuries, but nothing obvious was present. She squinted to be sure her eyes were not playing tricks. Sure enough, a faint white light surrounded Teyla's body everywhere the grass was touching. As she watched, the grass wilted, and some spots began to fade into a light brown. The princess was leeching the energy from nature.

Before Arden could process what was happening, the princess opened her eyes again with a gasp, attempting to get up. However, Arden laid her hands against Teyla's shoulders. Just like that, the need to shift disappeared, and Arden's body was fully under her control again.

"Hey, it's okay. You are okay. You lost consciousness for a few minutes there."

Teyla placed a hand against her chest, attempting to slow her breathing and calm down.

"I brought you outside and laid you down. The castle healers should be coming, as should somebody with water." Arden gritted her teeth in annoyance at how long they were taking.

Just as she had decided to call for more help, the maid came rushing back with the supplies and the healers. Arden stepped back to give them more space to inspect the princess and ensure she was fine. Her watchful eyes monitored everything they did for her, not giving them a second alone with her.

After several minutes of being inspected, the healers declared it a fluke faint—a phrase Arden chuckled at—and stated rest was in order, including limiting walks for the rest of the day. After the princess had downed three full cups of water, Arden eased up a little on her hovering.

"Princess, are you truthfully all right? I should have pushed earlier when you told me not to overstep; my negligence caused this mess and put you in danger." Arden dipped her head, ashamed. Even though she needed the princess alive and well for the mission, this shame came from a baser part of her soul. Arden had failed at keeping her safe, and the wolf inside was snarling in anger.

When she dared to look back up, there was no trace of anger or disappointment on the princess's face. Arden's shoulders relaxed incrementally.

"It is my fault, not yours." Princess Teyla sighed. "I knew I was feeling lightheaded. I didn't want to burden you or embarrass myself. Obviously, that's now off the table." She chuckled, her neck and face flushing.

Arden stifled a smile at how endearing she looked. "What is causing your lightheadedness?"

Teyla looked down before answering, "I am on my cycle. I am experiencing it heavier than normal."

Arden could sense the lie a mile away. To be sure, though, she discreetly sniffed, allowing her senses to stretch out toward the woman. The recognizable bite of iron was absent. Instead of challenging the princess, she merely nodded. "I see. I'm sorry for any pain your cycle is causing. Please let me know if you need any extra rags." Then, in a conspirator's whisper, Arden added, "Or if we need to steal some chocolate from the kitchen."

The loud burst of laughter out of the princess delighted Arden. Teyla gave her an amazed look, still smiling. "Oh, what a breath of fresh air having a female guard is!" Prompted by her guard's inquisitive look, she continued, "If I told any male about my cycle, lots of cringing and disgust surely would have ensued." She chuckled. "You simply asked if I needed more supplies and if I wanted to steal chocolate."

Arden allowed a soft laugh along with the princess, her serious demeanor cracking slightly. It was a real, genuine laugh, and Arden had shared it with her enemy. She was equally as amazed as Teyla, although for different reasons.

"Well, males would rather see an arrow protruding from an extremity than deal with a normal fact of nature." Arden rolled her eyes in exasperation. "Is that a yes to chocolate?"

Teyla sniggered—wholly inappropriate behavior from a princess from Cyrene. The pissed-off side of the princess was nowhere to be seen. Arden was proud to be the cause of her mirth, and her inner wolf was finally appeased.

A thoughtful look graced Teyla's face before she murmured, "Truly unique."

Arden fought a blush again as she helped the princess to her feet once more. Arden was pleased to see some color returning to her face and that her sweating had seemed to stop. She did not seem to be seconds away from crashing again. "Lead the way then, Princess. I am still trying to learn my way around." Arden blinked once at her involuntary admission, but Teyla did not seem to care.

"We will head back to my room so I can rest." The princess cranked her neck back toward Arden, her teeth flashing in the sun. "After a detour to the kitchens, of course."

The agent grinned at her devious smile. As they walked away, she scanned the ground and found the grass seemed completely normal, actually greener and healthier. Despite being visually reassured it had not happened, Arden felt in her gut that something else was happening. Something magickal.

Of all her thoughts thus far, that one was the most dangerous.

CHAPTER ELEVEN

AUDACITY & DANCING

After careful consideration, the Princess of Cyrene could admit that the half-formed plan she was in the middle of executing was incredibly reckless at best and potentially suicidal at worst. In her defense, it had not been her idea. Technically.

When she had overheard Harlowe excitedly talking about her bachelorette party with the other ladies in waiting, Teyla had a burst of longing so potent it had stolen her breath away. Of course, she had not been invited directly. Harlowe knew better than to suggest aloud that Teyla sneak out of the castle.

Neither of them was naive. It would require duplicitous actions for her to join any event outside the castle grounds. Teyla had stopped repeatedly asking to leave her gilded cage by the age of fifteen, shortly after Axel had died.

She'd asked yearly for her birthday and had been denied each time.

Of course, Teyla still snuck out to go on her undercover operations to *The Crevice* and other valuable outings. However, those felt different. She was making a positive impact on her people during those nights. The reward far outweighed the risk.

Tonight, she had taken an enormous, unnecessary chance for an undoubtedly selfish reason that only benefited her. She had climbed out her window and crept past the royal guards and city enforcement simply because she'd wanted to have fun.

It was so unlike her to be that audacious that she had questioned her sanity at least six times since she made the decision.

The guilt diminished when she finally arrived at the club and felt alive for the first time in years.

Harlowe's face lit up in elation—after a solid ten seconds of unfettered disbelief—upon seeing Teyla join the group.

All of this had only been possible because Harlowe had not invited the other ladies in waiting, a fact that Ruby had complained about rather loudly. Her fellow ladies had winced at the piercing pitch of her shrill bitching. The beautiful agent—whose name she had yet to learn—had rolled her eyes at the drama, eliciting a grin from Teyla. Harlowe had remained unwavering, claiming the bachelorette party was only for family.

Once Harlowe overcame her initial shock at Teyla's presence at this club, she ecstatically grabbed her into a bear hug, one that would never have occurred in the castle.

"Oh my gods, you came!"

Teyla's cheeks hurt from smiling so hard. "I came," she confirmed. "I wouldn't miss this for anything in the world, Harlowe."

Before her closest friend could respond, a tall brunette cut in, yelling over the thumping music. "Hey! My name is Rylin, this one's future sister-in-law. Who are you?"

Rylin's hip bump into Harlowe almost knocked them both off balance. Teyla laughed as she helped correct their tilting bodies, feeling more carefree than she could remember.

"Nice to meet you, Rylin. I'm Selene, Harlowe's friend from primary school."

The false identity had been one Teyla had used since they had become secret friends years ago. She rarely required it, but they created one just in case. Teyla was thankful for their foresight, especially as Harlowe's evergreen eyes twinkled in delight.

"First shot's on me, Selene. To the journey, bitches!"

"To the journey!" Teyla parroted Cyrene's customary salutation along with the rest of the female crew.

Teyla hesitated as she raised the acerbic liquid to clink against the other glasses, knowing logically that she should not imbibe. There were enough risks by just being here. She had put on makeup and a brown wig, but there was always a chance she would be recognized.

Her hesitant resolve disintegrated as Harlowe jumped up and down on her toes in excitement and shouted, "All of my favorite people are in one place!"

There really was no other decision for her to make after a statement like that. Teyla had not been anybody's favorite anything since her mother and Axel died. That elation was more than enough reason for her to tip the brown liquor down her throat.

The cheap fluid burned on the way down and the hairs of her nose, too, when she choked on the bitter taste. Rylin pounded on her back, then shoved a different cup in her hand.

Wary after that experience but needing something—anything really—to take away the remnants of that disgusting flavor, Teyla accepted the cup gratefully and gulped it. The previous alcohol's astringency was chased away by a refreshing, fruity taste.

"Thank the gods," Teyla breathed, the burning sensation pushing further down her esophagus and warming her chest.

Despite being halfway through her twenties, Teyla had never taken a shot. She was customarily allowed a single glass of wine or a solitary flute of champagne on occasion. Her father had always stated that drinking more than a single drink was classless.

A pleasant buzz settled in Teyla's head, and she felt

herself beginning to sway to the music in the background, shoulders dropping in relaxation. Anxieties about being out of the palace trickled away as the group laughed and took another shot.

In the back of her mind, Teyla knew she was being foolish. Her tipsy consciousness just could not bring forth a single worry, especially as the group meandered over to the dance floor. Her jaw dropped as Harlowe's friends began dancing together, far closer than propriety would dictate. The various balls and celebrations she had attended had never showcased people dancing in such a disreputable way, especially members of the same sex.

In Cyrene, it was illegal to marry within the same sex, but Teyla theoretically knew that moonlight rendezvous still occurred. Outside places like *The Crevice*, where illegal and immoral actions were abundant, she had never seen such provocative public dancing.

The energy inside the club was electric, and the hair on her arms stood up at the sensation. Harlowe animatedly spoke while tugging her to the middle of the dancefloor, not that Teyla could make out a single word she said. It was apparent that no response was necessary. Harlowe intertwined their fingers and raised their arms to the ceiling while they wobbled back and forth, giggling.

So lost in the overwhelmingness of everything, Teyla did not notice when Harlowe was pulled away with a different friend, nor when she lost sight of the rest of the group. The rhythmic music lulled her into a false sense of security, as if she were surrounded by bubble wrap and nothing bad could touch her.

Rough hands palmed her hips and tugged her backward. Teyla's midnight blue eyes opened as something conspicuously hard gyrated against her backside. A slow blink revealed no familiar faces, and undiluted fear sliced through the previously languorous haze she had become lost in.

The beefy hands touching her with an air of ownership

slid further down before squeezing her ass. She whirled around, ready to confront whatever entitled man had dared put his hands on her.

Instead, she gasped from a mixture of relief and surprise. *My agent's here!*

Her guard was inserting herself between Teyla and the stranger. She could not hear the first words that left the agent's mouth, but if the glare on her face was any indication, it was not nice.

Teyla was far more focused on the woman than the altercation in front of her.

"Why the fuck should I?" the man shouted, apparently incensed at whatever he had been told. Teyla looked cluelessly between the two, unsure what discussion they were having.

The agent slyly looked over at her before shrugging casually. Her lithe body sidled up next to Teyla, and she slung an arm around her shoulders.

"Because she is my partner, you intolerant douche canoe."

Partner.

A quick squeeze on her shoulder assured Teyla she had not misheard, and she pressed closer against the agent in silent agreement to go along with whatever ruse she was concocting. The blundering man was obviously drunk as he swayed precariously, narrowing his eyes at them, paying special attention to where their bodies connected.

Instinctively, Teyla curled in further against her agent's body, her left arm naturally sliding to rest on her abdomen. Except for the tensing of the muscles under the princess's fingertips, the agent gave no other noticeable sign of surprise.

"You have room for one more?"

Uneasiness caused Teyla's body to stop moving with the music, but the guard appeared unperturbed. Things were headed in an extremely dangerous direction.

Teyla's body was pulled closer to her savior, their bodies now chest to chest. In the back of her tipsy mind, the princess could tell that they were moving rhythmically along with a melodious tune.

"Listen, buddy. I'm not usually against a two-for-one special, if you know what I mean." The agent lobbed an insouciant wink his way, but her hands tightened on Teyla's waist in contradiction. "But my girl here is shy. Maybe another time."

Teyla rested her head on the guard's chest, studiously attempting to ignore how supple the breasts felt under her cheek. She just needed to trust that this agent was good at her job.

Trust did not come easily to her, but she found it increasingly difficult to focus and realized that she had little choice in the matter. A few moments after tucking her head under the agent's chin, the chest vibrated.

"He's gone."

Teyla wished the words were consoling, but she'd just been caught sneaking out. Even if the agent was not upset, her father was bound to be pissed once he learned of her escape.

The princess decided that the best course of action would be to meet the woman's wrath face-on. If this bachelorette party were to be the last event she attended, she would not end the night with her tail tucked between her legs.

Teyla tilted her chin up to face her but was startled to see the agent already looking down at her. Her breathing hitched as she realized their faces were mere inches apart. Oxygen continued to elude her when her sluggish mind registered the agent's features up close.

She isn't wearing a mask.

The same awed phrase looped repetitively in her mind as her eyes greedily took in all the features lit up in a kaleidoscope of hues. Amber eyes remained striking but less potent, with a multitude of colors flashing against them. Brown-sloped eyebrows raised as the agent mutely watched Teyla drink in her appearance. The princess's brown wig was captured in deft fingers as the agent looked contemplatively at the strands of hair.

"I prefer you as a blonde."

The woman's impish smile—partnered with the personal nature of her statement—pulled a disbelieving laugh out of Teyla. She had been preparing for a verbal lashing, not whatever that was.

Teyla's head tipped backward as she chuckled again with genuine amusement, not missing that her dance partner's attention dropped down to her neck and back up rapidly. She could not be sure what drew the woman's attention, not when the liquor was still making her mind feel boggy.

"So, *Selene*." The fake name was drawn out intentionally, and Teyla's face caught fire at her deceit being discovered. "What in the gods possessed you to think this was a good idea?"

Teyla had been waiting for this moment. Unexpected, though, was how relaxed she felt while being questioned. Maybe she could thank the liquid courage floating around in her body.

"I never thought it was a good idea. It was simply important enough to justify the means."

The truth settled like a weight between them, and Teyla began to step back. Warm hands grasped hers and pulled their bodies back together in a gentle rocking motion.

"What was so important to risk your life?"

The question surprised Teyla, which was starting to become a pattern. However, the guard did not look judgmental. If anything, she simply seemed curious, based on the slight cock of her head.

"I don't even know your name. I'm not going to share my deepest, darkest secrets."

It was a cop-out, and Teyla knew it. She was desperately trying to throw up flimsy boundaries to protect them both. The next words out of that sensuous mouth knocked those walls over as if they were made of paper.

"My friends call me 'A.'"

Friends. For some reason, it had never occurred to Teyla that A might have friends outside her job. Most people who worked in protection within the castle never seemed to leave.

A different thought stopped her train of thought in its tracks. Had Agent A just been here with her own friends, independently of Teyla sneaking out?

She quickly dismissed the thought, knowing it was A's shift tonight. Bothered by just how much she was shaken, she tried a joke to divert the topic. "Right. So, what should I call you?"

Instead of seeming bemused or offended at the implication that they were not friends, Agent A's smile grew, the corners of her eyes crinkling with the movement. Just like that, Teyla was captivated again.

"Around the castle, you can just call me Agent." A body bumped into Teyla from behind, pushing her further into their tentative embrace. "But otherwise, you can call me A."

"Fun!" Teyla blurted out before clamping a hand over her mouth. The damn alcohol was surely to blame for her loosened tongue. Still, the metaphorical cat was out of the bag, so she just went with it. "I wanted to have fun."

It sounded so childish once spoken aloud, and another embarrassed flush spread across her cheeks. Expecting mockery, Teyla kept her eyes trained on their shoes, feet nearly on top of each other. For a long minute, neither woman spoke.

"What have you not done yet tonight that you wish to?"

There was no way the agent was being serious. Yet her attention was steady and focused, as if waiting expectantly for an answer. Nothing about this night was making sense.

Apparently, booze made her far denser.

Before she had enough inhibition to stop them, words tumbled out. "I wanted to really dance with someone." Perhaps it would be possible for her to crawl into her own skin to escape her mortification. Teyla vowed never to drink hard liquor again.

Then again, Agent A looked far from upset, nor was she shaming Teyla. Instead, her lips pursed thoughtfully as she scanned the dance floor. As if reaching whatever conclusion she had been searching for, A nodded resolutely to herself. "All right."

"All right?" Teyla parroted back, dumbstruck.

"All right," Agent A confirmed once more. "But I have a condition."

A groan tore out of Teyla's throat before she could tamp it down, but the woman merely grinned at her petulant action.

"You can dance for another thirty minutes, but it has to be with me."

Teyla had a brief concern that her jaw was about to touch the gross floor. "You want to dance with me?"

Agent A shrugged, but the movement seemed more tense than it had been earlier in the night. "Why not? I need you to be safe, and I can't guarantee that when you dance with handsy strangers."

The logic was incredibly sound despite how ridiculous it was that they were even having this conversation. Never would Teyla have imagined having a negotiation over a dance partner.

"Take it or leave it, Party Princess."

Teyla scoffed at the apt sobriquet and lightly shoved Agent A's shoulder, exasperated. A loosely joined their fingers again and spun with the movement with far more grace than Teyla would have. The little shimmy she did made the princess laugh aloud, as it was so at odds with the club music playing over the speakers.

Teyla's mind was made up when the usually stoic agent crooked a finger in a come-hither motion while moving her hips in time with the beat.

Teyla's mouth dried as she pressed closer to those sensual hips, following the lead that was set for her.

Dear gods.

There was no way that the agent did not know how much sexual appeal she held. She was the embodiment of a femme fatale, and Teyla suddenly understood just how much one woman could change the atmosphere of an entire room.

Teyla's arms lifted, wrapping them loosely around the

taller guard's neck as hands settled on her own waist. Unlike the man from before, these hands did not wander, nor did they seem presumptuous. The agent was not directing her. Her hands were simply resting there, silently claiming the princess and keeping strangers away.

Teyla was not usually one for possessive actions, but this did not feel stifling in a controlling manner. It just felt protective, and the princess felt herself easing back into her pleasantly buzzed state.

As the music turned more upbeat, Agent A pulled away to spin her. Teyla could not fight the pang of disappointment at the space now between them.

What in the After was wrong with her?

Before she could think of a valid reason to press closer to Agent A again, she was spun in a half circle, and her back was pressed against the agent's front. The move was so sudden and unexpectedly intimate that Teyla was immediately on edge.

She was so distracted by the feeling of fingertips drawing small circles against her hips that she nearly screeched when words were spoken into her ear.

"Relax."

The command was soft, and Teyla knew intrinsically that if she were to pull away, she would meet no resistance.

"The man from before has just come back in the room, now accompanied by three friends. I suspect he believes he has been slighted."

Teyla did not respond but continued to dance while she casually glanced around the room. Sure enough, the large man was glaring at them while gesticulating animatedly.

"Well, fuck." Teyla sighed.

The chuckled breath against her ear made her shiver, a pleasant tingle going down her body.

"Succinctly put, Princess." The voice was smooth, like smoke swirling around her. It was getting unnaturally hot in here. "I suggest we put on a convincing show and then head out as if we are going home together. If they decide to jump us, I'll have more room to fight in the alley."

"Put on a show?" Her words sounded breathy to her own ears, and a flush spread to her rapidly rising chest.

"Just pretend. I promise I will not touch you in a compromising way."

Teyla wished she had a valid reason for the trust she already placed in this agent, but there would be plenty of time to analyze her reactions later. When she nodded her assent, she realized just how much space Agent A had been keeping between them.

There was not a single inch of her backside that was not pressed into Agent A's body, making Teyla feel lightheaded. She had wanted to dance tonight, but this felt akin to foreplay. Gods, her core was hot just from dancing with Agent A.

"May I touch your stomach?"

"Yes," Teyla breathed. As if she could say no right now. She ached for nothing more than Agent A to touch her.

A splayed hand pushed lightly against her stomach as their hips undulated together. Gods, she was *grinding* against her personal protection agent. Not only was she grinding, but she liked it. She more than liked it. A forbidden attraction she thought she had squashed long ago came rushing back to her in full force.

Lifting her left arm, she leaned fully back and allowed herself to enjoy the feeling of having another being wrapped completely around her. Teyla's fingers tangled into the brunette's hair, unintentionally tugging on it when she felt the hot palm brush against her midriff beneath her halter top.

Simultaneously, her breathing hitched and the agent's chest rumbled against her back, the music too loud for her to hear just what kind of sound the agent made.

Teyla was so hot. And wanting. And aching. Just as she felt Agent A's head dip to her again, she pulled the hair at the base of her skull again, harder and intentionally. Fingernails scraped her stomach as the agent exhaled a strangled noise against her ear, a delicious heat traveling from her abdomen straight to her core.

This was such a dangerous, intoxicating game, and Teyla's head felt heady from the power she felt. After Axel, she had not thought she could feel this hunger, but she felt ravenous. She let her head tilt backward and to the side, baring her neck to the agent.

Teyla could have sworn she heard a growl as lips pressed delicately just below her ear, and the hand on her abdomen slipped further down, teasing the top of her jeans.

"Fuck," Agent A cursed before pulling away, grabbing Teyla's arm and dragging her out of the club's side door.

The cool air against Teyla's flushed and sweaty skin cleared her head just enough to realize that she had basically begged the Agent to touch her on the dance floor.

They walked briskly through the alley, the dim lighting not helping visibility for the princess as she tripped on loose asphalt. Rounding a corner, she heard a door slam open behind them as many pairs of feet pounded the pavement.

Agent A abruptly turned and grabbed Teyla by the hips, hauling her onto a shoulder-height concrete ledge in a sitting position as Agent A stayed below. Blue eyes widened in wonder at the strength the guard had just exhibited without breaking a sweat, whose eyes looked like a burnt orange in the low lighting as she looked around and withdrew previously hidden weapons from beneath her shirt.

Princess Teyla had never found any person with weapons so attractive. As if sensing her thoughts, the agent locked gazes with her. Just how good Teyla thought Agent A looked down there, peering up at her from between her legs, was sinful.

The heat of A's undivided attention would have melted Teyla's underwear had she not already been soaked.

Agent A shook her head, as if pulling herself out of her thoughts and showed Teyla a weapon in each of her calloused hands.

"Blade or bullets, Princess?"

Teyla's eyebrows lifted high, but she accepted the sharp dagger, eight inches and serrated.

The woman grinned lopsidedly. "Excellent choice. Definitely had you pegged for a dagger kind of woman."

Teyla was unable to come up with a response before the belligerent man from the club and his lackeys rounded the corner. The agent turned around with her hands in her pocket, looking like she was just hanging out in a back alley. Teyla immediately missed the warmth from her body heat surrounding her.

"How can we help you boys?" Agent A drawled, a charming smile plastered across her face.

The man who'd laid his hands on Teyla stepped up, and she tensed as a gun waved in his hands as he responded.

"I want a turn; either one of you will do just fine."

The pure entitlement in his tone matched his greasy appearance. Teyla gripped the handle of the dagger hidden by her armpit, where she crossed her arms.

"I don't think that's necessary, sir," Agent A spoke with an air of calm confidence.

"It's no longer 'douche canoe' when I have a gun in your fucking face, is it, bitch?"

There had to be a way out of this shitty situation. Teyla's jaw tensed as his buddies roughed up the agent, taking her gun before shoving her back toward the wall. Agent A did not seem worried, but she could very well be putting on a brave face for her.

"Baby," Teyla began, and Agent A's attention snapped to her, calculating eyes scanning Teyla's face to figure out her plan. "If these handsome men want to watch, why don't we let them?"

A's eyebrow rose, assessing Teyla.

"That's a good start," one of the goons spoke up, chuckling as he grabbed his junk.

Teyla prayed to all the gods that abandoned her a long time ago for the agent to play along. She just needed to trust in her.

If the princess had not already been sitting, her legs might have given out when Agent A swaggered over to her. Her spine snapped straight when the agent's hands came to her own button-up shirt and began opening them one by one.

At the flash of lace, Teyla kept her eyes fixed on agent's face, refusing to watch her in any state of undress under these circumstances. However, as more red lace became visible, her resolve strained.

Fuck.

Was the agent always wearing sexy bras while guarding her?

The agent put her lips to her neck, her hands sliding down Teyla's chest between her breasts, avoiding touching her too intimately.

"Bitch, we can't see anything!"

The princess smirked as Agent A gripped the hidden handle of the knife while pressing a chaste kiss on her cheek. Teyla could swear it was a silent thank you.

Her guard whirled without warning, the dagger flying out and hitting the man's gun out of his hand. She was upon them before they could recover.

A punch to the solar plexus.

A knee to the groin.

A dislocated shoulder.

She moved like a wraith, and Teyla was unsure if she even touched the ground as she tore through each man with ease. The agent did not shoot or stab them, even after she recovered the weapons. She simply beat the shit out of them.

When all four men were groaning on the asphalt alley ground, the agent returned to her side. Her quick breathing was the only sign of exertion she showed despite the labor that had just transpired. Teyla's focus fell to the lacy red bra once before catching herself.

She cursed her shaky hands, either from the adrenaline from her flight or fight response or nerves over seeing this beautiful woman partially undressed. Maybe a combination. Still, she pushed all of that out of her mind as she reverently re-hooked every single button of the agent's shirt.

If she had not been here, Teyla would be dead, that much was for sure. She had been idiotic to sneak out just for Harlowe's bachelorette—Harlowe, who had disappeared with her other friends so long ago. Regret made tears well up in her eyes.

Upon seeing how upset the princess was becoming, the agent gently stopped Teyla's hands from refastening the buttons. "Hey, it's okay."

Teyla nodded rapidly, trying to wave off her concern.

"I have to admit, I have never had a woman cry at seeing my lingerie," A said dryly.

Teyla looked horrified. "No! That's not what— I'm not upset because… There's nothing wrong with—"

Agent A mercifully cut off her panicked rambling. "Ah, okay. You're crying because of how undeniably sexy my tits look in red," she deadpanned.

Teyla's sniffles turned into a snort. "Fuck off, A."

Her words lacked any real bite, and the agent's grin proved she knew that as well.

"Come on, Party Princess. Let's get you home."

Teyla let herself be picked up off the wall and led down several other side streets. As they walked, the streetlights became more numerous, as did the number of people ambling around. It was not until the agent opened the car door for her that Teyla realized they had never stopped holding hands.

CHAPTER TWELVE

LATE NIGHT RENDEZVOUS

Instead of capitalizing on the break the Reaper had finally allowed them to take, Teyla was ogling him from behind while he stretched. The first few times she'd been caught watching him, she'd claimed she was watching his technique. That lie fell flat as her thoughts wandered to what his physique might look like under his loose clothes.

It was official. Teyla was a little better than a dog in heat. Between this man and Agent A, over the past two weeks, she was constantly thinking about how it would feel to kiss them or how they might move between her legs. What had come over her?

It was not like she never pleasured herself in the privacy of her quarters. Still, over the past weeks, Teyla had found that she was not satisfied with her own hands.

When she did masturbate, she thought of them, leaving her aching for another's touch along her skin. Honestly, it was Agent A's fault. The press of her lips against Teyla's neck and the sway of their hips together were replaying endlessly in the princess's mind. Teyla fixated on the long fingers that had brushed the waistband of her jeans and felt that if she did not discover how they felt inside her, she might very well lose her sanity.

The Reaper was even more of a conundrum, but she remembered his wicked eyes as he had ground against her during the first installment of the competition. She watched how his body moved so fluidly as he demonstrated self-defense moves to her, and Teyla knew that his body would be strong and solid. The princess yearned to know what his body felt like pressing her down into a bed or underneath her.

How she wanted both of them was a mystery. For the second time in her twenty-five years of life, Teyla analyzed if she was interested in women. There had been a small infatuation before Axel, but she had chalked it up to just being a horny teenager.

Feeling out of her depth, Teyla had even attempted to do some research covertly in the library but had come up empty-handed. Same-sex marriage was a punishable offense, with a few death sentences carried out over the years. People had queer sex, as was evident at *The Crevice* and other clubs, but it had to be discreet.

After Axel, her future had been sealed by an edict to marry a foreign prince. Interest in a woman was not even permissible. Yet the longer Teyla spent around the agent, the stronger her attraction became.

Her phone vibrated in her pocket, distracting her. When she unlocked the phone to read the message, she grew confused at the message from Harlowe.

Oh my gods! I can't believe RYLIN told me about this before you did!!!!!

Teyla typed out a quick reply: *About what??*

Harlowe did not need to elaborate as soon as a picture came through. Disbelief had Teyla clicking the image to enlarge it.

Apparently, Harlowe's soon-to-be sister-in-law had snapped a photograph showing Teyla in a pretty compromised position in the club. Teyla remembered this moment, and it looked far more intimate without context.

Fuck that. She could not lie to herself. It looked exactly as intimate as it had been in real life for her.

The photo showed the princess leaning back into Agent A, one of her hands immersed in the agent's brown locks. The agent had one hand underneath her shirt where it had ridden up.

Teyla exhaled, her fingers flying across the keyboard: *Did Rylin send this to anyone else?! If Father sees this, Harlowe…*

Immediately, another message popped up from *Your Favorite Person In This World.* Teyla wasted no time to read it. *Of course not. I watched her delete it.*

Then: *just thought you might want to relive this SEXY moment!* Three winky faces followed.

The princess could admit that the picture was enticing. They certainly made a nice couple in the image. Teyla bit her lip, remembering just how erotic that moment had felt.

"What are you thinking right now?"

Teyla jumped at the Reaper's muffled voice as if caught by the chef sneaking out of the kitchen with sweets.

"N-nothing!" The squeak in her voice was far from convincing.

"I would be inclined to believe you if you did not have such a guilty expression on your face."

Teyla's eyes narrowed at the evident amusement in his tone. Although she had yet to see any features except his eyes, her imagination ran wild, filling in the gaps. Teyla was so sure he was breathtaking. His attitude was obnoxious, but she enjoyed their bantering most of the time. However, now was not one of those times.

"I don't need to share my internal monologue with a stranger."

"Oh, Princess, surely we are past strangers?"

Even the way he said the appellation felt familiar. She needed to shake off the tension eating her alive so she could focus. Sparring seemed like the next best thing.

"Let's go again." The princess stood up, shaking off the exhaustion in her limbs.

He stood up from his thigh stretch and shook his head. "You've had enough for the night."

Anger flooded her body, and she stomped her foot like a sulky child. "You do not get to decide when I have had enough!"

"I can see a physical burnout from a mile away. Your body is going to give out, and you will get hurt. I am not going to risk that."

The evenness in his tone made Teyla's irritation even worse. He was not raising his voice or even speaking to her aggressively. He seemed completely unfazed, proving she was not a threat to him, royalty or not. Before she could think the decision through, she lunged at him.

As if anticipating her outburst, he dodged to the side and stuck a leg into her path. As she hit the ground, she folded into a ball and rolled over her right shoulder before bouncing back up to her feet. The dagger was in her hand a second later as she attacked him repeatedly.

Each move was parried with infuriating ease as Teyla struck. She kicked out, her boot landing a solid hit to his abdomen. As he toppled backward, she followed him, straddling his hips as she pressed one dagger to the small sliver of skin she could see on his throat. Just as he moved to throw her off, Teyla withdrew a second blade and pressed it to his manhood, causing him to still.

"Don't even think about it," the princess raged, confused about her feelings for him.

Seemingly unworried about being bested, he watched her steadily. "Don't threaten somebody unless you plan to follow through."

"I plan to follow through, you bastard!" Teyla pressed the blade harder against his neck.

Instead of turning fearful, the Reaper leaned up, pushing it deeper into his skin. He locked eyes with her as blood swelled and dripped down his neck. He continued pushing forward until Teyla finally removed the blade in horror. His neck was bleeding steadily now, although he did not seem to care.

Cursing him soundly, she threw the two daggers down and applied pressure to his neck.

"What the fuck is wrong with you, you psychopath? Do you have a death wish?" Teyla's horror swiftly moved back to fiery rage. Raising her voice until she practically shouted at him, she continued to feel panicked as the bleeding continued and coated her fingertips.

"Calm down, Princess."

"Calm down? You won't stop bleeding!" Her eyes flew around frantically, searching for something else to help stanch the bleeding.

"For the record, I don't have a death wish. I need you to understand your limits before they get you killed."

His words were sharp, yet his tone was anything but. It was the softest Teyla had heard him speak, reminding her of the beautiful, nameless agent in the castle. When the blood finally coagulated enough that she knew he wouldn't bleed out, a huge sigh of relief left her, and she removed her shaky hands. "You are an asshole."

"I can be. But I'd rather be the asshole who kept you alive than the nice person who allowed you to get yourself killed. If you cannot kill, don't go for the kill. You are not better or worse off for it."

His eyes narrowed at her responding scoff.

"You can believe me or not, but you need to realize your limits. Don't go for the kill unless you mean it and know with absolute certainty you can complete it. Instead, cause enough injury to escape or call for help. You don't need to be the hero. You just need to survive."

Despite her best efforts, tears welled in her eyes. A torrential storm whirled within her, too many emotions twirling around to process. Teyla had never ended another being's life before, not even a spider.

The princess was unsure if a sudden foolishness overcame her common sense or if it was the gentle way he wiped the tears from her cheeks that led her to blurt out her confession.

"What if killing somebody turns me into a homicidal monster?"

As soon as the words exited her mouth, Teyla wished fervently that she could take them back. The vulnerability she'd just exposed could be used against her. When she scrambled off his lap, he did not stop her.

"I need to return to the castle before I am missed. Thank you for the lesson. I will see you at the next event."

Teyla's voice was curt as she sheathed her weapons and turned away from his body still sprawled on the rough ground. It was not until she was halfway across the clearing that she heard his whispered response.

"You are the farthest thing from a monster that I have ever met."

It took all of her self-control not to turn around and demand he expand on that statement, but she really would be missed in her quarters soon. Based on the rising moon, it was about to be midnight, when the night shift guards often checked the antechambers of her rooms to be sure nothing was amiss.

Privacy was a luxury she was not afforded.

Luckily, Teyla's secret workouts and lessons with him over the past several weeks had increased her stamina, allowing her to run back through the hidden path faster than ever before.

Just as she heaved her exhausted form onto the balcony with weak arms, a sharp rapping resounded through the wooden door.

Cursing colorfully enough to appall her mother in the After, Teyla quickly removed her coat—technically the Reaper's cloak from their first encounter that she'd decided to keep—and yanked her boots and pants off in record time.

"Teyla?"

That particularly revolting voice in her room at this time of night did not bode well. Nicolai's heavy footfalls thudded across the stone in the greeting chamber. She slipped into the bathroom on nimble feet, yanking on a nightgown and unstrapping one of her visible daggers as she went. In her haste, the tip of the blade scraped into her hand, a gasp escaping as she clenched her hand to mitigate the bleeding.

"What are you doing?"

His voice was much closer now, just outside her private chambers and far more urgent. Dread increased as she realized he would be able to smell the cut.

"I'm okay!" she called out breathily. "I am finishing up in the bathing chambers. Please wait."

Teyla's luck was ending as she heard him open the door despite her request.

Fucking bastard.

Her jaw clenched in irritation at his audacity and blatant disrespect of her wishes. Outside of making her life miserable in general, he'd fed off her for the past five years. During the last two, he'd begun making suggestive comments, growing bolder with each "playtime" session.

If the princess wanted to survive the night, she needed to be smart and as ruthless as her trainer had been instructing her should push come to shove. With renewed resolve, she exited the bathing chambers to face the second-worst monster in her life.

Nicolai was leaning against the side of the door frame in a casual, entitled posture. The suggestive smile on his face left the most putrid taste in her mouth.

It was a shame how handsome he naturally was and how easy he was on the eyes. His black hair curled around his temples, some pieces hitting his eyebrows. His nose was prominent but not unappealing. His brown eyes were framed with thick lashes, and his skin looked soft to the touch.

His villainy smothered any potential attraction. His

teeth were hidden right now, but Teyla knew that when he truly smiled, his fangs were slightly longer than most humans. Those terrifying fangs elongated into massive points when he scented fresh blood and fed. She was praying to all of the gods that existed that she had washed off enough of the Reaper's blood that he would not smell it.

"I just wanted to check on you after our last playtime," he began with a soft purr, standing on the threshold of the room and eying her bed briefly. "You smelled absolutely delicious when you left."

He reached for her hair, twirling a loose strand around his finger. Teyla carefully pulled the lock back and edged further away from him. His eyes dipped to the cut in her hand, his face resembling a rabid animal as he looked at her like she was about to be breakfast.

She was in such deep shit. He continued his monologue, oblivious to her internal battle to find a way out of this.

"I have been wanting to get you alone for a few weeks now, though that stupid new agent follows you around like a lost puppy, which you seem to enjoy. If you needed more attention, little lamb, you simply should have asked."

He had noticed the light banter and laughter between the new agent and her. If it caught his attention, he'd undoubtedly already reported it to the King. Teyla needed to deflect and diffuse this immediately. She walked across the room casually and lit one of the lanterns to allow more light.

"The girl agent? Whose name I don't even know?" Teyla was suddenly incredibly grateful for that now. "She's nothing more than an annoying gnat, flying around me and occasionally entertaining me. Her fumbling around amuses me. Forgive me for having a sense of humor, Nicolai."

Insulting her sweet bodyguard felt so wrong, but it seemed to placate Nicolai, as did utilizing his name without disdain. His mouth twisted with pleasure, disgusting her. If she managed not to throw up, she might just pull this off.

"She is quite annoying. Does that mean that I am still

your favorite companion?" He inched closer, passing through the doorway's threshold as he placed a nauseating inflection on the word.

Teyla backed up slightly, wanting to create space between them.

"As you are the only person I am allowed to speak to besides the ladies, I suppose so by default."

His smile turned predatory.

She involuntarily gulped, his sharp eyes tracking the movement as his smirk grew. He shifted forward even more, and she matched him step by precious step backward.

"Where are you going, sweet little lamb?" he questioned coyly. Her disgust grew tenfold as he slunk closer.

"You have always been my favorite too. You taste absolutely delectable."

Teyla took her eyes off him for a moment to assess her limited options. The main door was still ajar. Nicolai blocked the entryway, though, leaving her only option to go back further into the room to try to reach the servants' door. Screaming and fleeing would surely incense him even more. The only option was to play along and try to wound him enough to escape.

Attacking Nicolai would only cause severe repercussions, but the King only allowed Nicolai to feed on her during his arranged playtimes and never of Nicolai's own volition. The King enjoyed the power trip as she was forced into that humiliating role. If Nicolai attempted to govern the timing of her punishments, the King might very well kill the nightwalker himself. However, Nicolai had never preyed on her of his own accord and had conveniently made some kind of arrangement with her father.

Teyla's glance around the room cost her. Faster than her human brain could hope to process, using speed only granted to the moon-cursed, Nicolai breezed through the space between them and appeared right in front of her face. The stark smell of lavender hit her, a physical evolution of the nightwalkers to relax their prey. He took a deep breath, causing her to freeze in fear.

When Nicolai opened his brown eyes again, the sclera was tinted with red, the first sign of bloodlust. A slow smile spread across his face, his fangs elongating as she watched, tearing through his gums and causing a small trickle of blood to drip down his lips to his chin. Every instinct in her body revolted, begging her to escape.

Teyla needed to act.

"I've always found you delicious." She forced her voice to have a flirtatious tone, pretending she was talking to Agent A. The princess placed a hand on her right hip as she spoke, eyeing him up and down.

He halted his predatory advance, blinking in surprise. "Really?" His voice was laced with skepticism.

"Really. I think I've come to enjoy our little playtimes, Nic." She purred seductively as she slid her hand down her upper thigh. His eyes were raptly following that hand.

Shit. A different decoy then.

"Do you think you could have just a little taste now?" Teyla brought her left hand to the front of the loose buttons of her nightgown, undoing it to show the top of her cleavage. His attention shifted away from her thigh as he leaned forward to nuzzle her neck.

She forced herself to play the willing snack as she ever so slowly pulled up the hem of her gown to reach her dagger, trying not to alarm him. A sharp pain flashed through her chest as his teeth sunk into the top of her breast without warning. Teyla shouted at the intrusion, trying to pull away, but his grip on her was like a vice.

Damning the consequences, Teyla pulled her favorite dagger out of its thigh sheath and slammed it deep into his rib-cage. A strangled shout left him as he ripped his mouth off her. Teyla's hands scrambled to find purchase as she fell backward, frantically crawling away.

He hissed with rage, advancing with a preternatural speed. Nicolai grabbed her neck and lifted her, slamming her back against the stone wall. Black spots crowded her vision as her head cracked into the unforgiving surface. He backhanded her cheek. Disoriented, she fell, and her face hit the stone, this time on the right side.

Teyla cried out again as she felt the skin tear open from the rough stone, her bottom lip already split from the hit itself. Despite her struggling, he lunged and sank his fangs into her carotid. Her blood felt like it was boiling as his venom invaded her system.

It was useless.

She had tried to defend herself, and it backfired terribly. Nicolai was in the mindless state of bloodlust and would not be stopped from drinking his fill, including her feeble attempts. Her tears fell freely from pain, despair, and rage.

Suddenly, a loud snarl reverberated across the space, and Nicolai was yanked backward away from her. Whatever released that growl threw him so hard that he crashed into the other side of the wall, the plaster cracking. Teyla's legs were too weak from the venom running through her heart to support her, so she slid down the wall into a weightless heap. She hoped the paralyzing effects would wear off shortly.

Rapidly blinking her blurry vision away, the princess tried to make sense of what was happening. The shadow of a person fell across her, her rescuer stationed in front of her fallen body. A high-pitched scraping noise rang across from her, earning another guttural warning from the person standing guard.

"Stay down, you fucked-up abomination." The woman's voice was sharp as she verbally accosted Nicolai. Teyla was unable to distinguish the woman baring her teeth at him through her unfocused vision, but she appeared to be acting more animal than human.

Nicolai simply laughed, and Teyla struggled to focus on him. He was absolutely terrifying. His eyes were wild, crazed with bloodlust. He was not trying to hide his fangs in front of the woman. He was too far gone, craving and thirsting for blood.

Nicolai was planning on killing the woman. He might kill both of them under the influence of her blood. Teyla was the princess, but that never really mattered to him. Not when he was allowed to abuse and use her as he wished.

From what she could see of their struggle, he looked insane. Blood covered the lower half of his face, dripping down onto his tunic. *Her* blood. He'd drunk so much too quickly; it was no wonder Teyla was so lightheaded. She swallowed down another wave of nausea. Was the room spinning, or was it just her?

"Are you all right?"

What a peculiar thing for the woman to ask Nicolai. He was fine and also about to attack them. Nothing was making sense in her disoriented state.

"Teyla."

That was her own name. Frantic golden eyes glowing brightly in the room glanced at her briefly. Those eyes belonged to the very agent she was infatuated with.

"Thank the gods," Teyla breathed, relief clear in her voice.

The princess owed her more than a life debt at this point. Granted, it was highly unlikely either of them would survive the night for her to cash in that debt.

Yet, her loyal bodyguard was here standing as a physical barrier between Nicolai and her stunned, useless body. Agent A was willing to lay down her life for her.

"Watch out!" Teyla yelled out desperately.

Nicolai was crouching low and launched himself in the air toward them. Faster than Teyla thought was possible, her agent whirled around and lifted a hidden blade to block him.

Teyla could not decide if her mind was playing tricks on her as the woman seemed to move just as fast, if not quicker, than Nicolai. He yanked Teyla's dagger out of his side and swiped it toward her protector. Agent A blocked it with a long dagger of her own and used the momentum to strike toward his free side.

He howled in pain as the metal met its mark. Dark red blood erupted from the wound as she yanked the dagger free. Enraged, he attacked faster and faster, pulling out his sword and swinging it at her. The agent parried and dodged as well as she could but refused to leave the princess unprotected.

With a victorious shout, the tip of his sword sunk into her side.

Agent A's outcry of pain seemed to echo in the room. Nicolai leaned his head back and laughed.

Despite the excruciating pain she had to have been in, the agent took advantage of his distracted moment. She leaned forward, his blade slicing her further as she shoved her own dagger straight into his chest. He froze mid-laugh, a gurgling sound coming from him.

Teyla winced as Agent A took his sword by the hilt and yanked it out of her side. The squelching noise made her nauseated stomach finally lose its fight, and she emptied its contents all over the wall.

Agent A flipped his sword in her hand, pommel now grasped tightly. With an enraged shout, she swung it in an upward arc, chopping off Nicolai's head in one sweep. Before his head hit the floor, she was swinging again, still yelling a challenge. Again and again, she swung as she dismembered him piece by piece.

Teyla's legs finally stopped shaking enough for her to lurch upward toward her guard, and the princess slowly hugged her heaving form. Immediately, the agent stilled, lowering the gory sword, her body heaving with the force of her breathing. There was blood everywhere in the room. It painted the walls, the floor, and even the ceiling in arcs and splashes. She had been nothing but entirely thorough with him.

Despite the gore, Teyla continued to hug her from behind. It did not matter which of them the embrace was for because it felt nice. One of them was shaking from the trauma they had just experienced. It was probably Teyla. She felt A's body slowly relax in her arms as she leaned slightly back into the hug, laying her bloodied hands on top of Teyla's.

The agent gently pulled away and turned around.

To say she was covered in blood was an understatement.

Her hands and arms were the most saturated, her torso next. The blood splattered across her face only made her more savagely beautiful. Her mask had fallen off during the tussle, and Teyla simply blinked as she once again appreciated her entire face. Despite the circumstances, Teyla's throat grew dry at her beauty. This was a warrior in a woman's body, and as unhygienic as it was, she was extremely attracted to the ferocity still glowing in her eyes and the splatter of blood across her face.

The beauty in front of Teyla was reaching toward her and opening her mouth to say something when a scream sounded, startling them both. A maid dropped the bucket she was carrying as she took in the absolute carnage and fled the scene. The agent's mouth closed into a stiff grimace.

Without warning, she twirled away and bent down, snatching a dagger off the floor. She quickly wiped the blade off Nicolai's pants. Looking up and taking in the pained grimace on the princess's face, A froze and asked, "What? He was a burden on society and a terrible being. The least he can do is clean your blade." The agent flashed a grin before rushing toward Teyla. "Where do you keep your blade?"

Teyla blushed and hesitated, feeling ferociously embarrassed about her thigh harness for the first time.

Agent A must have sensed her apprehension because she added, "Quickly, Teyla. Guards will be here any moment, and this can't be seen. It's one hundred percent contraband for lovely princesses."

Deciding to focus on the fact that Agent A had just called her by name and called her lovely, she motioned to her right thigh. A's face morphed into surprised delight before dropping to her knee with her left leg propped up.

Seeing the woman of her dreams on her knee before

Teyla made the tangled energy in the princess's stomach transform into nerves for a wholly different reason.

Agent A quickly but gently bent forward and grabbed Teyla's right leg by the calf, guiding it to rest on her left knee. With reverence and slightly shaking hands, she gently lifted Teyla's dress on her leg, carefully protecting Teyla's modesty.

The princess's breathing hitched, and she nervously rested a hand on her throat, trying not to make any embarrassing sounds. Before Teyla worked up the courage to ask what she was doing, Agent A lifted the skirt section high enough to see the thigh harness, swallowing hard as a blush made its way to her cheeks.

Agent A lightly grabbed the harness and secured the dagger, pulling on the strap to tighten it. Every fiber of Teyla's being was focused on the feeling of the agent's touch upon her upper thigh. This was the most intimate thing that had happened to her in many years besides the dancing. Delicious heat spread down below her stomach, and Teyla exhaled a shaky breath.

Agent A parted her lips as if to say something, then inhaled and drew still as a rock. Without moving, she slowly looked up at Teyla through her dark lashes, her amber eyes positively glowing as she let out a throaty noise.

With the agent's neck exposed, Teyla could just make out a thin line of dried blood across her tan neck. Teyla's heart climbed into her throat as she recognized that same cut she'd given the man underneath her earlier in the night. Disbelief had the princess stepping back away from her. "Reaper?"

At the sound of her voice and the raw accusation coating that one word, something akin to panic flared in the agent's eyes. Her features grew hazy briefly before her left eye turned back into the startling blue Teyla had grown accustomed to, and the scar became visible. Her once rounded ears now showed the delicate curves upward that gave away her heritage.

The previous mirage had only one explanation, and the casual display of magick shook Teyla to the core. It should have been impossible for a magick wielder to infiltrate the castle walls.

Agent A and the Reaper were the same person, and she was Fae.

The sound of footsteps pounding toward them interrupted the potent dread, turning Teyla's muscles rigid. Within a heartbeat, Agent A's disguise was back in place.

Captain Farrow came forward, a familiar face in the royal ranks. "Come with us right away to explain yourselves to the King."

Agent A agreed without protest, amber eyes pleading as they looked into Teyla's. It was all she had time for before they were ushered out.

CHAPTER THIRTEEN

MIDNIGHT MEMORIES

The night was truly fucked. Arden had followed the princess back to the castle before beelining through the maze of servant halls to reach her own room. After quickly changing, she'd headed back toward the princess's rooms to ensure she was safe in bed before retiring for the night. Terror had rushed through her when she'd found the main door cracked open, then felt blinding rage to see that leech feeding on her.

Arden had lost herself in the feral protectiveness of a true alpha as she had hacked Nicolai to pieces. She would not risk his resurrection or recovery. No, for his sins against the princess, he would pay the ultimate price.

Arden had been too lost in her animalistic instincts to consider expanding the glamor to the wound the princess had marked her with. Now, her cover was blown. The Princess of Cyrene knew she could wield magick, and she was standing in front of the King of Cyrene.

Arden was facing a death sentence, and the King did not even know her name.

Not a soul in the throne room dared even to breathe too loudly. The silence itself was deafening. Arden could hear nothing except the blood rushing through her head. Her pulse was galloping a mile a minute, yet she forced her body to remain taut and her lips silent as she awaited acknowledgment from the King.

The murderer himself was sitting on his illustrious black throne, made from obsidian stone, placed strategically so that he was positioned far above the rest of the room. He had foregone a crown at this time of night—truly, early morning. If the distinctive white streak through his beard did not give away who he was, the arrogant posture did.

He was dressed all in black, blending in with his throne. His shirt was made of fine silk, embroidered with gold patterns. Long hair was tied into a knot at the back of his head, pristine, without a single strand out of place. He was leaning back on his throne, his elbows on the armrests, fingers steepled in front of him as he looked down across the room.

The throne room was huge, made to hold hundreds of people during formal events and celebrations. It also housed important funerals and official court meetings with the council. In special moments like these, it was a place to be tried and found guilty of crimes against the Crown.

Not many people were in attendance, which was probably a good thing for whatever was about to happen. Standing a few steps below the raised dais was the head of the council, a man whose name Arden did not care to remember. He was just the figurehead. No real power rested in the Council of Cyrene. Their tyrant was far too greedy to allow that.

Along with the head of the council, all five heads of the noble families were present, likely summoned by the King. The rest of the attendees were guards, herself, and Teyla.

Every bone in Arden's body yearned to kill the King now, while there were few guards present. This very well could be the best chance she would get for a long time.

Arden's voice of reason conceded that she could not win, not while in her Fae form and injured. Additionally, there were still more men than she could take on alone. There would come a time when he would pay for his crimes against her, her family, and her kingdom.

Begrudgingly, Arden could admit that today was not that day. If she made it out of here in one piece, she would personally ensure he would live to regret it.

The King leaned forward to place his elbows on his knees, his face pressing against his hands. The slight murmuring from the nobility immediately hushed in anticipation.

"Who would like to go first? Agent or princess?" His voice was quiet and calm, but Arden could taste the acrid, smoky taste of his rage along her tongue.

Keeping her head dipped in a convincing show of fealty, Arden took a step forward, ignoring the clanking of chains as she moved. Putting her wrists in manacles with chains to limit her movements was the first thing the guards had done as she exited the princess's rooms.

Arden was labeled an immediate threat. As saturated in blood as she was, it was not a surprise. The dried blood was now flaking off and making her skin severely itchy. Despite the shitshow this was turning into, she could not bring herself to regret saving the princess.

"I would like to explain what occurred from my perspective, Your Majesty." Utilizing the honorific set, every fiber in Arden's being ablaze with anger. This man was personally responsible for the death of her nation, and she was figuratively kissing his ass.

Her hands shook slightly, and she prayed to Mother Ambrosia that it would be mistaken for nervousness and not the blind fury hidden beneath her neutral expression. Arden needed to focus on the end goal: she would destroy his kingdom from the inside out.

Stick to the plan.

A slight nod was all the allowance she was given. Arden took a deep breath and released it along with her nerves, holding her palms up in supplication.

"I was completing my tasks for the night and realized

I had failed to gather my next assignment from the Captain of the Guard. I did not want to admit my mistake and appear foolish, so I attempted to track down Guard Nicolai. I remembered from this morning that he was assigned to the west wing of the castle. When I had looked everywhere else, I decided to check the hallway where the princess's quarters lay in case he had picked up an extra guard shift."

Arden purposefully avoided glancing at the princess as lie after lie left tumbled out of her mouth. It would take merely one word from her to derail Arden's entire defense, but it was a risk she had to take. Maybe Teyla would spare Arden to repay her for saving her life a few times, although Cyrenian royalty was not known for their mercy.

"When I arrived at her room, I found Guard Nicolai missing and her entry door ajar. Fearing the worst, I rushed in and found Nicolai on top of her. When I pulled him off, I found his face covered in her blood, fangs out, and his eyes turning red with bloodlust. I managed to fight him off with the blessings of the gods by catching him by surprise."

Truthfully, Arden was only able to defeat Nicolai because she had partially shifted, allowing her Lycan speed and reaction timing to come out. Had she not been relying on the aether in her blood, she likely would have been slaughtered. It was only because he was in the throes of bloodlust that he had not realized she had partially shifted in front of him.

"How did a human woman manage to escape unscathed from a vicious nightwalker?" the King questioned Arden, obviously suspecting she was not human.

Shit.

"I unfortunately did not evade injury, Your Highness. While I managed to take advantage of his distraction with the princess's blood and impale him in his chest, he did stab my side and throw me across the room."

Arden swallowed thickly, willing tears to fall from her eyes to seem weak and fragile like a human. She sniffled loudly and wiped her face with her bound hands before continuing.

"I was told growing up that to truly kill a nightwalker, it is through beheading, so I did that as well. I feared that it was not sufficient, so I dismembered him to ensure his demise."

When Arden finished her frighteningly inaccurate account of the event, she stepped back to the guards to allow them to feel the situation was under control. If she'd shifted into her wolven form, neither the chains nor their weapons could have stopped her without the assistance of quintessence-imbued silver to weaken her, but they did not know that. Instead, Arden tried to appear as docile and as human as possible.

The King's unblinking stare beheld her for an unnerving amount of time, assessing her and the recounting of the story. His face gave nothing away as he turned away from her and faced Teyla. Arden released the breath she had been holding and allowed her shoulders to relax a fraction of an inch.

"Daughter?"

As she stepped forward, Teyla kept her head high and met his stare. It was a feat very few people in the world dared. Arden's heart skipped a beat at her bravery.

"Father, I was returning from my washroom when Guard Nicolai arrived. I informed him of the impropriety of coming to my rooms at such an hour, yet he remained very… suggestive… and aggressive." She shuddered as she continued. "Despite repeatedly denying him, he restrained my arms and burrowed into my neck. Within a heartbeat, he bit me. I yelled out in pain and surprise, but nobody was around to hear me.

"He drank my blood quickly and held my arms down so I could not resist. By the time this brave guard showed up, I was dizzy, lightheaded, and confused from what I can only assume was rapid blood loss. From what I could see, she fought valiantly and protected me, causing herself injury. A maid must have heard the commotion and summoned the guards. That is all I know. I had no idea that Guard Nicolai was a nightwalker or how he had infiltrated the castle."

Finished, she stepped back as well and bowed her head.

Arden's knees wobbled in relief as she realized Teyla would not turn her in. The nobles began speaking loudly to each other; the news of a nightwalker in the castle was spreading terror like wildfire. The King held up a hand, demanding order.

His gesture was ineffective. Voices rose, speaking loudly over each other, each one demanding to be heard.

The fear was not unfounded.

Not only had a nightwalker been in the castle, but it had also somehow made its way into the royal guard. There could easily be more.

"Silence!" the King roared.

Immediately, all parties speaking froze; no one was a stranger to what often accompanied the King's rage.

"This is a simple fix. We will examine the body—well, what's left of it, anyway—and dissect it to discover how this nightwalker could hide its usual tell-tale signs."

A rumble of agreement rose from the heads of the noble houses. Nothing could be done until the investigation was complete.

"Now, we must decide what punishment is suitable for your princess for being so foolish and weak as to allow a nightwalker to feed from her."

Arden's head whipped up in shock before she quickly looked back down again. Why was he punishing the princess for getting attacked? It did not make sense. Arden's heart dropped to her stomach, thinking of what the punishment would be.

Arden had heard stories of the King's temper and his relishing of punishments for menial infractions. However, she could not allow the princess to be killed. It would derail all of the pack's plans and ruin any sort of redemption for her kingdom. Arden would shift in front of them all and attempt to kill the King immediately if it came to it.

Arden's whole body tensed as she listened to him continue.

"Tell me, agent, what do the commoners where you are

from, at the edge of our glorious kingdom, do as punishment for crimes?"

Arden's mouth felt as dry as cotton as she registered what he had asked. It was surely a trap, no matter which punishment she chose. Steeling her nerves, Arden met his beady gaze and provided the most honest answer.

"It depends on the severity of the offense, Your Majesty. It could be anything from being locked in a room without food to lashings or banishment when necessary."

The King's sadistic smile made Arden's hands tremble. She mentally chastised herself and stood even straighter. Arden would not show a single shred of weakness in front of any Cyrenian, least of all him.

His dark eyes looked Arden up and down, resting on her breasts for a long moment before turning toward his heir.

"Your lack of foresight and stupidity cannot go unaddressed, child. Step forward."

The princess obeyed, and Arden could clearly see her entire body shaking from fear. Apprehension tightened Arden's chest as she watched Teyla hold her head up proudly despite the tears rolling down her cheeks.

"Five lashings should be enough to convince you of your failure, I presume."

Arden could not risk any harm to the princess before her task was complete.

Without thinking through the sanity of her actions, Arden stepped forward in front of the princess and bowed at the waist.

"Your Majesty, I offer myself in the princess's stead. I failed in recognizing the nightwalker as well, and the princess was harmed because of it. Please accept my body in place of hers as recompense. I implore you not to punish her for my negligence."

Stormy blue eyes flashed toward Arden in shock, but she ignored Teyla's attention. She was not doing this for her, truly. Arden was protecting her investment in this mission.

His eyebrows raised in surprise before glancing at the nobles. "Lord Caine, what do you think?"

A rush of nausea turned Arden's stomach. Lord Caine was a savage brute. This was not going to end well.

As predicted, he spoke without mercy.

"Your Majesty, I think that five lashes would suffice for our princess, as she needs to learn, but I don't wish undue harm to her. This woman guard provides a good perspective on her own failings. I personally propose ten lashes to cover both her and the princess's oversights."

"Do the rest of the Lords and the Head of the Court agree?"

All of them nodded and murmured their agreement of Arden's punishment.

Ten lashes! For not killing a psychotic nightwalker before he revealed his predilection for blood.

Cyrene was just as ridiculously outdated and uselessly traditional as Arden had been taught. She found it extremely rewarding that she'd raided Lord Caine's residence and stolen information from him all those weeks ago. Surely, a single lord would see how absurd this was.

Most of the cowards kept their gazes fixated on their laps while Lord Caine smiled directly at Arden. She bristled in indignation at the challenge, and his eyes lit up at her glare.

Arden would take it. Then, she would report to the pack once she was healed enough. This was her role to play. She would do her assigned penance to protect the princess and save Orion.

"Ten lashes it is then." The King smiled, and it was not a thing of beauty. "Get the post and the whip, Lord Caine."

In Orion, the Captain of the Guard would dole out any punishments for his inferiors. Captain Farrow's eyebrows were furrowed, but he remained stationed by the King, ever obedient. This was obviously not a customary practice in Cyrene, either.

Once the wooden post was placed in the front of the

throne, the guards walked Arden over to it. They attached the manacles to the metal holders on either side of the post, which was designed to hold the victim up and cause more suffering as the skin stretched.

Lord Caine walked over to her, a malicious grin crossing his face. He removed a dagger from his side and sliced through her tunic, exposing Arden's back to the chilly air. A shiver wracked her body at the temperature change despite her wishes.

Lord Johan Caine's grin grew into a feral smile at her tremble, and she could hear him chuckle. Arden's apprehension grew, but she kept a stoic face. She had been through far worse than this and would not appear weak in front of the enemy's men.

Embracing her fate, Arden laid her face against the abused wood to avoid the momentum of the strike, smacking it into the harsh wood later. She tried to ignore the old blood stains on the wood, knowing her own would soon add to its macabre design.

"Make sure you count the strokes so we know you are mindful and paying attention to your lesson. Remember, this is for your edification. Yell it loudly so all can hear you." Lord Caine's voice was filled with barely contained sadism.

"Understood, my lord," Arden forced out between gritted teeth.

Without a preamble, the lashings began. The leather whip was made of three different pieces of leather combined into one thicker piece at the handle. Luckily, this whip did not contain any rocks or metal pieces, which was a small blessing.

Arden heard the whip soar through the air a split second before it made any impact. The pain seared her flesh, making her tense up and grit her teeth even more.

"One, sir." The debasement of counting aloud for the room full of pedantic men made Arden's ears burn. She knew the King was reveling in her embarrassment, and she forced herself to think of all the ways she would disembowel him later.

The next lashing landed directly upon the first one, and the skin tore open, releasing a spray of blood. That had to be a record, splitting skin open that fast. Arden clamped down on the whimper that threatened to sound at the fire.

"Two, sir."

Arden continued to count as he whipped her, legs giving out from under her by lash five. Her wolf was snarling so loudly in her mind that she could barely hear the King's laughter at the violence before him.

Still, she did not cry. It was taking every ounce of control to keep herself from shifting.

Instead, Arden thought about her family, brutally slaughtered. She thought of her nation and everything she was fighting to avenge. She considered how this pain was temporary compared to the pain Cyrene's King would face when it was time to exact her vengeance.

Arden would have pound for pound of flesh. This was her penance for all the lives she had taken and all those she would take before the end of this bloody journey.

Despite her disassociation, Arden counted, never missing a lash. By lash eight, her throat had gone hoarse from the effort not to cry or shout out. Her dignity would not be ripped from her despite the shame and pain accompanying each landing of the whip.

"Ten, sir," she finally rasped.

No part of her back was not screaming in agony. The burning sensation was everywhere. When the guards undid her manacles, the sound of her knees hitting the ground as Arden fell was far in the background. She had lost her hearing except for the insistent ringing that was almost as bad as the blows themselves.

The King sat there on his black throne, celebrating her anguish. Luckily, her tunic still covered her breasts.

"There you have it, girl. Thank the lords for the lesson and wisdom they've bestowed upon you today."

Not having any more fight in her, Arden echoed,

"Thank you, lords, for the benevolent lesson and wisdom you've bestowed on me tonight," barely above a whisper as her vocal cords, too, seemed to be muting.

Afterward, she added, "I will never forget it."

Arden said it neutrally, but it was a dark promise for what they did to her with their cowardice and cruelty. They would pay as much in retribution as their King.

Patience, she reminded herself.

Their time would come. Rushing her vengeance could ruin everything.

"You are dismissed, as are you, Princess. Be sure to see a healer, Teyla." The King waved her off carelessly and turned his attention away.

Every moment she struggled to stand stretched her flayed skin, but she bowed anyway. Arden walked stiffly down the hall, not bothering to cover her back. She would clean it up as soon as she could summon Xara.

Finally reaching her room, Arden pushed open the wooden door, grunting with effort. She lay face down on the creaky bed, content just to rest for a moment when a knock sounded.

CHAPTER FOURTEEN

THREE'S A PARTY

"Come in!" Arden raised her voice as she called out for the third time. She heard the wooden door open and a sudden inhale of breath.

"Oh, it looks so much worse up close."

Arden's eyes shot open, and she struggled to push her body up off the bed. "Princess! I had no idea it was you. Please come in."

"Stay down, you idiot. You're going to make it worse."

The ire in her voice was not lost on Arden. Obeying, she remained lying prone. All her senses were on high alert as she thought through how to explain this to the princess. Before Arden reached a conclusion, Teyla spoke again.

"I will make you a deal."

Arden cautiously turned her neck toward Teyla's guarded face, on edge as she waited for the offer.

"I will allow you the opportunity to explain yourself. If I believe you, I will summon help to care for your wounds and not report you to my father."

"And if you don't believe me?" Arden's voice was resigned even to her own ears.

"I will make you wish you had never stepped foot in my kingdom." Teyla's tone was a deadly promise.

Silence filled the room as Arden considered her ultimatum. It did not really seem that she had much of a choice but to reveal something to her. Teyla could not learn of all the plans, or everything would come crumbling down after literally years of planning and preparing. Arden would have to tread very carefully. "I don't know where to start," Arden admitted.

"The beginning is usually a good place." Teyla's quip caused the corner of Arden's mouth to curl despite the circumstances. "Why are you even giving me a chance? Why did you not tell the King about my use of magick? Surely, he would not have punished you then."

A very unladylike snort came out of the princess. "Don't pretend you believe the King is rational." A pretty pink blush graced Teyla's cheeks as she realized her faux pas. "Besides, you have saved my life on too many occasions for me not to consider you a potential ally."

It was not until the princess softly cleared her throat that Arden realized her own attention had been entranced by the lovely flush now spreading down Teyla's delicate neck. Arden's gaze snapped to pink lips as Teyla's tongue wet them. The princess looked nervous.

"Why don't you start by showing me which of your appearances is the authentic you?" Her gentle offer made Arden shudder as she nodded in agreement. Arden could not tell why she was so nervous for Teyla to truly see her. She was well aware that she was scarred and imperfect, but until this moment, it had never bothered her.

Teyla kept rapt focus as Arden released the glamor on her features once again, relaxing fully as she let go of the mental strain of holding the quintessence. Arden wished, not for the first time, that she could read Teyla's thoughts as the princess took her time looking her over.

The agent worried her lip nervously as the princess studied her face carefully, as if trying to identify any evidence of a remaining mirage. Without asking, Teyla brought up her hand and tilted Arden's face slightly to look at the heinous scar that bisected her left eyebrow and temple. Shame caused Arden's ears to flame, yearning to cover the ugly proof of a previous failure.

Arden's self-deprecating thoughts rapidly trickled out of her brain as Teyla gently traced the scar with a reverence Arden had never experienced.

"How did you get this?" Teyla's question was not cruel, simply curious.

"That's a story for another time, Princess. For now, just know it taught me a valuable lesson."

Teyla's face contorted, thinking to push Arden for an answer then changing her mind. She traced the scar along the side of Arden's shaved head to its end right above her pointed ear.

As if in a trance, Teyla's fingers lightly ghosted the curved tip of her ear, no longer rounded like a human's. Arden shuddered down her entire body, and Teyla quickly pulled away in alarm.

"Did I hurt you?" Teyla's blue eyes were wide with worry. The pure innocence in that look convinced Arden to be honest.

"No," Arden spoke through gritted teeth as she struggled to remain still despite the desire that had just been stoked. The agent needed to switch the topic immediately. "I am here to protect you from any who wish harm upon you."

"Why? You are not from Cyrene." Arden shook her head, and Teyla continued. "I know now why your accent seemed so familiar yet foreign to me. You are from Orion."

A sense of panic flared in Arden's chest, but honesty seemed the only path ahead. Arden could sense that lying now would shatter the very fragile trust she had managed to forge. "Yes."

"Why do you wish to protect me? I was under the impression that all Orionians hated Cyrene." Her blue eyes seemed to search the depths of Arden's soul.

"Many do, although that is because it is easier to lean into their hatred than to understand the nuances behind the fall of our kingdom's grandeur."

"You mean to claim you are not one of the majority that hates Cyrene?"

The vulnerability on the princess's stupidly perfect face made Arden's heart stutter. It would be so easy to mislead her, but her soul was so weary from all the lying over the past two decades. The truth was, Arden wanted to confide in her. "Yes." Her voice was emphatic as she internally begged Teyla to believe.

"Why have you not tried to kill me when you've had numerous chances to? My father is solely responsible for the fall of your kingdom."

"True, your father is. It would be naive and honestly ignorant to blame you or your people for the crimes of your King. I may be many things—an asshole definitely included in that list—but I refuse to be foolishly blinded by vengeance. You are not your father, a fact I have seen repeatedly in the weeks of knowing you as a competitor and guard. You are kind and altruistic, and I have discovered I need to protect that for Cyrene to ever have a chance of recovering from its sadistic ruler in the future."

Teyla rocked back on her heels in surprise at the stark honesty.

Arden meant every word spoken, although she did omit the plan to steal Teyla from her home. Hopefully, Teyla would never know until the time was right. Arden was unsure what the Council of Elders planned to do with her, but it had to be safer for her in Orion than here.

Already, Arden had saved her numerous times, and she had only been around the princess for just under a month.

The minutes trickled in silence as Teyla processed everything said, and Arden could not help but fidget as she awaited the verdict for her fate.

Finally, Teyla released a deep sigh and nodded her head before leaving briefly and sending a summons for a healer. When she returned, they sat in semi-comfortable silence as they waited.

Deciding that staring at the princess in silence was bordering on creepy and obsessive, Arden turned her attention to the room. She blanched as she noticed a pair of dirty underwear haphazardly thrown over the chair. Arden was suddenly hyper-aware of the heat spreading across her face as she swallowed thickly.

"What is wrong?" Teyla asked inquisitively.

"Nothing." Arden's answer was too quick to come off as natural.

Teyla's eyes narrowed suspiciously before she scanned the room to determine what caused such sudden embarrassment. A shit-eating grin grew on her face as her eyes landed on it. "I have seen women's undergarments before, you know." She was teasing, mirth lacing her voice. Arden's blush pooled in her cheeks, surely a dark crimson by now.

A peel of laughter broke free from Teyla, one of the most beautiful sounds Arden had ever heard. She would gladly embarrass herself regularly to hear that sound from her chest. Arden was in such deep shit.

Embracing the teasing, Arden added, "Maybe, but you haven't seen my undergarments."

Teyla's laughter subsided, and her intense focus glued Arden to the bed. Arden yearned to know what the princess was thinking.

Teyla looked anywhere but at Arden. "That's not quite true."

Arden was pulled back into the memory of unbuttoning her shirt in that dim alley and teasing the princess.

Teyla cleared her throat. "Your quarters are quite… cozy. I can't believe I have never seen them before. You've been in mine so many times."

"Well, I am to protect you, Princess. Of course, I've

been to yours." Arden paused as a heavy shame crushed her. "I am sorry for the mess I made there. I hope you don't have any issues staying in there again after the walls and floor have been deep cleaned."

Arden had painted the walls in blood. It would take hours to get all of it off. It was not a pretty sight. Teyla's room was now a blood bath. Outside, insistent rain was pounding the ground, and Arden thought of dragging herself out there to be healed by nature, perhaps by Mother Ambrosia herself.

Before Teyla responded, rushed steps came pattering into the room. Xara skidded to a stop, sloshing water onto the floor in her haste. Her curly hair was wild, and she was still in her nightgown, not bothering to change into proper attire in her haste to arrive.

"A! Are you okay?" Xara rushed out, scrambling over. Arden grinned in delight at seeing her packmate so unexpectedly.

Teyla raised her eyebrows. "Wait." Teyla's brow furrowed as realization dawned. "You are the girl from *The Crevice*!"

Fuck. Before Arden could weave a believable tale, Xara answered.

"After Arden rescued me, I realized I wanted to use my second chance at life to help others, so I joined the castle staff as a healer."

Teyla pursed her lips and took Xara in. "I'm glad you have found purpose after the horrors you faced. Please tend to *Arden's* wounds. She has a wound on her right side from a sword and was whipped on her back. She will need salt and water to cleanse it and a salve to help stop the bleeding and keep it from infection."

Xara gave an affirmative nod and left to gather the rest of the supplies.

Arden wished to ease the tense silence surrounding them in her absence. "You know, with the burning pain in my back, I had already forgotten about getting stabbed," the Fae said, moving her tattered shirt to look at the wound. The blood had begun to coagulate.

"I have not forgotten a single injury you have suffered on my behalf," Teyla said gravely.

"Oh, lighten up, Princess. I could be dead. This is worlds better."

"You could also only have a sword injury and not have been whipped half an inch from consciousness."

"Yes, well, it's already happened. Please stop being so serious. Let me talk to the easy-going Teyla instead of the Princess of Cyrene while I'm in all this pain."

Teyla looked at her, deep in thought. After a minute of standing there, she leaned forward. "Arden, would you like me to distract you while your friend cleans your wounds?"

The offer was sincere, and the use of her full name took Arden's breath away. "I would like that very much."

Xara scurried back into the room and closed the door, clutching antiseptic, healing salve, and more clean rags tightly to her abdomen. She quickly surveyed the room before falling into business mode.

"A, here's a chair. I need you to sit on it so I can reach your side wound as well," Xara ordered, her voice leaving no room for debate. "Also, I need what's left of this shirt to come off. It's in the way."

Xara turned around to prepare her items and offer Arden a semblance of privacy. A deep blush settled on Teyla's features as she realized the agent was about to strip.

"I, uh, have some tunics in the chest over in the corner, if you would be so kind as to grab me one. Preferably black, in case I bleed on it," Arden offered.

Teyla nodded and quickly walked to the chest. "Of course."

With the princess distracted, Arden glanced toward Xara's preparations to find the young girl already looking at her. Xara's eyebrows raised teasingly as a smirk slid across her face. Arden rolled her eyes and sent Xara a stern look, the message loud and clear: not a word. Xara simply shrugged and smiled, going back to folding cloths.

"Is this one all right, Arden?" Teyla held out an over-sized black tunic.

Arden flashed her a reassuring smile. "Looks great."

With a soft grunt, she stood and grabbed the chair. She hissed in an intake of breath as the clotted wounds broke open when she lifted the chair and turned it around. Arden straddled the seat, the back of the chair against her front, for easy access for Xara. She laid her arms across the top of the backing and rested her chin upon them. As long as Teyla stayed on the other side of the chair, her front would be covered by the chair.

Teyla grabbed a second chair near the fireplace and sat directly in front of Arden, less than a few feet away. It was too close to be deemed casual, yet the intimacy soothed her, considering the situation. Teyla needed to be close to truly provide any distraction for the agony she was surely about to feel.

"Does anybody have a knife I can use to cut off the rest of this shirt?" Xara asked, knowing damn well Arden always had knives. Before Arden could direct Xara toward one, Teyla spoke up quickly.

"I do." She lifted her skirt briefly and unsheathed her beautiful knife.

The grip was made from pure onyx, with metal on the pommel and cross-guard for durability. It was primarily black as a starless night with thin white streaks within it. The blade itself was made from traditional steel but was beautifully crafted. Overall, it was a durable blade, withstanding most things outside of an exceptionally hard blow. Its sentimental value showed, as there was an inscription on the blade.

Xara quickly cut off the rest of the tunic, leaving Arden bare from the waist up. An overwhelming sense of embarrassment returned with renewed vigor, especially as Teyla's attention dipped to the chair and back up.

"So, Princess, how are you going to distract me?" Arden asked with a nervous laugh, even as her chest tightened with anticipation.

"How would you like to be distracted?" Teyla asked coyly.

This woman will be the death of her. Arden knew exactly how she wanted to be distracted, but that definitely would not happen when she was injured or with an audience. If she ever got that kind of chance, she'd want privacy as she made the princess cry out in pleasure.

Teyla nervously began to chew on her lip as if she could read Arden's very dirty thoughts.

Shit.

Surely, Arden did not say any of that out loud. She quickly looked over to her packmate's face, which was completely focused, revealing nothing had been spoken aloud.

"I think I would like to hear more about Teyla. Not the Princess of Cyrene, just Teyla. I want to know what makes her this compassionate woman and what makes her tick." Unlike Arden's other thoughts, this felt far safer and a much more respectable way to pass the time.

"There's not much to learn," Teyla said with a woeful laugh.

"Please, Teyla."

Even Xara paused. Arden could not remember the last time she'd said please to anybody. Yet here she was, saying it to her blood-sworn enemy. Xara quickly carried on, not saying anything. Arden was in such deep shit. She would get cornered for answers by Xara sooner rather than later.

A defeated sigh passed the princess's lips. "Fine. But I'm only doing this until she's done. Deal?"

"Deal," Arden quickly agreed, feeling giddy.

As Teyla settled back into the chair and crossed her legs, Xara spoke up.

"Get ready, A. This is going to hurt."

The words had hardly left her lips when the first antiseptic-soaked cloth was pressed against the shredded flesh. As prepared as Arden was mentally, her body still tensed up, and she cried out in pain. Arden quickly closed her traitorous mouth, clenching her jaw repeatedly as she worked through the searing pain from the antiseptic. It was essential for cleaning out any infection, but damn, it hurt, and the bleeding began anew.

Teyla leaned forward from her reclined position and grabbed Arden's hand in hers.

"You can squeeze if you need to. You also can cry out if you need to. Don't try to take it silently just to save face in front of me."

Arden nodded, not trusting herself to speak. Xara laid another cloth on a new section of her back, causing a whimper to escape.

Teyla took this as a sign to begin her distraction. "Baby Teyla was quite the wild child, believe it or not." She chuckled with fondness at the memory. "My mother always encouraged me to speak my mind, stating that 'a good queen knows when to speak up,' so I needed the practice. The King was not very fond of this method, but he loved my mother dearly and allowed it. He wasn't always who he is now. He used to play make-believe with me and carried me around, so it felt like I was flying. He was gentle and soft and… I'm sorry. I digress. Let me restart.

"Once upon a time, there was a little girl who loved to speak her mind. She was strong-willed and fierce, never accepting an answer without resounding proof. She asked 'why' about everything and drove her tutors crazy with her endless questions. She was carefree but studious, wild but always careful. Her mother liked to call her a walking contradiction."

Arden felt the burn of Xara cleaning her wounds, but it felt far more distant as she listened raptly to the story Teyla was telling. There was pain behind her voice but also a certain happiness at reliving the memories.

"Everything was perfect until the day the Orionians murdered her mother, and the war began. The King turned into a brutal killing machine. He murdered so many of the Orionian people without discretion or mercy. It was—and still is—a senseless loss of life. Fervently against her father's massacre of the culprits after they were caught and found guilty, the princess spoke up in a council meeting, requesting that the war be ended."

Arden clamped down on the correction begging to be released. The people of Orion never killed the Queen of Cyrene. She had always been told that the King killed the Queen and covered it up. Did Cyrenians really not know the truth? Despite her heartbeat kicking up, Arden said nothing, fighting the urge to interrupt by focusing on the fire igniting her back.

"She was only six years of age and was laughed at by the Council and the King. They demanded more blood in retribution for losing the Queen. So, they murdered the royal family, only to discover much later that the Princess of Orion had escaped and had begun to rally the remains of their kingdom. So much loss, and so many paid for the crime of a few. The King has never been the same, nor has the princess. She lost her voice and confidence, her wildness was tamed, and she lost who she was."

She paused, her eyes lined with silver. Arden squeezed her hand, encouraging her to go on with a slight smile.

Teyla sucked in a deep breath.

"She stayed lost for another two decades or so until she met an unlikely ally who is drawing her out of her shell again. It terrifies her, but maybe finding herself again will be the first part of healing her kingdom."

"Maybe," Arden murmured.

Xara spoke up from behind her. "I have good news and some not-great news. Which do you want first?"

Teyla answered for Arden.

"Good news first. I think I could use some of that." She laughed nervously. That last confession had taken a lot out of her.

"The good news is that your back is all finished! The

healing salve is on, and the fresh bandages cover the wounds to protect them from dirt and infection. I cannot wrap them fully until your side is taken care of."

"And the bad?" Arden asked through clenched teeth, unease rippling through her.

"Your side needs to be sewn shut. The cut is thin but very deep and won't heal properly unless we close it manually. Do you think you can withstand the pain?"

Xara's mouth was tugged into a frown as she searched Arden's face. It felt odd to have somebody care so deeply for her well-being.

"Of course, I can. I'm basically invincible, remember, little one?" Arden said with far more bravado than she felt. She winked in false confidence.

"Evidence to the contrary."

Arden whipped her head back toward Teyla in disbelief. There is no way that the princess just muttered that sarcastic remark. Teyla was not looking toward her but had a suspiciously growing smirk. Arden stuck her tongue out at the princess childishly, resulting in her letting out that beautiful, damning laugh.

Arden smiled as her wolf chuffed proudly.

Realizing she still needed to reassure her packmate, Arden urged her on, "Seriously, Xara. Let's do this now. We don't have much of a choice." She added gently, "I trust you."

Xara smiled briefly at her before shifting back into healer mode. "Princess, can you grab something for Arden to bite on? This is going to hurt really badly."

Immediately, Teyla was up and searching through the room for something durable to bite down on. Eventually, she came back with a leather belt. She held it out to Arden, waiting expectantly. Stubbornly, she shook her head.

"I'm fine, ladies. I don't need to bite down on something like a damn horse does a bit."

Teyla raised her eyebrows.

"You will bite down on this because the girl you claim is

like a sister told you to." Teyla gently but firmly grabbed Arden's chin and guided her mouth to the leather. The princess's thumb tapped the side of her jaw, a silent command to open. And damn her, Arden did as she was bid to.

It really brought a whole different definition of being whipped.

"If that isn't enough reason for your stubborn ass to listen, then you'll do well to remember I am still a princess whom you serve. You will do as you are told when it comes to your health and safety."

Arden huffed out an annoyed breath and allowed the leather to be placed in her mouth. She slowly bit down, flexing her jaw as she glared at the princess.

"Good girl," Teyla praised.

A rush of warmth rushed to her lower abdomen at that. Teyla had said it so innocently. There was no way she meant it the way Arden had reacted to it.

But fuck, she liked the way those words sounded coming out of Teyla's mouth. On top of it all, she was saying them about her, to her.

It was euphoric.

Arden would probably do almost anything Teyla said if she got praised like that every time.

Before either of them could say anything further, although what she even could say was a mystery, Xara interrupted.

"Brace yourself, A. Here comes the needle."

A new, deeper level of pain came with the first puncture of the needle. It was like being stabbed all over again but without the adrenaline that helped her through it the last time. The string Xara was using to suture her up slid through her skin sickeningly. Arden released a strangled groan around the leather, tears springing to her eyes.

Teyla immediately responded, bringing her chair even closer. She hesitated for a moment before wrapping her arms around Arden's neck, bringing her in for a hug. Their heads were so close that Arden could feel Teyla's breath on her forehead.

"Tell me," Teyla murmured so that only Arden could hear. "Why were you blushing so hard when I told you that you were being good?"

Mortified, Arden felt that blush betraying her again. Teyla had not only noticed her reaction earlier but was now calling her out on it. What could she even say to a princess who likely had no sexual experiences and definitely should not know about her infatuation with her?

Arden craned her neck a bit from where it was resting to see the princess's eyes sparkling. Xara stood up fully to grab a different supply. Arden seized the brief moment of reprieve and took the leather belt out of her mouth to speak.

"Um… it's really, uh." She coughed, uncomfortable and embarrassed. "It's just not something I am called often, so I was surprised. And pleased."

Too far behind the princess to be seen by her, Xara mouthed the word "pleased" back at Arden, raising her eyebrows meaningfully. At Arden's mutinous look, Xara's own hand clapped over her mouth to muffle the snickers threatening to sound. Arden could hardly stay annoyed as she beheld Xara's deep chocolate eyes so bright with humor.

Seemingly oblivious to their silent conversation, Teyla hummed. "I see." She continued to assess Arden. "So, it is something I should say to you more often so you know my appreciation."

Yes.

"No!" Arden paused, taking a breath.

"Liar," Teyla whispered, her eyes sparkling with mischief.

Teyla cocked her head slightly to the side as she assessed Arden. They could be kissing if Arden simply raised her head another few inches. She mentally slapped herself for the thought and realized she must be delirious from the pain.

Arden moved to pull back out of the embrace when

Xara started to stitch another suture, quickly putting the leather back in her mouth to bite. Teyla began to rub Arden's shoulders in consolation and comfort. Her tensed muscles relaxed at the sweet touch.

Finally, Xara laid the supplies down and sighed. "That's the best it's going to be, A. Do you want to look at it before I cover it up?"

Nodding in the affirmative, Arden stood up to go to the small mirror. Teyla exhaled a startled squeak. She dared a glance toward the princess and found her with her hands covering her face.

The fact that she was attempting to preserve Arden's modesty warmed her heart. "Sorry, Princess. I forgot I was not wearing a top. I'll let you know when it's safe to look again."

Without waiting for an answer, Arden gingerly walked over to the mirror. True to her word, Xara had covered all her back wounds with white cloths that were already slightly saturated with sanguineous fluid. Arden leaned slightly to the left and lifted her right arm, grimacing at the discomfort of the movement.

Xara had done a marvelous job sewing her side together. The wound itself was slightly oozing but was mostly held together. Though never having done any kind of wound care experience before now, Xara's work thoroughly impressed Arden. The pack would be thrilled that they finally had a healer.

Nodding at Xara, Arden lifted her arms gingerly as her friend finished wrapping long strips of fabric around her torso, holding everything together. When she was done, Arden felt uncomfortably restrained in her movements, but the pressure was vital in helping the bleeding stop. Her torso was bound from just above the navel and up, crisscrossing over her shoulders to help the bandage remain on.

"Okay, Princess. I'm all covered up. Literally. I can barely move."

Teyla removed her hands from her face, her mouth twitching in amusement.

"Can you help me put on that black tunic now instead of laughing at my expense?"

Teyla's smile grew. "I wasn't laughing." She made her way over and helped slip the shirt over the bandages.

The chair was covered in blood. Arden really hoped the maids would be able to get the blood out. Otherwise, she would be reminded of being whipped every time she returned to the room to sleep. Granted, she hoped she would not remain in this kingdom for more than another two months, tops.

"Well, now that I know you are okay, you should get some sleep," Xara spoke, gesturing to the bed.

Arden brought her in for a very gentle hug, kissing the top of her head. "I am eternally grateful to you for your services and forever thankful to have met you, pup. You go to bed too. It has to be around three in the morning, and you have to be up soon to service the castle."

Xara's doe eyes found the princess, raising her eyebrows meaningfully at Arden before bidding Teyla goodnight and leaving the room. Arden was about to lie down when a thought sprung across her mind.

"My gods, you don't have a place to sleep right now! Please, take my bed. I can sleep in the other chair."

The princess ardently shook her head. "You are injured, and I am indebted to you for saving my life. You deserve and need the bed. Please sleep in it." She continued to press. "Seriously, that's an order."

Arden shook her head fervently. "I'm sorry, Princess, but this is an order I must disobey. Take the bed. I sleep in these chairs all the time."

A trivial lie. With a sigh, Teyla settled into Arden's bed. The agent pushed back all the thoughts and indications that came along with that and settled into the chair.

After an hour of tossing and turning on the chair, Arden heard Teyla's tired voice speak up.

"Come and get in your bed, you stubborn ass. There's enough room for us both, and I can't sleep with all that shifting around."

Arden was too exhausted and in too much pain to argue. She simply lay down on her left side, facing away from the princess. Arden drifted off to sleep as soon as her head hit the pillow.

CHAPTER FIFTEEN

PHASE II

The princess groaned and nuzzled her warm pillow, clinging to the last remnants of sleep. She was not expecting the pillow to squeeze back. Discombobulated, her eyes snapped open as she tried to pull away without success.

Memories came flooding back as Teyla registered that the vice-like grip was not a pillow but the strong arms of the Orionian woman holding her body closely in her sleep. Arden's face was so relaxed as she rested, something Teyla had not had the pleasure of seeing until now. The night before had been a whirlwind, and Teyla had been more focused on Arden's injuries and comfort than anything else.

For the first time since they had met, there were no hard lines across Arden's skin or obvious reservations. She looked much younger and more innocent like this. The wicked-looking scar along the left side of her face seemed so violent, clashing against the soft glow of the morning light filtering through the window. Her unbound brown hair splayed across the pillow tantalizingly, and Teyla's fingers itched to wrap themselves amongst the strands.

The princess had never seen the agent's hair down, and

all she wanted to do was play with it, maybe tug on it again to see Arden's reaction up close. Teyla shook her head to clear those lustful thoughts and concentrated on how they'd ended up in each other's arms.

Sometime in the night, one of them must have gravitated toward the other's body heat, and now they were cuddling. She was cuddling with Arden. She invited a woman who hailed from Cyrene's biggest enemy kingdom into bed, and they'd intertwined extremities.

Teyla should be freaking out that she was in bed with the enemy, not fantasizing about actually bedding this woman. Yet, she could not bring herself to regret the circumstances. Arden hailed from Orion but had abundantly proven herself with the sheer number of times she had protected Teyla during the competition and as her personal agent.

Teyla had just experienced the best night of sleep she'd had in decades and was currently cocooned in the body of the woman she was lusting after. On top of that, the princess no longer needed to feel guilty about pining after two people at once. *They are the same person!* This was all a win as far as she could see, as was last night after the lashings.

She had followed Arden to her quarters to check on her, which was obviously the right decision. The woman was in rough shape and was clearly not going to tend to her wounds herself.

Teyla had tried to distract her from the pain the best she could, which was the least she could do since Arden had taken the beating on her behalf. Teyla's toes curled as she recalled how Arden had reacted to being called a "good girl." While the princess had pretended to be oblivious at first, she knew exactly why the Fae reacted so viscerally. For the sake of research, Teyla had recently smuggled a contraband book out of the library that spoke about various kinds of sex, and one of them was about submission and phrases dominant partners often said.

While Teyla had not intended it sexually at first, she

could tell how much Arden enjoyed it by how flushed she had become. Her own body had gotten excited at the prospect, and she was grateful Arden did not notice. Teyla was definitely going to tell her how "good" she was far more often.

Arden shifted. Teyla quickly closed her eyes, hearing Arden's deep breath in, and felt the moment her body tensed up at their cozy positioning. After a few seconds of Teyla's heart pounding in her ears, Arden relaxed.

"I know you are awake, Princess. You breathe differently when you are asleep." A long pause, then, "That sounded super creepy. I'm sorry."

Teyla huffed out a laugh and took in just how relaxed and content Arden appeared.

"So, why are you just cuddling with me in bed while awake?" Her tone was playfully accusatory, and Teyla was happy that Arden was not angry.

"I actually tried to get up when I first woke, but your arm had a death grip on me," Teyla joked.

"Well, you are really warm and comfortable. What can I say?"

Teyla secretly wished it was because Arden wanted to be close to her, too, but decided not to respond. As she pushed up again to get up, Arden groaned. Teyla immediately moved the hand that was perilously close to her stab wound and apologized profusely in horror.

"It's okay, Princess. It actually barely hurts now," Arden placated.

Teyla was unsure if she could believe the agent, who appeared clearer-headed and much more sentient than last night. That was suspiciously quick. "Let me look at your wounds," the princess demanded.

"I'm not sure that's the best idea. I do not have anything extra to wrap them up with."

Arden had a point. Their little healer was not present and would be unavailable as the castle staff bustled around, prepping for the competition later today. Still, Teyla could not shake the feeling that something was off. Arden should be in a lot more noticeable pain.

"Then, please allow me to undo just a small section to assess your wounds. Especially since you are expected to perform well during today's competition."

"Trust me, Princess. I always perform well," Arden bantered casually as she rolled over onto her stomach.

Teyla inhaled sharply, thinking about all the ways Arden might perform well and which ones she really wanted to participate in. Trying to act normal despite the dirty thoughts in her head, the princess gently unraveled an area of the outer bandages.

Her jaw dropped at what was uncovered.

After several moments of silence, Arden asked, "What is it? Is it worse than you thought?"

The truth could not be further from that. The flesh was knitted together and scabbed over, with some light pink scarring on the outer ends of the wounds.

"Your wounds are already healed beyond what they should be," Teyla managed to choke out. It was unreal. It simply could not happen. Unless Fae could heal this rapidly, there was no natural explanation. It would only be possible with magick.

Fear caused her stomach to sink like a heavy rock in the sea. Her hands trembled as Teyla pulled them away from Arden's injured back, blinking rapidly as if that would change the objective reality right in front of her.

Arden abruptly stood up and walked to the mirror to see for herself.

"Can your kind heal this fast?" Teyla's voice was a shaky whisper as Arden's eyebrows raised.

Arden's lips turned down as she swiveled back toward the princess. "Fae and Lycans can heal at about double the speed of humans, but even they would take at least a week or two to heal entirely from these injuries."

"Did you heal yourself with whatever magick you possess?"

She looked at Teyla with something akin to pity. Whatever truth she was about to hit Teyla with would not be good. "The ability to use quintessence to heal is incredibly rare, Princess. I know of fewer than five beings that have ever possessed the ability to repair injury. It is not my gift."

The implication remained unspoken between them. Even with her Fae ability, only one other person could have healed her that fast.

Mercifully, Arden did not push Teyla to share the secret she had been concealing from every single soul since her mother had died. It did not truly matter if she confirmed what Arden was thinking. The agent now knew, and Teyla had never been more at risk. "If my father finds out, I—"

Arden cut Teyla off, putting her hand on the princess's shoulder comfortingly. "I understand. I have no desire to put you in harm's way. You have spared me from the wrath of your King, and I intend to return the favor."

Teyla's knees wobbled at the relief, threatening to make her cry.

Arden delicately wrapped her arms around her, unsure if Teyla would allow it. The simple act of kindness was enough to open the dam holding the princess's tears inside, and she fiercely returned the hug.

Mindful of Arden's injured back, Teyla placed her arms around Arden's hips and held her tightly, tucking her face into Arden's chest as she sobbed. Arden simply rubbed her hand in circles soothingly and cradled Teyla's head to her heart.

Finally, the crying calmed into occasional hiccups. The princess self-consciously wiped her face as she pulled back, realizing she had just broken down in front of Arden. The agent's thumbs came up to Teyla's face and gingerly wiped away any last traces of her fear. Teyla rolled her shoulders back and lifted her chin as she tucked away the vulnerable side of her.

"Now, let's talk about the second phase of this fucking competition today. Where should we meet?"

Arden pulled up her hair in a quick bind, grabbed her leather baldric, and placed it around her waist instead of over one shoulder as she usually wore it. Sliding a sword into its scabbard, she answered. "Let us meet by the refreshment station on the south end of the arena in two hours. We can talk about a plan and adjust it as needed when the King announces the objective."

It was a solid plan. Arden walked to the wooden door and grasped the handle before pausing and tilting her ear back toward Teyla. Her very pointed ear. "Princess…"

"Your ears!" Teyla blurted out, rudely interrupting her. Arden's sensuous lips curved upward at the corners in amusement at the outburst, pulling Teyla's attention to them. "Also, your eyes are still gloriously night and day, and you don't have on your mask, which will get you whipped again for sure."

The words kept tumbling out one after another. Arden's teeth flashed in the light as that small grin grew into a full-fledged smile.

"Are you worried about me, Teyla?" Her teasing voice lilted like a soft purr, the princess's name sounding borderline indecent.

Teyla felt her mouth water, and she shifted uncomfortably. "Absolutely not," she spluttered as Arden's rich laugh rumbled through the tiny space between them. "I am just making sure you don't die for my own very selfish wish to remain alive."

Arden chuckled at the defensive tone, her shoulders shaking with the force of her mirth. Despite herself, Teyla began to laugh with her. If the princess thought Arden was gorgeous when she was her usual, reserved self, then she was absolutely breathtaking when joyous.

Arden pinned her bottom lip between her teeth harshly as she tried to reign in her amusement. For the first time, Teyla noticed her slightly elongated fangs.

Unlike with Nicolai, Teyla's body did not respond in fear. Almost in a trance, Teyla eyed them as she imagined what it would feel like to run her tongue over the tips of Arden's incisors or to have them scrape gently against her neck. The longing to feel those teeth against her flesh was shocking, and Teyla took a small step backward to negate the sudden urge she had to jump Arden's bones.

Arden cocked her head inquisitively but respected the increase in space. She opened her mouth to say something, but the words seemed to die on her tongue. Instead, Arden cast Teyla a knowing look and smirked smugly.

There was no way she could know what Teyla was thinking, surely. Teyla waited for Arden to call out her odd behavior, but the agent simply closed her eyes to concentrate. Within mere moments, her features were altered back into a convincing human appearance. Matching amber eyes found blue ones once she was done weaving her mirage.

Teyla noticed rather possessively that Arden did not hide the mostly healed slice Teyla had made to her neck with a magickal mirage or clothing. It was practically on display.

Teyla felt a twinge of guilt knowing she should not feel so satisfied that she marked Arden for others to see, even if it was simply a battle wound. The satisfaction far outweighed the guilt, though. Arden would bear Teyla's mark for at least another few days, even if it did not cause her to scar due to her Fae healing abilities.

When Arden finished securing a mask to her upper face per castle protocol, she elaborately curtsied at Teyla with a flourish of her arms. "I am ready to serve you, my princess."

Teyla snorted at her antics and headed toward the still-closed door. Before the princess could open it, a soft hand landed on hers, halting her.

"I just wanted to say thank you, Teyla. You not only spared me, but you also healed me, intentionally or not. I would be in far more pain or even dead without you. It is not a kindness I expect to forget any time soon."

Her earnestness caused Teyla's throat to close, so she simply nodded, speechless, and gestured toward the door.

Arden released her hand with a slight squeeze and opened the door for Teyla. Apparently, chivalry was not dead, after all.

As soon as Arden left Teyla in her now clean room with several guards stationed outside, the princess called for her maids. When Teyla realized Xara was among those summoned, she flashed a secret smile at her. When the bath was drawn and breakfast delivered on a large wooden tray, Teyla dismissed each of them except for the young girl.

The princess rushed through cleaning her body and hair, knowing she was bound to become filthy again today from whatever the King had designed. Once out of the bath, dried, and garbed in undergarments, she called Xara into the bedroom. Xara immediately set to combing through her hair to get all of the gnarly knots out of the golden strands.

"Did you fight a battle in your sleep, Princess?"

Xara's quip relaxed Teyla as she realized the girl would not treat her like a porcelain doll after last night's events.

"Hardly. Last night, I had the best sleep I've had in forever."

"I would, too, knowing Arden was there to protect me."

Teyla's eyes shot to hers via the reflection. Xara's brown eyes were the picture of innocence despite the amused flickering within their depths.

"How did you even know that?" Teyla grumbled in defeat, slouching in the chair as she crossed her arms. Deeming it safe to continue working, Xara began to pin the long locks up gently.

"I may have seen Arden on her way back from your rooms, and I have never seen her so expressive." She continued in silence while Teyla searched for a response.

"It isn't like anything illegal happened. We just slept in the same bed."

"No need to get defensive, Princess. I mean no disrespect."

Teyla winced at a particularly hard tug and followed

with a quick apology. Xara continued to speak.

"Even if something did happen, I would simply be happy for Arden. She has been physically alive but dead in her heart and soul for so many years of her life that I am afraid she doesn't even know how to live, only to survive."

The most dangerous emotion filled Teyla's heart as she listened to Xara: hope.

The girl continued to talk as she finished Teyla's hair. "Anyways, I am glad to see both of you are still alive and well after last night. I hope things continue to stay that way after the competition today."

As soon as Xara finished, she bowed and left the princess's rooms, leaving Teyla with far more questions than answers. Teyla knew she should be focusing on preparing for today's challenge, but her mind spun as she ate quickly.

Why had Arden been merely surviving for so long? Who had injured her face so severely? What was her magickal ability? Was Arden really happier after being around her? Was she just as puzzled at the heated tension between them? If Teyla kissed her, would she kiss back?

These obsessive questions haunted her.

It was not until Teyla signed in under her alias at the registration tent and walked to their rendezvous point that the anxiety of the competition caught up with her. She was pacing back and forth twenty feet from the refreshment vendor when she caught sight of the agent dressed as the Reaper.

Teyla felt relieved. She'd been unsure after their tense night and morning if Arden would actually show up. She shook her head in disappointment at her own doubt of Arden's character. The agent had proven her allegiance countless times.

Once they made eye contact, Arden tilted her head toward a far more vacant patch of land. Teyla followed her at an inconspicuous distance through the buzzing crowd. Once far enough away from most people, Arden halted and waited for Teyla to catch up.

"I have it on good authority that the ring is filled with

various weapons. If I had to guess, we are going to be judged on our handling of them."

"All right. What are they?"

"As far as I was told, there are swords, guns, and javelins. Have you ever thrown a javelin?"

The urgency in her voice was not lost on the princess. Teyla's responding grimace was enough.

"Fuck," Arden swore, kicking a rock with her boot. "Do you know how to wield your hidden weapon?"

"What the hell is that?"

"You know, your special *gift*," she urged, her two-toned eyes widening with meaning.

Oh. She was referring to Teyla's magick. It was surprising to hear anybody even mention it. She had been so tight-lipped about it. A small pressure lifted off her shoulders at having somebody to finally discuss it with.

"I have never used it to harm somebody before, and even if I did, it would be obvious what I was doing. But I never want to use it for harm. I am a pacifist at heart." Teyla hedged around disclosing what kind of magick she had control over, purposefully being as vague as possible. Not only were other people milling around, but Arden also had not revealed her particular brand of magick.

Turnabout was fair play.

The exasperated breath Arden released informed Teyla just how frustrated she was, but she did not push further. "Why is it so important for you to win this competition?"

Arden's question caught her off guard. Teyla had anticipated the agent telling her to withdraw from today's event, not trying to understand why the princess needed this.

Teyla took a deep breath. "I need to take hold of my own future. The King has decided my fate for far too long, and I will not be forced to marry a man against my will. Love is the only thing that cannot be taken from me."

"I see." Arden stared out across the clearing with a distant look, deep in thought. "Let me show you how to properly throw a javelin. However, unfortunately, my magick cannot aid you in this."

Arden walked over to a fallen tree branch and picked it up in her gloved hands before weighing it. Deeming it sufficient, she placed it in Teyla's right hand.

"Grasp the area just behind the middle of the branch. Now hold it up using your shoulder as a support for its weight."

Teyla listened intently as the agent walked her through the best footwork and showed her how to utilize her hips to increase the force of the throw. Just as Arden was going over how to aim, the trumpets heralded the King's announcement of the event. They paused, walking closer to listen while Teyla took embarrassingly deep breaths.

This time, the arena was a lot smaller, easily allowing stands for the audience to be erected around another oval area. There were targets along both long sides of the oval, with a sparring area cleared out in the middle. The royal section was raised higher above the main crowd. Teyla assumed it was to stroke the King's ego.

The King was dressed in stunning silver and navy-blue robes, so splendid they must have cost a fortune to have tailored. He was growing out his light brown beard, with his signature white streak down the left side of it. All men of the family had this genetic trait, something the King used to complain about but appeared to be embracing now. He stood up from his seat, and a hush came over the crowd. The anticipation was palpable.

"Ladies and gentlemen of Cyrene, welcome to the second installment of the King's Competition!"

A roar rang out, the crowd impatient to discover what this round would bring. A contagious round of stomping began in the furthest point of the stands, quickly gathering popularity. Soon, the entire stadium was rocking their seats, calling for the competition to begin. Miraculously, as the King began speaking into the microphone again, the rumbling noise subdued.

"Your patience has been much appreciated. This next round will be far simpler and more precise, focusing on individual skills with different weapons. Each competitor will be tested on their skills with a gun, a javelin, and a simple sword and shield. The competition will occur in four waves, with a total of two hundred men competing.

"We will start each wave with fifty men. The first station will be pistols and will be graded by each man's ability to accurately hit the center of the target. They will have three chances, and the top twenty-four men will go on to the next round."

The crowd was hanging on every word, exhibiting the level of rapt attention she knew the King was thriving under. Teyla wondered absently why he was testing their ability to use weapons.

"The twenty-four successful men will move on to javelin throwing, with the same rules applying. The top ten men will move on to the third and final round. They will engage in direct combat with each other, utilizing real swords and shields. Whoever deals a 'fatal' blow wins. The top five men from each round will move on to the next segment of the competition."

Silence fell over the crowd. Today, the competitors would thin from two hundred men to twenty, if Teyla was doing her math correctly. That was an extraordinary amount to cut in just one round.

A shout rang out from the crowd.

"How do we know who wins each round?"

The King smiled, as if anticipating this question. "To aid in this testing, we have our own royal guards in the ring at each station. They are experts in each field. What they say goes without question. Anybody who wants to contest a decision can come to me directly."

More silence followed. The King frowned—never a good sign.

"Do you not trust your King?" he roared. The crowd immediately began making noise again, sensing the danger of remaining silent.

"This exercise is to ensure that your future king has the ability to protect you. The prince will prove his skill and his worth in direct combat versus commanding a larger battlefield. Never will the future royals of Cyrene fall like the last queen did."

A somber silence fell among the crowd and nobility. If they had made a sound, Teyla could not have heard them over the roar of anger screaming in her ears. The King should not bring up her mother to justify his every decision. Her death was personal, and he continued to call it up to the masses to exploit their support and sympathy.

Teyla felt a light touch on her shoulder, her body tensing until she realized it was Arden. The princess slowly released the breath she had been holding in and gingerly unfurled her fists. Her nails had bitten into the skin from clenching them so tightly. After finishing his speech, the King returned to his throne, and the first round began.

Arden was in the second group, and Teyla was in the third. They had been assigned to their respective groups during registration. With nothing to do but wait, they wove through the crowd to get a better view.

The first group included Lord Johan Caine, who unfortunately demolished the rest of the men. He was the uncontested star of the last round, defeating his opponent in a record two minutes. He had the advantage—the King had told the nobility what the challenges were a week in advance so they could practice.

It was unfair. Surely, they assumed they could rig this competition and marry her off to one of the nobles. When the second group was called forward, worry crawled down her spine like an insect. Teyla grabbed Arden's hand as she started toward the arena. "Try not to die on me, okay?"

"Anything for you." Arden winked at her before pulling away completely.

Was she flirting? Surely, that was flirting.

Murmurs broke through the crowd as Arden entered

the arena in all black, the mask completely obscuring her facial features.

She walked with a swagger and confidence that only came from a history of knowing she was the best. Teyla had seen her fight a few times but had never had the chance to study her fully in action. Excitement thrummed as Teyla watched Arden stroll over to her assigned area in the first station, picking up the handgun.

Arden checked the clip, the chamber, and other specs before setting it back down.

Shrugging and rolling her shoulders, the agent stretched a bit, much to the enjoyment of many women in the area. A sharp pang of jealousy flared as Teyla heard their appreciative remarks about her physique. They were unaware that Arden was female, but the way they objectified her was infuriating. Finally, the first round began.

Several of the men's first shots did not even hit the target, which was embarrassing compared to an expert like Arden. Her first bullet hit the outer rim of the innermost ring before she slyly looked around the clearing. Was she intentionally shooting worse to blend in with the other contestants?

With her Fae abilities, Arden easily found Teyla in the crowd. Unable to do anything but encourage her, Teyla mouthed a message she hoped Arden would be able to decipher despite the distance.

Fuck them up, Arden.

Arden nodded sharply before aiming the gun again and firing two shots in rapid succession directly into the middle of the bullseye. The women around Teyla erupted into cheers at her success, but when Arden turned back to her section of the stands, her attention was solely focused on the princess.

Butterflies fluttered in Teyla's stomach at her attention.

Teyla clapped along with the others as the twenty-four top contestants moved on to the javelin throwing section. Arden tossed one of the javelins up in the air and caught it, spinning it in her hands rapidly.

When given the signal to begin, she cocked her arm back, took a short running start, and hurled the javelin toward the target. She looked completely unfazed as it landed in the center of the target again. Many of the men hit the edges with sheer brute strength. Undeterred, her agent continued to throw javelins, finishing second place in the round. With ten men left to skirmish, they paired the other top-placing man against Arden.

A hush enveloped the spectators. They could have heard a pin drop throughout the stadium as the men followed directions to their assigned areas and were handed their weapons. Arden was composed as she placed the shield on the ground, seeming to decide against it. She gave the sharp sword a few practice swings before resting, simply watching her opponent warm up.

The opponent was a large man, built like a horse. His torso was massive, as were his arms. He was made to crush things, and Teyla worried that Arden would be next due to her injuries. Arden cracked her neck casually as the brute swung the sword elaborately. Teyla could not tell what he was saying to Arden from this distance but based on his laughter and the laughter of men closer to the arena, it was diminishing and unkind.

Because of her mask, Teyla could not be completely sure that Arden was not responding, but she seemed to stand as still as a statue, refusing to give in to the ramblings of her opponent. Hardly a single soul appeared to be watching the other competitors. They were hungry for drama and excitement, and it was clear just who would deliver it.

Finally, the guard leading the station shouted to begin, and the men leaped into action. The sound of scuffling boots was audible against the sound of steel striking steel. The beast of a man charged at Arden, who simply sidestepped him. Enraged at his opponent's adept maneuvering, the large man bellowed and swung his sword.

The crowd leaned forward in their seats, cheering for Arden or the other man; Teyla could not tell who the crowd favored. The Orionian deftly blocked the blow and moved out of the way again. She did this time after time, never going on the offensive. It was almost like she was toying with the man, simply showing him how easily she could dodge the onslaught of attacks.

Teyla tried to picture what Arden would consider the best tactic against this hulk of a man. It came to her suddenly as Teyla realized Arden was tiring him out. She was much slimmer and faster, and her stamina would outlast his, especially as he swung with what seemed to be full force.

Arden's shift to offense was almost imperceptible. One moment, she was standing back, dodging yet another brute force attack, and the next, she was at the man's back, kicking behind his knee.

As the giant fell, Arden smacked his heel with the flat of her sword; had she used the blade's edge, she surely would have severed it. As it was, blood flowed from the split skin, and the man screamed his pain. Arden utilized the man's kneeling body to propel herself in front of the man and rested the sword underneath his chin: a fatal blow.

The audience yelled their approval. Arden raised her arms above her head in celebration before turning to the royal section of the stands and bowing deeply at the waist.

Distracted as she was, there was no way she could see the large man getting up behind her and grabbing his sword in answer. Teyla barely had time to gasp before the brute brought the sword down startlingly fast directly at Arden's head.

The Fae woman must have heard the shift in the crowd or the crunch of the ground underneath her opponent. She dodged out of the way just in time. She whirled around, spraying rocks and dust everywhere.

In quick succession, she brought her sword down upon her opponent three times. The first swing hit the giant's knee, forcing him to drop again. The second was the sword pommel aimed at his gut, knocking the air from his lungs. Lastly was a well-aimed hit across the back of his head with her elbow.

For the last hit, she did not hold back any strength and knocked the man out cold.

Arden stood over him like an avenged soldier, glaring down at the man in righteous fury. Only once the man took a breath did she look away. She waved at the crowd again, which was in a bloodthirsty frenzy of applause, but she was much more subdued this time.

After she bowed one more time toward the royals, she left the arena, ignoring the people trying to stop and talk to her. None of them dared follow her after seeing what she was capable of.

Teyla blew out a relieved breath, releasing the tension in her shoulders. That was far more intense than Teyla had anticipated. Her father was discussing something animatedly with Lord Caine. Teyla could not wait for her phase of this competition to be over.

CHAPTER SIXTEEN

SNEAKING & SCHEMING

Arden snuck through the city, keeping her cloak wrapped tightly around her and her charge. It would be easier and faster not to bring Xara and simply update her later, but that was not how things worked in a pack. Arden refused to dishonor Xara by asking her to stay, so they crept through Silas in the dead of night.

They traveled through the city's slums, far less likely to be stopped and questioned there. The slums functioned mostly on a "do not ask and do not tell" policy. When somebody saw something strange, they did not ask what was happening, and the favor would be returned if the city enforcement officers came asking around about suspicious behavior. Only gold would sway this code they lived by.

They fit in with the other inhabitants of the slums. They gave a wide berth to the people who drank and fought in the streets. Arden was armed to the teeth, a myriad of weapons stowed outside of her cloak to warn people away. Arden would not hesitate to use them if necessary. Arden and Xara were simply the shadows and nothing else.

Without incident, they reached the wall of rock housing the entrance to the den. Sweeping the foliage away, Arden entered the darkness of the yawning crack barely large enough for a grown man to fit through. After several paces and a slight curvature, a dim flicker of light became visible, and she waited impatiently for her eyes to adjust fully.

Before she could process the movement, she was tackled to the ground. Despite the searing pain in her back from her landing, she ruffled Jace's hair affectionately. "Hey, asshole, how are you?"

He scoffed and pushed up off of her. "I've been fine. Helping win glory for our pack and whatnot."

"Yeah, glory." Arden rolled her eyes as she also rose to her feet. "More like flexing your muscles around women in between rounds, you horn dog."

Arden had said it playfully, but he bristled at the derogatory name. Wolves were vastly different from dogs. "Hey! You can't blame a guy for wanting to make sweet, sweet love to a woman in desperate need of attention," he defended himself with a lascivious smile as she playfully shoved his shoulder.

"Whatever, Jace. Let's go find your sibling and the others. I'm sure there are a lot of updates all around."

He laid his arm over her shoulder as they descended deeper into the partially underground den. The others were already gathered in a semi-circle, awaiting their return. She smiled sheepishly at Maximus, who sent her an exasperated look.

"Now that everybody is present," he began, shooting another pointed look in her direction. "Let us begin."

Theo shifted forward slightly and began his report aloud in his human form.

"All right, men and women…" A rumbling cut him off. Everybody turned toward Aeri. Aeri had not previously had an issue with that greeting, but their body language was pure aggression: blunt human teeth bared with anger and chest puffed up, heaving.

Theo normally did not handle challenges well. Instead of growling back, he flashed his teeth and tilted his head in silent submission. Just a fraction, but it was enough to appease Aeri, which was good considering that was the most submission Theo had ever shown.

He cleared his throat and began again.

"All right, men, women, and… thems?" He looked over to Aeri and waved his hand toward them. Once they nodded in approval, he continued.

"Unfortunately, I don't have a lot of progress to report. I have made some headway with the rebels within the city, but the primary group of rebels, the Ghosts, are hard to reach. I have spoken with their lowest-ranking members, and hopefully, we can meet the leader and come up with an exit strategy once we get the princess. I think the one thing holding us up is a reliable way out of the castle and Cyrene as a whole with the princess. We have a clusterfuck of variables that even Aeri cannot plan for.

"I do have a lead on how the castle is getting their information on Lycans. It sounds like they have feelers out in the community, and their ears listen for whispers about people who have shifted by accident or show any signs of being moon-blessed. The Ghosts have intel on where they are taking these innocent people, which is another reason why we need to track them down and join their ranks."

He nodded to Aeri, indicating it was their turn to give updates.

The young Lycan perked up immediately. "We have three main points that are causing contention with planning. First, we need a reliable exit strategy. I am not even sure that we can trust the Ghosts to lead us to safety. No offense, Theo." Aeri carried on with their report, ignoring Theo's annoyed growl.

"I don't trust people outside our pack to have our best interest at heart. Any one of them could double-cross us. We need extensive information on each person we let in on the plan and substantial leverage over them. Get that and a way out, and our first problem is solved. The second issue is—"

"The competition." Jace cut off his wombmate. "Are we planning on completing the competition and stealing the princess then? Or is this just a diversion to allow us time to strategize and allow Arden to get closer to the princess?"

Arden had indeed grown closer to the princess. Far closer than was acceptable for a multitude of reasons, but she could not seem to resist whatever force pulled her toward Teyla.

It was infectious being around her. Also, incredibly dangerous and foolish. Arden could easily lose her objectivity about what was needed or become too emotionally invested when they ultimately decided to leverage Teyla's life for their land back. That option no longer seemed viable.

Arden needed to discuss it with Maximus. He had always guided her with wise advice in the past.

Aeri continued. "Thirdly, how the hell are we going to get the princess to come with us? It's not like she is going to come quietly, and we cannot exactly knock her out for five hours while we escape."

The Lycans sat in a circle, passionately debating diverse options, all of which had major issues. Some would surely get them caught, and others were downright bloodthirsty—thanks to Theo—but Arden listened to them all. Only once the disagreements escalated did she speak up.

"I have thoughts for all of these concerns." The din quieted. Arden did not raise her voice but deliberately, slowly, and calmly laid out her plan. "For our getaway, I agree that we need to utilize the Ghosts as much as possible. That particular rebel group is the widest known organization and has remained in operation despite years of the Cyrenian Crown trying to eviscerate them. They are good at what they do. However, I doubt they will meet with any of us."

"What the hell was the point of saying all that, then?" Theo asked, throwing his hands in the air.

"Because they won't meet with just any of us; however, I would place good money on them wanting to meet with the Reaper."

Silence.

After a blissfully quiet moment, Maximus responded. "That is… actually a promising idea. Would you be going undercover, as you know the nefarious details of your kill list?"

Arden answered. "I think it depends on what they say to the proposal. If they want verification of the work I've done as the Reaper, I should go. If they are looking for proof of a strong ally, I believe it should be Theo. Men traditionally view other males as stronger than women and would default to that ideology when considering allyship."

"I agree with that logic. What else do you have thoughts on?" Max urged her to continue.

"We should finish the competition. If we can win it, several of us can be alone with the princess at one time. Well, alone with the princess and her assigned personal agent." A grin stretched across her face at her successful infiltration of the guard. "Which shouldn't be an issue."

Xara took her hand and squeezed it reassuringly. Arden tightened her grip on Xara's and finished her thoughts.

"Lastly, I still have some of that vial of sleeping draught that I used on those patrolling Lord Caine's countryside residence. Aeri, could you make more with an increased potency?"

"Yes, I could. I'll need to find more ingredients at the black market."

"Good. We also need to test it on some scumbags down here in the slums. The elixir amount we currently have is only for an hour. If we need to increase the strength, we need to make sure it won't kill her."

Theo muttered under his breath. "That'd be easier than this shit."

Arden's voice became caustic. "We are not going to kill her. We need her alive as a bartering tool to regain our lands and protect our kind. Stick to the plan."

Theo bristled, reacting to her tone and words. "It's not up to you, Arden. If we need to kill her, the point will still get across with her severed head returned in a basket."

A deep growl thundered through her chest as she readied to launch at her brother-in-arms. A small hand holding hers squeezed tightly. Arden's rage grew, and her claws slid out, ready to attack Theo for his insolence. A soft gasp broke through her red-tinged haze.

As those claws came out, they pierced Xara's skin. Arden's stomach heaved in dread as she retracted her claws and bundled Xara into her lap. The impending brawl became the furthest thing from her mind.

"Xara, I am so sorry!" Arden lamented. "Why didn't you let go? You're only human. You cannot get in the middle of a Lycan spat!"

Xara's big brown eyes were filled with tears she refused to let escape. She hugged Arden, wrapping around the agent's torso like a bear would its mother.

So quietly that Arden could barely hear it right next to her ear, Xara whispered. "Your feelings for the princess were about to be revealed. Calm down."

Arden stiffened at the command but heeded it. Xara was right. Somewhere along this journey, Arden had begun to care about the enemy's daughter. If the pack caught on to her hidden desires or the important details she had been hiding, they would never trust her again. Then, Theo really might have Teyla killed. Arden took a deep breath, squeezing Xara once in thanks, and pulled herself together.

"I apologize for my outburst. I have not slept well between my work in the castle, as the Reaper, and in the competition. You all know that this directive was provided by the Council of Elders and Princess Calliope herself. We know how hard we have all worked to get to this point, and I will not disobey a direct order from our future queen."

Theo crossed his arms with a scowl but said nothing more. Encouraged, Arden continued. "I genuinely believe keeping the princess alive is imperative to our cause. Unless something critical changes that, I think we should stick to that plan."

"I believe your passion comes from a good place, Arden, but reign it in. We are all on the same side," Max chastised. "We should stay with the plan of keeping Princess Teyla alive. She is not the one who murdered our families. The King of Cyrene did. It would behoove us to remember that."

Xara's small voice spoke up. "I think Arden is forgetting an important update for you guys."

Everybody turned to her, who now sat beside Arden with her injured hand lying limp in her lap. Truly, the wounds were superficial, but they did bleed like a rose thorn poke would. Arden could not think of anything she had forgotten. "Arden got flayed for killing a nightwalker."

Immediately, snarls rang around the room, even from Aeri, who was normally the most passive. Nightwalkers were a Lycan's sworn enemy. If they could have their way, they would have all of those soulless creatures eradicated. The Orionians had come close to eliminating them from Lycan territory before the kingdom's downfall.

Arden clarified. "It is true. The whipping part was as terrible as expected. Worse still is that there were nightwalkers in the castle that were moving around undetected. I was next to this nightwalker posing as a guard for weeks and could not pick up his scent. I am not sure if they are masking it with herbs like I have hidden my own scent before, but there was no trace.

"He even drank the princess's blood," she continued. "I fear there are more within the castle, but I cannot find a way to identify them. They may even exist within the royal ranks. Shit, the King could be one of them. He whipped me for killing one, saying that it was because I failed at identifying the threat and protecting the princess. I worry we are up against far more than one dead nightwalker."

Arden skipped the part about taking the lashings for Teyla and the princess healing her. The prospect that there could be more nightwalkers in the castle changed everything, yet it changed nothing. Ultimately, it meant that their escape might be much harder. Discussions broke out with this added information, but Arden continued.

"The palace is trying to come up with a team to work on identifying nightwalkers. Hopefully, I can glean information from them that will aid in our plan."

Theo scoffed. "Well, apparently, you have a plan for everything. Might as well let Arden be team leader since she is taking charge of this entire operation."

Arden swallowed down her anger and replied coolly. "Everything I have said tonight has been a suggestion and, as always, is up for debate and a vote within the pack. There has been no usurping of imagined power here. I respect and fully support Maximus's position in our pack."

Theo snorted, but Arden knew it was facetious. He stood up, rolling his shoulders back and tilted his neck side to side, popping it. He shook out his head, more lupine than male at that moment.

Arden did not let his blatant disregard of her outwardly ruffle her. Instead, she turned toward the leader in question and stated, "I actually have matters to discuss with you that do not involve the pack. While you sit on all of this information provided by the hard work of our pack, may I have an audience?"

Formal words for a formal request: no other pack members allowed. This was a discussion between the alpha and a submissive wolf in the pack.

"Of course, young one." Max's deep, gravelly voice soothed her anxieties. "Come. Let us meet in a place with slightly more privacy."

Arden shifted Xara as if she weighed nothing. She truthfully was quite light when Arden tapped into her Lycan strength. She ruffled Xara's hair with her hand fondly.

"You two better keep a close eye on her." The undertone was clear. Xara was the pup of their pack.

Jace smiled down at Xara and said in a conspirator's tone, "It's okay. We are going to teach her how to gamble, aren't we, little one?"

Arden laughed before elaborating. "Then you really

need to keep an eye on her. She will run you dry playing cards."

Jace's dropped jaw was comical. When Arden turned back toward Maximus, she was still chuckling. She waved a hand ahead of them, beckoning him to take the lead and choose their destination.

They walked through the small den under the sprawling vines and followed the rocks that had been laid as their code to outline the path to the hidden entrance. They moved into the grove where the foliage was triple canopy and felt privacy was protected. For several long minutes, they did not speak as Arden struggled to find where to start. The air was turning brisk, the first sign of autumn she had seen.

Her love of colder weather came from her home in Orion. It was cold most of the year due to being high in the mountains, and she used to play in the snow with her father every winter. She had adored letting her wolf loose to howl into the crisp outdoors, greedily breathing in the first scents of the season.

The leaves were still rustling pleasantly when Maximus spoke.

"What is weighing so heavy on your mind, Arden? I have known you for nearly thirty years, child. I know when something is bothering you, even when you try to hide it."

There was no smugness, simply stark honesty. It was a quality she had always admired. While Arden was still young when her parents were murdered, Maximus never spoke down to her but always addressed her with candor, patience, and respect.

Pushing aside her fear of being judged, she began. "Teyla can wield quintessence, but I don't know if she contains gifts beyond healing."

He was the epitome of calm, as usual. He paused his walking momentarily before resuming at the same leisurely pace. They circled the clearing twice before he spoke again.

"True healing magick?" His voice was laced with skepticism. "What evidence do you have?" A demand for more information. Not a challenge, but clarifying and computing data.

Arden informed him of the grass wilting, then recovering stronger than before when Teyla had collapsed. She explained the scourging and how she woke up mostly healed after being by Teyla's side. She even recalled how Nicolai could hardly control himself once he had taken a sip of her blood and, once consumed, how he appeared stronger than other nightwalkers Arden had fought.

Throughout her recollection, Maximus stayed silent. Then, "Theo believes we should kill her. He believes it just as emphatically as you feel he is wrong. In light of her being a wielder, his position is more favorable considering the threat she could pose to Orion. Tell me why he is wrong upon our overdue return."

"She is pivotal to all we have planned." Arden's entire body vibrated with barely leashed rage at the thought of Teyla being harmed at the hands of the pack.

"Yet, if we returned her dead carcass, hacked to pieces, it would send a very definitive message to the King of Cyrene." His voice was devoid of emotion, making the threat more potent.

Arden bared her teeth at him, grabbing his arm and pulling him to a stop. "Nobody. Touches. Her. But. Me." The words were strangled through gritted teeth. Her chest heaved up and down as she fought the impending shift.

Maximus did not back down. He stepped closer until her nose was almost touching his chest. Despite her five-foot-ten-inch height, tall for a female, he towered over her, physically dominating her space.

He growled softly. "Then, tell me why."

Arden's blood sang with the challenge, demanding retribution for his blatant disrespect. It rushed through her ears as she tried to calm her erratically beating heart. Arden took a few slow, deep breaths.

She deferred to Max in the pack out of respect and necessity. She was not here to play leader of their little cabal. Her sole purpose was to bring the princess back to Orion's capital and present her to the Elders. Arden's alpha instincts were not helping this situation.

She took a step back from him, submitting to his questioning. Attempting to dominate those who dared to defy her had only caused mayhem in the past, and she would not make those same mistakes again. Her fingers itched to touch the scar marring her face.

"She is everything to me."

Arden's shoulders caved in at the quiet admission, and she glared at the ground. If she looked up and saw his disappointed face, she would hate herself even more than she already did for this weakness.

She toed the grass anxiously as the full weight of speaking the confession aloud settled on her. When Maximus said nothing, words began tumbling out of her even faster.

"I know she's the daughter of the man who destroyed our lives, and our pairing is possibly the worst idea to ever exist and—"

Maximus's hand raised, cutting her off. "What does being in her presence feel like?"

Arden's mouth snapped shut, caught off guard. That seemed completely irrelevant, but she trusted him not to mock her, even if he was angry. He would never disrespect her or their bond that way.

"It feels like when you take a sip of fresh water after a long day and suddenly realize how parched you actually were. You did not realize you were thirsty, but now it's all you can think about." Arden flushed at the cheesy comparison. "I feel like I need to be around her all of the time, consequences be damned. She walks into the room, and my world lights up. It is as if everything was in shades of gray until she's there, and everything becomes a radiant kaleidoscope of color."

Her stiff muscles relaxed as relief flooded her system from finally talking about it with somebody she loved and trusted. He would know what was wrong with Arden and how to fix her infatuation. Once Arden started talking, she could not stop, nor did she want to.

"I simultaneously love and hate when she is near because I cannot focus on anything except her and her wants and needs and comforts. I can't figure out what is wrong with me, to feel so strongly about a woman I barely know, who is the blood-sworn enemy to our Crown."

Arden took hold of a bright red wild lily, tugged it from its place nestled into the soil, and held it to her chest and heart.

When she finally scrounged up enough bravery to peek up at him, Max was beaming. Tears overflowed as her throat threatened to close up from the visual reassurance that he was not damning her. They began walking again, this time with Arden a half-step ahead of him, feet feeling lighter than they had in weeks as she carried the flower.

"Arden, I am so happy for you. I want to console you and say that there is nothing wrong with you for feeling this way. It is such an incredible gift from the Mother to find a gods-blessed mate."

Arden tripped on her own foot as his words registered. He snatched her arm and pulled her back up as he belly-laughed at her shock. Arden's mouth opened and closed several times like a fish on land as she was at a total loss for words.

"It probably was not obvious because she would not be able to feel the bond as clearly as you. You also might not have realized it with scent alone. Have you touched her?"

Arden balked at his question, her eyes bulging. "No! And it would not be any of your business!" she sputtered, turning the shade of the lily she was holding.

"Oh, shit. No! I didn't mean it like that!" Max shook his head frantically. His blustering made him seem younger. "I meant skin-on-skin contact, like touching her hand," he said softly.

Arden scratched the back of her head awkwardly in equal parts mortification and relief. "Oh. Thank the gods." Her voice cracked, and she cleared her throat. "Our skin has touched many times."

Maximus hummed in thought. "You might not be able to tell in your human form. It may require your Lycan senses. I could be wrong but based on how your father spoke about your mother, I believe it is the same."

He suddenly stopped walking and pulled her in for a tight hug. "I cannot wait to meet the woman the gods deemed your equal. Based on your brief description of her magick, I don't think she is simply a witch. It might be improbable, but I think that Teyla could be—" His sentence was cut off with a thud. Arden tilted her head backward to look up at him.

Maximus, the man who had rescued her from a burning building, who taught her to fight and hone her anger into a vengeful outlet, who raised her since she was orphaned, had a bullet hole in the center of his forehead. A trail of blood began to trickle out of the wound. Time slammed to a jolting standstill.

That moment of horror cost Arden.

Masked men ran out from behind the trees from all sides, yelling their challenges. Arden shouted a hasty alarm to her packmates as they descended upon her.

It was clear they were well-trained. Unfortunately for them, Arden was livid.

Arden embraced the pure animalistic need to kill and let it consume her as she became a whirlwind of fury. She ducked under the first sword that slashed toward her head, and she had a serrated dagger palmed in each hand in the next breath.

She dove between two men lunging at her, simultaneously slicing them through their abdomens, disemboweling them. Without taking a moment to rest, she was moving again, sprinting toward her next adversaries.

As she ran, the tell-tale click of a cocking gun resounded. Half a thought sent water out of her canteen into a wall in front of her. At the clenching of her hand, it solidified into impenetrable ice.

Arden heard the bullets smack against the stalwart

defense as she spun in place and hurled one dagger, burrowing it into the neck of a man running from the sight of her magick. She jumped and kicked the icy wall with all her might, shattering it into hundreds of pieces.

Arden commanded those sharp shards to remain in the air as she tracked the remaining six men running away in zigzags, yelling out to each other. There was no mercy in her soul.

There was only whatever was left of her vengeful heart as she became the executioner on behalf of the male they took from her. Six deft flicks of her wrists sent the ice soaring through the space and embedding their points into each man.

Their pained cries fed the monster, demanding their agony.

It was over within minutes. Arden stood there in the clearing where she had just been hugging her mentor and friend, her chest heaving, drenched in blood that was—for the most part—not hers. Arden stalked over the still-steaming bodies of the men she had butchered but paid them no mind.

The sounds of whimpering and jagged breaths led her to the only man she'd struck in the torso. He had given the order to flee. Arden placed a foot on his wounded abdomen as she knelt by him. His scream was music to her ears. She gripped him by the hair on his scalp and pulled his head up to look her in the eyes.

Whatever he saw there made him flinch. Arden ground her heel even harder into him and yanked his face covering off. She recognized this man.

"You are from the competition," Arden hissed, recalling the man who had tried to attack her when her back had been turned at the last event. His hideous face had been burned into her brain. He sneered at her despite his predicament.

"I should have known you were some fucked up thing of nature, you harlot."

He spat at her, and Arden did not so much as move to wipe the glob of saliva sliding slowly down her cheek. "Why are you here?"

When he clenched his jaw and looked away, a lethal calm settled over her. Arden released his hair, shoving his face back into the dirt, and grabbed a wickedly curved dagger from her boot.

"Here is how this is going to go, you piece of shit. You answer all of my questions, and I'll let you die with your dick still attached to your body. For each question you don't answer or get wrong, another sliver will go missing from whatever little you already have."

His face turned purple with anger. "Fuck you!"

"I'm glad you made that choice."

He paled as Arden brought the curved dagger to his groin, a wrathful sneer pasted to her face as his screams began anew. The mindless, repetitive motion lulled her into a hazy, bloodlust trance.

A gentle hand on her hand brought her out of whatever headspace she had sunk into as she had carved up the human man. However, Jace's face held no judgment for her actions but simply a grim understanding. He cautiously took the slick blade out of her hand and pulled her to her feet by her elbow.

"Do you want to see him before we lay him to rest?"

All thoughts of the man she'd just butchered fled Arden's mind, and she rushed over to Maximus's fallen body without another word. She had been so focused on avenging him and finding out how the hell they'd found them she had forgotten to remember to return to him.

Arden fell to her knees next to his corpse.

The shot was well-aimed. Half of his face was covered in sticky blood, his mouth still open mid-sentence. He had died instantly, she was sure. Yet, Arden could only sit there amid the brush, weeds, and corpses, cradling his body in her arms as sobs wracked her.

The rest of the pack slowly gathered around her. Arden looked frantically for Xara through her watery vision to find her wrapped protectively in Aeri's arms.

Xara's deep brown eyes were wide with something akin to fear as she saw the carnage Arden had created.

Jace and Theo prowled through the morbid scene with purposeful steps, stopping periodically to check for a pulse or kick a corpse. With each man declared deceased by her fellow Lycans, another tally was carved into Arden's heart.

How many more people would she kill before she returned home?

Arden was a monster in a wolf's skin. For her kingdom's revival, she would become a monster and worse, even if she suffered damnation in the After for it.

Oblivious to her self-deprecation, Theo grunted once with approval, his nose flared as he scented the wind. His burly form was intimidating even in an open space. He did one more sweep of the area before he crouched down by Arden and gestured toward the bodies.

"You made a mess, Arden. You need to help clean it up." He spoke in an authoritarian manner that spiked her temper.

"Maximus's body is not even cold, and you're already seizing your chance to be pack leader. Typical." Arden's snarl was a clear indicator of her feelings. Max's marred head lolled to the side when she moved to stand up, instantly stopping her in her tracks.

Xara's attention was still glued to Maximus's gory face. Arden's poor healer could do nothing to help him now. Feelings of worthlessness swelled again, and Arden bit her tongue hard enough to draw blood, the sting of pain grounding her. What was the point of her years of training and becoming a harbinger of death and destruction if she could not protect the people she loved?

Theo's voice was tight with anger. "Somebody needs to step into the role now that Maximus is dead." He took in the remaining members of the pack. "It's no secret that I've been vying for this position but believe me when I say it brings me no pleasure to attain it under these dreadful circumstances.

A pack without a leader will crumble. You know this, as it is innate to who we are. I will take on this mantle and attempt to honor Maximus every step of the way."

He looked down at Arden's kneeling form. "You are hurting and grieving right now, so I will overlook your disrespect. But I meant it. This mess needs to be hidden and cleaned up after. There can be no trace. Let's get to it."

Jace and Aeri murmured among themselves before the blond spoke. "It rained over in the grove about a mile north of here yesterday. The dirt will still be soft for a mass grave."

Theo considered before agreeing with Aeri. Immediately, the pack began hauling bodies down the mile trek, made significantly easier by their Lycan strength. Xara made herself useful by grabbing underbrush, sticks, and pine nettle from further away to cover the dirt scuffled by the skirmish. Arden's heart sank even more as she beheld the red lily crushed in the mud.

When Arden dumped the last body into the shallow grave, she returned to Maximus's limp form. At some point, somebody had closed his eyes. He almost looked like he was sleeping—if Arden simply ignored the bullet hole. Arden gathered his belongings off his body with reverence and care.

She strapped his favorite dagger to her hip, adjusting to the new weight that did not compare to the grief pressing down on her shoulders. As she shifted, a flash of gold caught her attention. Arden lifted his head and retrieved the glimmering jewelry from around his neck.

A soft gasp fell from her lips as she beheld the royal medallion with the Orion crest. The identifiable shield with a wolf and sword shone in the moonlight. If he had been caught with this, he would have been identified as royalty and put to death immediately. Arden wondered if the Council of Elders gave it to him to honor his role in this mission.

A glance confirmed none of the pack had returned yet, so Arden quickly placed the medallion around her neck and tucked it beneath her black shirt. She made quick work of Maximus's final dwelling space and placed him under the ground.

It was twilight and a cool breeze had picked up, blowing the brush and dried dirt. Arden felt the landscape was grieving along with her, with them. One by one, the pack gathered around the grave in a solemn circle. Xara was stifling her cries, furiously wiping the tear stains from her face.

Each member took a turn saying something about Maximus and his values. Some choked up and could not finish their sentiments. When, at last, it was her turn, Arden swallowed around the lump in her throat.

"Max…" she croaked. "Thank you for being the family I didn't have and teaching me to be who I am. I would not have made it this far without you. I will spend each breath of the rest of my life attempting to have even a fraction of the integrity and empathy you had." As she finished the solemn vow, she tossed a handful of dirt onto him. Following her lead, each pack member copied the motion until he was covered.

In proper Orionian tradition, each laid a rock they found suitable on the shallow grave as a sign of respect. In Orion, during an actual funeral, the body would be completely covered in rocks to entomb the respected person. The presence of so few stones was a slap in the face of his legacy.

Arden's stomach turned leaden. He deserved better. With his particular service to the Crown, he would have been buried in a prestigious sector of the Orion cemetery. Nothing as fancy as the royal section, but something befitting the honor he deserved.

Theo cleared his throat. "It is too dangerous to meet back up any time soon. Let's gather after the royal ball. I will send information via our spies as to where and when closer to the time. Stay safe."

The dismissal was clear. Arden wondered for the fiftieth time since Maximus's untimely demise how ecstatic Theo was finally to be in charge and call the shots. There was an air of electricity from the tension among the pack. It was likely that Jace supported Theo, but did Aeri?

It did not truly matter. Theo spoke with his gut and not his head. Any leader of a pack needed to be level-headed and even-tempered. Theo certainly did not fit the bill.

It makes no difference now, Arden mused. It was done. Theo had the pack's buy-in for now. She would not sabotage the competition or their plans just because she did not like Theo.

She was not blind. He was a brute, and he hated her. It would be uncomfortable, but she had no choice but to bear it until she figured out an alternate plan.

This pack was no longer trustworthy to have the mission or her well-being as their top priority. Theo was raring for blood. Arden would stay with them and obey Theo as far as her morals would allow to ensure she knew of their movements. When the time was right, she would just have to sneak Xara and Teyla past their noses.

Arden grabbed Xara gently by the arm and knelt beside her. "Are you all right, sweetie?" Arden rarely used terms of endearment with people. Beyond the oath of fealty that was sworn, she could feel in her soul that Xara trusted and supported her. Somebody with loyalty beyond the oath was rare, and she planned to treasure that.

"You used magick, A." Her worried face looked up toward Arden as her bottom lip trembled.

Arden exhaled a gusty sigh as she realized Xara was correct. She had not even considered the risks.

Foolish. So incredibly foolish.

If Maximus were still here, he would be telling her off himself. Arden swallowed at the fresh stab of pain and forced herself to answer. "I did, and I shouldn't have. My actions might have put us all at more risk. Will you forgive me, little one?"

"Yes." Xara's voice was small as she answered, barely above a whisper. "And yes, I am all right."

"Impressive." Trying to compliment her, Arden added, "If I were thirteen and had just seen a friend's dead body, I would be freaking out."

Instantly, tears swelled in Xara's eyes.

Arden cursed her terrible coarseness with children and rushed in to hug her. "Oh, Xara, I'm so, so sorry. I don't think before I speak sometimes."

Or most of the time.

Xara was on the same wavelength as she responded with a thick voice. "Or all of the time."

Arden barked out a relieved laugh. They quickly entered the den, grabbed the scant things they'd each stored there, and headed back to the castle.

CHAPTER SEVENTEEN

PHASE III

Her fingernails cracked against the hard stone as they scrambled to find purchase against the steep ledge she was clinging to. The crowd cheered as a flash of bright red hair signaled another contestant reaching the top of the cliffside successfully.

Teyla was not surprised that the challenges were becoming more treacherous, but she had not truly expected to make it through to this round. Despite Arden providing the crash course into javelin throwing a few weeks earlier, Teyla had been convinced she would get eliminated.

Relief had flooded her when her attempts at least struck the target, even though they were far from the center mark. After Teyla had disarmed her opponent, she'd been struck stupid by the proud glint in Arden's eyes as she clapped.

The King had elected to test agility with this round. The cliff in question was notorious for claiming several deaths per year. Many of Silas's children were injured as they braved the treacherous climb on a dare.

Only fifteen minutes prior, one of the competitors had lost his grip and fallen, and the visual of his femur tearing through his skin would be seared into Teyla's brain for a long time. After this day, only five men would remain. Hopefully, two of those would be women in disguise.

The pressure was ramping up, and based on the frenzied yelling and betting, the spectators felt it too.

Teyla was glad Arden had recommended this route up the cliff face. The other competitors chose the easier-looking path but were fighting each other on the way up. Several men had already been pushed off. It was just the two of them on this side, and all of Teyla's sneaking out and climbing up the side of the castle had certainly paid off since she knew how to scale a wall.

Giving herself a moment to catch her breath, she checked on Arden for the hundredth time since the start of this round. Something was wrong.

While Teyla had to remind herself that they were still mostly strangers, she had been relatively confident in her ability to read the agent. Yet, now, Arden was completely devoid of emotion or expression.

She seemed closed off. Not much had changed about her exterior. Physically, she appeared all right, although Teyla did see a new bandage peeking out from under her long-sleeved shirt.

Arden's flat affect bothered Teyla. Over the past several weeks, the princess had thought they were becoming unlikely friends. Today, they felt oceans apart.

The weather was turning gray and cloudy, matching Teyla's worsening mood.

A familiar, dry voice snagged her attention.

"Hey. Are you all right?"

Teyla almost let out a humorless laugh. How ironic that the person she was worrying about was asking her if she was okay. Teyla opened her mouth but paused. Saying anything could result in Arden pulling away. It was best not to risk it. "I am fine. Just worried about the weather." Her muscles screamed at her from holding the awkward position for so long.

Arden growled, "I swear, if I get soaked while I'm on

this fucking cliff, I'm going to be pissed."

Arden adjusted her grip somewhere below Teyla.

"I'm sure you'd look pretty while wet," Teyla grumbled in annoyance.

The princess clamored up the sharp edges again but paused at Arden's silence. She turned to her friend.

Arden was as rigid as the statues in the courtyard. Her eyes were comically wide, and Teyla sorted back through what she'd said to get that reaction. The princess was adjusting her grip when it hit her. "Oh, my gods! I just meant that you are always so attractive that I'm sure you will still look beautiful if we get soaked, whereas I would end up looking like a drowned rat!"

Teyla watched a one-sided smirk grow as Arden listened to her rambling explanation. It was truly unfair how devilishly sensual that made her lips look, and Teyla suddenly wished Arden had not pulled off her face covering while they climbed as her thoughts grew lustier by the second.

Teyla could not recall anyone ever spontaneously combusting from embarrassment, but by the molten heat spreading throughout her body, she was sure she'd be the first.

With annoying ease, Arden scaled the rocks until she was adjacent to Teyla. Her shit-eating grin refused to wither under Teyla's glare.

"So, you think I'm beautiful, huh?" Her words ended in a teasing lilt, and her eyes shimmered for the first time all day. Teyla would embarrass herself a thousand times to see Arden look like that.

"I would not use that description."

Arden's smile did not waver. "You just did."

"Fine. I misspoke." Teyla shrugged nonchalantly, hoping it would not betray the speed of her heartbeat.

Arden continued to match Teyla's pace as they climbed, always a few feet below the princess. Teyla had a suspicion it was so the agent could catch her if she slipped, which warmed her heart in a way she would rather not consider. Teyla could finally see the summit. A burst of energy revived her aching muscles with renewed vigor. They might actually make it.

"All right, I'll bite. What did you *mean* to say?"

"I had a plethora of descriptors to choose from, really." Teyla's snarky reply was punctuated by a grunt as she strained her arm to reach the next rock. "Decent, lackluster, completely plain–"

A sharp gasp escaped her as the rock underneath her left foot crumbled. Teyla's body lurched harshly to the side, her legs dangling helplessly, swinging by one hand, her heart plummeting with the crumbling rock.

Teyla's swinging momentum stopped as a warm body pressed against her, holding her firmly against the rock slab, bracketed between four straining extremities. Sharp breaths heaved through her lungs at the realization that she had been a hair's breadth away from falling to death.

"It's okay, sweetheart. You're safe. Take some deep breaths."

Holding both of them to the cliff, Arden spoke against Teyla's ears. Teyla closed her eyes and tried to follow her command, matching the agent's chest rising and falling against her back.

Once the princess regained control of her faculties, she turned her neck to look at Arden. Teyla had completely miscalculated exactly how close their mouths would be and felt Arden's breath against her yearning lips. Arden searched her eyes for a long moment. Maybe she was looking for Teyla's sanity.

"All right. Let's get moving. Two men have already made it up, and we need to be in the top five to continue."

Arden did not mention the minor meltdown nor the fact that she'd just saved Teyla's ass.

Again.

Once Teyla had a firm handle on the stone, Arden pulled further away and motioned for her to continue up.

They climbed the rest of the way in silence, and Teyla nearly wept once her body was lying on solid ground again. Her bones felt like mush.

Arden helped her stand and rushed them toward the blue flag. As they drew closer, Teyla counted the tally marks of those who had made it. Five men had already advanced. Protecting her had cost Arden a spot in the competition.

The realization made Teyla stop in her tracks. Had Arden not been babysitting her, she would have made it. The ease with which Arden had clambered up the cliff left no space for doubt. Teyla felt a hand grab her upper arm, and she allowed the agent to drag her past the finish and toward the tented section of the crowd. "I am so sorry," Teyla breathed, misery wracking her body almost as fiercely as the ache from her muscles.

"Stop. I knew I likely would not advance. Protecting you was far more important than the King's games."

Arden had pulled up her mask once more so Teyla could only see the earnest look in her eyes. Arden meant that.

Her altruistic sacrifice dumbfounded the princess. She thought Teyla was more important than whatever her purpose had been in sneaking into the competition in the first place.

"I lied earlier," Teyla blurted out.

"Oh. Okay. What about?" Arden took a step back, her arms crossing in a guarded manner.

"I did have a lot of words to choose from, but I was too nervous to say them, so I called you ordinary. But you are far from mundane. You are exquisite, and it would be my honor to be your friend, if you'll have me." Uncertainty had quieted Teyla's last few words to a whisper. She saw Arden's hand slowly reach out to her, allowing her ample time to pull away. The princess did not want to deny her anything and took her hand as Arden gently pulled her closer.

"I have already considered you a friend, secretly, for longer than I care to admit." Arden's admission squashed the remaining nerves Teyla had left. "Thank the gods."

Arden exhaled a husky laugh at Teyla's obvious relief and released her, and the princess's hand felt lonelier than ever before.

"Where are you going, darling?" The word felt foreign in Teyla's mouth but felt so right when applying it to her lovely friend.

Arden's attention snapped back toward Teyla, stunned.

With false bravado, the princess continued, "What's wrong? I thought we were using pet names now, *sweetheart*," she teased. It was as if Teyla was possessed. Never in her life had she made a passing complimentary comment toward a romantic interest, let alone boldly flirted with one. Enraptured, Teyla watched as Arden swallowed hard at the comment. She watched the movement all the way down her throat and watched, entranced, as the beads of sweat trailed down to her collar.

Teyla sent thanks to whatever gods had blessed her with this humidity. Sweaty Arden was incredibly arousing. The mental image of licking that sweat from her neck banished all other thoughts.

When Teyla finally managed to look away from her neck, she saw Arden fiercely staring at her, and the stark desire trapped there stole Teyla's breath away. The princess desperately hoped Arden's magick did not involve an ability to read every thought inside her head.

Time slowed as Arden's ravenous gaze moved down her body, taking in every minute detail, and then moved back up again. Teyla's breath caught in her throat, and Arden's slight head tilt confirmed she'd heard it.

"Do you know what they say about playing with fire, Princess?"

Teyla mutely shook her head as she shivered with pleasure from Arden's raspy voice.

"You need to be careful, or you will be burned."

Teyla stepped back into her alter ego. She would not allow her agent to win this round of verbal sparring. "Maybe I'm a pyromaniac."

Arden's surprised laughter filled the air, and some of the tension left with it. Teyla rolled her shoulders to release her pent-up energy.

"So, *friend*, what is it you would like me to call you?" Arden asked, a teasing lilt still in her voice.

Teyla tilted her head to the side as she thought about her answer, playfully tapping an index finger against her chin as though in deep thought. This felt so reminiscent of their interaction in the club.

"Within the castle in front of others, I'd like you to refer to me as Princess, or Princess Teyla, or even Your Highness, if it pleases you." Teyla paused, partially for dramatic effect and partially because she was nervous about being so forward.

"In private," Teyla continued, lowering her voice. "You may call me Teyla, sweetheart, or any other sweet pet name you desire."

It felt like harmless flirting, but if they were caught by anybody exchanging these words, the consequences would be disastrous. She had no notion if Arden would act on her desires. There was truly only one way to know.

Teyla summoned Arden even closer, putting her mouth a hair's breadth away from Arden's ear as if exchanging a secret. The princess took a steady breath and finished, "If we wind up in bed together again for any reason, you may call me anything you like."

Arden's entire body tensed up, and she exhaled sharply. Teyla leaned back, fighting down the embarrassment from what she had just insinuated.

Nothing had happened the last time they'd been in bed together, even though in the peaceful moments after waking, she had hoped something would. For over a month now, Teyla had fantasized about kissing her. When Arden did not respond, Teyla feigned indifference. "How's that for playing with fire, Arden?"

"You are nothing like what I expected," she murmured, as if more to herself than out loud.

Before either of them could further the exchange, screaming began. Both of them sprinted toward the royal stands. They stopped a safe distance away so as not to be seen by the King. A guard covered in blood was leaning over with his hands on his knees, gulping down lungfuls of air.

"Speak!" the King's command was thunderous.

"It's the maids," he gasped out. His body was wracked with shakes as he continued. "They have been butchered. By the kitchens. Please, somebody go."

Arden spun toward Teyla, reaching for her hands with surprising gentleness, considering her frantic appearance. Teyla had never seen her so rattled. She allowed Arden to tug her toward a stallion draped in fabric and adorned with the royal crest secured to a nearby tree.

Understanding dawned on her. Xara.

Arden made quick work of the ropes. Teyla struggled not to think about the punishment if they were caught stealing this steed.

Arden hoisted her up into the saddle by her hips and settled behind. Teyla wasn't familiar with the kitchen staff, and though she felt sad for them, she was distracted by the strong thighs around her.

Stealing a horse made a lot of sense, as cars stayed in bumper-to-bumper traffic. Arden raced them over the sidewalks, sending people jumping out of their way, and Arden rode them back to the castle grounds with the speed and skill of a master horsewoman.

Arden deposited Teyla quickly back into her room before racing off again. She was gone before Teyla could even remind her to be careful.

The princess paced for over an hour until she finally settled in one of the plush chairs. She tried and failed numerous times to read a book. Worry kept feeding her worst-case scenarios, and she was up, pacing again.

Arden had been gone for three hours when a knock on the door sounded. Teyla jumped to her feet, running to open it. Arden tore off her dark cloak as she entered. Why was she always covered in blood? This time, it was evident that it was not hers. Teyla quickly closed and locked the door behind her. Arden stood in the middle of the greeting room, staring blankly at the floor.

"Was it Xara?" Teyla asked quietly, painfully aware of the shake in her voice.

"She is alive and okay." Arden's voice shook as well, likely from relief. "The guard was right. Four girls were butchered. Not to be grotesque, but their bodies did not have even an ounce of blood left inside them. It appears there's another nightwalker on the prowl."

Teyla cursed colorfully. These nightwalkers were ruining everything, as per usual. She did not understand why her father could not keep his underlings under control.

Teyla longed to tell Arden all that she knew, but she had been forced to take an oath of secrecy. Teyla regretted that moment of weakness more with every passing day. Each of those girls' deaths was on her. She should have let him kill her instead of allowing all of these innocent lives to be lost, she thought, disgusted with herself.

"Why did they allow you close enough to see the bodies in that much detail? I am sure if you were seen snooping around, you would not be standing here with me right now."

"They would have had to catch me in the act to stop and punish me. I arrived several minutes before the guards did. I spent the rest of the time walking around the castle searching for anything that could clue me in as to who this monster is," Arden said. Pausing for a moment, she gulped. "I have heard bad news. As of an hour ago, the King has decided you will stay sequestered in your room until the ball in three nights' time to keep you safe. I will be here around the clock to continue our lessons and help keep you from dying of boredom. There will be double the number of guards outside your doors."

"What?" Teyla asked dumbly. The King could not be serious. "I can't leave my room for three days?" she repeated slowly.

Arden winced, ratcheting up Teyla's anxiety, and the

agent held up her hands in surrender. "His will is ours, Princess."

All the fire left Teyla. There was no point in fighting it, and this was hardly the worst thing the King had done to her. She would survive this. Besides, three nights alone with Arden sounded amazing. Teyla halted. "Why would the King approve you to remain here?"

Her guard grimaced. "I might have left out one small detail earlier. The girls were butchered right outside my quarters."

A horrifying thought gripped Teyla. "They might have been trying to get to you, and when you were nowhere to be found, they turned to the maids who happened to be nearby."

Arden solemnly nodded. "Those poor children were slaughtered in my stead. As an act of 'goodwill,' the King has decided I will dorm here on your chaise. He stated there was a clear target on my head for killing Nicolai, and as I was the only guard to have survived a nightwalker, I was best utilized here as extra protection."

There was a nightwalker in the castle trying to kill Arden, and it was highly likely it was per the King's directive. Teyla could not figure out what game he was playing by forcing them to quarantine together. The blood-soaking Arden caught her attention again.

"Arden, I will start a shower for you and have somebody grab you fresh clothes." She smirked to lighten the mood and added, "You might as well be clean if I have to be here with you for three days."

Once the water was hot, Arden went into the bathroom to clean herself off. Finally, fresh clothes arrived for her. Teyla ignored her rapid heartbeat as she took them into the bathroom. She averted her eyes from the shower and laid the clothes on the sink.

"Thank you, sweetheart."

Teyla bit her lip to keep from grinning like an idiot. Before she thought of a response, Arden continued, "You told me I could call you that in private."

She was right. Teyla was totally screwed and trying ardently to keep her imagination from fantasizing about how sweet Arden was being while bathing in her shower.

Naked.

Definitely not thinking about it.

"You can. It just took me by surprise." When there was no response, Teyla added, "Enjoy your bath."

The princess practically sprinted out of the bathroom and back into the safety of her bedroom, her body flaming with desire. While Arden was occupied, Teyla put on her own nightwear. She grinned devilishly at her reflection, the thin white negligee hugging her curves.

As Teyla climbed into bed, the end of the sleeping gown rose high on her thigh, and her body tingled as she wondered how Arden would react when she saw it.

The subject of her obsession came out shortly afterward in a beautiful blue shirt and pants. Arden had left her hair down, and it was already curling beautifully. The agent did not even glance her way before settling down on the chaise.

Confusion and disappointment warred within Teyla. Maybe she had misread Arden's body language before, and Arden's teasing truly was platonic. Self-conscious at how foolish she had been, Teyla rolled on her side, curled into a small ball, and fell asleep.

CHAPTER EIGHTEEN

ORANGE SPICE & EVERYTHING NICE

The smell of smoke was suffocating in the bedroom.

For a moment, Arden thought she had left the wood fireplace going in the common area again. Somehow, the workers must have forgotten to snuff it out when making their rounds before bed. She breathed in that charred scent one more time before opening her eyes.

Through the smoke-induced fog, she could see with perfect clarity every detail of her room. She marveled at her ability to see the paintings of wolves that hung on the wall. There was one, the alpha, who was pure white, standing majestically in the frame. He commanded respect and attention. His eyes seemed to hold the knowledge that no animal should contain.

To his right sat a slender female, the luna. She was his mate and his most loyal defender. Her ashy coat was speckled with a lighter gray on her chest, and her amber eyes sparkled with an air of authority and grace.

Arden should not have been able to see anything at this time of night. Another sickening moment passed before she heard distant screaming from inside the house.

Her eyes welled from a tidal wave of fear and the relentless smoke. She reached into her lap to pull her stuffed animal closer, taking comfort in it. Its fur was matted from being loved so fiercely. With tears cascading down her face, she slid off the bed to the floor.

A yelp escaped her as the soles of her feet were singed from the tiles. She always complained to Mommy and Daddy about how cold the tiles became in the middle of winter. Instead of that biting cold, she was now tortured by unbearable heat.

She quickly scrambled back onto the bed, clutching her precious toy to her chest with an iron-like grip. Her brain felt muddled and foggy as she desperately searched the room for anything to help her reach the door. As she looked around, the screaming abruptly stopped. A sob rattled in her chest as she threw her blanket onto the floor between the bed and the door.

She backed up on her bed until her back met the cool wall, her legs trembling from fear. As she prepared to run and jump, the door flung open with such force that it splintered into pieces.

She shrieked and crouched into a ball. A figure landed heavily on the floor for hardly a moment before forcing his labored body to his feet. His rattling breaths gave way to deep coughs that sounded painful. He quickly scanned the room desperately before his eyes landed on her shaking figure. Despite the circumstances, he smiled briefly.

"Thank you, Mother Ambrosia!" His voice wavered with relief. He jogged over to her and clasped her hands between his own.

"Honey, it's Max. I know you are scared, but we need to leave. Now."

A shred of relief entered her heart as she recognized one of her daddy's most loyal packmates. Agonizing fear swirled in her gut. Something was very wrong.

The urgency in his voice and her relief overridden by fear spurred her into action. She wrapped her arms tightly around his neck as he sprinted toward the window. The scent of the smoke wafting in from the door he broke down was overpowering, and she began hacking relentlessly.

"Fuck," Max fervently said, wiping at his irritated eyes.

He set her on the edge of the window before running into the closet and grabbing a shirt. Before she could protest, he tied the shirt around her head, effectively covering her nose and mouth. As he leaned in closely, she could make out every detail in his brown eyes, noticeable against the dark soot covering him.

"Honey, listen to me—" He broke off as she struggled against him, her terror rising again.

"Listen, sweetheart. I know you are scared, but I need you to be brave. You're such a big girl." He smiled softly as he spoke, faltering with his next words.

"You are in immediate danger. Our pack has been attacked. The house is on fire, and there are people looking for you right now. We need to get you out of here. You are the most important person for me to protect."

She whimpered as he spoke but tried to listen. She trusted Max. She nodded silently, afraid to speak.

He wasted no time stepping back and shifting into his wolf form. She recognized his tawny fur immediately and those brown eyes that remained the same regardless of the form he took. He lowered onto his stomach, and she did not hesitate to jump on his back. Once he was sure that she had a tight grip around his neck, he took several steps back further into the room. She released a quick squeak as he took off into a sprint and leaped through the windowpane.

The crunching sound as he landed on the forest floor below was sickening, and Arden could not tell if part of his leg had broken. Without pausing, he took off into a run, turning away from the burning house behind them.

She glanced back at the wreckage they were running from. The wind whipped her face relentlessly, but she hardly registered the pain. Their house was engulfed in ravaging flames, and she could see that the fire had entered her bedroom where they had been mere seconds before.

She turned to face forward when movement in the front yard caught her attention. Mommy was being forced onto her knees in front of a wicked-looking man. Daddy was struggling against four more men, straining against their hold. Her eyes glistened with tears as she spoke.

"M-m-max. Mommy and Daddy are outside. Some men are hurting them. You have to go help, Max!" Max's ears twitching backward was the only indication that he heard her desperate plea. He did not stop but ran even faster away from the house.

She sobbed and yanked at his fur so hard it tore in her fingers. Besides a slight whimper, he did not acknowledge her but kept running away, farther and farther from her parents and their burning house. She could not understand why he was refusing to help her parents. He loved them.

She was still crying when she looked behind them again. With her enhanced vision, she could still see her daddy thrashing against the men, desperately trying to reach his mate. The conflagration taking over their house caused a startling silhouette of the figures in front of it. For the first time, she wished she could not see clearly at such distances.

Her enhanced eyesight beheld the vicious grin that spread across the leader's face as he laughed at the sight of Daddy on the ground.

The flash of silver alerted her to the dagger that was pulled out, flickering in the reflection of the fire. She could only whimper as the man grabbed Mommy by her hair, forcibly turning her around to face her husband. She could see Mommy on her knees, shaking but saying something to her mate.

Even with Max running as fast as he could, it was not enough to avoid her seeing the man slice open Mommy's throat from ear to ear. A haunting, ear-splitting howl from Daddy was the last thing she heard before Max carried her away into the forest.

Arden woke up, gasping. That particular flashback had not haunted her in a very long time. It was not truly a nightmare but rather a forcibly relived memory. She felt disoriented as she woke, not recognizing her surroundings.

Suddenly, a hand was on her. Arden twisted out of the grasp and took the intruder down with a swipe of her legs. She fell on top with her fingers wrapped around a throat.

"Arden! Wake up!" the intruder yelled out desperately.

Arden's face contorted, absolutely feral, as she lost herself to her most animalistic instincts. The agony from her dream was still howling in her ears, and the suffocating cloak of smoke was still curling around her nose. The person under her began smacking her hand, wriggling around, trying to escape from underneath her.

A growl ripped from Arden's throat, lips pulled back over her teeth in a snarl. Both of her hands found the flailing arms of the threat and quickly pinned them above the head. She squeezed her thighs harder around the person's hips to force stillness.

Arden grasped around in vain for a knife, then shoved her face into a neck near the carotid artery. Her fangs elongated as she began to shift into her wolf form, ready to tear out the throat.

As Arden readied to bite down for the kill, the sweetest scent permeated her nose.

The voice in her head demanding her to *kill, kill, kill* was suddenly silenced, giving her a moment of quiet to think. Every modicum of her attention honed in on the divine scent wrapping around every fiber of her being.

It was a subtle mixture—vanilla and orange—infused with a kick of cinnamon. Arden knew that scent, though she could not place it while her wolf was clamoring so loudly in her head. In her partial shift, her wolf was much closer to the surface than usual.

Safe. The person this scent belonged to was safe.

This realization retracted her canines back to their standard human size and ceased her low growl. Curiosity pulled her back into her cognizant mind, wondering who it was that felt safe to her wolf. Few had ever earned that respect. From where her mouth was poised, Arden could sense nothing but the rapid pulse galloping along her victim's neck.

Cautiously, making small movements, Arden lifted her head and eyed the intruder, who lay there frozen still, taking small, shallow breaths. Blonde hair was sprawled against the floor from the tussle. Arden could tell now that it was a woman. Why would a woman whose scent correlated with safety be trying to kill her?

It took another horrifying moment of waking up and shaking the last smoky tendrils of the dream off to realize just who she had pinned under her. Arden immediately released the wrists of the Princess of Cyrene.

She had become lost in her memories, and it almost cost her everything.

Arden could not bear moving off of Teyla until she discovered what injuries she had caused. Her hands rushed over Teyla's skin, starting at her hands, still limply lying above her head. Softly, deftly, Arden's fingers gently turned the princess's hands over as she scoured over her for even a slight injury.

Satisfied that her hands were unscathed, Arden's fingertips ran down Teyla's arms, checking every inch of skin she could see. When Teyla's upper extremities were sufficiently assessed, Arden moved to her neck and torso. Relentlessly, she checked and double-checked that her actions had not harmed Teyla. If the princess were injured, Arden would never be able to forgive herself.

She was so lost in her own horror that she did not realize she was chanting under her breath while completing her frantic search. "No, no, no, no, no."

"Arden, look at me."

"No, no, no," her muttering continued.

A soft hand gripped her face, forcing her to look at Teyla. Sparks flew at the contact, a steady, pleasant sensation dancing along her skin. Arden froze on the third check of Teyla's neck and met her eyes.

The deep blue color instantly soothed her even as Teyla's touch ignited her skin.

Where Arden anticipated anger, there was none. Instead, this generous being was comforting her despite nearly getting killed by a night-terror-frenzied assassin.

As Arden's mind slowed its frantic thoughts, she realized what position they were in and how little Teyla's negligee left to the imagination underneath her. Arden's fear sluggishly turned to arousal as she greedily took Teyla's body in.

Arden leaned further back as her fingers played with the neckline of Teyla's nightgown, tracking each rise and fall of her barely restrained breasts. Orange, vanilla, cinnamon.

Mate.

The hunger in Arden grew ravenous as Teyla's arousal permeated the air.

"Just to clarify, are you about to kill me or fuck me?"

Arden shook her head to rid it of the rising desire and looked down at the princess incredulously. "What?"

"You look like you're about to devour me, and I want to know if I need to prepare for the After or the best sex of my life."

Teyla's blunt statement sent Arden reeling. The princess's excitement told Arden that she wanted this, but the agent needed to hear her say it.

Arden pushed off the floor and offered Teyla her hand. The princess accepted the help to stand before pulling away.

"I can't believe I misread this. Again." Teyla's exasperation was evident, her voice low.

Before she could spiral, Arden picked her up and wrapped one of Teyla's legs around her waist. Teyla jumped up and fully wrapped her legs around Arden's waist, and Arden groaned at the feeling of their bodies pressed so tightly together.

"Or not?" Teyla questioned breathlessly as Arden carried her over to the bed. The halfling gingerly crawled up the expanse of the bed before depositing the princess with her head landing on the pillows.

"It would make me a special kind of idiot to do anything with you on the floor. You deserve an experience fit for a queen and nothing less."

Teyla searched her eyes briefly before surging up and pressing her lips into Arden's.

Arden felt her control evaporate, heady with lust. Teyla's lips were so much softer than she had ever imagined.

Arden pulled away, chuckling at Teyla's disappointed frown. When Teyla tried to force Arden's head closer, the agent pinned her hands once more. "You are a vixen, Teyla. I was going to make our first kiss gentle."

The sight of Teyla biting her lip almost unraveled what little self-restraint Arden had left. She regained her balance with knees on either side of Teyla's hips and one hand loosely restraining Teyla's fingers. Entranced, Arden trailed across Teyla's bottom lip with her thumb, pulling it gently away from her teeth.

Teyla coyly licked the tip of Arden's thumb. Arden shuddered, her breath catching in her throat. Her thumb dipped further into Teyla's mouth, and the princess tilted her chin downward. The hunger in Teyla's oceanic eyes fed Arden's soul, burning as Teyla twirled her tongue around Arden's thumb and then sucked with a yearning gaze.

Delicious heat dove straight into Arden's core. She did not breathe until Teyla released her thumb from inside her wicked mouth.

"What if I don't want gentle?"

Arden thought Teyla's voice, gravelly from her desire, might very well kill her. Her wolf pleaded with her to claim the princess, but she drew the line. Arden would only claim her once Teyla knew everything about her and still desired her. Teyla wanted the freedom to choose her own life partner, and Arden refused to be like the men who wanted to take that freedom away from her. "What do you want, Princess?"

"You." Teyla strained against her hold, and Arden immediately released her arms. "I want all of you—your passion. I want to see you lose control for once."

"Teyla…" She felt the princess shiver underneath her. "You don't know me, and once you do, you will not like me. I have killed people without batting an eye. I don't want you to regret this later. I need you to be sure."

"Will you kill me?" Head cocked, Teyla lifted an eyebrow inquisitively.

"Never," Arden swore wholeheartedly. "But there are other ways to get hurt." A tsunami of sadness rose with her, waiting to crest with the princess's rejection. It was better this way.

"Then, I am very sure that I want you right here and right now."

Reading the hesitation keeping Arden in a chokehold, Teyla tilted her hips until the agent was lying next to her. The princess raised her hands, stopping just before touching Arden's face. Only once Arden nodded her permission did Teyla touch her, tilting Arden's head to expose her neck.

Only for her would Arden allow this. To Teyla alone would she submit her entire being. The one made for her. The other half of her soul. Teyla did not know it yet, but Arden was wholly hers for the rest of her life.

Teyla's mouth grazed Arden's neck right at her pulse point. Her blunt teeth scraped teasingly along Arden's skin as she slowly perused upward, along her jaw. When Teyla reached her mouth, she paused once again, her lips hovering just above.

Arden locked eyes with her and moved to close the gap, Teyla's eyes fluttering closed as they met. Their mouths moved together as they explored each other, breaths mingling. Arden felt Teyla's tongue swipe along her bottom lip, a request and a demand. Arden's left hand found Teyla's side, softly touching her and learning her curves.

Arden opened her mouth, Teyla's flavor bursting along her taste buds. She would never be able to eat oranges again without thinking of her mate.

Arden's mouth turned ravenous as her restraint snapped. Teyla pressed impossibly closer to her as her hand made its way back up Teyla's side under the nightgown. She was so soft.

When they finally pulled away, both of their chests were heaving for air. Teyla's panting made Arden feel bold. Arden kissed down her neck to her collarbone as the agent's thumb caressed the side of Teyla's breast.

Teyla's light gasp made Arden's chest rumble in satisfaction. Arden circled closer to the center. She could see Teyla was aching, her back arched, shoving her chest closer to Arden.

Arden pulled back enough to watch Teyla's face as she finally grazed her pebbled nipple. Teyla's thighs squeezed together as a breathy moan escaped her. It was the most exciting noise Arden had ever heard, and she planned to make Teyla repeat it many times that night. "Take this off, sweetheart."

Teyla sat up slightly, slipping off the sheer nightgown and tossing it aside. The princess lay naked except for her panties. Her cheeks blossomed with color, but she did not hide herself as Arden took her in.

"Exquisite." Arden felt drunk with desire as she appreciated the princess.

Teyla was curvy and plump and offering herself to Arden like a snack on a platter. Arden planned to eat her fill.

Arden gently pulled off her own blue shirt, shuddering as Teyla watched with blatant anticipation. Arden shoved off her pants until she, too, was only in underwear. Arden had never been self-conscious about her body until this moment, but she forced herself to be still.

"Arden…" Teyla's said with awe. "You are stunning."

The yearning in her burning gaze sent a fresh wave of desire through Arden, who moved until her body was wedged between Teyla's legs. She ran her hands along Teyla's thighs and over her hips with a veneration she had never shown another living soul.

"Teyla, I'm giving you one last chance to back out. If you choose to, it will not hurt our friendship. But once I get a taste of you, my obsession with you will only grow stronger."

"Thanks for the warning, but I am a grown woman, and I know what I want. Plus, I kind of like that you're obsessed with me."

Arden kept her eyes on Teyla's grinning face as she slid Teyla's underwear down her legs. As Arden lowered her mouth directly below her core, Teyla's sweet and spicy scent grew stronger. Arden groaned and finally, *finally*, tasted her fully. Once she started, she could not stop.

Teyla's hips bucked against her face, so Arden banded an arm across them to keep them still. She paid close attention to what made Teyla react and squirm the most. Teyla had covered her mouth with her hand to muffle her noises of pleasure, but Arden could easily hear her moans and whimpers.

Arden continued to pleasure her even as Teyla's thighs

tightened around her head and her back arched off the bed. As the princess's breathing slowed down and her legs went limp, Arden gradually slowed her ministrations.

Gods, she tasted divine.

Instead of being satiated, Arden wanted more.

She lowered her mouth back down below Teyla's core and dragged her tongue through the wetness in one long lick. Teyla moaned uninhibited and tangled her hands into Arden's hair passionately.

Arden nipped at the inside of her thigh as she teased Teyla's opening with one finger, barely applying any pressure. She smiled into Teyla's thigh as her hips undulated and the princess groaned.

"Arden, please."

"Please, what, precious?" Arden purred as she pushed her middle finger inside and withdrew it. Teyla's gasp was music to her ears.

"Fuck! More."

Arden's soft laugh was seductive. "More what, baby?"

Teyla's hands in her hair tightened. She tugged Arden's face upward, drawing a deep moan from Arden at the slight pain.

The princess cupped Arden's jaw as she looked pleadingly at the older female. Arden was almost overwhelmed by the pure need on her face.

Almost.

"Arden, please. Fuck me."

As soon as the words left the princess's mouth, Arden's finger entered her again, taking mercy on Teyla.

"Such a dirty mouth, Princess. I love it."

Arden continued to whisper soft encouragement as she added another finger and increased her thrusting. A strangled whimper left Teyla's throat as Arden's fingers curled inside of her, hitting her sweet spot.

Noticing Teyla was whispering something, Arden leaned closer to hear her name being spoken reverently on repeat as

Teyla approached her second climax. A shudder went down Arden's spine at the sheer delight she felt as she worshiped Teyla's body.

Feeling Teyla's walls flutter, Arden knew she was close. She pushed Teyla's leg open wider, allowing Arden to kiss and bite along Teyla's neck and collarbone. Her other hand found one of Teyla's nipples and tugged it as her fingers curled into her G-spot again.

The princess's body stiffened as her orgasm crested under Arden's stimulation. Her hands dug into Arden's hips as Teyla bit harshly into her shoulder to silence her shout.

Arden prayed the marks would scar, particularly Teyla's bite, as she slowed down her ministrations, pulling Teyla gently through her climax.

Once Teyla's body became pliant again, Arden removed her fingers carefully. Teyla wrapped her arms around Arden and pulled her into a languid kiss, far less frenzied after her orgasms.

Arden nuzzled into her neck and relaxed as she listened to Teyla's heartbeat slow down to its usual cadence. The princess's fingers were playing with Arden's hair idly, the rhythmic motion melting Arden's heart.

"I have wanted to touch your hair since the last time we were in bed together," Teyla whispered.

It felt unreal that she had been interested in Arden for that long. The agent knew her own infatuation had come before she recognized their mating bond and only grew stronger with it, but Teyla had no supernatural explanation. It did not seem possible that anybody could want Arden outside of her usefulness to them.

"You can play with it as much as you like when we are alone." Arden looked up at the princess and gave her a quick kiss.

When Arden tried to pull away, Teyla followed until she was lying on top. When her lips left Arden's and her hands began exploring, Arden lifted her chin to look at Teyla.

"You don't want me to?"

Arden's heart ached at the disappointment on Teyla's face. "Trust me, Princess. I want nothing more than for you to touch me. But there is no obligation to. I feel honored and privileged to have made love to you."

"M-hmm. Noted."

Teyla's mouth roamed up Arden's jaw until reaching the shell of her ear. A loud moan tore through Arden when the princess licked the curved and slightly pointed helix. Arden's head fell limply on the pillows at the sensation of Teyla's hot breath against her ear. "Arden, darling. You must be quiet. We wouldn't want any of the guards to come investigate."

Arden's hand balled up tightly against the blanket, and she pressed a pillow firmly against her mouth as Teyla began learning her body. Teyla's delighted smirk at her reactions was imprinted onto Arden's brain as tantalizing desire filled her body. Already far closer to orgasming than she would care to admit after pleasing Teyla, Arden sighed in rapture at hearing the hushed noises of her mate claiming her.

CHAPTER NINETEEN

EUPHONIOUS

She hated the stifling heat of her greeting chamber and the sweat sliding down her neck in beaded droplets.

They had only been participating in what Arden had coined "endurance training" for twenty minutes, and Teyla was already drenched in sweat. Her body odor was far too prevalent for her liking, and she knew Arden could probably scent it.

Arden's skin looked supple and cool despite doing the same exercises. Teyla's emotions warred with each other, barraged with jealousy and disappointment.

The princess held a difficult fighting stance for so long that she asked to call time, but Arden laughed, saying it had only been two minutes.

Already, Teyla's thighs shook with exertion, and she was beginning to regret asking for training sessions. Her body would never be as strong as Arden's, no matter how long and stringently she worked out, but maybe she could hold her own against human opponents.

Teyla's eyes slid over to the woman, taking up every space in her thoughts. One leg was slightly in front of the other as Arden maintained a squat with all the ease in the world. Teyla huffed an exasperated breath through her nostrils.

Arden's eyes cracked open, and a grin greeted her. "Don't give me that look, Teyla."

"What look?" She feigned ignorance.

"The look that says you hate me right now."

Arden's carefree laugh warmed Teyla's heart, and Teyla marveled at her own feelings. After their intimate tumble in the sheets, Teyla had fallen asleep in Arden's arms. Ever since they had awakened that morning, Arden's entire countenance had shifted, and she appeared incredibly satisfied. Throughout their miserable training, Arden had laughed and smiled more than the princess had ever seen. "You woke me up before dawn." Teyla scowled to shake off the sentiment. She continued stubbornly, "It is inhumane to get up prior to the sun."

"You asked for this. It will keep you safe in case I'm ever not there, which will only be if I am dead," her agent stated matter-of-factly.

"Arden!"

"What? If I am ever injured or, yes, dead, I need to die knowing you can protect yourself." Her tone was as serious as the statement itself.

Teyla quit arguing and focused on how badly her legs were burning and shaking.

"And three… two… one… time's up." Her lover's voice sounded not a moment too soon.

Instead of rising up gracefully from the squatted position like a proper lady and princess, Teyla plopped down onto the floor to rub her shrieking muscles. At the sound of footsteps coming toward her, she looked up and accepted the glass of water from Arden's outstretched hand.

"Drink. Staying hydrated is important for your body." The sight of Arden's throat as she swallowed a gulp of her own water was incredibly provocative. That sight alone made Teyla thirsty.

"Also, I wouldn't sit there if I was you. You should move so your muscles aren't stiff tomorrow."

Arden's pupil rolled her eyes but followed the instructions without verbal complaint.

So, their routine for the next three days was formed. Every morning before dawn, despite Teyla's protests, they began endurance training, consisting of mindful movements with only body weight to fight against. Arden walked Teyla through a very structured and specific set of movements, from lunges to squats to sitting on the wall with their legs spread parallel to the ground.

While it was the worst part of training for Teyla, her personal agent hardly seemed winded at the end of each section. Every afternoon, Teyla's entire body screamed in anguish, and she needed to soak in hot water with magnesium salt flakes to ease a fraction of the pain.

After the endurance section came hand-to-hand combat. Arden taught her countless different techniques to throw a punch, block, and turn an enemy's momentum against them. After the first day, she specifically focused on what motions came easiest to Teyla, tailoring the training to her abilities. When the princess tightened her abdomen while pivoting and pushing harder with her legs, she could shatter any assailant's nose with her elbow, a blow Arden had only just managed to dodge.

When they broke for food, they chatted, sometimes delving deeper. Teyla especially enjoyed learning about Arden's upbringing—on the rare occasion she would share. After digesting and hydrating, it was back to training on the princess's favorite subject: blades.

Arden went slowly, going over the proper way to handle a dagger for over an hour on the first day. Once she declared Teyla was safe enough not to stab either of them accidentally, it was on to offensive and defensive moves. With each practiced slash with the obsidian dagger inscribed with the phrase from her mother, Teyla felt closer to her spirit in the After.

Falling into those training sessions felt as natural as wearing a second skin, her blade already feeling like an extension of her arm. Arden even admitted she was impressed with how fast Teyla had improved in just a few days. The praise made Teyla giddy.

After physical training, the princess attempted to stay on top of her studies. Per the King, quarantine was the perfect time to continue the stringent academic lessons, so the various tutors brought materials daily. It was increasingly suspicious that she had not been summoned back to the King's office for whatever torment he might concoct.

The best part of the day was when she would fall into bed exhausted, pulling Arden in with her. Every night, she fell asleep to her lover rubbing her sore muscles as Teyla's head lay on her chest.

Three days and three nights had passed like this, and despite being trapped inside her quarters, Teyla loved the routine. On the fourth day, she woke to the sun shining through the windows and realized something was amiss.

At the glaringly obvious lack of a warm body next to her, Teyla jumped out of bed and rushed to the living area, her steps faltering abruptly. Music was playing softly, and not a tune she recognized.

Curiously—and cautiously so as not to startle Arden—she peered around the cracked door.

The music was not coming from the speakers or from a musical streaming service like she had initially suspected. The melody emitted from the ivory keys was breathtaking.

The pianist's posture showcased her practiced discipline, properly at attention yet swaying as artfully as the story she was creating with the notes. It would be a disservice to call what she was doing playing piano.

Arden's fingers moved with adept, graceful ease, caressing the keys as if they were a loved one. She took her time with the melodic phrasing, patient and unhurried. She was clearly an expert and did not rush or quicken the notes due to anticipation.

The piece opened with lumbering pianissimo tones

from the lower register. The dissonance of the music caused Teyla's heart to ache, feeling a bone-deep sadness push against her as if it were her own experience. It was reminiscent of Teyla's past hardships and anguish.

Memories transformed into more soothing recollections: her mother comforting her after she'd broken her wrist, dancing with Harlowe at her bachelorette, watching her father smile at her artwork for the first time. Enraptured by the past, she realized that her recollections were transforming into the tone of the melody.

Arden's head began to nod softly.

As the arrangement approached its crescendo, it filled the space like a living entity. Energy buzzed like a livewire, the hair of Teyla's arms rising. She stood transfixed as Arden's hands danced quicker across the eighty-eight keys, transcending from soul-wrenching to hopeful in the span of a few notes.

The princess felt a piece of herself she had thought lost awaken with interest as the tension increased. As the climax at last shouted its victory, Teyla heard the music clearly for what it was: *hope.*

It crested over her like a wave, and tears of sorrow and joy flowed freely from her eyes. The passionate hands slowed until one last clear note rang out, its lasting resonance filling the small room. A lingering exaltation of triumph over grief followed in the quiet of the aftermath.

Arden's eyes were closed, hands still poised over the keys. Her head was tipped back slightly off center, and she breathed in and out deeply. Teyla yearned to know what she was thinking about.

A camera snapping interrupted the meditative atmosphere like a gun going off. Teyla grimaced apologetically as Arden's eyes flew open in surprise.

"I am so sorry. You just looked so ethereal and peaceful, and I just wanted to freeze this moment to remember." Teyla was incredibly embarrassed and flustered that her phone's sound had been on. It was nearly always on vibrate. She cursed her bad luck and walked to rest a hand on Arden's shoulder.

"It's okay, Teyla. Did you like it? I've been composing it for many years, but I feel that it has evolved into something I'm very happy with."

Arden had never appeared so bashful as she glanced up. Teyla realized Arden really valued her opinion.

"I loved it! It evoked such intense emotions for me and—" Teyla paused her sentence abruptly, her mind working a mile a minute. "Did you just say you wrote it?"

The agent simpered and nodded shyly, endearing her to the princess even further.

"That is… indescribable. Incredible. Impressive."

"Did you happen to discover a thesaurus or learn what an alliteration was in your sleep, darling?" Arden laughed as she was shoved to the side for her teasing, and Teyla could only shake her head with her own delighted humor.

Mindlessly running her hands through Arden's hair as her head rested lightly against Teyla's abdomen, the princess felt that she could become used to this easy companionship. The comfortable moment was shattered with a concerning thought.

"Why did you not wake me for training today?" Teyla inquired, confused as to why their routine had been disrupted. The answering grimace on Arden's face made her stomach sink.

"A messenger came while you were still asleep. Apparently, the King advised that you spend the day getting ready to look as he wants you to look." Arden's words were hurried, clashing against the confident way she had just played.

Teyla's suspicions immediately rose. "What *exactly* did his note say?" she asked, her voice clipped.

Arden sighed and closed her eyes, obviously disturbed. "He said you needed all day to prepare and try to look presentable."

The truth shouldn't have hurt after all this time, but Teyla felt the bite of the insult all the same. A hard swallow valiantly fought back the sting of tears forming. She turned away to hide it but felt a hesitant touch on her wrist.

Arden's thumb moved back and forth soothingly, and some of the tension left Teyla's tight shoulders. When she no longer felt like she was about to cry, the princess faced her once again.

Arden was patiently standing there. Her eyebrows were snagged in the middle, brought down in a picture of concern. Still, she said nothing. She simply waited there, weathering Teyla's emotions in camaraderie. "Um, Princess…"

Before Teyla could ask what was wrong, she saw it.

Floating there just above Teyla's palm was a small but very prominent ball of light. It was pure white, brighter than the sun outside, and she instinctively knew it could burn just as easily. Teyla's eyes widened in surprise at the shock of wielding magick without meaning to.

Instead of appearing concerned, Arden's blanched with shock. Teyla's dismay at this secret finally coming out increased, and the ball grew in kind. Anxiety rose rapidly until her chest was tight with pain. The ball became bigger with each frantic breath taken until it encompassed her entire hand.

"Arden, release me!" Teyla all but yelled fruitlessly.

She felt wild, out of control, and this *thing* reacted in kind.

"Sweetheart, you're not going to hurt me." It was the confidence in Arden's voice that soothed the vortex in her mind. She wished for it to vanish, but the magick did not heed her.

"Teyla, look at me."

The command caught her attention, but Teyla could not tear her eyes away from the growing ball of power outside her control.

"Teyla."

She wanted to listen, but the light was far too close to her lover's hand. Teyla's breaths became short and sharp gasps, barely allowing her to gulp down enough air.

"Look. At. Me." Arden's voice was rough and compelling.

Instantly, Teyla obeyed. Taking advantage of the brief victory, Teyla focused on Arden's perfect face, not allowing herself to fall back into the pit of fear she had nearly succumbed to.

Arden's eyes were brighter than normal, maybe reflecting the sphere's light. Her right eye was like liquid gold, and she had never seen such a vibrant light blue hue in the left. Teyla forced out a deep breath and then another as she attempted to strong-arm her own body into regulating. As her fear subsided, the ball of light shrunk steadily until it was no larger than a copper coin.

"Do you want this light to go away, Teyla?"

"More than anything right now." Her voice was low.

"Close your eyes and tunnel into your body until you find the strongest section of the aether you can feel." Arden was calm and supportive. "Mine is usually most prevalent in my sternum. It almost feels like a fine vibration."

"I can't." Teyla exhaled a breath, lips trembling as she began to cry.

"Yes, you can. You've harnessed the quintessence with your aether before, I'm sure. You are not finding it because you are so panicked."

Teyla pulled away, bringing the ball of light to her chest. "You'll get hurt!"

"No, I won't," Arden stated matter-of-factly. "You cannot intentionally harm me just as I can't harm you."

"We won't know that for sure about this…" she paused. "This abomination."

Arden shook her head resolutely. "Teyla, this is not an abomination." The agent's voice and features softened. "It is a beautiful, raw power, and it is just as much a part of you as water is to a stream. You will not hurt me because you do not want to, and it will obey."

Before she could bite back a retort, Arden moved.

One moment, the Fae was standing in the doorway, and in the next blink, she was on her knees in front of the princess, hand snuffing the light out. Teyla tried to pull her hand back, but Arden was too strong. In fear, Teyla's other hand flew out and slapped Arden harshly across the face.

The agent's head whipped to the side from the impact. Teyla's hands flew to cover her mouth, horrified. Arden's shoulders began to shake, and Teyla's brain started to fly through what she could possibly say. She was stopped in her tracks by the laughter bubbling up from Arden.

Her lover slowly brought her head back up, then threw it back, laughing even harder. Teyla was frozen, worried Arden had gone insane. Already, there was a red mark blooming from the smack, offering a bright, rosy tint to her left cheek. The princess crossed her arms and stood there, dumbfounded, waiting anxiously for Arden to stop laughing.

After a few moments, the laughter faded, amusement still glinting in Arden's eyes, touching her cheek in amazement and smiling broadly.

"Okay, I deserved that." Another chuckle. "You pack a hell of a slap, Princess."

"Arden, I am *so* sorry for—"

"Defending yourself?" she cut Teyla off. "You have absolutely nothing to apologize for. I am so proud of you. Seriously, Teyla. You had great reflexes, and I am seriously impressed. And look, your tiny light is gone."

Teyla twisted her hand slowly back and forth, analyzing it and looking for any sign of the light.

In a more somber tone, Arden spoke again. "It will only react negatively to your fear," she said gently. "But you can become its commander, and it will obey."

"How do you know that, Arden? Truly. Just because Fae can control their magick doesn't mean I will ever be able to."

The agent led her to the chaise, and they sat down. Once settled, Arden took a deep breath, released it, and began.

"In Orion, magick is not a cursed word or a horror story told to kids to get them to behave. It is a sacred, beloved thing."

Arden searched her face. After a minute of silence, Teyla encouraged her to continue.

"We grew up hearing about the wonders of quintessence and the weight it carries for those who are gifted and chosen to carry it. But we were not afraid. Those who have elemental magick bless the lands and are respected and honored.

"I once knew an exceedingly kind and caring witch named Lila. She blessed our lands with abundance for decades from her magick. She told me that her magick was akin to her soul. She couldn't survive without it, and likewise, it cannot function without her. You control your magick. It reacts to your feelings and will honor your will as long as it is respected and cared for. It is a precious, beautiful gift. Just like you."

There was much to unpack there, but Teyla honed in on one word. "Did you just call me beautiful?" Her voice was raspy, thick from holding back more tears. Arden let out another adorable laugh.

"I did. You are the most beautiful person I have ever met, inside and out. As is your magick."

"You're just saying that because we slept together," Teyla dismissed.

"That is absolutely not true, Princess."

Teyla refused to look at her. Her comment had been hurtful, and she could not understand what possessed her to act so dismissively toward Arden. Teyla knew she was insecure about her body, but Arden had never outright lied to her.

Finally, Arden sighed in resignation. "Would it make you feel better to see my magick so you don't feel so alone in this kingdom?"

She could tell Arden was completely serious. Teyla quickly double-checked that her doors were locked and secured before nodding enthusiastically. Arden scrutinized her for a moment longer before cracking her fingers. Teyla took a few steps away so they were standing across from each other.

Unblinkingly, the princess watched Arden's hands for the first sign of magick. Her breath caught as a ball of water formed in Arden's upturned palm. It was enchanting. The water was continuously swirling but remained contained in its spherical cage.

As Arden moved her wrist, the fluid followed, becoming a floating cylinder. She directed it around Teyla's arm in a spiral before silently calling it back.

"Is it cold?" The amazement was clear in Teyla's voice.

"It can be." Arden shrugged, as if that were not the most fascinating thing she had ever said.

"Tell me more," Teyla pleaded.

The dancing water wove in and out of Arden's fingers. "Well, technically, I can only control the water itself. Over time, and with a lot of training from others who are far smarter than me, I realized that I could command the water particles to vibrate slowly or quickly. That vibration alternates the temperature."

The water formed the shape of an arrow before solidifying and dropping into Arden's waiting hand. She offered it to Teyla, and the princess' hand shook slightly as she accepted it. The ice was as cold as she was expecting, but as she ran her finger along the arrow shaft, there was not a single flaw in the sculpture. It was smooth as glass. When she held it back out to Arden, it turned back into water before vanishing.

The casual display of such impressive control was as frightening as it was dazzling. For the first time since they met, Teyla understood just how easily she could have been killed by Arden from her magick alone, let alone her deadly fighting skills.

"Do you think my magick is an abomination?" Arden asked, repeating the verbiage back to her. "Or that I am for being able to wield it?

"No."

"You are not either. Quintessence exists in all things, whether there are wielders around or not. The only difference is that we wielders can feel it in our bodies and bones."

Teyla knew that particular feeling she was referencing. It

was like a living, breathing entity within her. She just struggled with controlling it.

"Someone is here." Arden's head turned toward the door moments before a loud knock sounded. Teyla nearly jumped out of her skin, knowing they'd been talking about and performing magick illegally just a moment before. It was eerie how well Arden could hear.

"Come in!" Teyla's voice was raised loud enough to be heard. Arden stepped further away as five housekeepers entered the room, three of whom were carrying a dress.

"Now that you have proper company and guards outside, I will take my leave. I will see you at the ball tonight." Arden nodded and walked to the door after her proclamation.

Teyla murmured goodbye, well aware that Arden would hear it and know she was thinking of her as Teyla surrendered to the hectic onslaught.

CHAPTER TWENTY

MASQUERADE

Although Teyla was loath to compliment him on anything, her father knew how to throw a party.

The great hall was dressed in glimmering metallics with royal purple accents. Clusters of overflowing, blossoming flowers were intertwined with robust foliage and manipulated into large wreaths wound with gold thread adorning the stone walls.

The massive wooden doors to the hall were lined with copious boughs of garland, and twice the number of torches were lighting the room as usual, their flickering flames reflected in the mirrored floor that she adored so much.

As Teyla appreciated the waving firelight, the dark indigo hues tinting the floor had her gaze turning up, mouth falling agape at the ceiling, which was decorated like the night sky, with more paper mâché stars than she could hope to count.

The decorations were admittedly opulent, but they served to represent the event. Even the castle servants and workers were hardly recognizable, every speck of their skin covered in gold and silver paint, eliciting the same sense of anonymity that the masks provided the rest of the guests.

Long tables stretched across the right side of the hall,

filled with food and overflowing flutes of champagne. It was decadent and fitting for a party worthy of celebrating a future king and the unveiling of their princess to the public.

Teyla gracefully turned down the offer of a dance from another masked face for the fifth time tonight. It was a very felicitous concept to have the theme of the night be a masquerade party. As all workers in the castle wore face coverings daily, she had overheard many people gossiping excitedly at the prospect that the princess was in their midst.

It seemed no expense had been deemed too great. Everyone in attendance thus far was wearing their finest outfits. For the rich, that meant silks in every color of the rainbow—emerald green, lapis blue, scarlet, shining onyx, and fuchsia.

For the proletariat, neutral dresses and suits that were—at least—not covered in dust and grime. Only a few of the less fortunate people were allowed into the great hall; the rest of them remained outside, surrounding the castle, celebrating nonetheless. No phones were allowed into the castle, and the Royal Guard acted predominantly as security that night, metal detectors in hand.

"Hello, Princess," a low voice murmured.

She would know that voice blindfolded.

Keeping her eyes low in submission per the King's requirements, the first thing she noticed was gold-heeled shoes that wrapped around delicate feminine feet. Those same feet were resting in the same fighting stance that she herself was standing in, taught to her by her favorite tutor.

As Teyla's eyes trailed up, she could not help but appreciate the beauty of the black dress that was so simply adorned with glittering jewels. It was stunning and more provocative as her eyes continued their journey up. She was sure the men at this party had already noticed the slit in the dress that stopped mid-thigh and were ogling at the show of bare skin, and an ugly spear of jealousy and protectiveness shot through her.

The dress's bodice had even more glittering pieces, and the corset hugged her body closely, displaying a delicious amount of her chest as well.

An intricate black mask largely hid the lady's face. The entire right side was completely covered by feathers from her hairline down to her jaw. The left side was a classic hard mask lined with black fabric to make it more comfortable. That side was covered in little gemstones and matched the sparkling dress beneath it.

The clearing of a throat reminded Teyla to stop blatantly checking her out in the middle of a public gathering. Still, damn it all, she looked mouthwatering, and the princess could not halt the mental image of those legs that had been wrapped around her less than twenty-four hours earlier. "Arden?"

The woman in question's smirk broke into a fully formed grin, white teeth flashing, the canines slightly longer than the rest of her teeth. "In the flesh, Your Majesty," she quipped.

Teyla whipped her head around, surveying the crowd. The entire multitude except one noble person had strayed away to dance as the village fiddlers had begun playing.

When Teyla turned back, her eyebrows rose in surprise as she once again took in the whole of Arden's regalia. She looked delectable, but why she'd decided, tonight, of all nights, to wear something this provocative eluded Teyla.

"You look… absolutely breathtaking, Teyla," Arden whispered reverently, only loud enough for her ears.

Heat rushed to Teyla's cheeks at the compliment. Nobody else had commented on her appearance, not even the maids. She ran her hands along the skirts, smoothing the deep forest green folds self-consciously. For once, her father had allowed her to pick the color, and she chose the color of Arden's people to pay homage to her in a secret way only they would know.

"As delicious as you look, is there a reason you chose tonight to dress up so… scandalously?" Teyla kept her tone level. She did not want Arden to feel like she was being judged. The agent never did anything without reason—she was learning.

Arden took a deep breath before answering, annoyance so well masked that had Teyla not known her micro-expressions so well, she would have missed it. "It was a request from the King."

Teyla understood the hidden remark. The King did not ask for anything. He demanded it. Those who disobeyed found the consequences to be very, very uncomfortable, like the ten lashes Arden had experienced before. "Why?" she questioned.

"He stated that I needed to blend in, although I am certainly drawing more attention than not in this skimpy thing. Not to mention these six-inch heels."

Teyla huffed lightly at the obvious disdain.

Arden continued, "I am assuming that it is a test of some kind. Perhaps to see if I would disobey for propriety's sake. Regardless, I still have my dagger, so I feel mostly all right."

Teyla's eyebrows furrowed in confusion. The dress was very form-fitting until the skirt of the dress, and even that had a slit in it. The back was also open and showed the various welts on her skin that would soon fade away to nothing but scars.

Understanding dawned on Teyla, and her core lit up at the thought. Teyla's imagination helpfully supplies an image of Arden wearing a leather thigh harness; it was so sexy Teyla felt she'd melt into a puddle. Arden's heated gaze bore into her, and she knew her lover could tell exactly in what direction her thoughts had turned.

Arden stepped further away. Suddenly, an unwelcome hand touched the small of her back, and a suffocating wave of cologne hit her.

Lord Johan Caine stood beside Teyla, touching her like it was his inherent right to do so. She would have recognized him even with a mask on, though he deigned to remove his before the King gave the order. The brush of his hand was too possessive and suggestive to be identified as anything but a claiming gesture. Teyla swallowed the bile that rose and turned to him, forcing a polite but bland smile.

"I was unaware that the King had so generously hired harlots to entertain us tonight."

Caine's comment was clearly directed at Arden, and Teyla vividly imagined breaking his nose for the derisive way he spoke to her.

Momentarily forgetting herself, the princess replied with a patronizing smile. "I don't think the King could pay her enough to service you, My Lord."

A stormy glower thundered over his face.

Lord Caine scoffed. "Who knew the bitch had bite? Regardless, I would never let my cock near a thing like that." He waved dismissively toward Arden, as if she were dirt under his shoe. Teyla's blood boiled.

"At least the King is paying me," Arden spoke disparagingly. "Your mother gave it away for free; undoubtedly how you came about."

The hand on Teyla's lower back tightened as the lord's face reddened alarmingly.

"My Lady, may I request this first dance?" His deep voice felt as oily and wrong as the hand still touching Teyla.

There was no real choice. The insult of refusing him would be far worse than suffering through a song. Teyla extended her hand to grasp his upturned fingers. "Of course, My Lord. It would be my pleasure."

She spoke the words with the practiced ease of somebody who had been playing court games for their entire life—somebody just like her.

As he led them into the throng of dancers, Teyla could not help but glance back to find Arden already disappearing in the crowd, keeping an eye on her at all times. Knowing Arden was there allowed her shoulders to loosen as she strolled through the dance floor.

Surrounded by members of the nobility and laypeople alike, the instruments sounded, and the dancing began.

She allowed her body to go through the motions of the dance she could have performed while asleep. As they moved around the room, she caught flashes of Arden in the crowd, never far, watching Lord Caine with barely restrained disgust. Teyla looked back at the man in question.

Lord Caine had deep eyes like soil and brown hair that he styled slicked back. He had a tiny white scar that slashed through his right cheek, and she felt a pang of jealousy that she had not caused it. His lips were bent in an almost permanent sneer.

After she saw the way he'd relished whipping Arden, she understood why the King had taken a fast liking to him when his father had passed away recently. Her disdain toward him had simply grown.

As they danced, his slimy hand drifted lower and lower until it was groping her posterior. Teyla was disgusted and trapped. She could not remove his violating touch from her ass without causing a scene. As she contemplated her options, a throat cleared behind her.

"Lord Caine, please remove your hand at once. People are watching, and the King surely would not appreciate the rumors that the princess is impure."

Teyla dared to peek up at his face and was glad she was not on the receiving end of that glower. Risking a glance behind her, Arden looked completely relaxed and bored, like she did not care at all about the level of disrespect she had just committed.

"The King will not care, as I am about to win the competition and enjoy my prize."

At the end of his sentence, Lord Caine squeezed Teyla's ass even tighter and pulled her closer to him by the wrist, causing her to yelp out in pain. Teyla knew she would be bruised later.

Arden's face was absolutely murderous. She crept up to him, saying, "Remove your hand before I remove it permanently." As she spoke, she bared her teeth at him in a challenge.

For his part, Lord Caine just laughed. He let go of the princess's waist and shoved her toward Arden. Teyla tripped in the heeled shoes, but the agent caught her effortlessly and helped her regain her balance.

"I will remember this when I am king. I will have a lot of fun breaking you apart." He glared at Arden.

Arden looked impassive, unfazed by the threat. "It would behoove you to remember that pain you sow is pain you reap. I will personally ensure that anything dealt is felt tenfold." Arden's polite smile would appear amicable to anyone watching their exchange, but her eyes were filled with dark promises of pain and suffering.

The lord laughed and turned away, melting into the crowd like the haunting spirit he was. Arden turned toward her, inspecting her from head to toe. "Are you all right?"

Teyla's anger flared, and only the reminder that the King was present kept her from smacking Arden for the second time in the past twenty-four hours. "Of course, I'm all right! What are you thinking, challenging a lord like that?"

Teyla saw Arden wince like she had been hit. Her brave lover, who had killed people and stood up to the most ruthless lord in Cyrene without batting an eye, had winced at Teyla's words. Apologies immediately began to bubble out of her mouth, but Arden spoke over her.

"It is my duty to look out for you. I take that to mean physically, as well as protecting your mental state, your image, and anything else that could harm you. Including creepy bastards like Lord Johan Caine." She took a steadying breath. "I take my role very seriously. Damn the consequences, as long as you are happy and safe. I care for you, and I'm glad to risk my well-being for you."

Teyla did not know what she did to deserve that kind of devotion. She was spared from replying as another man asked for a dance. The princess acquiesced to his request as she was bound to do, but her eyes remained on Arden until the crowd consumed her.

The rest of the night went similarly. Teyla danced until her feet had blisters and her legs felt like they would give out. She ended up dancing with most of the competitors and plenty of other laypeople as the night went on.

Finally, Teyla was pulled to the side along with the rest of the nobility, all of them standing to the left side of the throne. The King stood from his seat on that giant throne, and silence followed.

A lone cough was heard from the gathering people as they waited anxiously for their princess's reveal. Teyla felt herself shrink back at the prospect of so many people staring at her. The mask was a comfort after so many years of being outside of the limelight.

Her father appeared regal that night, wearing a deep purple and silver ornate robe. His beard was groomed meticulously, and there was no sign of the vile monster inhabiting him. His dark hair was slicked back, and it struck her again just how much she took after her mother. Teyla was her replica in all ways but one: her blue eyes came from her father.

As the King began speaking, she felt her anxiety grow into a living being. Arden was nowhere to be found, which added to her worries.

Her lady-in-waiting elbowed her harshly and jerked her chin toward the King.

"What, Ruby?"

"I said… Princess, come meet your devout people."

Berating herself for missing the first cue, Teyla walked gracefully up the steps to the throne, where several people awaited: the King, with obvious annoyance in his eyes, a young boy holding a golden pillow with a tiara on top, and the Head of the Council.

The tiara was made of pure gold with sparkling amethysts and diamonds around its wreath. It glinted and glittered in the lights of the Great Hall, tantalizing her. Sorrow overshadowed the moment as she remembered her mother's smile the last time she had been allowed to touch it.

Teyla stood with her back perfectly erect, shoulders back, and head held high. The King continued with his pretty speech.

"Here is your princess, who has been forced into seclusion for decades! I present her to you in good faith so that the remaining competitors might know what they are fighting for."

He gestured for her to come forward. Teyla obeyed like the perfect pet he had trained her to be. The Head of the Council's gloved hands picked up the tiara from the golden pillow and balanced it on her head. It was a tad too small, but it would do well enough for the theatrics tonight.

With the heavy weight on her head, Teyla faced the King once more.

"Behold—your Princess Teyla!"

With his declaration, he ripped off the mask obscuring her features. The crowd gasped at the reveal, then broke out into cheers. The Great Hall had a wild energy in it. The room reverberated with loud cheers and shouts from the crowd. The King was reveling in it, arms spread wide as if gathering strength from their blind adoration.

A tingling feeling began along her spine, the hair on the back of her neck rising. Teyla warily searched the room for any sign of what was off. She was unable to locate Arden, but the sensation was growing worse.

A small voice in her head spoke. *Watch out. Something is wrong.*

Halfway down the grand hall stood an unfamiliar man wearing an all-black mask in the crowd. He just stood there amongst the people hollering and jumping and bumping into him. He stared at Teyla intently, a small smile breaking out across his face at her attention.

Now that she had seen him, she could pick out more men with black masks in the crowd, each one creeping forward through the masses. Teyla took an uncertain step back, unsure of what to do. If she were wrong about the threat of danger, the King would be furious. If she were right and did nothing, people could get hurt.

As she took another step backward, a high-pitched scream sounded above the rowdy mass of people. Teyla tracked the sound to find a common woman covering her own mouth in horror as she looked up toward the dais. She was looking toward the King.

The crowd's screams grew louder as more people followed the woman's line of sight.

Heart thundering in her ears, Teyla turned just in time to see the Head of the Council's decapitated head hit the platform before the rest of his body did, bouncing grotesquely down each shining stair. Right behind his crumpled body stood another man with a jet-black mask on, armed with numerous blades and grinning maniacally.

Blood splattered his clothes, as well as the once beautiful staircase leading up to the throne. For one terrifying moment, Teyla could not think, could not breathe.

Panic set in, causing her breaths to become too shallow and quick.

Run.

There was no clear escape route.

Hide.

There was nowhere to hide from these men who now knew her face.

Fight.

The word whispered through her. Teyla had barely begun training. She would certainly die if she tried to kill them.

Arden's voice rang through her head this time, words from weeks ago sounding clearly in her brain.

Cause enough injury to escape or call for help. You don't need to be the hero. You just need to survive.

Arden promised she would always protect her. Teyla just needed to buy her some time to reach her through the absolute mayhem erupting as terrified people knocked over banquet tables in their rush to escape. The princess shut down any doubt about Arden still being alive and resolutely stood her ground as the man approached her, swinging his sword around as he laughed.

"Scared, little girl?" he crowed, his excitement about cornering her obvious. She remained silent, waiting for the moment to strike. She did not have any weapons, but her body could cause harm just the same.

He swiped his sword up toward her face.

Now.

Teyla darted forward and spun, ramming her cocked back elbow straight into his nose. She felt the crunch of bone as it broke and quickly dove out of the way of his other hand. Her body knocked into a table as she hastily retreated, a bowl of round fruit toppling onto the floor.

The figure in black tripped on the rolling fruit. "You bitch!" he snarled, his words slightly garbled from the river of blood running down his face.

Satisfaction at the sight elicited a grin from her. If she were going to die today, at least she would take him with her.

Teyla's smile seemed to enrage him further as he swung his sword savagely, his eyes hungry for blood. After narrowly avoiding his blade twice, her heeled feet tripped over a limp corpse, sending her flying backward.

A gurgling noise sounded above the din. The pool of red her hand was soaked in was either the burgundy punch or blood. She forced her attention away from that thought in time to see a dagger stab through the man's throat, severing his spinal cord. The dagger was yanked out, and the man careened off the platform.

Arden's face was splattered with more blood than the dead man lying on the floor between them. How many people had the agent fought as she battled her way to her? *Why was she always covered in blood?*

Teyla's relief quickly deteriorated as four more men surrounded them. Arden merely cracked her neck and wiped her dagger on her expensive, beguiling dress, which she had tied above her muscular thighs. With her legs in a fighting stance, dagger in hand, and feet still in heeled shoes, she released a fierce growl, more animal than human. The men—as one—charged.

CHAPTER TWENTY-ONE

STILLETOS

Arden wiped the dripping blood from her brow in time to see two men attacking from opposite sides. She quickly lunged forward, deftly parrying their blades mid-air and landing behind one of them. Before he could turn around, her blade was at his throat as she sliced his neck open from ear to ear. As he fell, she tackled the second man and stabbed him in the heart.

Twisting for good measure, Arden yanked it out of his chest and looked for the others. She snatched his fallen sword, spinning it threateningly, grateful that metal detectors had precluded guns. She slid her dagger into its thigh harness and held the sword with both hands, angling it toward the last two men.

One yelled out and ran toward her, while the other ran toward Teyla. Arden whipped out the dagger, and it hissed toward the man lunging for her mate. His head whipped back, the blade embedded deep in his skull. As he collapsed, the dagger was still vibrating from the force of the throw.

Arden's balance was off after chucking the dagger, and the last man capitalized on her shaky footing. The skin on her palm tore open as she batted his sword away from her torso. She cursed and moved backward, nearly spraining her ankle.

Gods damned heeled shoes.

With two more arcs of her sword, the rebel was hacked apart. Arden did not even spare him a glance before rushing over to Teyla, who was still sprawled out on the ground.

"Hey, Princess, don't freak out on me yet. We have a little way left to get back to your rooms."

Teyla accepted the offered hand. Arden pulled her to her feet, quickly assessing the rest of the hall.

People were still panicking, trying to exit the Great Hall, their screams of fear reverberating. It appeared that there'd been no discretion from the rebels as nobility and laypeople alike had been killed.

The King's guards had immediately surrounded him and escorted him out of the hall while everybody else had been left to fend for themselves. Once safe in his chambers, the King gave the order to "Finish the rebels but leave some alive."

Bodies littered the floor everywhere. Blood flowed freely over the tiles.

The guards were steadily gaining ground on the rebels as more loyal Cyrenian men joined the fray. By her quick headcount, there were still around thirty rebels left fighting. Most of the rebels were fighting the guards near the hall's main entrance.

Bullets began hailing down on the guards, guests, and rebels alike. Arden grimaced. *There goes our minor advantage.*

Through the shattered glass windows, she could see the gunmen shooting sporadically at the people below. The front entrance was a death trap. There had to be another way.

"Come on, sweetheart. We have to keep moving. More will come."

That seemed to shake Teyla from her frozen stance. Palming Arden's dagger in her hand, which Arden had pulled from a dead man's face, the princess inspected herself. Her gorgeous dress was ruined, her entire body was shaking, but her pale face was focused. She was scared but ready to die fighting if necessary.

However, she would not be dying tonight. Arden would

make sure of it.

The agent pulled Teyla flush behind her, raptly monitoring the situation. Her wolf was snarling to be let loose and destroy the threat. For the first time since her arrival, she was relieved there was some sort of spell around the great hall that nullified magick. Arden would not have been able to suppress the shift with her mate in such immediate danger.

Sweeping her gaze across the hall, Arden noticed a small nondescript door near the back of the room, behind the dais. Leaning backward and craning her neck while keeping her eyes peeled for danger, she spoke to the princess. "Teyla, do you see that door behind us to the right?"

"Yes, I see it. It is a servant's door."

A flurry of bullets whizzed by, making the decision for Arden. She clutched Teyla's left hand in her right and surged forward, dragging her along. "Hold on, Princess!" Teyla's death grip on Arden's wrist proved she understood. Arden sprinted toward the door, holding back just enough to appear human. Teyla raced to keep up, tripping over her heeled shoes.

They zig-zagged through a spray of bullets as they ran, and more shouts rang out from behind, growing closer and closer with every breath. A glance verified that more masked men were on their tails.

"Fuck," Arden muttered to herself.

Teyla turned and cursed as well. Hearing her fiery princess speak so colorfully delighted Arden despite their treacherous situation.

When they reached the door, the men were only twenty feet behind. Arden opened the latch and shoved Teyla through, slamming it closed against a hail of bullets.

There was nothing within the corridor to brace against the door, and her back was burning from the bullets that shattered through the door and into her flesh. They would not kill her, but fuck, they hurt.

Teyla tugged on Arden's gown. Eyes fixed on the door, preparing for the onslaught of men certain to come through it,

Arden tilted her head. "Kind of busy here…"

Another insistent tug had her turning, annoyed.

Behind them, with his face buried in the neck of a laywoman in a brown dress, was Lord Johan Caine.

He slowly looked up from his meal and smiled, bright red arterial blood running down his face and neck. His two sharp cuspids were touching the bottom of his lower lip.

Without warning, Arden shoved Teyla into the alcove just as the door behind her exploded open.

Three heavily armed and hooded men raced in. Arden looked to the left at the men, then toward the right to Lord Caine, who was still grinning with those bright red eyes. Before the men could decide who to attack, the lord moved too quickly for Arden's Fae eyes to track. He seemingly vanished to the shock of the hooded men, the woman's body dropping to the floor, only to reappear by the broken door.

His clawed hands latched onto one of the men, pulling him close. The man shouted and struggled against his hold.

As he tried to pull his arm away from the nightwalker, Lord Caine gripped his arm and shredded it with his claws, degloving the skin and revealing bones.

The masked man screamed in agony, still fighting the fierce grip of the lord. The screaming stopped suddenly as the lord tore out his throat with his teeth.

Teyla's gasp of horror was drowned out by the outraged roars of the man's cohorts. They turned their blades on the nightwalker with renewed fervor, managing to land a few hits before they were swiftly dismembered.

There was no way the women could sneak past Lord Caine without a fight, but they could try.

Keeping her face calm, Arden leaned against the stone of the alcove and crossed her ankles, the perfect picture of boredom.

Lord Johan Caine grabbed a bloodied handkerchief from his vest and dabbed his chin, ever the picture of sophistication despite the gore surrounding him. Arden looked around at the carnage lazily.

"Well done, Lord Caine." She paused, forcing her lips into a savage grin. "You made short work of those rebels. I commend you."

He looked at her, head cocked, as if she was a specimen to be studied. His tongue swept out, gathering the blood from his lips and swallowing it.

Arden did not break eye contact with those bright red eyes, unwilling to avert her attention even for a second. Still, he said nothing.

"Since you have done all of the hard work for me, we will be taking our leave." She nudged Teyla in the opposite direction of the shattered door and forced her steps to be leisurely, never turning her back on Lord Caine as Teyla walked away.

"No." His voice echoed in the small space.

Arden halted but urged the princess to continue her retreat.

"Stop." His voice thundered in the hallway.

Teyla listened immediately, and Arden mentally cursed their astonishing bad luck. The agent tightened her grip discreetly on the hilt of the sword.

"No, sir. I don't think we will," Arden answered coolly.

Lord Caine sneered. "You will do as you are instructed, mutt."

Arden's heart froze in her chest. She had been taking the scent nullifiers for months. There was no way he should have been able to scent out her heritage.

He released a terrible laugh, chilling her to the bone as it echoed in the servant's hall.

"Did you think you were discreet? I had suspicions after you killed Nicolai, but tonight, I confirmed it by how quickly you moved." He took a long, deep inhale through his nose. "I can smell it on you now, ancient, yet new—enticing and magickal."

Lord Caine stepped forward. Arden retreated, matching him step for step.

"I never liked you, but knowing you are Lycan filth, it will be even more enjoyable to kill you."

She heard Teyla's inhalation of surprise at his words but tuned her out and kept her body in front of Teyla's. Arden was still too close to the spell that prevented her from fully using magick or fully shifting into her wolf, but lesser magick worked.

Allowing the partial shift to occur, Arden sensed her claws growing as her teeth slightly elongated. Just as the shift finished, she darted to the side, Lord Caine missing her by mere inches in the narrow corridor.

Arden's instincts to kill and protect screamed in her skull. Noises became louder tenfold, and she could see each tiny drop of blood on the ground.

He jumped toward her, his razor-sharp talons tearing into her left shoulder, embedding deep into her muscle. She snarled and shook him off.

Arden lashed out with her claws and swung her sword into his ankle. His scream of pain and anger was music to her ears.

He countered the attack. Their bodies were a blur around the room, growls and snarls sounding out as they fought. Arden could hear the skirmishes throughout the great hall, clamoring through the shattered door.

Just as her sword was inches from his heart, he twisted enough to grab it, stopping the attack. His claws wrapped fully around the blade embedded in his hands, and he yanked backward, pulling it fully from her grip.

He backhanded Arden's face, her body flying off of him and slamming into the ground. She applied pressure to her shoulder and knelt in supplication as she discreetly looked for another weapon.

Lord Caine smiled cruelly while she fidgeted on her knees in front of him.

"There is no saving you," he spoke with glee.

Arden finally stilled and brought her glowing eyes to meet the lord. She allowed a small smile. "I'd expect nothing less from a brute like you."

As he leaned down to bite, she attacked. Heeled shoe in hand, she rammed the sharp heel straight into his eye. His face screwed together as his mouth contorted in a scream.

Arden quickly stood up, her vision blurring as she became lightheaded. Lord Caine lay there on the floor, writhing in agony. Eyeing him one more time, she limped toward Teyla, checking that she was all right.

"No!" Teyla screamed. Caine's arms wrapped around Arden like a vice as he bit her neck.

Arden's legs collapsed under their shared weight, his venom weakening her as it entered her bloodstream. His fangs were ripped from her neck as his body suddenly flew backward several feet, wrapped in a brilliant, white light.

"You will never touch her again." Teyla's voice was as dark as an abyss, the words as hard as flint as she spoke to Lord Caine.

Arden looked toward Teyla in disbelief. The princess's hands were outstretched toward Lord Caine, brows furrowed and teeth gritted in pure rage. Instead of glowing blue, her eyes were completely white. Arden could not even see her irises or pupils. Her face was lit in stark relief from her magick. Shadows suddenly covered them, and Arden blinked rapidly to see what was happening.

The lord was no longer encased in Teyla's magick, but he was not moving from his slumped position.

"Kneel."

Teyla's command thundered in the space, and Arden watched in awe from her sprawled place on the dirty floor as he was forced to comply. Arden was no longer in the presence of her scared princess. In her place was a righteous queen.

Caine's shallow breaths were raspy as his head lifted to look at Teyla, undiluted fear on his face and filling Arden's nostrils. Her mate's outstretched hand slowly balled into a fist before she allowed it to drop to her side. His veins began to glow, a muted light gathering beneath the skin. It gradually grew brighter and brighter until his red eyes turned pure white.

His body spasmed as every single vein and blood vessel ruptured simultaneously. His face was a permanent, soundless scream until he was completely incinerated. Only ashes remained, floating down to rest on the tile.

Arden had never seen anything like it.

She breathed through the venom lighting up her insides and gripped Teyla's hand until the princess released her hold on the magick, and her white irises turned back to their stunning blue hue.

A crooked smile lifted Arden's lips as she continued to look at the princess in complete wonder. "Is now a bad time to tell you that I have never been so turned on in my life?"

CHAPTER TWENTY-TWO

DUALITY

Arden left Teyla's side and toed at the rebels' bodies, appearing wholly human again, with no sign of claws or pointed ears. Dark humor laced her voice. "Normally, I would behead them since they were bitten and potentially injected with venom, but there is no chance they are coming back as nightwalkers being this dismembered."

Relieved to see that she was well enough to make jokes, Teyla offered up a small, exhausted smile. That smile dissipated as she caught sight of the woman Lord Caine had been feasting from. She was exsanguinated, not a single drop of blood left in her body. She was so pale, so lifeless. Yet her glossy eyes seemed to stare into Teyla's soul. Haunted, Teyla couldn't look away.

Arden came back over and wrapped her warm embrace around Teyla, wincing as the motion tugged on her wounds. The princess sank into the embrace for a moment before stepping back. "Let's go, Arden."

Foregoing their cumbersome heels, they crept barefoot silently through the castle.

The rebels were still infiltrating the castle. Each time

they were close to another hallway, the sounds of fighting grew louder and door after door was blocked. Doubling back and finding new, unexplored routes was simply exhausting.

Teyla's heart was palpitating. Frustrated with their slow pace, she was sweating profusely in her dress, and her skin felt itchy from the dried blood flaking off.

At last, Mother Ambrosia blessed them, and they stumbled into her room. Five guards were stationed outside, ready to fight any rebel who made it that far into the castle. Teyla briefly wondered if her father had afforded her the protection out of love but quickly dismissed the sentiment as the King's motive occurred to her—no one would want to win a dead princess.

Upon entering the room, Arden dropped into an armchair, panting slightly.

Teyla walked over and put a hand lightly on Arden's back, the agent flinching at the pain.

"Oh my gods—he bit you." Teyla could see the puncture wounds. Her heart raced. Had that nightwalker turned her beloved? She backed away, her heart breaking, and held up her dagger, trembling.

Arden raised her tired eyes to hers and grimaced.

"He did," she said. Arden watched warily as Teyla paced across the room, never lowering her guard.

"You're going to turn into a nightwalker." Teyla was overcome with uncontrollable terror, barely able to breathe.

"No, I won't."

Teyla's hand shook, her eyes wide, studying Arden. She rasped incredulously, "You don't know that for sure." Arden looked beat up and diaphoretic. Her eyes were glossy, and she shivered. Concern washed over Teyla, but she kept her distance. Teyla had never turned into a nightwalker because Nicolai had never injected his venom into her. She highly doubted Lord Caine had shown Arden that same consideration.

"I cannot be turned into a nightwalker, Teyla."

"Explain." Arden opened her mouth, but Teyla interjected. "No half answers. I want the full truth."

Teyla's pacing resumed in Arden's long silence. Teyla turned, furious, to demand an answer when Arden finally spoke.

"Sit. You'll need it for this."

Teyla crossed the room and sat in the armchair across from Arden in the living area. The chairs were a light beige color, and, in the back of her mind, she hoped the blood would not stain them.

As she sat down, her legs buckled. Teyla's grip on the knife's hilt loosened slightly, the tip dropping lower as she watched Arden.

Arden twisted in her seat to face her fully, leaning in with her elbows on her knees. "Normally, I would ask you to swear an oath of secrecy before telling you any of this." Teyla sat up straight. The dagger's point raised again as Teyla glared at Arden, a frown across her face. *Another damned secret.*

Arden continued slowly, "But I doubt you would agree to that."

Teyla eased back again.

"Instead, I am asking you to keep this secret of your own free will, trusting that you have my best interest at heart."

The princess's voice shook from nerves. "Okay."

"I'd like to get through all of this without interruption. Can you agree to hold any thoughts or questions you have until the end?"

"Yes," Teyla breathed, trepidation creeping higher in her chest.

Arden sighed for one more long moment and then began speaking her truth. "A very long time ago, a goddess named Ambrosia felt very alone. To ease this feeling, she created children whom she called witches. Ambrosia wanted these witches to be made in her image, so the gift of magick flowing through their veins only passed through the female line."

The princess interrupted her, annoyance flaring. "I already know that history. Why are you telling me this?" Teyla really did not want to hear about how she was a witch.

Despite her rigors, Arden responded patiently. "Because it is pertinent to what I am about to tell you about myself."

Teyla winced sheepishly in supplication. She'd already broken her promise of silence and forced herself to remain quiet. Holding back an admonishing grin, Arden continued. "Blessed with an abundance of gifts, the witches rejoiced and honored Ambrosia, calling her the Mother. All was peaceful for centuries. Eventually, the witches became lonely as well and used their combined magick to create moon-blessed creatures called Lycans, a shapeshifting race. The Lycans were loyal and protected their witches and their packs.

"One day, a witch named Laelia, who was not content, went down a dark path. During this journey, she used blood from the Lycans and created a nightmare of a creature, which she named nightwalker, as these moon-cursed beasts could only hunt during the nighttime. Eventually, nightwalkers and Lycans alike evolved, turning into the creatures they are today."

Despite Teyla's whirlwind of emotions, confusion won out. Every history book she had ever been forced to read and copy verbatim had claimed Lycans and nightwalkers were both moon-cursed.

"Because nightwalkers were crafted utilizing Lycan blood, the venom in the fangs of a nightwalker will not turn a Lycan. Instead, the Lycan will get extremely sick: fevers, chills, sweating, vomiting, you name it. So, I will not turn into a nightwalker due to this bite. I am just about to get extremely ill."

"I thought you were Fae." Surely, Arden had not been lying this entire time about her heritage. Noticing Arden's chagrined expression, Teyla realized she was about to be sorely disappointed, and her confusion morphed into a feeling of betrayal.

Arden saw Teyla's grimace and explained, "I *am* Fae. That was not a lie. Being Fae is how I can manipulate magick."

"But?"

"But I am only half. My mother was Fae, but my father was a Lycan. Instead of having a different animal form, my other form is my wolf." Arden shrugged, as if her explanation was the simplest thing in the world.

Teyla's mind reeled as she tried to understand everything. Various pieces that had puzzled her about Arden for the last few months slowly came together.

The growls and snarls she made when she was angry, her ears that were slightly pointed but not as sharp as Fae she'd seen in picture books, and even her different colored eyes—all pointed toward the duality of her nature. The longer Teyla considered it, the clearer it became. "Prove it." Teyla lifted her chin resolutely. She would not be denied this. Arden had lied by omission, and the princess needed to see it for herself.

Arden sensed her resolve, and she nodded. "Ready?"

"Ready," Teyla warily confirmed.

Arden's eyes began to glow, which Teyla now knew meant she was channeling her magick. The tips of Arden's fingernails grew into sharp points, and her canines flashed as she spoke.

"This is a partial shift. I can tap into my advanced senses and move exceptionally fast, but I mostly retain a Fae form. Does that make sense?"

Understanding jolted Teyla; she had seen Arden partially shift countless times. The first few times she had thought the glow was a trick of the light, but Arden had partially shifted many times to protect her. The risk she had taken, performing magick repeatedly in Cyrene to protect the princess, was monumental. "Yes, it does make sense," she whispered.

"Good. Now, I'm going to fully shift. I won't be able to talk to you, so please don't scream or stab me."

Despite her worry, Teyla's lips twitched in amusement. Only Arden would make being stabbed sound like a mere inconvenience.

Without any more preamble, Arden shifted.

A soft, warm light flared momentarily as the magick took hold. It was over before her next blink. One moment, Arden had stood there partially shifted, and in the next, there stood a giant wolf.

Teyla reeled back in shock from her size alone, but she did not scream. She had asked for proof, and Arden had supplied it.

Arden's eyes remained the same colors in this form, and they held an intelligence that only sentient beings possessed. Her fur was the same brown as her hair, a lovely hickory color, except for a thick stripe of silver on the left side of her head.

It struck Teyla that it was the same path as the scar on Arden's face. Her paws were the size of Teyla's two hands combined, and the claws protruding from each toe were huge. The wolf's head came up to her chest.

The wolf eyed her warily, as if unsure whether or not to approach. Instead, she opted to lay down slowly as if to indicate she meant no harm. Teyla realized she was shaking then, from nerves and exhaustion alike.

"Arden?" she quietly asked the wolf.

Giving a large, wolfy smile showing off her impressive teeth, Arden nodded up and down. Her tail wagged back and forth once, but she did not rise from her place resting on the carpet.

Steeling her nerves, Teyla cautiously walked over, focusing on putting one foot in front of the other. Her instincts were telling her to run away as fast as she could. This wolf was an apex predator, and her most basic instincts told her she was the prey. Still, she trusted Arden.

Finally, she stood in front of the wolf, who was still lying there patiently. She cautiously knelt in front of Arden and offered a hand for her to sniff. It occurred to her immediately how silly she probably looked to Arden. Her agent was not a timid hound that needed to be placated. Arden—Mother bless her—sniffed the hand anyway before licking it.

Teyla squealed with laughter at the tickling sensation of the pink tongue darting out and wetting her fingers, and some of her anxiety eased. Although her instincts were still trying to play tricks on her, she knew inherently that Arden would never harm her, even in her wolf form.

Her hand stretched out again and rubbed Arden's head right between her ears. The wolf's chest rumbled in satisfaction. Feeling braver, Teyla scratched behind one of her ears. Arden's fur there was exceptionally soft. The fur along the rest of her body and extremities proved far coarser.

As Teyla continued to pet her, Arden rolled onto her back, offering up her belly. The princess bit back a smile and rubbed her gently, Arden's eyes closing in bliss. After several minutes of interacting with her in her wolf form, Teyla was ready. "Shift back, Arden. We have a lot to talk about."

CHAPTER TWENTY-THREE

INAMORATA

Arden promptly shifted back into her Fae body at her princess's command. She still felt wary even after Teyla had reacted so well to her wolf.

What she had not been expecting upon taking her wolf form was just how strong the mating bond had felt. As soon as her furry feet touched the floor, she felt the powerful, loving connection, as if their souls were tethered.

The amplification of her devotion to her witch alone made her head spin. Every lonely part of her fractured soul felt mended, and she knew at that moment that Teyla was truly her other half.

Where Arden was callous, Teyla was kind. Where she was merciless, Teyla was gracious. Where the princess was uncertain, Arden was confident. Everything she disliked about who she had become was more than made up for in Teyla.

She had wanted to howl in triumph and announce to every soul on this continent that Teyla was hers, and Arden belonged to no one else. However, when she looked at Teyla and saw only apprehension and fear, her exaltation came to a screeching halt. Teyla did not feel the bond. Arden would not force it. Teyla had confided that she wanted the chance to marry for love. Arden just hoped that she could prove herself a worthy suitor.

"So… Lycans still exist." Based on Teyla's voice, Arden could tell she was processing out loud. Although it was not a question, the agent nodded affirmatively in encouragement.

"And you are not just Fae, but also half Lycan."

Another non-question, and another incline of her chin. Arden covered her smile with her hand at how adorable Teyla looked right now. She did not want the princess to think she was laughing at her.

"Being a Lycan gives you superhuman strength, which you have been using to protect me this whole time. It's how you were able to keep up with the nightwalkers in a fight." Teyla paused, tapping a finger on her chin. "Lycans are essentially shapeshifters that change into wolves. Are you still yourself when you're a wolf?"

Arden chuckled. "Yes, Teyla. I am still myself."

"I mean, are you cognizant like you are when you are human?"

Arden bit down her desire to respond immediately and took a few minutes to think about the question genuinely. The fact that Teyla was inquiring instead of screaming and running away was a massive step in the right direction.

"I have two bodies that I can inhabit, but I am always myself. I am aware and understand things just like I always do." The princess opened her mouth, but Arden continued. "I always have more animalistic tendencies in my brain—like fighting, growling, scenting—but they become more prominent in wolf form. Does that make any sense?"

"I think so," Teyla answered carefully. She walked back to the armchairs and took a seat, and Arden followed suit.

"I have always been told that Lycans were mostly extinct. Is that true?"

They were treading dangerous waters with this line of questioning. Teyla was her mate, but she was also the princess of the kingdom that had nearly destroyed Arden's own. She needed to be honest without giving away too much intel.

"Your father slaughtered many of my kind during the war, including the king of Orion. The Orionian army was able to fight back once he lost the element of surprise. I would say that at least half of the Lycan population was eradicated and a good portion of the Fae as well. Orion is still predominantly human but with far fewer magick wielders. That loss is something that Princess Calliope has been focused on for many years."

"So…" Teyla shook her head in disbelief. "The world as I know it and my entire life is a lie, a deception made up by the King. None of it was true."

Arden winced, unsure of what to say. She was right. The King of Cyrene had created a narrative that fit his agenda and lied to her about it for the entirety of her life. That level of betrayal ran deep.

Teyla whipped her head up from where she had been staring at her hands. "The attacks on the outskirts of the border. If your princess is focused on rebuilding, why is she authorizing razing and looting in my most defenseless towns and communities?"

Arden's forehead wrinkled as she tried to temper her pity. Teyla did not need to be sheltered right now. She needed the harsh truth.

"As far as I am aware, Princess Calliope did not order any of those attacks. The reports I had received indicated injuries and puncture wounds that were most consistent with nightwalkers."

Arden watched Teyla's mouth open and shut repeatedly. It would be amusing if it were not so heartbreaking. The need to comfort her overpowered her. Arden could no longer fight her instincts, nor did she want to.

She wrapped her arms around the princess, ignoring the searing pain in her shoulder from the fighting earlier. Teyla was more important than any discomfort. "I'm so sorry, Teyla. I can't imagine how you're feeling. But let's get you a bath drawn up. I'll check with the guards to see if the rebels have all been taken care of."

Arden chatted with the guards outside the door for a few minutes before closing it again.

"What did they say?"

"The rebels have been either killed or taken for questioning. The siege is over. Additionally, they sent for a maid to gather hot water for your bath, as the raid knocked out a lot of the plumbing in this part of the building."

Arden's knees gave out as she finished. The venom from Lord Caine was kicking in. Her whole body ached and shivered. Running a hand across her forehead, she felt sweat accumulating heavily. Teyla jumped up from the chair as Arden hit the ground.

"Your injury. You are getting sick." Teyla fussed, making Arden lay down as she placed a cold wet rag on her febrile forehead. Through a haze, Arden felt comfort over Teyla's soft touch.

A knock at the door sounded, and several maids came in with fresh buckets of water. All of them turned pale at the sight of blood on the princess and her agent. Keeping their heads down, they focused on drawing up a bath and setting out fresh clothes for both of them. Teyla quickly went to the bath as Arden staggered to her feet, watching on wobbly legs as the maids put out fresh linen on Teyla's bed.

"Thank you very much, ladies," she murmured. "Is Xara all right?"

A sharp slice of shame went through her gut as she realized how long it had taken her to check in on her blood-bonded sister.

One of the blond maids spoke, looking down at her own feet. "She is okay, agent. She is helping tend to the injured in the Great Hall. They set up a giant temporary infirmary."

Tears filled Arden's eyes at the relief coursing through her. Xara was not only safe, but she was also helping others.

Typical of Xara and one of the many reasons Arden adored her. "If you happen to see her, let her know that the princess and I are all right, please."

The blonde nodded, and the maids filtered out of the room.

After her soak, Teyla came out of the bathroom with sleeping clothes on, wringing out her wet hair. "All yours."

When Arden tried to stand independently without success, Teyla offered her shoulder to lean on as they walked to the tub. She delicately removed Arden's blood-soaked dress, gently peeling it away from her injured skin. Arden could not even find it in her to feel embarrassed as Teyla's eyes focused on the many injuries. When Arden finally clambered in, the water was still lukewarm. She closed her eyes from the pleasant temperature.

The agent jolted back into consciousness as Teyla lathered the bar of soap across her arms and chest, scrubbing her body in gentle circles. The princess paid special attention to her face and fingernails, as they had the most blood on them. When Arden's body was sufficiently clean, Teyla poured a sweet-smelling citrus soap into her own hands.

She did not bother asking permission to touch Arden's hair this time, and a small smile stretched Arden's lips, which the princess remembered she could touch whenever she wanted. A low moan escaped her mouth at the enjoyable scratch of Teyla's nails along her scalp. The princess gently tilted Arden's head backward and poured clean water from another bucket over her head to wash out the fragrant soap.

Arden's eyes drifted open at the gentle kiss on her lips. It was not ravaging or hungry. It felt simply like Teyla was grateful they were still alive. Arden's eyebrows rose as she looked down. The bath water was a hideous color of rust from all the blood and dirt, but she was certainly clean enough.

Teyla helped lift her out of the tub, and Arden tried to dry off with the towel wrapped around her, favoring her right shoulder. Shifting into her wolf had made the wound even worse. The claw marks had embedded deeply into the skin but had already coagulated. Luckily, Arden could not see the bullet holes that littered her back. They would heal soon enough, the metal having been pushed out of her skin from her natural Fae powers.

Arden was annoyed that she could not inspect the bite mark on her own collarbone but assumed that if it were concerning, Teyla would have mentioned it. Patted down enough, Teyla helped her into a loose shirt and shorts before helping her back toward the bed. Teyla halted when Arden stopped walking.

"What's wrong, Arden? Are you about to pass out?"

Arden could see Teyla's beautiful blue eyes were filled with worry as she looked up and down to see what was wrong. The fact that Arden was half Fae and half Lycan surely terrified Teyla, but Arden could tell she still cared. "I can't sleep in your bed."

"Don't be ridiculous. We've shared a bed before, and you're injured."

"I can't. I might be unconscious for a while, and I can't risk somebody coming in to see me in your bed. It would ruin your image if word got out, even if nothing was happening."

The princess pursed her lips as she glared at Arden until she begrudgingly led the agent to the chaise. It was not the most comfortable thing, but it was far better than the ground. Once Arden was supine, Teyla fluffed several pillows to put under her head and grabbed a blanket.

Arden snagged Teyla's hand as she turned away. Teyla turned to her, and Arden smiled through the pain blurring her vision. "Thank you for helping me and not stabbing me when I shifted."

Teyla's mouth morphed into an amused grin, and she touched Arden's cheek. "You would have done the same for me."

Her hand on Arden's face and her slight grin was the last thing the agent remembered before passing out.

The next several days were a blur, only short clips floating around in Arden's skull. The only constant thing was the fire burning her alive from the inside. Her whole body felt aflame like quintessence-imbued silver had entered her blood. She was delirious with pain, not able to keep track of the days. In the few moments after the fire had faded, a bone-deep freeze settled in.

Arden could recall a woman shaking her awake from her half-dazed state and hauling her into a luscious bed; flashes of a worried face, brows furrowed as the woman laid a cool, damp cloth on her forehead. The woman sometimes spoke, but everything was muffled and fuzzy, and Arden could not read her lips. There were also times of bolting up and vomiting in a bin, the woman holding back her hair and rubbing slow, comforting circles between her shoulder blades.

Those sweet flashes of memories kept her going through the inferno under her skin. Arden could not remember the woman's name but knew deep down that she was her mate. Wherever her mate touched, sparks flew, and pleasant shivers ran up her body, dulling the raging conflagration.

Finally, after an eternity of burning, she cooled. After a while, Arden realized she could feel her body again, the burning sensation fading. Even when sensations returned, it took her a long time to gather the courage to move a finger, convinced and terrified that if she fidgeted, the fire would return.

Only once she dared to move did she believe the fire was truly dying down. As she wiggled a thumb, she heard the rustling of fabric, the groan of a chair, and a faint sigh. Her eyes cracked open a sliver as they adjusted to the light, making out blonde hair. Teyla's head was propped up on her hands, elbows digging into the mattress. Her sky-blue eyes had deep purple circles beneath them. Her hair was a mess, and she was wearing the same clothes as the night Arden had passed out from sickness.

Arden frowned and slowly blinked, displeased at the state her princess was in.

"You were sick for three days with me caring for you night and day, and the first thing I get is a frown?" Teyla asked quietly, rolling her eyes in exasperation. Arden cracked a small grin at her antics. "There's that beautiful smile I adore."

Arden flushed. Teyla had never spoken to her like that before. She was never so direct in her compliments. As Arden thought about it, she could not recall Teyla ever referring to her as beautiful. The thought made Arden's heart flutter.

"Thank you," she began, her voice raspy and aching. "I was out for three whole days?"

"Technically, three days and seven hours, but who's counting?"

Another joke, and Arden's smile grew in response. She loved this playful side of her princess. "Can you tell me what all happened?" Teyla bit her lip as she thought. It was easily the cutest thing Arden had ever seen before.

"The abridged version? You were not lying about how sick nightwalker venom made you, nor that you would not turn."

Arden remained silent, waiting for the rest.

"Fuck, baby, I was so scared," Teyla breathed.

The admission seemed difficult for her. A burst of happiness went through the halfling from head to toe at the term of endearment.

"Arden, you were *really* sick. I was able to help your superficial wounds heal by accident as I lay with you, but I didn't know how to wield the quintessence to heal you fully or help with your sickness. You kept fevering and vomiting and losing consciousness. I had to forbid anybody from coming in, even the maids because you kept shifting between your two forms!"

Arden's giddiness slammed to a halt, her smile dropping. She had not shifted unintentionally since she was a baby.

"I had a lot of time to think about what you told me while I took care of you. At first, I was livid that you had the audacity to flip my world upside down by telling me everything I know is a lie, then just passing out and becoming unresponsive for days on end."

Arden grimaced, nodding in understanding. That would have been awful if the situation had been reversed.

"As time passed, I realized that wasn't really fair to you, as you had literal poison in your blood. So, I started comparing what you told me and what I've been taught and realized the overarching stories were not too different. My father has told many lies throughout his regime, especially to me. He has hurt me and relished in causing me pain for years now, and then he tells the public how much he adores me."

A vicious snarl erupted from Arden, though her dry throat protested the action. The King was actively abusing his daughter. Suddenly, Teyla's trepidation about meeting with him on the agent's first day as a guard made sense. The growl became louder as her wolf instincts demanded retribution for the harm he'd caused.

"Oh, hush with that before you bring the guards in," Teyla chastised, smacking Arden's arm lightly. Eyebrows shooting up in surprise, the growl cut off.

"Now, as I was saying before I was so rudely interrupted…" Her eyes sparkled with laughter. "The King lied to me? Big surprise there. Add it to the ever-growing list. You shifted in front of me, so obviously, you are not lying. So, I believe it's possible that you are telling the truth about our history."

Arden hardly dared to breathe. It was more than she could have hoped for.

Teyla continued, her voice shaking. "You were delirious in your sickness, calling out for somebody named Max. You also often called out for your mate."

Time stopped, along with Arden's heart. Roaring sounded in her ears, and panic rose in her like a wave threatening to crash down.

"While humans do not call anybody their mate, we do have husbands and wives." Teyla's voice became softer. "And I am not thoroughly familiar with the concept of mates in regard to your kind, but I believe it is something quite intimate." She drew her shoulders back. "I wasn't aware that you were with anybody. Please forgive me for taking advantage of you and your kindness."

She turned away, and Arden's panic grew. "Teyla, wait!" she yelled louder than she'd meant to. Teyla froze but did not turn back. "Please. You are misunderstanding the situation. I am not with anybody, nor have I been in many years." Desperation turned her voice hoarse. "Please," Arden whispered again.

The distress in her tone must have been evident as Teyla finally turned to face her. The princess's eyes were guarded as she waited expectantly for an answer.

Arden gulped, gathering courage. "Sweetheart, it's you. *You* are my mate, my other half. No one exists apart from you."

CHAPTER TWENTY-FOUR

AGONY

"But I am a woman," Teyla took a step back and sat on the bed, her knees feeling too weak to stand.

"You are. In Orion, many couples are the same sex. We are not as antiquated as Cyrene, and it is not against the law to be a female loving a woman."

Teyla sat frozen in shock from the truth Arden had just dropped. Arden was the first woman she had ever been with, and Teyla had become nauseated as she realized Arden quite possibly had many female lovers before.

Arden took the silence as incredulity. She continued, carefully seating herself closer and pulling the blanket over both of them. "I cannot say I was not surprised, but I know it in my soul. You are my mate."

Teyla formulated the next sentence carefully. "What exactly is a mate to Lycans?" Her lover sat quietly, and Teyla's dread grew. So close yet oceans away.

Finally, Arden answered reverently, as if in awe at the concept. "A mate is the equivalent of finding your other half."

The surety of her voice soothed Teyla's anxiety.

"A mate is to be cherished, loved, and provided for.

When a Lycan meets their mate, no other person matters to them. Their sole affection and devotion reside with their partner. Their mate is their world." Arden paused there, taking a moment to herself. "You are my world."

Teyla's heart ached inside her chest. Teyla was stunned by Adren's sincerity. She didn't feel worthy of the adoration Arden was expressing.

As if reading her very thoughts, Arden enveloped her hands. "Listen, Teyla. I love you. I know you can't say it back yet, and that's okay. But I know how I feel." Her thumb stroked the back of Teyla's hands gently, the fondness of her touch apparent. Arden's fingers whispered over her skin with the reverence of a priestess at a temple. "You are deserving of so much more than I can offer you." There was a note of sadness in her voice. "You deserve more than a person like me. But the Mother has other plans. You are destined to be mine."

It all felt so heavy, the weight of this new knowledge pressing down on Teyla, making it hard to focus. Teyla was resistant to this mating claim. She did not want the Mother or any other goddess making her decisions for her. She wanted a say in them. She *needed* the freedom to choose something. It felt just as oppressive as her father not allowing her to pick a husband.

"Is it such a bad thing to be with me?" Arden asked in a low voice.

Teyla saw that Arden was crestfallen. "Arden, my hesitation has nothing to do with you. It's about losing my ability to choose to be with the one I love based on my own feelings, not because you have some…possessive claim on me."

Arden sat up straight, the anger in her eyes making the princess shrink back. "It is not a 'possessive claim.' It is a rare and precious gift. One I will not allow you to defame simply because you do not understand it," she snarled.

Teyla leaned back, affronted by her tone. In all the situations they had been in together, Arden had never snapped quite like that.

"I am not trying to force the bond onto you. I recently

discovered it myself and was not even going to share it with you. But now you know. I will give you space to sort it all out in your mind. Let me know when you're ready to broach the topic again."

Arden threw the blankets off them and swung her legs over the side of the bed. As she stood up, there was a sudden loud banging, and the door swung open.

In came a dozen guards, all in their royal gold uniforms.

"What in the gods' names are you doing, barging into my quarters like that?" the princess snapped, appalled by the level of disrespect.

Captain Farrow stepped forward, hand still on his sword pommel. "The King requires Agent Arden's presence immediately."

Fear and dread had Teyla rounding the corner of the bed, holding her palm out at Arden to remain where she was. The princess stepped toe to toe with the captain and glared with authority. "You could at least pretend to have a modicum of decency instead of breaking the latch of *my* door like a bunch of surly brutes right after a siege of rebels and a night-walker attacked me in this very castle. Did it even occur to you that I might *need* that lock for my own protection?"

"But…"

"Of course, you didn't. That would take using your brain. What is this meeting even about?"

Farrow closed his bearded mouth and looked sheepishly down at his boots at her verbal baratement. Her chest heaved with anger, and he quickly answered in her moment of silence. "I am not privy to my King's agendas or purposes, nor do I need to be, Princess. However, Agent Arden has been summoned, and she will come with me."

"I am your princess," Teyla snapped, her anger growing. "You owe me the same respect I have given you."

Farrow had been the captain of the guard for the last decade. They were not strangers, and she could see the shame in his downcast eyes. The other guards were looking at each other from behind their commander, unsure of how to respond or proceed.

Arden stepped forward, avoiding Teyla's silent command not to move, annoying her. The agent's hair was still unbound, its messy brown waves spilling across her face. Her shirt was wrinkled and disheveled from sweating through it. Her feet were bare, and the dark bags under her now matching amber eyes were stark against her pale face.

"I am happy to come whenever the King calls me, as always. Please lead the way."

Teyla pushed the sting of betrayal down. Arden was being the smart one right now by not causing more issues.

"Then, I am coming too," she declared, looking just as disheveled as Arden did. She hastened to make herself semi-presentable. Taking care of the agent for three days straight had not been light work. She had barely rested.

One of the guards in the back protested, "Princess, there is no need for your presence."

"You will have the fortune of receiving it anyway. Lead the way."

Peripherally, Teyla could see the corner of Arden's lip curl in amusement before she grew stoic once more. The guards turned around and escorted her out like a common criminal. Anger and fear swirled within Teyla, battling for dominance. Eventually, fear won.

She needed to keep up her haughty appearance, looking like an annoyed and entitled royal brat. If the guards, or worse, her father, suspected how much she cared for Arden, Teyla would lose her.

The princess petulantly crossed her arms, huffing loudly and followed the group. She kept her eyes on the back of the closest guard's head to keep from staring at her friend—her mate, if she bought into the "fated souls" ideology.

It was an awkward and quiet walk, the guards remaining silent with grave faces instead of their usual chatter. Clinking armor filled the corridors as the group somberly headed to the throne room, and Teyla was immensely grateful when they finally reached it. Sooner was better than later when waiting for an ax to fall.

Her father graced the tall and formidable black throne. He was drinking something from a goblet, ignoring the procession as they entered. When they reached the center of the room, everybody bowed, including Teyla. The stone tiles beneath her feet used to be gloriously white back when she was a child. However, they now took on a slight pinkish hue from all the blood spilled, despite the staff's best efforts to scrub it out.

"Rise." His voice floated over them, sounding ever so regal, typical of what she expected from him. It always threw her slightly off-kilter, how proper and put together he sounded versus how vicious he could become.

Her adrenaline was pumping through her. Teyla had always felt antsy before the King, but for the first time in her life, it was not for her own well-being. The guards moved to line the dais, a few returning to the door. They were not keeping people out. They were keeping everybody in.

"Well, this is a surprise. I asked for one person, yet two showed up. Explain."

"My King, I—" Captain Farrow started.

"I came here of my own choosing, Father," Teyla interrupted, and Captain Farrow wisely snapped his mouth shut. The King's eyes were such a dark blue in the low lighting that they were almost pitch black.

"Continue," the King demanded, his voice booming throughout the room. Leaning forward from his black throne, he gave her his sole attention, his eyes sinister for her pain.

"Your guards busted open my door, breaking the latch, and attempted to keep me in my room. As it so happens, I did not feel safe behind a broken door with nightwalkers feasting around the castle or after the recent siege. I knew that I would be safer here with this many guards than anywhere else in the castle."

It was a lie told more for his sake than her own. His

people, including his personal guard, were unaware of the nightwalker that commandeered this throne so many years ago. Only those in his inner circle were aware.

Teyla had stumbled upon it accidentally a few years ago when she came to this very room unannounced as her father had feasted on a woman barely older than she was at the time. Instead of killing her, the King demanded an oath of secrecy. If she had refused, he threatened to turn her into the very monster he was. If death had been an option, she would have chosen it gladly.

The King answered, "Very well. As this pertains to your personal agent, you are permitted to stay." His deep voice was calm. Later, Teyla would learn if she was to be punished for her actions.

"Come forward, guard." The King's voice was soft, as if speaking to a lover.

Teyla's breathing nearly stopped. This voice always precipitated murder. Arden walked closer to the throne with her head still bowed in reverence.

"I'm sure you are curious as to why I asked you here."

Teyla nearly snorted. There were never requests from her father, only demands and the expectation that they were obeyed.

"Speak." His voice hardened. He would not ask again.

Arden answered, "Your Majesty, I must confess that I am confused but honored to be invited to be in your presence."

"Drop the act." Each word was painfully enunciated. "The last time you were here, I had you whipped. Surely you have not forgotten so quickly?"

"I have not forgotten the lesson you supplied me, Your Highness. I think about it regularly to better myself," Arden responded smoothly, her voice never faltering. She continued to look down at the stone steps leading up to the throne but never directly at the man gracing it.

"Clever words for a clever person. Do you remember who gave you those lashings?"

"I believe it was a lord, My Liege, but I admit I was too busy thinking about the whipping to notice who was holding the end of the whip."

The King chuckled, and Teyla cringed. He had not laughed since before her mother had been slaughtered.

"Then, I suppose it is a waste of time to ask you if you have seen Lord Johan Caine around the castle?"

Teyla clasped shaking hands behind her back, evidence of her unease. Arden answered, her composure still the epitome of calm.

"With all due respect to the lord, I could not distinguish him out of a lineup of the other lords. Additionally, I have not run into anybody but the princess since the siege. I was injured and have been laid out for the last three days."

The King tilted his head, a predator fixated on potential prey. Admiration at the bravery of her lover stole Teyla's breath. When her father looked at her like that, Teyla quaked. Arden's back was straight, and her shoulders were loose, looking like the perfect picture of innocence.

"Pity. You were my number one suspect as to his disappearance."

Teyla's mouth gaped. This was intended to be an execution. She held still.

He used the past tense. Was it possible that Arden got herself out from under his sword? Could it be that they would walk out of this throne room without blood being spilled? Teyla did not dare to hope.

"In fact, I have had many suspicions about you, some of them big and some small. The most problematic one—except for Lord Caine's disappearance—was the concern about you as a rebel sympathizer at best, a rebel leader at worst."

Arden was many things that would justify the death penalty to the King, but she was not a rebel. She was loyal to Teyla. Arden might be a magick wielder hiding in plain sight, but she had done nothing but protect the princess since the day they met.

"You blew that theory apart during the siege. You had ample opportunities to kill the princess or take her hostage, yet I got it in my reports that you continually protected Teyla. You did so despite your lashings from the last time you mishandled a blade. Still, I was not convinced."

He stood up and took one purposeful step down before stopping, looking down at Arden.

"So, I tortured the surviving rebels for three days, gathering information from them about the rebel operation they've named the Ghosts. Three days of slicing into them, enucleating their eyes, and breaking bones, all for them to give me the name of their informant. Imagine my surprise when it was not yours. In fact, when I asked about you directly, none of them knew who you were."

He advanced another slow step. Teyla breathed in through her nose and out through her mouth as she warily watched her psychopath of a father.

"Ergo, I have tentatively decided to test you to see if you merit my trust."

"Whatever it is you require, my King, I do so happily."

"As it turns out, I have captured the informant those incompetent imbeciles named. After days of trying to glean information from them, I have gathered all I can from them about the Ghosts and their plans to usurp my throne."

His voice rose with his anger, and the princess took a small step backward. Arden remained still as he continued down the steps until he reached the main floor.

He motioned over a guard and unceremoniously grasped the handgun from its holster.

Arden flinched.

"I am told that you know the fucking brat—"

Teyla balked at his use of profanity.

"—who was trying to destroy my reign!" He took several deep breaths, as if trying to contain his anger. Not a soul dared even to blink too loudly.

"So," he continued, his voice much more subdued. "If

you are not a rebel, you will kill this individual for me." He clapped twice, and the side doors to the throne room swung open.

Teyla's world stopped spinning.

Xara was borderline unrecognizable. Chunks of her deep brown hair had been ripped from her scalp. Her right eye was completely swollen shut, pus oozing out from around it. The right side of her face was -swollen, as if multiple bones in it had been crushed. There was a definitive boot mark along her cheek.

They had forced her to walk naked throughout the castle. The guards leered at her, making Teyla nauseated. She was just a child.

The princess could not tear her eyes away from the travesty of injustice in front of her. Several of Xara's fingers were bent the wrong way, and two of them appeared to be missing entirely. Words had been carved into her flesh.

Filth.

Peasant.

Rebel.

Traitor.

Harlot.

Her ankle was clearly broken, yet they were forcing her to walk on it. Teyla's hand flew up to cover my mouth as tears flooded her eyes. She quickly wiped them away, hoping nobody had seen them.

Once Xara made it to the center of the room, the guards escorting her threw her on the ground and spit on her. Arden's jaw flexed as she marked every single one of the guards' faces, the only sign of anger or discomfort she made.

Teyla could not fathom how Arden remained so stoic. Teyla had seen them together, and they cared for each other like sisters.

Desperation had Teyla stepping forward to stop whatever horror was occurring. "Father, this has to be some kind of mistake." He did not deign to even look at her as she spoke.

The princess tried again, not ashamed of her pleading intonation. "Father, she is but a child. Please— "

"Silence." His voice seethed. "Do you intend to challenge your king?"

Arden's head shook almost indecipherably at Teyla.

Teyla bit her cheek until it bled as she attempted to hold her tongue, and she cast her eyes downward. "No, my King. Please forgive my insolence."

Xara remained lying where the guards had roughly tossed her, silent tears streaming down her face as she noticed the gun in his hands.

The King cracked his neck and faced Arden once more, lazily gripping the gun.

"I am told you two know each other, that you are like family."

"That is correct." Arden's voice was hoarse.

"Am I to be expected to believe that you were unaware of your 'sister's' rebel inclinations?" he spoke lowly.

"Yes." Arden's answer was clipped but not disrespectful.

"Interesting." He mused aloud, as if they were discussing something during a dinner party. "Luckily for you, your 'sister' corroborates that same story. Unluckily for you, I do not fully believe her."

Arden, at last, looked away from Xara as she turned her attention to the King.

He held out the gun toward Arden, grip first. "Kill it."

Teyla could barely believe that he was further debasing Xara by calling her an "it." The princess' own fury rose in her as she helplessly watched the scene unfold. She was utterly useless. She had attempted to deter him already twice. Interrupting again would not only get Xara killed but also put Arden in harm's way.

Her horror only grew as Arden took the proffered gun. Disobeying his direct order would result in her immediate death. Teyla screamed internally to stop, although she knew it was pointless.

Arden took the required steps to stand right before Xara, but she hesitated.

"Please, Arden," Xara whispered brokenly.

For the first time in her life, Teyla saw everything profoundly clearly, without the filter of her standing and privilege as the Cyrenian Princess.

Xara was not begging to be spared. She was pleading for death. She was asking the friend she loved dearly to provide her relief from her pain and suffering while offering her forgiveness for having to do it.

Arden's hands shook.

Teyla's smart, brave mate was shaking. At that moment, the last piece of her soul tethered to this man was released.

She had always been compliant and submissive to her father, even when he hurt her. Teyla had convinced herself that she could do nothing to change things.

However, this felt different.

For this moment, and all the others like it, the princess would remain passive no longer. She did not know enough to wield her magick now, but he would atone. She did not know when or how, but one day, she was going to be the one to make the King pay for every single moment of pain he caused tenfold.

Arden knelt in front of Xara, and Teyla's chest ached with the respect of that decision. She would not stand over her like Xara was beneath her. She got down to the girl's level as an equal. Arden grasped Xara's shoulder, squeezing it once. There was no trace of fear on Xara's face; only thankfulness and love shone in her eyes as she looked up at Arden.

Xara whispered one last sentence to her friend.

"Long live the Queen."

As soon as the words were out, Arden pulled the trigger, grunting from the recoil as the bullet went through Xara's head.

Blood gurgled up through the girl's lips, yet she smiled up at Arden. Within one breath, Xara passed. Her body slumped forward, falling onto Arden's kneeling form. The agent's face was blank as she offered the gun back to the King.

His eyes lit up in feral delight at the grotesque mess he had created, and he accepted the weapon. His lips grew into a closed-lipped smile. "Interesting," he repeated thoughtfully. He swept his robe back and ascended back up to the throne. "Leave me."

Immediately, the guards walked away. Arden stared down at Xara's body. Teyla grabbed her hand while the King's back was still facing them. It was ice cold, as if all the blood in it had run out. Teyla gently tugged it, then released it. Arden's eyes were dazed as she stood, following the princess out of the room.

Teyla glanced back one last time as the throne room doors began to close behind them. The King smiled, his fangs elongating as he stalked back down the steps toward Xara's body. Teyla swallowed down the bile threatening to choke her and raced them back to her room.

CHAPTER TWENTY-FIVE

FURY

"How dare you give them her name!"

Her closed fist pounded Theo's chest. He grasped her wrists tightly to prevent another swing. Enraged, Arden threw her head back and whacked her forehead on his nose.

Theo threw her across the den, holding his nose. Bright red blood poured out, and she smiled sadistically.

"Arden, calm down!" Aeri yelled.

"Theo, don't!" their twin said as Theo stormed back to Arden.

Arden's tattered heart welcomed the violence. She had felt nothing but numbness the past few days. Now, though, she felt pissed. It was a welcome change.

Arden ducked as his fist swung for her face. He was big, but she was far nimbler and faster. Rage sang in her blood, driving her fist into his already broken nose.

Theo roared.

"Guys, stop! Let's talk like respectable people!" Aeri pleaded.

Theo shifted into his wolf form and tackled her. Arden hit the den floor, and the air left her lungs, his maw snapping forward. She tucked her legs and kicked him in the stomach, pushing him off. She transformed in an instant, snapping her teeth. Both wolves circled, ears held low in warning.

"What the fuck happened?" Jace asked, holding his arms out in front of him warily. He stepped protectively in front of Aeri to prevent accidental injury.

Arden lunged, missing Theo's neck by mere inches as he reared back. Then, as one unit, the twins moved.

Aeri jumped on Arden, holding her down as Jace tackled Theo. Both siblings grunted as the wolves struggled to stand back up, muscles bulging with effort. Jace growled, and everyone paused.

"Shift back, damn it! Let's have a fight like civilized fucking Lycans."

Arden fought to get out from under Aeri but did not want to hurt them. She only wanted to hurt Theo. She stopped struggling, and her body shuddered as she shifted back into her Fae body. Aeri held her down. Theo rolled his eyes and shifted back as well.

Simultaneously, the twins released their charges and grabbed clothes, throwing the articles at each of the naked forms.

"Change," they said in unison.

Arden pulled on the men's clothes carelessly and folded her arms in front of her, glaring at Theo.

"Arden, *calmly* explain what you're talking about," Aeri demanded.

She took a few deep breaths, seeing red. Her body trembled with rage, but she complied.

"Theo gave the Ghosts Xara—" Her voice broke. Stuttered breaths followed as tears filled her eyes. "Xara's name."

"You did what?" Jace turned to Theo incredulously.

Theo ran his hand through his hair on the back of his head, shrugging. "I had to!"

Arden growled at his defensiveness.

He threw up his hands. "I did! The Ghosts were not

going to work with us until I gave them the name of a contact we had within the castle. Right now, that leaves Arden and Xara. So, I picked!"

"Where are the rest of your spies? The ones gathering the intel on the underground operation?" Aeri queried.

"Gone. Dead. I don't know. I have not heard a whisper in weeks from them."

"When were you going to tell us this?" Aeri asked, shocked.

"When I needed to. I figured out a solution," Theo snarled, his chest heaving from the strain of keeping human form while riled up.

"Your solution got Xara fucking killed," Arden snapped.

Everybody froze.

"What?" Theo blanched.

It was so quiet in the den she could clearly hear the chittering of insects. Arden gritted her teeth as they ached, begging to shift.

"You. Got. Xara. Killed," Arden spoke slowly, her voice dripping with venom.

"What happened?" Jace demanded.

Arden walked several steps away, not fully trusting herself not to attack Theo again. "The siege at the castle. Did you all hear about it?"

All three Lycans answered affirmatively.

"We heard it was a bloodbath," Aeri said softly. "We didn't know you were alive until you came here tonight."

"It was. From what I have discovered, the onslaught was designed and played out by the Ghosts in an attempt to kill the Princess of Cyrene and wreak general havoc, I guess. I know they have dissented from the King's decisions for decades, but they have never organized an attack of this scale or caused as much needless death." Arden paused, looking each of them directly in the eyes. "They failed."

"You killed rebels?" Theo exploded. Jace laid his hand

on his chest again, pushing him back a few steps. "That's crossing a line, Arden! That's killing our own kind!"

"They are not our kind!" Arden shouted back. "We need the princess alive! Despite that little fact—*they* tried to kill *me*. Repeatedly. Did you want me just to lie down and let them gut me?"

Theo remained silent, but Aeri held out their hands to placate her. "Arden, nobody wishes that. Please continue and explain what happened to Xara."

Arden started to sob at the sound of her name. She felt the fiery rage cooling. All her anger disappeared, replaced with shame and anguish.

Arden continued, "We both survived the attack. Cyrene's Lord Johan Caine turned out to be a nightwalker. I got bit. He injected his venom into me, and I was out for three days. Three days of not knowing my own name, I was so delirious. Three days in which the rebels were being tortured by the King, giving him anything he wanted so he would stop. They gave him her name."

Aeri tentatively stepped closer and ran a hand along Arden's back to soothe her as the sobs continued.

"She had been tortured. I could barely recognize her face. They defiled her body and used it in every way. After I saved her from being sold into slavery, she was raped by countless men. She was beaten and bruised so badly. The King demanded I finish her off to prove I wasn't a rebel as well." Arden's voice wavered again.

"She begged me to kill her," she rasped out. "So, I did. She was on her way to the After anyway. If her bleeding hadn't killed her, the infection would have."

She brought her accusatory glare back to Theo. He had the decency to, at least, pretend to be bothered.

"You gave them her name. You all but killed her. She was a member of our pack!" Arden spat.

"She was just a human girl! She was never part of our pack," Theo retorted.

The twins looked at Theo, their faces mirroring their mortification at his statement. Jace stepped away from him. He looked over at Arden. "Theo didn't mean that, Arden. He's just in shock."

She looked down at her palm and stared at the scar that represented their oath. It no longer cast a slight iridescent glow. It had no need to now that the other half of the oath was dead. Instead, a line slashed through it, and it was a beefy red color, a testament of her failure to protect Xara. She closed her fist around it.

"That human girl saved our hides by not giving any information away about our pack. So, what's the plan now?"

"There is no plan anymore that involves you," Theo bit out.

"What?" Aeri asked, Jace looking just as confused.

Theo continued. "Arden, you are hereby banished from this pack. You attacked your alpha and protected the princess of our sworn enemy over helping the rebels. You obviously do not have this pack's best interest at heart anymore, nor are you supportive of the cause. So, get out."

"You will never be an alpha in any way that matters." Arden's tone was caustic as she walked backward away from him. She had not trusted the pack since he'd taken over, and now, she could see her instincts had been right. She glanced at the twins. "Let me know if you two ever pull your heads out of your asses about this fucker."

Aeri and Jace said nothing as she turned and ran back to the castle.

CHAPTER TWENTY-SIX

PHASE IV

"Welcome to the final installment of the competition!" the King spoke from his platform, towering above the crowd. Frenzied cheers followed, with those in attendance ecstatic to finally learn who their future king would be. "One last event stands between your final four contestants to reveal who is strong enough, cunning enough to become your Heir Apparent to the throne!"

The response from the masses was deafening. Teyla had never seen so many people packed so tightly together, with children hoisted up on their fathers' shoulders and men shoving each other for a chance to be closer to the wooden beams outlining the arena.

"Our contest had to be postponed while our kingdom was restored after the attack of the hateful rebels. However, we are now ready to resume our pageantry and finish our games. Today's competition will be a show of agility, strength, and skill! Your future king needs to possess these abilities to produce a worthy heir for the next generation of our rule."

The noblemen chuckled. Teyla's stomach turned sour.

"Today, we shall witness a talent unlike any other. Today, these men will joust!"

Following the King's proclamation, a procession of six men on horses paraded in from one entrance of the ring. The flag bearer rode in front, waving the royal crest. Then came the competitors in twos, each man waving toward the crowd from the back of their steeds, soaking up the attention. Taking up the rear was another flag bearer.

The group rode their horses around the arena several times as people clapped and hollered, attempting to catch the momentary attention of their future Heir Apparent. The arena was electrifying.

Despite the worry in the back of her mind about how to get out of the arranged marriage, Teyla was spending all of her concentration on Arden. The agent had been withdrawn and uncharacteristically mute for the past two weeks.

The princess knew she was still grieving Xara, and she could not begin to pretend to understand the depth of her sorrow. However, Teyla needed to bring her out of it, for both their sakes. The princess wanted to lessen Arden's grief just as much as she needed the agent's entire focus if her plan to flee was to be successful.

A ringing sounded out, and the games began. The nobles surged to their feet as the first two men galloped toward each other, their jousting lances aimed at their target. The crowd booed in disappointment as they both missed. Each man swung his horse around and readied for the next bell, signaling round two.

"Agent Arden, who do you believe will win this round?" The princess was worried she might be ignored, but Arden sidled closer.

Arden murmured, low and husky, "The man in the red is going to win this round."

Teyla's heart fluttered at the sound of her girl's voice after weeks of silence. *Her girl.* She liked the sound of that. "What makes you so sure?" Teyla knew next to nothing about jousting. It only recently began to gain popularity in Cyrene but was extremely well-known in other neighboring kingdoms.

"The man dressed in red, Landon, is holding his jousting lance correctly, with it tucked tightly to his side. The man wearing purple is Griffon, and he is relying on his shoulder and forearm strength versus his core. Even if he got a lucky hit with a grip like that, the lance would fly out of his hand instead of breaking on his competitor's suit."

As Arden finished her analysis, the next bell rang. The horses galloped toward each other at breakneck speed, their riders undulating to the rhythm of their horses. Griffon held his lance awkwardly, and the tip hit Landon's stomach plate before ricocheting off. Landon hit his opponent's right shoulder, and the lance shattered. A deafening roar came over the crowd as they leaped to their feet.

While both men stayed on their horses, Landon's lance had broken, sealing his victory. After three months of prior success, Griffon was now out of the competition.

His head hung low as he steered his horse out of the ring, some spectators jeering at his failure. Teyla found their behavior disgusting, as she did most men. At least, those Teyla had been around had been far from impressive.

Workers quickly removed the shattered wood pieces from the horses' path. The next contestants, garbed in yellow and green, respectively, took their places as they waited for the bell.

"So, oh wise one, tell me who will win this round?" Teyla glanced at Arden for an answer.

The competitors urged their steeds into a gallop, each lowering his weapon.

"It pains me to say this, but Hemmings. The man in yellow."

A cracking noise echoed as a lance made contact with armor. The man dressed in green accents almost fell toward the left before righting himself on his horse. Hemmings dutifully wore the yellow fabric around his biceps to distinguish him.

Hemmings was shaking his head, as if disappointed

with his performance. Both men settled into the arena's edges as they were given new lances.

"You don't like Hemmings? Why will he win? I think the green guy was holding his stick properly based on your last commentary."

"Stick," Arden repeated with mirth as she huffed out a short laugh. "It's called a lance, Princess. Hemmings is an ass, but he is stronger and has better aim. Holden did not even land a hit that round."

"How do you know all of their names?" Teyla asked suspiciously.

"Research," Arden replied.

Teyla's eyes narrowed, but she let it go. "Just because Hemmings is currently winning doesn't mean Holden cannot make a comeback."

"Maybe not, but it is unlikely. Hemmings is superior in every way."

"You say that like you know him personally," Teyla joked. Arden stilled, refusing to look back at her. Maybe she did actually know him. *What if they had been a couple?*

The princess leaned forward to catch her gaze, but Arden studiously watched the ring. Arden was definitely hiding something. Teyla possessively hoped it was something else.

Holden started toward the center again. It looked like his lance was aimed at Hemmings's chest. At the very last second, the tip of his lance was thrown up, and he landed a direct hit on Hemmings's helmet.

The impact threw Hemmings's entire upper body backward, but he surprisingly managed to stay on the horse's back. Upon closer inspection, Teyla noticed that his feet were caught in the saddle's stirrups. His lance fell to the ground as he went limp. The arena went silent as they held their breath, waiting for Hemmings to fall off his horse.

With a loud groan, he regained consciousness. He pulled himself back up and righted himself in the saddle. A hit like that should have put him out for a long time. He was exceedingly lucky.

He ripped off his helmet, and a gasp swept through the crowd. His temple was already bruised, and his left eye was beginning to swell.

Despite his injury, the women screamed for him. Teyla noticed his jaw was sharp enough to cut rocks, and his long, flaming red hair was beautiful. His face was swelling quickly enough that she'd be surprised if he could still see out of his left eye.

Hemmings leaned over his horse and spit blood out of his mouth. Next, he yanked on the reins of his horse and led it over to the assistant in the corner. "Another lance. Now!" he yelled, anger amplifying the volume. Holden had removed his helmet to wipe away sweat and was currently slack-jawed at Hemmings's recovery. The aid nearby nudged him and handed him his lance.

This time, Hemmings flew like his horse had wings, lowering his lance until it was parallel with the ground. It found its mark in the middle of Holden's chest, who flew backward ten feet. Teyla gaped at the velocity of his hit.

The King clapped his hands, his face lit up at the ferocious brutality. Teyla's stomach curdled. Two men rushed into the arena and grabbed Holden by his arms, dragging him out. Another ran in to calm his horse. Hemmings raised his hand in triumph, beating on his chest as the crowd became ecstatic.

Of course, Arden's prediction came to fruition. The woman had yet to be wrong about anything in this competition. Teyla smiled at her, shaking her head in fake annoyance. Arden's own lips curved upward in a semblance of a smile, her amber eyes twinkling under her mask.

One of the most annoying ladies-in-waiting leaned toward them from her seat. "What are you two smiling at?" Her nasal voice pierced the air. Arden winced, and the princess coughed harshly to cover her laughter.

"Hello, Ruby, how are you today?" Before Ruby could apologize for her lack of cordiality, the princess continued.

"I am smiling because I am so excited for my betrothed to be announced. Agent Arden has been helping me guess who will win."

An easy enough lie. However, it seemed Ruby was not satisfied.

"Agent, what are *you* smiling at?"

Teyla sighed heavily in annoyance. Ruby's mother, Lady Constance, indulged her at every turn. Constance proclaimed that her little Ruby was truly a precious jewel and deserved to be spoiled as such. It was nauseating, and Teyla ruefully wished she could tell her off just once.

Arden simply smiled widely at Ruby, showing all of her pearly teeth.

Ruby bristled at the disrespect, her voice climbing an entire octave. "Agent! You have been spoken to by a noblewoman. You *will* do as commanded and speak when told to!"

Arden's head cocked. She got up and sauntered the rest of the way over to Ruby. While her attitude was dangerous, a thrill went through Teyla as she anticipated the agent's reaction. Arden knelt between them, elbow resting casually on her knee.

"I apologize for your misunderstanding. I only answer to my queen."

Ruby's jaw hung open, and Teyla's followed suit.

Her *queen*. Not princess.

Queen.

Xara's last words came hauntingly back. Was Xara referring to Teyla or Princess Calliope of Orion?

Ruby's face was as red as her namesake, and the princess was impressed that steam was not shooting out of her ears.

The lady erupted. "That is blasphemous to the King! And I won't allow you to speak in such a way in front of me. Teyla is not a queen. She is just a princess!"

Arden's face was as rigid as steel at the insult. "You will find, milady, that Teyla is anything but 'just a princess.'"

"There you go again! You feel comfortable calling the princess by her given name instead of her title. You insolent pig! You will learn your place, or I will teach it to you!" Ruby's chest rose up and down at her outburst.

"You spoke the princess's name with an equal amount of familiarity. Perhaps it is you who needs to learn their place," Arden spoke with a lethal calmness.

"Arden!" Teyla admonished.

The nobles were beginning to come back from gathering their refreshments. A few were just out of earshot.

Ruby sneered at Arden. "Ah, well, I'm not surprised at this attitude from you. You must feel entitled and emboldened by your close relationship with the princess. I heard a little rumor that you were found in the princess's bed one morning. I wonder what the King would make of that debauchery." Ruby displayed a big, smug smile.

"Looks can be deceiving, and assumptions can be deadly." Miraculously, Teyla's voice was steady as she attempted to reason with her. "It would be a shame to falsely accuse your princess of something."

When Ruby did not respond, Arden leaned threateningly close to her. Teyla quickly laid a hand on her arm, trying to calm the agent down. Some of that rage seemed to melt away at her touch. Arden rolled her shoulders and leaned back again out of Ruby's face.

"That's right, Teyla. Call your bitch back."

"Enough," Teyla snapped.

"You do not want to go to the King." Arden's tone was soft.

"Oh, I think I do," Ruby crowed gleefully.

Arden bared her teeth.

"Have you told Farrow it's his yet?" Arden looked pointedly at Ruby's abdomen.

Ruby's self-satisfied smile disappeared. Arden continued her taunting.

"Better yet, how about I break the news to mother-dearest? I'm sure Constance will be thrilled. I suppose congratulations are in order?"

The blood drained from Ruby's face, and panic flared. Teyla surreptitiously looked at the lady's stomach. She might have gained weight, but she did not look with child. Yet, based on her reaction, Arden was spot on. It would ruin not only Ruby's reputation but her mother's as well.

"Or," Arden said calmly. "Let's call a truce and agree to allow rumors to remain unearthed, yes?"

"Yes, please," Ruby breathed out.

"Good. It's settled. Now go find somewhere else to be before I change my mind."

Ruby scurried off toward the refreshments, shoving her way through the other nobility, eliciting annoyed protests.

"How did you know she is with child?" the princess questioned.

Arden shrugged. "Her pheromones have changed."

"You can smell the change in her pheromones," Teyla stated in disbelief. "Was Farrow a lucky guess?"

Arden smiled wickedly. "Their scents have intertwined."

Sudden dread hit her. "Can you…" Teyla trailed off as heat rose to her cheeks. She chose her words delicately. "Scent other pheromones?"

Arden bit her lip, smirking. "Yes. I can always tell if your scent has changed."

"Even when…" Teyla could not force herself to finish.

"Even then. I have basked in your tantalizing scent every time you've been wet for me." Arden licked her lips as if reliving a memory.

The princess's eyes widened with embarrassment as she realized just what Arden was probably remembering. Teyla covered her face with her hands; the knowledge that Arden could scent her arousal was both embarrassing and exciting.

Arden breathed deeply, her miraged amber eyes growing dark as she groaned.

Hot desire flashed through Teyla even as she flushed up to her ears. The way Arden was looking at her made her core feel like molten lava.

A loud crash came from behind them, and Teyla jolted in surprise. Blinking a few times and clearing her throat, Teyla turned to see a drunken patron had overturned a refreshment table. It gave her a minute to breathe and calm herself.

Swallowing, she turned back toward Arden. "Maybe if you're a good girl at dinner, I'll let you have me for dessert."

Any uncertainty she'd felt at uttering such erotic and evocative words was instantaneously overcome when she saw the visceral shudder that rocked Arden.

"Tonight," Teyla promised, winking.

She settled back in the chair as the rest of the nobility returned to their seats. The match for her betrothed was going to begin soon. She needed to focus for now. Later, Arden would be hers. She would make sure of it.

CHAPTER TWENTY-SEVEN

CHAMPION

Settling back into her seat with refreshments, Arden took a long draught of water from her cup, still scenting the intoxicating orange spice and vanilla. Teyla's arousal was perfuming the air, and Arden was distinctly glad there were no other Lycans within the nobility. Arden wanted to keep that scent all to herself.

Teyla smiled. "Stop making that satisfied face this instant. I find concentrating on anything but you unbearable when you look like that."

Teyla's cheeks were dusted with a pink hue, which Arden found precious. "Why is that, Princess?"

"Would you like the appropriate answer or the crass one?"

One eyebrow raised in surprise at her teasing. This side of the prim and proper princess was reserved just for her.

"I think I'd like both, if you would be so inclined to humor my curiosity."

"I could deny you nothing, it seems." Teyla stood from her seat, bringing them closer together as the rest of the nobility also stood in excitement for the next round. The princess pulled out a decorative fan, waving it in front of her face to obscure her words from all others. "The polite answer would be that I find your face mesmerizing when you look pleased, whether that be happy, giddy, or otherwise charming."

Arden's mouth watered as Teyla spoke, the craving for her only intensifying as her voice dropped lower.

"The more accurate reason is that I find you incredibly tantalizing like that and can think of nothing but what your face looks like when I fuck you."

Arden choked on the sip of water she had taken, spewing water all over her dark shirt. The agent coughed as quietly as she could as a few of the nobility turned to glare.

Arden held a hand up in a silent apology as she struggled to evacuate each droplet from her trachea. Teyla's shoulders were shaking with silent laughter at Arden's predicament. Arden shot her a dirty look as she wiped her mouth with the back of her hand. "You are an absolute vixen!" Arden whispered, causing the princess to laugh even harder. The agent rolled her eyes at her mate's obvious merriment, fighting a telling smile of her own. "I suppose it would not help you to know just how incredibly wet I am by that then."

Teyla stiffened, those delicate hands tightening in the folds of her dress. Her scent grew stronger again, and Arden risked a glance to find her chewing on her bottom lip.

"I'll just have to find out tonight."

"It is now time for the final match of this glorious competition!" the King exclaimed, standing from his seat several rows away from them and effectively ending the quiet teasing. "Let us meet your finalists!"

The gate on the right side of the arena swung open. Jace came out, waving at the crowd as the King announced his fake name. Arden grimaced in sympathy.

He looked like shit.

His eye was swollen shut from the swelling, the area surrounding the socket already a deep shade of purple. His sharp cheekbone was split open, angry red splotching surrounding it.

Despite the wounds, Jace smiled arrogantly at the crowd as they showered him with adoration. He walked around the perimeter before stopping at the ground just under the King's platform. He bowed low at the waist, holding the genuflection for several seconds before standing up and folding his arms behind his back.

"And now, Hemmings's competitor. Landon!" the King's voice boomed over the arena, and the opposite gate opened. Landon jogged out, his red tunic as bright as Hemmings's hair. The crowd was equally loud for Landon, but Arden focused on Jace.

As if feeling the heat of her attention, he locked eyes with her. He inclined his head slightly, and her body sagged with relief. She might be kicked out of the pack, but he still respected and cared for her. It was enough.

Arden zoned out as the King droned on, fortifying the basic rules of jousting and what would qualify as a point. Then, an unnecessarily prolonged pause caused the hair on the back of her neck to stand up.

"Whoever wins this round will not only be crowned victor but as Heir Apparent to the throne of Cyrene!"

Arden discreetly looked around but saw no active threat.

"The wedding ceremony between my daughter Teyla and the victor will occur in two nights' time. And we will feast in celebration."

"What?" Teyla's disbelief was potent. That was exceptionally soon. Arden was running out of time.

"To end the competition with a flare, this final fight will not end by knocking the opponent off his horse. Sometimes, being royalty demands making tough decisions. To prove you can do what is best for your people, you must decide what you are capable of. There can only be one future king. This fight is to the death."

Gasps rippled through the crowd, but Arden had seen

enough of his brutality to remain unfazed. Her concern for Jace grew as Landon warmed up. Jace was stronger, but he was also young, injured, and largely untested. Landon was a finalist for a reason.

Each man swung up onto his respective horse and grabbed his lance. Landon pulled on his helmet, but Jace forwent his. Arden doubted he could even fit it over his damaged face, but the risk of death increased substantially. The ringing sounded, and the horses were off galloping at full speed. She exhaled a shaky breath when both men missed; her nerves were just about shot.

Landon whipped his horse around with a swift tug to the reins. Without taking the usual thirty seconds to regroup, he headed back toward Jace at breakneck speed.

Jace did not have time to raise his lance before Landon was upon him. With impressive agility, Jace shoved himself into a crouch in the saddle and threw himself over the opposing lance, tackling Landon straight off his mount.

A plume of dust rose from their impact on the ground, and they grunted in pain. Within seconds, Jace rolled away and heaved himself to his feet. He shook his head back and forth to clear it—his head had hit Landon's breastplate during the scuffle.

His competitor pushed himself to his feet, grimacing and holding his right flank where he had landed. He spat on the ground as he stomped on his lance, snapping the end off into a jagged spear.

Landon stalked forward and swung, the weapon narrowly missing Jace. Their boots scuffed the dusty ground as they parried, Jace dodging the strikes and throwing punches of his own.

Growing frustrated, Landon kicked rocks and dust up into Jace's eyes. Momentarily blinding his opponent, he thrusted his broken lance into Jace's shoulder. Jace's shout of pain caused Arden to tense up as she silently bore witness to her friend's pain.

The human released a cruel, delirious laugh as Jace struggled to shuffle backward. Jace's hand gripped the wood protruding from him, and he roared in anger as he ripped it out. Jace swung the wood as hard as he could against Landon's skull.

The crack was audible, as was the sound of Landon's limp body collapsing to the ground.

Jace did not waste a moment, throwing punch after punch into Landon's face as Jace bellowed. The arena grew completely silent except for the sound of Jace's knuckles meeting flesh repeatedly.

A deep sadness filled Arden's heart. Her people were not ruthless killers, nor did they lose themselves to bloodlust like nightwalkers. This was a reaction driven by his wolf to avenge the harm and disrespect bestowed on him by Landon.

Finally, Jace punched his final blow and slumped over the pummeled body. His adrenaline had run out, and Arden's heart broke as she watched him realize what he had done.

His naturally bright red hair was a soaked crimson color, as were his face, hands, and tunic. The crowd had been excited for the challenge but had not anticipated the grotesque truth of what a victory would entail.

"Does he breathe?" The King sounded bored.

Jace placed a shaking hand on Landon's chest.

"Yes." Jace's voice sounded broken.

Arden blamed herself for suggesting they enter the competition.

"Then finish it."

"As you wish, Your Majesty."

Jace reached for the broken lance once more, now covered with both of their blood. It was so slick from the gore that he nearly dropped it when he lifted it.

Jace leaned down and whispered something in Landon's ear. When he was finished, he brought the wooden stake up with both hands and brought it down with all his might directly into his opponent's heart. Landon took one last breath and was no more.

CHAPTER TWENTY-EIGHT

PREPARATIONS

A loud screech sounded as Teyla kicked back her chair from the table. The nobility stopped their conversations at the interruption. She had been required to join this celebratory dinner, but she could not stomach sitting here for one minute longer.

"Father, I must retire. I have many plans to make tomorrow to prepare for my wedding ceremony."

He dismissed her with a careless fling of his hand, shooing her away. She did not wait for him to change his mind. She nodded politely at the ladies-in-waiting near her, smirking as Ruby studiously looked down at her plate.

Her feet broke into a small jog after she exited the room, anticipating being wrapped in Arden's arms. Just as she turned another stone corner, a hand clamped down over her mouth, and she was dragged into a small closet. Teyla struggled against the tight hold as her attacker shoved a broom through the door handle, effectively locking them in.

"Shh, Princess. It's me."

Her body went instantly limp at Arden's words.

The agent released her as soon as she stilled, and Teyla twisted in her arms, shoving Arden's back against the stone wall, caging her in with her own arms, thrilled when the agent did not fight it. Arden's answering grin excited her, and she shoved the ridiculous castle-required mask up to her forehead. Arden's hair stuck up in messy wisps around her mask, and Teyla adored her even more for it. "You scared the shit out of me, darling."

Arden leaned in for a kiss, but Teyla pulled away from her teasingly. She was not going to get away with it that easily. Arden pouted, and the princess laughed softly. "I am ready for my dessert, Teyla."

Arden's impatience was cute. Teyla could not help but want to taunt her more while the agent allowed her to be the more dominant partner. "I see," the princess murmured, kissing Arden's jaw as she squirmed. "Were you a good girl, like I asked?" Teyla barely recognized her own voice, which dripped with desire.

"Yes, Teyla."

Arden's exasperation was adorable, but Teyla doubted Arden would appreciate being called adorable to her face. The princess hid a smile in the crease of Arden's neck, caressing her breasts lightly with the tips of her fingers. "Good. That pleases your queen." The stark desire in Arden's eyes was gratification enough for that sly comment.

"Did referring to you as a queen bother you, love?" Arden's hands, calloused from the constant handling of weapons, ran up and down Teyla's neck as the princess continued teasing her, enjoying her soft panting.

"Not at all," Teyla assured her, sliding her hands underneath Arden's shirt and along her well-defined abdomen, feeling her muscles contract beneath the teasing touch. "It just surprised me. I feel very cherished that you view me so highly."

Arden's head thumped against the stone when Teyla traced the soft V shape along the curve of her hips, brushing along the waistband of her pants.

The princess dragged her nails lightly against her skin, grinning devilishly at her as Arden's hips bucked forward. "Patience is a gift, Arden." Teyla tsked at her.

"One I have never possessed much of." One hand fisted the princess's hair at the back of her neck while the other gripped her jaw, bringing Teyla into a scalding kiss.

This kiss was not gentle or loving like their first time together. This was a claiming. Arden's tongue opened the princess's mouth, exploring, craving, yearning to devour her lust.

Pleasure erupted over Teyla's body with passion. She matched Arden's energy, letting her know that she chose Arden through the thrusting of her tongue. Her mate tugged on her hair, and Teyla moaned as Arden kissed down her neck.

Lifting her lips from Teyla's, Arden held a hand over Teyla's mouth to muffle the sound. "You have to be quiet, dearest."

Her Fae nipped along Teyla's collarbone and chest, tracing a path to the tops of her breasts. Noticing Arden thought she had the upper hand, Teyla finally pushed a hand through the confines of her pants. Teyla's fingers traveled through the soft hair before sliding through Arden's wetness. Teyla shivered. "Fuck, Arden. Is this all for me?" she purred, her fingers wet from Arden's lust as she removed them from between her mate's legs. The agent's chest was heaving, and Arden's face flushed as she beheld the evidence of her desire on Teyla's fingers.

"Of course."

Arden's husky growl threatened to undo Teyla. The princess leaned away, bringing her damp fingers to her own lips as she tasted Arden for the first time. The sweet and tangy flavor danced along her tongue, and her eyes closed.

When Teyla hummed in pleasure, Arden's control snapped. She spun them around until Teyla's back was scraped by the uneven stones. She pulled down the top of the princess's dress until her breasts were freed from their confines.

Arden's strong arms flexed as she lifted Teyla by the backs of her thighs until her legs were wrapped securely around the agent's waist.

Teyla interlocked her ankles behind Arden and pulled them flush against each other as Arden's mouth covered her nipple. The princess's back arched as her underwear was swept to the side, and Arden's long, deft fingers entered her at last. Teyla felt Arden's smile against her chest.

The agent looked up through her brown eyelashes, monitoring every minute reaction to her ministrations.

Arden switched to the other nipple without changing the pace of her slow, deep thrusts. Teyla could not silence the soft whimpers from the pleasure Arden was wringing from her body. When Arden's hot mouth left her chest, Teyla groaned in protest—but Arden did not leave her wanting for long.

Lips pursed, Arden gently blew on her exposed nipples, causing them to harden. A mischievous, lopsided grin crossed her face. Before Teyla could inquire about it, a crisp cold settled. The princess yelped as the moisture from Arden's mouth hardened into ice around the peaked tips of Teyla's chest.

Just as it started to become uncomfortable, Arden's hot tongue laved away the slight bite of pain, transforming it into immense pleasure.

Another finger entered Teyla as her lover repeated her licking on the other nipple, driving Teyla nearly insane with need.

"Please," the princess begged.

"What do you want, Teyla?"

Annoyance had the princess glaring heatedly before Arden's fingers distracted her again. The agent's other hand gently circled Teyla's clit, never fully applying pressure. The princess had never begged for anything in her life. This woman was going to ruin her. "Please make me come."

Arden beamed up at her, and the reaction alone was worth the begging. Arden shifted until she was kneeling before Teyla, pressing her harder into the wall for balance. Carefully moving so her fingers did not leave Teyla's core, Arden rearranged the princess's right leg to be propped over her shoulder, nudging her other leg to follow suit.

Without breaking eye contact, Arden placed her face between Teyla's soaked thighs, her tongue replacing the hand on her clit. Applying direct pressure with her mouth brought Teyla right back to the edge she wanted so desperately to fall over.

"Arden…" the princess moaned quietly, unable to voice her impending orgasm. Arden hummed in understanding, the vibrating mixed with the curling of her fingers, making Teyla's vision flash white as the dam holding her orgasm broke.

Teyla held her breath from the blinding pleasure, sure that if she breathed, she would yell out and get them caught. When her core relaxed, Teyla released the air threatening to rupture her lungs and blinked sluggishly. Arden slowed down her fingers as she gently licked Teyla clean.

When Teyla's shaky legs could stand and she knew something other than Arden's name in her hazy brain, Arden pulled away fully and drew Teyla in for a sweet, gentle kiss. Her body was thrumming pleasantly from the orgasm, but this kiss fed her soul.

Arden loved her.

It was evident in every word she spoke, every touch and every decision.

"Are you going to fall over, Princess?"

"I don't think so."

Assured Teyla was not about to topple over, Arden searched the small closet for something. When she found it, she bent down to grab it.

"Open your legs one more time for me, Princess."

When she obeyed, Arden gently bathed her with a scented damp cloth. Arden rinsed the towel, perfuming the closet further, and wiped her own hands and face. Still basking in the afterglow, Teyla grinned at Arden—she was one very satisfied woman.

Arden shucked off her shirt and pulled on a fresh one, bringing Teyla back to the present. The cloth, the basin of scented, tepid water, a new shirt, and a broom to conveniently lock them in.

"You planned this little rendezvous!" the princess accused, lips curving into a grin.

"If I said yes, would you be impressed or a little freaked out?"

Teyla shook her head in disbelief at Arden's planning and forethought. The fact that she'd wanted Teyla badly enough to plan this escapade made her love Arden even more.

Teyla was attempting to tame her hair, but her fingers froze at the revelation. She loved Arden. The thought should have terrified her, but it did not.

Loving Arden was illegal, dangerous, and potentially unethical if she considered their different kingdoms. None of those concerns really mattered as much as the epiphany that Teyla loved her.

Arden noticed Teyla's wide eyes and panicked. "Shit. I'm sorry. Did I push you too fast or do something you didn't want to? I thought because of our conversation earlier that you would—"

Teyla's lips silenced the agent's rambling as she kissed her with abandon. When Arden's surprise faded, she kissed her back. The princess pulled away when she needed air, and Arden's furrowed eyebrows made Teyla laugh.

"What was that kiss for?"

Teyla wanted to tell her that moment, but the timing was wrong. Not right after a mind-blowing orgasm. She didn't want Arden to think it was due to her post-orgasmic haze.

"You amaze me," Teyla said simply, shrugging. "Let's go to your quarters to talk about the betrothal."

Arden's mood instantly plummeted, but she did not argue. Her enhanced ears could hear no footsteps, so they crept out of the closet and hastened to Teyla's room.

Once there, Arden secured the latch and gestured for Teyla to sit on the bed. "I know you want to be in charge of your own future relationships. I want that for you too. But I cannot let you marry him!" Arden cried out, looking a little panicked.

"Surely you know by now that I choose you."

Arden's sigh of relief cut the building tension like a knife.

Teyla carried on. "I have an idea how to avoid this marriage."

"As do I."

Arden pursed her lips, and Teyla thought she looked entirely too kissable.

"Would you like to go first?" Arden leaned forward.

"How about at the same time?" Teyla counter-proposed.

"On the count of three, then," Arden responded, smiling softly. Silently, she held up her fingers as she counted down.

Three. Two. One.

"Run away with me."

"Help me escape."

The silence was deafening. Then, as each processed what the other had said, they erupted with unrestrained laughter.

No fucking way. Teyla could not believe her ears.

Once the giggles calmed down, Arden clasped Teyla's hand somberly. "There's a lot I need to tell you. Things that may make you resent me or even be scared of me. I don't want to downplay how these revelations could affect your faith in me. Getting you out of this castle and this kingdom is my biggest concern. It will be hard. It may be painful. I need you to trust me every single step of the way."

A frown tugged down Teyla's lips as she tried to sort through her emotions. Only one thing truly mattered. "Did you lie about loving me, being my mate, or that you would never physically harm me?"

Arden fervently shook her head. "Never. I would *never* lie to you about that."

"But there are other lies?" Teyla pressed, needing to hear Arden say it.

"There are many lies of omission, but I have never lied to your face." Arden was graver than the princess had ever seen her. "I have bent the truth for your protection and mine, but once we arrive in Orion safely, I will tell you everything you want to know."

Teyla listened for the little voice in her gut to tell her to run from Arden and never look back, but it never came. The agent had never allowed harm to come to her. People showed their true colors repeatedly. Teyla had seen hers. "Okay. If we make it out alive, I care for you enough to give you the benefit of the doubt as to your intentions. But as soon as it is safe to do so, you *will* offer me the entire truth and nothing less."

"You have a deal."

Preparations were rapid as Arden went through a list of every contingency plan she had created. They needed to leave within the hour as people slept to have a sufficient head start by the time the palace realized Teyla was missing.

Arden gave Teyla a thorough list of items to pack, then left to steal provisions from the kitchen.

Teyla giddily ripped off her dress and changed into a comfortable shirt and pants.

The princess had just finished tying up a travel bag when she heard a dull thump from the back corner of the room behind her. All senses went on high alert, and Teyla froze as she strained her ears to hear anything else.

She silently shifted her feet until her body was against the front wall. She stealthily slid her dagger out of its sheath on her right thigh. Her fingers began to tremble as Teyla allowed her long shirt sleeve to cover the blade and beheld the three warriors stepping out of the servant's door.

"Perhaps your customs differ from mine, Sir Hemmings, but in this house, it is considered an affront to the Mother and the gods to see your betrothed prior to the wedding ceremony, especially appearing within her bed chambers."

If he was surprised that she recognized him, he gave no indication. The person on the far right looked startlingly similar to Hemmings. Wombmates were exceedingly rare in Cyrene, but removing the varied hair color and the bruising on Hemmings's face from the fight, they were nearly identical.

The man in the middle was huge, the threat of violence radiating from him within the bedroom's four walls. His chest heaved up and down, and he was seething.

"Surely, you must now know my true name is not Hemmings, Princess." The redhead cocked his head to the side, the gesture subconscious yet hauntingly familiar. A brief look between them confirmed they were all supernaturally still, a trait Teyla had never seen in human men. She had seen Arden do that same head motion. These people were Lycans, if she was not mistaken.

"I had a suspicion," the princess admitted, carefully replicating the bored yet slightly amused persona she had witnessed in Arden. "I do not wish to be rude. You know my name. I would like to know yours so I do not continue to refer to you with an incorrect moniker."

"You don't need our names, bitch," the hulking male in the middle snarled, taking a thundering step forward. Teyla flinched, but his companions each grabbed his arms and hauled him back toward them.

"Enough, Theo. We need her alive," Hemmings reprimanded the giant named Theo, who shot him a scathing look. Ignoring his companion, the Lycan with ashy hair answered Teyla.

"What need do you have for our names, Princess?" His voice was soft compared to the others.

"If I am going to be killed by three males—Lycans, right?—I would like to go to my grave knowing my assailants' names."

The redhead's eyebrows rose at her flippant comment. "The attractive one you are speaking to is Aeri. They are neither man nor woman, so mind your words." The irony of him calling his identical wombmate attractive was not lost on her.

"My apologies. I didn't mean to offend." Teyla inclined

her head toward them. Aeri returned the gesture as their brother continued.

"You have already heard the big guy's name. My name is Jace. For the record, we are not intending to murder you tonight unless you uselessly fight back or resist."

"I dare you to try to run, girl," Theo growled.

The corner of Aeri's mouth curved upward at the blistering look Teyla sent Theo's way.

In Teyla's opinion, he might be intimidating, but he had nothing on Arden. "It would appear it is in my best interest to simply go along with your plans, then, Jace." Her voice quivered slightly as she realized her time was up. Arden would not return in time.

Theo tackled her, and all of the training with her mate had her reacting instinctually. Her hand clenched the dagger tighter as she swept an arm up at him. The blade made contact, but her head smacked into the ground.

Teyla's vision doubled as she tried to scramble backward. His fist connected with her face, sharp pain radiating from her bones. He was hauled off her before another punch could land. A sharp prick in her neck left her drifting out of consciousness.

CHAPTER TWENTY-NINE

WRATH'S EMBRACE

Arden had been tracking their trail for two days and two nights, hardly pausing for sustenance or rest. Knowing her pack, they didn't take a car—plates could be recognized. No. They took horses, for sure.

The sky was turning purple and orange on the third day when she caught the faint sound of their feet crunching against the branches and leaves underfoot. Her furry ears swiveled, tracking the direction, deftly slinking through the underbrush.

When the group was making camp for the night, Arden released her own packs from between her jaws and shifted back into her Fae form. Biting back a sigh as her muscles groaned from stretching into a different form, she pulled on some clothes. As she buckled and strapped various weapons to her body, she counted them; it had become a meditation of sorts that calmed her before any fight.

Seven deadly blades of assorted sizes, weights, and serrated ends adorned her. Two wicked swords strapped along her back, creating a deadly X across her spine. Two thin daggers graced her forearms, and a long knife was clasped to each hip. One more throwing dagger was on her right thigh.

A secret eighth one she wrapped between her breasts to keep secure close to her heart. The onyx handle soothed her. It still carried Theo's rusting blood and scent. Pride at her mate's savagery rose before she locked her emotions away.

She had forgone any firearms, knowing they would bring far too much attention.

Arden had lost her cloak along the way, opting to drop the unnecessary weight. With her coarse fur, she had no need for it while running as a wolf. As the cold winds blew her old pack's scents toward her, she longed for its warmth. The only reason they were not already dead was the reassuring spiced orange and vanilla scent that danced along the breeze.

Arden left the bags on the rocky terrain and crept toward the campsite, just outside the light from the fire. She quickly noted where each person was and what weapons they had within arm's reach. Sauntering forward, she was as prepared as she would be.

"I like the new edition to your face, Theo. It's a definite improvement."

Three Lycan heads whipped around in her direction. Arden's previous pack mates deftly sprung to their feet in a trained fighting stance. Theo's face had an impressive gash from the edge of his jaw to his temple, his eye cloudy from the injury. It was fresh, still crusty from dried blood, and Arden knew her princess was the cause. "The only thing that would improve it is if I had been there to witness it being inflicted."

Theo growled. "Of course, you're here. You're like a fucking leech."

Arden merely smirked at the insult. "It's not the worst thing I have been called." She casually shrugged, noting his growing annoyance. "I may be a leech. But I am a leech dedicated to the Crown of Orion."

"Why are you here, Arden? We completed the mission without you." Aeri's voice was solemn. There was no pride or glee in their words. It was the only thing currently sparing them.

"A mission that was not given to you to complete,"

Arden added.

Teyla's frown tugged her heartstrings, and Arden's jaw clenched as the flickering fire lit up the large bruise on her face. Jace and Aeri shifted, taken aback.

Jace frowned. "What are you talking about?"

Arden did not look away from Theo as she answered Jace, quoting the script by memory. "The Council of Elders bids Maximus and Arden to enlist the help of a pack to aid in their mission of capturing the Princess of Cyrene and bringing her back to Orion."

Aeri interrupted, "We know the decree."

Arden continued, "This mission is of utmost importance and should be completed using any means necessary to bring her back alive. As the Council decrees it, so must it be done."

The twins turned to Theo in shock, who rolled his eyes in response.

"You were the only one who saw it before it was burned," Jace accused, narrowing his eyes. "We continued to follow you once you banished Arden because you assured us it did not matter who brought her back, nor if she was dead or alive."

Theo winced at the betrayal in Jace's tone.

Teyla looked between all of them, raptly paying attention as the tension became more volatile.

Theo released a crazed laugh. "You have had some haughty ideology that you are more important than everybody else ever since I first met you. Maximus doted on you and allowed you to believe it unchallenged." His face contorted in disgust. "I am not such a weak male."

The air inside her throat turned so frigid it burned at his defamation of Maximus, and the temperature of the air dropped swiftly. Aeri and Jace looked around for the source, but Teyla stared directly at her.

Arden stared Theo down. "You should know better than to sling insults and allegations prior to doing your own reconnaissance, Theo. Do you even know anything about me, whom you speak of so disparagingly?"

"I know plenty about you, mutt."

Aeri stepped between Theo and Arden, hands extended. "He did not mean that, Arden." The derogatory slur on her heritage rang in her ears, and she added it to the ever-growing list of items Theo would atone for before she was finished with him.

"Actually, I did," Theo sneered. "I found it funny that Maximus, who carried a seal of approval from the Council, vouched for a young girl I had never heard of. That might not have been so unsettling had our numbers not been so depleted. I knew most Lycans assisting the covert missions in Cyrene. But I had never heard of you."

He began slowly stalking sideways, with Arden mirroring him step for step.

"It wasn't until I began working closely with the Ghosts that I found out your name only began turning up a few years ago. There was not a single record or piece of information about you prior to that. I knew then you were not who you claimed to be."

Metal sang as he withdrew his sword from its sheath at his hip, gradually spinning it around through the air as he continued, each pass growing closer. Arden did not bother handling her own swords.

"I'd carried suspicions about you for years, but the Ghosts proved I was right. Imagine my delight when Miss Perfect's lie was discovered, proving she was not who she claimed to be. So, I orchestrated the attack on the castle and gave them your description. I had hoped they would succeed in getting rid of you."

Jace and Aeri were mute from shock. Arden's suspicions were at last confirmed, and in front of an audience, no less.

"At least now I get the satisfaction of killing you myself." Theo surged toward her, but his torso fell forward, his hands hitting the ground. Cursing soundly, he stabbed the ice encasing his feet. Each piece he chipped away, Arden replaced until he shouted with anger.

Having enough of his petulance, she released the tight hold she kept on her true ranking. For the first time in three years, Arden allowed the alpha dominance she held by birthright to seep into her voice.

"Enough."

The command rang clear through the encampment, and its effects were instantaneous.

The brute struggling against the icy hold stopped his thrashing as each muscle locked up of its own accord. The siblings immediately dropped the hilts of their weapons, pure confusion on their faces.

Arden took in the forest air as the burden of hiding her true self lifted off her shoulders. It had taken her years of practice and many failures to suppress her ranking and power around others, especially Lycans.

"Who are you?" Jace whispered, fear and amazement lacing his voice.

"An alpha."

It was not a full answer, but Arden was more focused on her mate. Teyla's eyes darted to each person, trying to ascertain what was occurring. The alpha command didn't affect Teyla because she was human, but it seemed Teyla could tell the Lycans were bound to obey Arden. Even if she were a Lycan, Arden would never take Teyla's freedom of choice away.

"Princess, please come here." Arden softened her voice as she held out a hand, palm turned upward. A request, not a demand. Never with her mate, her equal.

Arden's knees felt weak as Teyla held her head high and came to her side. Arden cupped Teyla's bound wrists in a comforting gesture, rubbing a thumb across her skin. She palmed the dagger from her thigh and gently cut through the rope, revealing burns from the chafing. Her stomach turned with guilt as she beheld each injury she had not been there to prevent. "Please forgive me for taking so long to get to you. Each of your wounds is a testament to my failure."

Teyla's fingers gripped Arden's chin and lifted her head from its submissive bow. The princess stood on her tiptoes to rest her forehead against Arden's as an intimate gesture. "You are not responsible for the actions of others. Thank you for coming for me."

"Always," Arden promised.

They pulled apart, but not before Arden laid a delicate kiss on Teyla's head, mindful of her hematoma.

Jace's pallor was stark against his bright hair in the rippling firelight, while Aeri had a soft smile on their face.

Theo laughed maniacally as he beheld Teyla in Arden's embrace. "Of course, you've fucked that enemy bitch."

"Mind your mouth, you fool!" Aeri snarled, but the warning came too late.

Arden's hand flew out and grasped Theo's jaw forcibly. When he struggled against her hold, she squeezed harder, fracturing his mandible. At his outcry, Arden grabbed his tongue and tugged on it harshly until it was fully extended.

"As it seems you are incapable of controlling your tongue while in the presence of royalty, I will do it for you."

Theo's eyes flared in panic as her knife flashed in the moonlight. Without mercy, she severed through his tongue. Arden ignored his screams as she tossed the unattached muscle into the campfire before stepping away. Arden turned to Jace. "Stanch the bleeding and make sure he doesn't choke on his own blood or vomit. I want him alive to face Princess Calliope."

Arden waited for his timid nod. Then, she turned toward her beautiful mate and picked her up with one arm beneath her knees. Arden carried her the entirety of the ten-minute walk to a nearby lake in silence, allowing Teyla's presence to calm her down.

Arden concentrated quintessence through her fingertips to warm a small section of the lake water as Teyla stripped, wanting it to be a comfortable temperature for the princess to rinse off in. Arden followed her after undressing and sank until the water covered her shoulders.

"Why did you cut off his tongue?"

"He called you a bitch." Arden's shrug rippled the water. She dropped beneath the water's surface to wet her hair. Admittedly, she was stalling having to face the repercussions of her violent reaction. She stayed under long enough for her body to burn for air.

When she breached the surface again, Teyla wrapped her arms around Arden's neck and nestled into a full-body hug. Arden averted her gaze, worried that the princess would no longer want her now that she knew just how vicious Arden could be.

Teyla bent her neck until Arden looked at her, turning Arden's face toward her when the Lycan tried to turn away again.

"He called you much worse." Teyla pressed, the lilt at the end indicating she wanted Arden to explain further. Arden sighed in defeat.

"His opinion of me doesn't matter. It made me angry, but they were just words. If anybody else speaks poorly of you, I will react in kind."

"You are going to cut out the tongue of every single person who speaks ill of the Princess of Cyrene while in Orion?" Teyla's musing was playful, the twinkling in her eyes hypnotizing.

"Of course not!" Arden defended. "I am perfectly capable of rationality. I may decide to simply kill them instead."

Teyla snickered at the brash statement, and Arden could not resist pressing her lips to Teyla's from the sheer joy of hearing her laughter.

"So… you didn't tell them we are mates. Was that intentional?"

Arden's sly glance found hers, one eyebrow raised. "Maybe."

Teyla shook her head at the lackluster response, leaning back in the water until her golden hair floated in a wreath around her.

It hit Arden again just how lucky she was to have found her mate. Mother Ambrosia must have made a mistake if she thought Arden was deserving of the princess.

Once they were both relatively clean of blood and grime, Arden carried Teyla out and deposited the water droplets from their bodies back into the lake.

"I will never get used to seeing such a casual display of magick." Teyla smiled at her own wonderment. She had so much to learn and see after being isolated for two decades. Arden vowed to show her the world, if Teyla allowed her to.

Arden trekked back to the campsite, carrying Teyla despite her protests that she could walk just fine.

A few minutes out, the princess touched Arden's cheek. "Do you have any more ground-quaking secrets I should know about?"

"Yes."

"Tell me!" Teyla urged, reminding Arden of their previous agreement.

"Once we are safe, I will." Birdsong echoed around them as the night settled in like a blanket. Arden hoped their joyous melody was an apropos prelude to her return to her beloved home.

CHAPTER THIRTY

MERCY'S REQUIEM

"I seek counsel with the Elders immediately."

The Orionian guard looked at Arden unimpressed as she requested a meeting with the leaders of Cyrene's most hated enemy.

"All meeting requests must be processed through the proper channels. Last minute demands are not permitted."

Jace and Aeri exchanged a look of annoyance as they repositioned Theo back on their shoulders. The Lycan was still alive and breathing, just as Arden had demanded. A different guard kept looking between the prisoner's blood-soaked shirt and his swollen face, piecing the clues together.

"I know the requirements, sir. Send a messenger to inform them that Arden has returned home from her mission. They will want to know."

He glared at Arden but nodded to a young boy. The kid ran, shifting into a wolf pup mid-stride. Teyla jerked back, reeling in surprise. Seeing that nobody else seemed astonished, she felt foolish.

This was Ashwood, the new capital city of Orion, which rose after the initial Cyrenian siege. Solaris, the capital city prior to being ransacked two decades ago, remained abandoned. At least, that was what Jace had whispered as they'd walked through its busy streets. Everybody seemed comfortable with Lycans shifting.

Arden leaned against the wall with her foot kicked up behind her as the group waited. She appeared calm and collected physically, but Teyla could practically feel the nervous energy from her. The princess took her hand, hoping to comfort her. Based on the smile Arden sent her, the effort was noticed and appreciated.

When the small gray wolf with lanky limbs returned, he shifted back into his human form, already accepting the pair of pants offered to him. Apparently, Lycans were quite comfortable with nudity.

"The Elders sent for you, lady." He inclined his head, barely winded after his run.

Bronze coins flashed in Arden's hand before passing them to the runner, ruffling his messy hair. "Thank you, pup."

Arden raised her eyebrows expectantly, and the guards opened the throne room doors, the heavy wood groaning with the movement. She hesitated only a moment more before stepping past the invisible border of the room.

As Teyla crossed through the door frame after her, she felt the weight of magick tingling along her limbs before it vanished.

Teyla's eyes were as wide as the wombmates had been at the unwelcome feeling. Arden seemed unbothered as she walked toward the nine figures lining the dais. Teyla gathered that the lady sitting on the throne had to be Princess Calliope, but four guards mostly obscured her figure.

Teyla's unease grew at the clanging of the doors closing behind them. The foreboding feeling of walking into a predator's den was potent. What possessed her, the Princess of Cyrene, to walk directly into the presence of the Princess of Orion and expect that she would not be harmed or killed?

Sensing her distress, Arden's hand squeezed reassuringly. The various figures' attention focused on their joined hands, and the realization struck her. Arden was not just comforting her. She was claiming Teyla as hers in front of her elders and Princess Calliope.

The fact that no one objected spoke magnitudes of her mate's importance to Orion's most elite members. When they stopped a respectable distance away, Arden, Jace, Aeri, and even Theo knelt. Teyla's pride demanded she do nothing. She was royalty in her own right. Still, that pride was her father's. Teyla's mother taught her that respect given was respect earned.

Teyla bowed her head low for three seconds before raising it along with the rest of the group climbing to their feet.

A woman who looked like she had one foot in the After stepped forward. Teyla's stomach climbed to her throat as the crone's piercing green eyes scanned the entourage before settling back on Arden.

"Where is Maximus?"

Arden's eyelids shuttered momentarily, as if the pain was too much to bear. "He has been laid to rest in Cyrene, Elder Amelaide."

"No..." she gasped.

Teyla saw the grief on her wrinkled face; it was harrowing to witness. For the first time since entering, the other elders shifted and murmured to each other. Whoever this man Maximus was, he was important to Arden and the kingdom.

Without asking, Teyla's lover took the stairs in large strides and knelt before Elder Amelaide.

Arden pulled a golden chain with a pendant from around her neck and placed it in her wrinkled hands. "I could not bring him home." Arden's voice cracked. "But I brought back his medallion so that we may honor and remember him and his service to the Crown."

The elder's hands closed around the necklace and brought it to her chest.

Tears fell down Teyla's face at the raw emotion in the room. A part of her marveled that emotions were not punished here as they were in her kingdom.

Elder Amelaide patted Arden's head before stepping backward. Immediately, Arden was on her feet and helping the old woman to a chair near the throne itself. Others assisted until the woman, clutching the medallion like a lifeline, was seated and settled. Arden jogged down the steps irreverently until she was by Teyla's side once again.

"Have you accomplished the tasks you were sent to complete?" A male voice rose this time.

Arden answered, "I have on both counts, Elder Thalter. But before we get to that, I have brought a Lycan male here to face punishment for his crimes against the Crown."

"Bring him forward."

Tension bracketed the space as Jace and Aeri hauled Theo to his feet and dragged him to the center. They left his side as he swayed in place.

"Theo Whitelark is accused of treachery in the highest degree, plotting a scheme to get me killed and attempting to kill the Princess of Cyrene against this Council's directive."

Teyla watched Theo shake as each allegation stacked on the other and felt something akin to pity before she remembered that he'd attempted to murder her.

"How do you, Theo Whitelark, defend your actions?"

Upon his nonsensical garbling, the Elder scowled.

"I forgot to mention that for his insolence, I cut off his tongue." Arden grinned slyly.

"How do you expect him to provide a defense if he cannot speak?" This female voice sounded younger than the others, and Teyla was startled to see it belonged to the Orionian princess. An exasperated sigh left the royal. "You are just as much trouble as you were before you left three years ago."

Arden explained, "I have brought others who witnessed his confession." A slow, mischievous grin formed. "And I humbly disagree, my lady. I am far worse now."

The princess rose from her seat and waved off her guards, who were attempting to encircle her again. "Shoo, all of you. We all know that with her home, I am safer now than I have been in the past three years."

Teyla pressed her lips together to hide a smile at the loving familiarity between Princess Calliope and her guards. One of them rolled his eyes, eliciting a laugh. A pang of longing ran through Teyla at the intimacy she might have known in another lifetime.

"Come here, you tyrant, and give your best friend a hug." Princess Calliope opened her arms.

Teyla was at a loss for words as Arden met the princess halfway down the steps and embraced her tightly. The Lycans next to Teyla seemed similarly astounded.

Oh gods.

They were far too familiar with each other. Another unwanted and unbidden wave of territorialism swept through Teyla at the thought of her mate's past lovers.

"Love, join me, please." Arden beamed with a wide smile as she gestured to Teyla.

Despite her apprehension, Teyla joined them, body on high alert. She relaxed incrementally when Arden slung an arm around her waist.

"I want to introduce you to my stunning mate, Princess Teyla of Cyrene."

The room instantly broke out in loud arguments between the Elders, and Teyla shrank into Arden's arms.

Amid the mayhem, Princess Calliope smiled widely at Arden, shaking her head. "It seems you have much to share about your time away from home." Her attention turned toward Teyla. "It is my honor to meet the female Mother Ambrosia created to be this one's other half." She poked Arden's stomach as she spoke, the gesture so familiar and normal that Teyla returned her smile.

"The pleasure is mine, Princess. I hope to live up to the expectations of being her mate."

"Princess? I'm not the princess. I am Brynn, Calliope's older cousin." The female took one look at Arden's sheepish face before throwing her hands in the air. "Calli! What were you thinking, bringing her all the way here without telling her?"

"You are older by six months," Arden scoffed. "And I was *thinking* that I didn't want to scare her off when she just started trusting me!" Arden threw her hands up in the air, mimicking her cousin.

"Oh, yeah. Great call. You can just terrify her in front of the Elders!" Brynn accused, her blue eyes narrowing.

They argued back and forth, but all the noise faded in the background. She'd called Arden by a different name. Previous clues played in the background of Teyla's mind.

You may resent me. I bent the truth to protect both you and me.

She staggered a half step back, gathering both women's attention. Theo's accusation floated forward.

Your name only began popping up a couple of years ago.

How could she be so naive? It was all laid out right in front of her, but Teyla had been blinded by Arden's affection and the overwhelming desire to trust that somebody had her best interest at heart for once. Arden did not exist before she came to Cyrene. That name and background were fabricated.

Arden reached for her, but Teyla could not stand her touch.

Teyla took another step away, but Arden continued to try to grab her hand.

A storm of emotions swirled through Teyla. Betrayal. Anger. Hurt. Mistrust.

When Arden's fingers grazed her arm, Teyla's hand struck Arden's cheek. The force of the slap whipped Arden's head to the side, and the guards immediately drew their weapons.

"Stop!" Teyla heard Arden—or rather, Calliope—command. "If any of you touches a single hair on her head, I will hang you over the gate by your entrails."

"Charming." Brynn, the Orionian pseudo-princess, muttered, earning herself a glare from the true Heir Apparent.

"You threaten your own people? Have you been in

Cyrene so long you forgot where your loyalties lie?" the male Elder protested.

"I make no threats, Elder. Only promises." Calliope's voice was clipped as she corrected him.

"She just harmed royalty! That cannot go unpunished!" Elder Thalter continued to push for retribution.

Calliope rose to her full height, a red welt forming on her cheek from the slap. The man looked away from the anger he beheld.

"Thalter, are you challenging a direct order from your Heir Apparent? Or is it more accurate that you are suggesting we harm our future queen?"

Calliope's voice was the soft intonation that Teyla had only heard her use before a fight.

However, the familiar voice was helping Teyla process that her Arden was Princess Calliope.

Thalter gaped at Calliope's words. "That human girl is the daughter of the man who murdered our king and queen! She will *never* be your consort, let alone our queen. Our people will not allow it!"

Elder Amelaide spoke up from her chair. "It is not up to our people or this council. We agreed under oath that if Calliope were successful and returned with Princess Teyla, Callie would be crowned. While the manner in which she accomplished her task was a bit… unorthodox, the facts remain the same. As Calliope's mate, Princess Teyla *will* be crowned Luna and Queen."

Enraged, Elder Thalter shifted into a huge feline predator. Two giant fangs framed his chin as his lips curled back, exposing his teeth as he snarled. Amelaide did not even bat an eye.

"Guards, seize him."

Elder Thalter swiped at them with his claws and bucked against their grip, to no avail. "Detain him in his quarters until the council can reconvene regarding his future."

Calliope observed Amelaide's decisions quietly, allowing

her to determine the appropriate management of the elder.

Teyla's anger about being lied to about her mate's identity softened as admiration took its place.

Few royalty deferred to their councils, and Teyla hated how easily she'd begun to appreciate Arden's—Calliope's method of ruling.

Maybe Teyla had overreacted. Calliope looked at her longingly before stepping further away to give her space. As soon as the doors closed behind the still-snarling feline, Calliope's attention refocused on the matter at hand.

"Since that debacle is now temporarily resolved, I call forth Jace and Aeri to speak about their experiences of Theo's crimes. As I have brought the allegations forward, I remove myself from the voting council."

Jace stepped forward, his sibling joining him as they both bowed deeply in fealty to Calliope. Teyla snorted in annoyance—the Orionian princess herself tracking the sound.

The crooked grin Teyla loved so much appeared, and Teyla's eyes narrowed at how annoyingly cute her mate was. Calliope's smile grew at Teyla's glare, unperturbed by her bad attitude.

"Arden—" Aeri elbowed Jace in the ribs. Jace quickly corrected himself. "Princess Calliope speaks only the truth. Theo continuously planned on killing Princess Teyla, even going as far as suggesting dismembering her."

Calliope's growl silenced him.

Aeri continued, seeming less wary. "We captured her, injected her with sleeping serum, and made it three days before Princess Calliope caught up. Upon her arrival, Theo admitted he knew your orders and that he had provided the Ghost rebels with Princess Calliope's description so that she would be killed. He then attempted to do it himself."

"Do you swear under oath to the Crown that all you have said is accurate and truthful?"

"I do," both wombmates echoed. They stepped farther back as the elders gathered around the throne where Calliope's cousin Brynn was again sitting. It did not take them long to make a decision. Elder Amelaide walked forward to provide the verdict. Teyla had a suspicion that she was the head of this council.

"The Council have unanimously agreed that Theo Whitelark has committed treasonous acts to the Orionian Crown. As such, we defer punishment to our Heir Apparent."

Calliope turned her burning eyes on Teyla.

"Princess Teyla of Cyrene, what recompense do you deem appropriate for Theo's crimes against you?"

"I think the permanent scar on his face and the loss of his tongue is enough atonement."

Calliope nodded before stalking behind Theo and shoving him to his knees. She gripped his hair, forcing his head up sharply. He groaned as his neck wrenched back at an uncomfortable angle.

"Consider yourself lucky that my mate is so forgiving. You certainly don't deserve her mercy after you threatened to chop her into pieces."

Jace and Aeri winced in shame, tilting their heads down. Calliope leaned down, only stopping once her lips were mere centimeters from his ear.

"Unfortunately, I am not so forgiving."

The dagger she produced tore through his chest without warning, deep red blood spurting from the wound. It went in again just as suddenly, the force of it knocking his torso back into Calliope's legs.

His hands scrambled to find purchase against her, grasping for even a scrap of fabric to tug on. Calliope spoke for all to hear, each sentence punctuated with a new wound. "Theo Whitelark, you have been found guilty of treason by our elected Council of Elders. In addition, you condemned an innocent young girl to days of torture and humiliation at the hands of our greatest enemy, a child who was blood-sworn to me. You attempted a coup to kill your Heir Apparent."

Teyla grimaced as Theo was meticulously butchered

with each punctuated sentence. This was not just revenge for petty grievances. No, the woman in front of her was a queen in her own right, demanding retribution for the crimes against her kingdom. There would be no clemency for him. Teyla was watching mercy's death and requiem.

"Worst of all, you laid hands on my mate, who is your future queen. You attempted to end her life. For that alone, I cannot absolve you of your crimes. I strip you of your Orionian status, mark you as a rogue, and condemn you to death. Consider this your repayment per pound of flesh."

Withdrawing one of her twin swords, she beheaded him. Nobody spoke nor moved to clean up the mess. When Calliope raised her head, there was no sign of the woman Teyla knew. Calliope carried herself as royalty.

"Let this be a lesson for all present to learn. I will not be lenient if any living being attempts to lay a hand on what is mine. This is my future bride, *your* future queen, and I expect each and every one of you to lay down your life for her as you would for me."

She dropped the hilt of her sword and stalked purposefully toward Teyla.

Teyla's instinct was to flee, but though Calliope's eyes were resolved, Teyla saw no remaining violence in their depths. She stood her ground, waiting to see Calliope's next move and looked up as she stopped a foot away.

"My queen," Calliope whispered as she dropped to one knee at Teyla's feet, looking down in deference. Reeling from disbelief, Teyla remained frozen as every Orionian emulated her, words of loyalty falling from their lips.

Calliope—Princess and Heir Apparent of Orion—was humbly submitting to her, as was her court. Finally raising her head, Teyla's mate sent her a smug smile, biting her lip to keep from laughing at Teyla's dumbfounded expression. Climbing back to her feet, she extended her hand to Teyla.

Teyla slowly accepted the proffered truce and let Calliope lead her out of the throne room.

CHAPTER THIRTY-ONE

ABSOLUTION

"Was anything real?" Teyla's question was full of insecurities, and despair rolled off of her in waves.

Callie hated that she was the primary cause of it. The deceit was all her fault, and although it broke her heart, she knew it had been necessary. Callie needed to allow Teyla time to feel the betrayal and come to her own conclusions.

Callie was not above reassuring her, though. "My love," she spoke softly, timidly, not wanting to run her princess off. "My devotion to you is the most real thing I have ever committed to."

"Tell me everything, *Princess*," Teyla breathed, and Callie saw it for what it was—one last chance to give her the full, unedited truth. Teyla, more than anyone, deserved it.

Calliope sighed as she leaned against the balcony railing overlooking the courtyard, feeling more at peace than since she'd left despite the tension between them. She watched pups chase birds, each other, and their own tails as their parents chatted around the garden.

Callie began. "I was ten when my parents were slaughtered in our country home in Romalta, a city many miles from here. Somehow, our location had been divulged, and Cyrenians set the manor on fire. Maximus, my father's beta and advisor, managed to grab me and escape, but not before I watched them slice open my mother's throat."

Teyla laid a hand on her arm, and Callie knew she understood. The gentle touch made her hopeful they could salvage this relationship. It would be easier to excavate her own heart from her chest than to let Teyla go.

"My training was…intense, to say the least. Max told me that the only person I could rely on to protect me was myself. So, he arduously honed my physical prowess and my ability to tamper my alpha ranking. Trusted Fae taught me how to manage my magick. After seventeen years, I went to the Elders to petition for the right to claim the throne.

"Many were against it, saying I was too young and inexperienced. I had not completed the rite, which is required of all royalty before they are eligible to be crowned. It was actually Amelaide who suggested I offer myself to complete the near-impossible mission of infiltrating our enemy's lands and capturing the princess. Arrogant as ever, I told them it would be done within months. Little did I know it would take three years of meticulous planning even to get my first glimpse of you." Teyla laughed at that, and Calliope knew how cocky she must have come off to Teyla when they'd first met.

The sky began taking on more vibrant hues—the first sign of dusk.

Callie continued. "All my years of being the vigilante, the Reaper, hunting down slave owners and pedophiles for coin to help run our rebel operation faded away when I realized just who was chasing me out of *The Crevice*. Imagine my surprise when the princess I was sent to capture turned out to be nothing like her father. She cared deeply for her people, put herself at risk to protect the innocent, and had a spirit that amazed me. Instead of taking you then, I let you go.

"Months of training you, competing in that fucked up tournament, and secretly becoming your guard repeatedly proved just how worthy of the crown you were. I knew at that point that I would not force you to do anything, unlike every other person in your life had done. I wanted you to decide to leave with me."

Teyla was silently crying as she listened, but Calliope did not stop. Once she started, the words just started pouring out of her. Teyla deserved to understand every single half-truth she had told.

"When I told Maximus about you and the inexplicable draw I felt to you, he was the first one to suspect you were my mate. Since I had never fully shifted around you, the bond was barely noticeable and had not snapped into place. But by the time he suggested we were mates, I was already well on my way to falling in love with you.

"I knew nothing about the siege and was furious at how close you'd come to getting hurt. Theo kicked me out of the pack after I broke his nose for giving the Ghosts Xara's name. At that point, we were already out of the competition, but Jace was still a finalist, so I focused on adjusting my plan to get you out."

Calliope ignored her own tears welling in her eyes from the pain she was recalling. Max and Xara's dead faces haunted her.

"It was my idea to use the sleep serum on you," Calliope admitted with a grimace. That caught Teyla's attention.

"Really?"

"Yes. But that was before I really knew you!" she elucidated.

"Ah, yes. That little detail." Teyla's voice was dry as she nudged the small opening of the balcony with her toes. "Anything else you want to come clean about while we are here?"

"One hundred and thirty-one." The confession chagrined her.

"One hundred and thirty-one what?"

"Cyrenian people who have lost their lives at my hands in the last three years." Birds chirping and pups yipping filled the chasm she'd just placed between them. "No women. No children, and most of the men I only killed after confirming they were terrible people."

"You know the exact number?"

"Worried I'm missing a few?" Calliope laughed humorlessly. "I am sure. The one time I counted incorrectly, Xara corrected me immediately. I confessed to her what number I knew at the time, and from then on, she kept me accurate and honest. Anyway… I just thought you should know just how much of a monster I really am."

Callie did not bother to mask the bitterness she was feeling. That number did not include any others outside of Cyrene. Her soul was blacker than the depths of wherever it would be sent once she died.

Sweet arms encircled her from behind.

"A monster would not know the number of lives they have taken," Teyla said, turning Callie around in her arms. "Thank you for telling me."

Callie studied Teyla's furrowed brows. Pink lips pulled into a slight frown, and Teyla looked delectable. Teyla's tongue flicked out to wet her bottom lip, and Calliope found herself leaning in, their mouths hovering inches apart.

"You deserve better than me, Teyla. And I'm sorry I lied to you about who I am."

The depths of the blues in her eyes swallowed Calliope. She saw in the setting sun just how many various hues they contained for the first time. How she had not noticed before astounded her. As if Teyla heard her internal begging, she inclined Callie's chin until their lips faintly brushed.

"I'm still mad at you," she whispered against Callie's lips. Callie groaned as Teyla's tongue swept across them as she licked her own lips again.

"I know." Gods, did she know. Callie knew she deserved Teyla's anger.

"And I expect you to make it up to me for many…" A quick kiss. "Many…" Another kiss. "Many years."

The last kiss was firmer, and Callie gasped as she felt Teyla's blunt teeth nibble on her bottom lip. Teyla's words registered, and Callie pulled away.

"Years? You really mean that?"

As an answer, Teyla took Callie's breath away with a scorching kiss.

Callie's inner wolf howled in delight at the acceptance and forgiveness. It was only once they separated that the howling was not entirely in her head.

The Lycan families were cheering at their affection. They hadn't realized all eyes were now locked on the couple on the balcony. Teyla flushed and hid her head against Calliope's chest as their bodies shook with embarrassed laughter. Once the hysterical giggles settled down, they swayed in a content embrace.

Teyla gazed at her mate. "So… what's next?"

"Well," Calliope's voice trailed off as she thought. "I will officially claim the throne with you by my side, figure out how the nightwalkers are repopulating and evolving so rapidly, and continue to rebuild Orion."

"And overthrow the King of Cyrene to save my innocent people?"

"While looking fine as hell doing it, no less."

Teyla laughed again. Lightly, she punched her shoulder and watched Callie jokingly rub the area while shaking her head. "Of course. Easy. What could go wrong?"

Calliope gathered her princess in front of her, resting her chin on the top of the blonde head as they watched brilliant streaks of orange and pink cross the sky. Callie had been secretly terrified of what might come, but a peace like never before settled over her.

Calliope had a purpose. She had a mate. She had a plan.

She would save both of their peoples, help her queen take her rightful throne, and bring peace to this endless battle.

Teyla tilted her face backward to Callie, a hopeful smile gracing her lips. "Let's begin."

Acknowledgements

The person deserving magnitudes of my appreciation is my supportive partner, Bex Randel (they/them/theirs). I started off this journey with a confession to them that I had started writing a story that might turn into a novel. They encouraged me to just focus on writing and stated that if it was never published it would still be just as valuable and amazing for the simple fact that I had created it. They also never became annoyed with my numerous requests for their feedback about diction, descriptions, or concepts I was working on (a miracle, as there were a lot!).

I also owe many thanks to my editors, who offered me tangible feedback to improve this novel to the quality it is today. These wonderful editors include Christopher Cervelloni, Deborah DeNikola, Randee Gleason, Rose Winters, and Kate Popa.

I'd also like to highlight my friends Ross Overacker and Hannah Randel. I appreciate your willingness to beta read my story and being endlessly supportive along the way.

To my beautiful pups Naomi Marie, Hazel Louise, and Olive Rose – thank you for keeping my lap warm while I did countless rounds of editing and writing, and for always being willing to distract me from writer's block with a game of fetch or kisses.

Dearest Reader: words cannot express how grateful I am that you took a chance on a novel from a queer debut author. Every human that has read this book has helped further actualize my dream of becoming a published author. I hope you love these characters as much as I do.

Made in United States
Troutdale, OR
07/02/2024